MATTHEW A. CARTER

THE
BANKER
—WHO—
DIED

Ordering Information:

Quantity sales. Special discounts are available on quantity purchases by corporations, associations, and others. Orders by U.S. trade bookstores and wholesalers. For details, contact the publisher at the address above.

Editing by The Pro Book Editor
Interior Design by IAPS.rocks
Cover Design by Garin Ray Publishing House

ISBN: 978-1-7330500-2-9

1. Main category—Fiction/Thrillers
2. Other category—Fiction/Thrillers/Crime

First Edition

PART ONE:
IN MOSCOW

CHAPTER 1

S TANLEY McKNIGHT STOOD IN FRONT of the fogged-up bathroom mirror, trying for maybe the hundredth time in his life to make out the worn letters on the blade of a razor. That straight razor was all he had left of his great-grandfather. A family heirloom, but a useless one—he had never learned to shave with it. Stanley's grandfather, however, had held to that morning ritual and used the razor all his life. Even on his deathbed in San Francisco General Hospital, he had nearly given the Russian Orthodox priest a heart attack by pulling it out from under his pillow during his own last rites. Struggling to open it with fumbling fingers, he tried to say something, but all that came out was a bubble of saliva from his blackened lips. The priest shrieked and started frantically crossing himself, the sleeves of his cassock flapping like wings. Stanley's mother, standing beside him, had taken the razor from her father and handed it to Stanley.

"He just wants to be shaved with this," she reassured the priest, addressing him as "*Batyushka*" or "Father" in the Russian style.

Stanley liked the word, which he hadn't heard before. Many years later, when he was studying Russian at Berkeley, he learned another name for a Russian Orthodox priest, "Pop," which he thought sounded much funnier.

Stanley sighed and opened the bedroom door. He was instantly hit with the smell of cigarette smoke. Just as he expected, his wife, Christine, was still in bed, wrapped in a sheet, the little breakfast table strewn with her usual mess. She was holding a cigarette in one hand and a large cup of coffee in the other.

"My coffee's gone completely cold. Will you make me some more?"

"You'll have to make it yourself." Stanley opened the cover of the secretary desk, pulled out a narrow drawer, and slid the razor inside. "I'm already running late."

"But you found time to play with that stupid razor of yours." Christine flicked her cigarette ash into the cup.

"Would you please quit smoking in bed?" Stanley closed the lid of the desk, turned the key, thought for a moment, and then put it in his jacket pocket. "If you flew thousands of miles here just to pick a fight..."

"Darling, you've forgotten our fights already. They all start the same way—with you criticizing. You're a drag, is what you are. Don't smoke in bed. What's going to happen if I smoke in bed?"

"You could start a fire, for one. And anyway, I don't like the smell."

"Damn it, Stanley. Who's falling asleep? I've got a plane to catch too. I have to be out of here in forty minutes."

"I didn't know that," said Stanley.

"I told you about it yesterday. Several times. Surely, you didn't get that drunk on three glasses of wine?"

"Not from three glasses, no."

"You see! There you go. You never agree with me. About anything. You argue—you always have to argue."

Stanley fell silent and started rocking from foot to foot. This sparring was pointless. They could go back and forth this way for hours without ever getting around to what they really needed to say.

His cell phone vibrated. A hoarse male voice informed him in German that his taxi was waiting downstairs.

"I have to head out," said Stanley.

"Ok, bye." Christine pulled another cigarette out of the pack, leaned back on the pillow, and lit up. "Be careful in Russia. I've heard it can be dangerous. Especially for such a handsome Yankee."

"I'll try my best. When are you planning to fly over to see me again?"

"I don't know. I don't like Zurich. It's a dreary, boring place. I don't understand how anyone can live here."

"I work here."

"So I've heard. Work comes ahead of everything else with you."

"Goodbye, Christine."

"*Auf wiedersehen*!" Christine said derisively, but then she added: "Have a good flight."

Stanley couldn't get their parting out of his mind the whole half-hour drive to Zurich's Kloten Airport. Each time he left his wife, he was genuinely relieved. But when he saw her after a long separation, whether she warned him in advance or just showed up unexpectedly, as she had this time, he felt almost happy.

At the airport, Stanley checked his bags and walked past endless fast-food restaurants to zone D. Before he reached his departure gate, he stopped in front of a bar called the Montreux Jazz Café.

A slightly disheveled man of about fifty in a dark-blue suit and brightly colored tie sat at a table facing a television on the wall. The man was finishing his beer as he mechanically scanned through email on a BlackBerry, a half smile never leaving his face. *The world is my oyster*, that grin seemed to say. As he scrolled, he would glance covertly at the women passing by, raising his glass slightly in salutation and muttering something to himself every time he saw a pretty one without a companion.

"Isn't it a bit early for drinking?" Stanley asked, putting his travel bag down on a chair and sitting on the one beside it.

"Where we're going, at this hour of the day they're already drinking vodka." The man unwillingly detached himself from his phone and looked through Stanley at yet another pretty girl walking past. "The flight's delayed. How about a beer?"

"Sparkling water, please. Ice on the side," Stanley said to the Indian waiter who had walked up.

"Another Heineken for me, and make it quick." When the waiter left, Pierre Lagrange, the senior managing director of the bank Laville & Cie, finally transferred his full attention to Stanley. Lagrange regarded him with what seemed to be a mixture of arrogance and distrust, although Stanley might simply be imagining things. He was about six feet tall and heavyset, with a disproportionately large head, short gray hair brushed back, and the friendly smile of a cannibal. His figure inspired fear and respect in the bank's employees.

New beer in hand, Lagrange tugged the knot of his tie to one side and unfastened the top button of his shirt beneath it. The tie wagged its tail, briefly flashing a Hermès label to the world.

"How's your new life in Zurich? Is everything to your satisfaction?" Lagrange asked more amiably, staring down at his BlackBerry again.

"Everything's just fine. I rented an apartment recently, and I'm enjoying the city."

"You're enjoying Zurich?" Lagrange wheezed slowly, keeping his eyes fixed on his phone. "I've never heard such nonsense. Zurich's a shitty little village, a rest home for the elderly. You can enjoy Paris. You can enjoy New

York. You can enjoy Hong Kong, Havana, and even Moscow, if it comes to that. But Zurich's like an old mother-in-law who tosses a bit of cash your way on holidays and promises you a good inheritance when she dies, if you behave yourself. You hate her, but your greed is stronger!"

Stanley shrugged and stared at the screen, which was showing a Billie Holiday concert with the sound off. Lagrange came from a family of French aristocrats, and he regarded the world with the superiority of one of the elect. He had been exiled to Zurich as a result of some scheming among the bank's partners, sent from the Geneva headquarters to expand the Russian client department.

"Did you have time to prepare for Moscow?" Lagrange quickly finished his beer and ordered a double Scotch. "I'm putting a lot of faith in you, my friend. Russian clients are a particular breed, and they need a nonstandard approach. But if you do well here, you have a good future ahead of you."

Five months earlier Stanley had received a call from a headhunter he knew, a man he met occasionally at the pub. The headhunter had suggested that he drop everything in London, including his career as an investment adviser with Goldman Sachs, to move to Switzerland.

The name of the bank Laville & Cie had meant little to him. A classic private Swiss bank specializing in the ultra-rich, it was one of the top-ten Swiss banks in terms of assets. Founded in 1878, it had a long and glorious history, and new clients needed a minimum of $20 million to open an account there.

Stanley had immediately been offered a role as a senior investment adviser, the title of director, a "welcome bonus" of 250,000 francs, a fixed salary of 350,000 francs, and a guaranteed bonus of the same amount at the end of the first year. Taking taxes into account, it was a lot more than he could have counted on from Goldman in London. He accepted at once.

Exactly two months after Stanley had started there, Lagrange called him into his office. August Landmesser, the account manager for Russian clients, had been killed in an accident. His Maserati had rammed through a barrier on a mountain highway near Lake Geneva and plunged into the lake.

Somebody in the bank had to take over Landmesser's Russian clients, and Lagrange had decided that Stanley McKnight was the man for the job. "First of all, you're not Russian, even with your roots, and Russian clients prefer foreigners as their private bankers," Lagrange explained. "But you do speak good Russian. Second of all, I know that Goldman has to have toughened you up, and you need balls of steel to work with fucking Russians. So, do you have the balls for this, McKnight?"

Lagrange had little liking for Russian client managers in general, and the female variety in particular—he thought they lacked professionalism. These latter were generally Russian or Ukrainian women who had married Swiss men in the '90s, or, as Lagrange called them, "babushka bankers." The babushka bankers were quite useful at the start of the new millennium, when the influx of Russian money into Switzerland was at its peak. They didn't have to apply for permits to work in there, and they were fluent in German or French; Swiss banks hired them as client managers en masse, despite their total lack of banking experience.

McKnight was quickly transferred from his position as an investment adviser to that of client relationship manager responsible for acquiring new clients from Russia and the post-Soviet states. The main difference in the role was that now he had targets, specifically, to bring in $250 million in net new assets per year.

As an investment adviser, Stanley's work had a narrow focus: he consulted with clients on their securities portfolios and nothing more. No fuss, no muss. Now he was in a role where he had to attract new clients, to essentially be a hunter, the hardest possible job in the private banking industry.

There was some good news, though—he didn't have to start from scratch. Management bestowed a dozen of Landmesser's clients on Stanley and gave the rest to his new colleagues at the Russian desk.

Boarding for their flight to Moscow was announced, and a long line formed at the gate.

"Damn it, where is that little Swiss shit?" Lagrange rattled the ice in his glass, leisurely sipping the rest of his Scotch.

A young investment adviser named Bernard Mueller, assigned to work with Stanley, was supposed to be flying with them.

"I can't believe it—did he oversleep, or what? Anyway, Stanley, let's go. It's time to board."

The packed business-class cabin smelled of strong liquor. The stewardesses, in their dark, formal uniforms and bright scarves, glided silently between the rows. When one of them placed a glass of Macallan in front of him with a perfunctory smile, Lagrange took a gulp and proclaimed, with an enthusiasm born of Scotch, "Stanley, you have no idea the opportunities that are coming your way! You'll be thanking your lucky stars that we plucked you out of the Firm and gave you the chance to work with us!"

"To tell you the truth, I had to think long and hard before accepting this job."

Stanley was not, however, being fully honest here. He had not been enthused at the prospect of waiting around in London until a promotion finally came his way. It would have been two years at the very least, assuming that nothing happened to him before then, of course, along the lines of, say, losing his mind sitting in an office twenty hours a day. That offer from Laville & Cie had looked like a welcome way out.

"I had to think long and hard," Lagrange repeated, a mocking edge to his voice. "Do you know how many people we hired to the Russian desk last year? No? Not a single one. If it hadn't been for old Landmesser meeting a sad end, you would still be selling investment funds to retirees from Monaco. But"—Lagrange paused for emphasis, taking a sip of Scotch, and continued in a loud whisper—"the stars were on your side."

"You're probably right that I am lucky to be here."

"Do you want to have an easy life?" Lagrange asked, suddenly grabbing Stanley's hand and squeezing it tightly. "Then always stay with the herd and lose yourself in the herd. Thus spoke Lagrange!" The Frenchman, already quite drunk, raised his glass and gave a booming laugh, frightening the stewardess. That laughter quickly turned into a rasping cough and back again to mirth.

Stanley freed his hand, wondering how to handle his boss in this state.

"Ok, let us speak plainly." Lagrange went on in a calmer voice, seeming to pull himself together. "All the more so since the Russians you'll be working with don't like to beat around the bush, either. But why am I telling you this? You're Russian. You should know."

"Well, it's my great-grandfather who was Russian—I'm an American," Stanley reminded him.

"I had one client from Russia try to convince me that even a single drop of Russian blood changes the entire body. The blood of the Russian tsars, for example, was no more than one twelfth Russian, but they were no less beloved by the Russian people for that."

"I might quibble with the 'beloved' part," Stanley interjected, looking out the window to the snowy Swiss mountains below. "A hundred years ago those same people staged a revolution and butchered not only the tsar, but his whole family. Clearly not an act of love."

"That's just family drama. Lenin was getting revenge for the death of his brother," Lagrange retorted, undeterred. "And anyway, all things are subject to interpretation. Whichever interpretation prevails at a given time is a function of power and not truth. I, for one, am convinced that it's your great-grandfather who will help us set up good relations with our Russian clients. How did he end up in California, by the way?"

"My great-grandfather? He was a captain in the White Army. He was in Siberia when it became clear which way the wind was blowing, so he made it onto the last ship out of Vladivostok."

"He must have had a rough time of it?"

"From what my grandmother told me, he found his feet pretty quickly. He was a skilled electrical engineer, and he spoke English, so he got hired by the Bell Telephone Company. And later married an American."

"An unusual story for a Russian immigrant," said Lagrange, sipping his Scotch. "They usually keep to themselves and marry Russian. And they like to settle places their countrymen have already tested out. It's like they're always expecting a trick or a trap. Right, Bernard?"

"Sorry, I didn't catch that?" The young man had made it on to the plane at the last possible moment and was now frantically revising a client presentation on his laptop in the row behind them.

"I said," Lagrange shouted over his shoulder into the gap between seats, "Russians are always looking out for traps. You've already had some experience working with them."

"Yes, they're always afraid of being cheated, but also of being made to look the fool."

"You've got that right," said Stanley with a laugh. "Russians are always on guard, because they know how easily they do it to each other."

"That," Lagrange replied more soberly, "is why we are trying to arrange the best conditions for Russian clients at our bank. They must feel relaxed and at ease. There are very wealthy people among them, Stanley. Very. Wealthy. People."

"I'm aware. I spent the summer studying Russian in Moscow twelve years ago. It was noticeable even then. We Americans don't like to flash our cash around, but the Russians love to."

"Here's what I'll say to you, boys," said Lagrange, warming to his role as mentor the more he drank, "Do you hear me, Bernard?" he shouted over his shoulder again, knocking over his glass at the same time. "Remember this: Russians don't want to be rich. They want to be richer than other Russians."

Stanley and Bernard exchanged a glance and nodded in silent agreement.

The stewardess walked down the aisle with a smile frozen in place, handing out immigration forms to the passengers. The plane had begun its descent.

CHAPTER 2

S TANLEY REMEMBERED MOSCOW'S DOMODEDOVO AIRPORT very well from when he'd left Russia many years ago. He had heard something about its reconstruction since then but hadn't paid too much attention—something was built or renovated, nothing out of the ordinary. But when they exited passport control, Stanley was stunned. The space around him looked more like a stadium than an airport; all that was missing was the football field. It might not have surprised him so much in Zurich, one of Europe's largest airports. But here, in Russia?

"Where are we?" he asked, more to himself than to Lagrange.

Pierre, somewhat preoccupied after his three-hour aerial bout with Macallan, didn't understand the question.

Pierre and Bernard had moved over to a crowd surrounding a television mounted on the wall, everyone watching the screen with intense concentration. The same incident was being shown repeatedly, from different camera angles. The footage, taken from security cameras, was blurry, and the movements of the people in it looked jerky, unnatural. All five or six cameras had captured the scene from above. The setting seemed to be close to a hotel or restaurant. A flashing neon sign with the enormous silhouette of a bear would occasionally enter the shot. The bear was holding a tray.

Each video fragment started with the appearance of a car, from which two men in suits emerged. A couple came out from under the awning of the establishment, walking toward them, a man and woman dressed in light-colored clothing that blended their silhouettes into the well-lit space behind. Two more men followed them, in dark suits like those coming from the car.

"Those guards are idiots!" someone in the crowd scoffed loudly. "Who closes a perimeter like that?"

At that point, a gray ball of something that looked like smoke or dust flared up and burst across the whole screen.

"A stun grenade," announced another expert from the crowd. "M-84. American. And now those idiots are out of the game."

For several seconds, the image on the screen was covered with a trembling white haze, and then the contours of figures around the car began to show. Suddenly, another car appeared in the corner of the shot. Judging from its disappearance in a matter of seconds, it was traveling at maximum speed. White flashes flew out of the car in the direction of the group walking out of the building. The recording cut off there, and the scene began again from a different angle.

"McKnight!" called Lagrange. "Come look over here. Can you read the scrolling text below? It's moving too fast, my Russian's not good enough."

"I'll try," said Stanley, and began translating aloud. "Ok. An opposition leader. His companion's condition is not serious. All four guards getting... got...hospitalized. A former member of parliament. He did not survive."

"People rarely do survive two bullets to the head," a man remarked sarcastically in Italian-accented English. "Welcome to Russia."

Pierre shot the Italian a disapproving glare before taking Stanley's elbow and steering him toward the escalator. Bernard, loaded with suitcases, staggered along behind, afraid of getting lost amid the sea of taxi drivers aggressively volunteering their services.

In the time it took them to reach the exit and find their driver from the hotel, Lagrange managed to deliver an entire lecture on how various authoritarian regimes around the world dealt with political opposition. He spent five minutes detailing the types of political murders committed in African countries and how they differed from those in Latin America. According to him, the victims were always targeted because they had stopped playing by the unwritten rules of engagement between the existing government and the political forces striving for power.

"The first thing that ambition does is turn off the future victim's critical-thinking skills," Lagrange said. "He starts to believe that all this noise surrounding him, the media, human rights activists, the UN, the US State Department, and other decorative elements, are some kind of shield. One he can hide behind in the event of real danger. And it gets worse after that—he starts to lose his instinct for self-preservation. After all, he's got these big tough guys around him with guns in their holsters and pockets full of fancy devices. And hundreds of cameras are watching all of this. The victim forgets that there are real people behind every instrument. And there are real people behind his guards—their superiors, their instructors, their employers. Take that man they just sent to meet his maker—why did he leave through the front door! I knew him a little. He was a wealthy guy. We struck up an acquaintance. They laid it out for him a couple of years ago—that's how the Russians do it. Then a second warning, the last one. This guy seemed to understand that they weren't playing games. So he settled down, dialed it back to an acceptable level. But then a couple months ago he comes out with an interview saying he's going to expose corruption. Ok, great, go ahead and expose it. That's fine. That's why he's got that silver tongue, so the folks back home can be shocked by his revelations and believe in justice being done. But why did he have to name names?"

McKnight was only half listening to Lagrange; he had little interest in this covert political warfare. He'd read enough about it already. If Russians had their own rules of doing business, he would play by them.

"I remember a Russian saying that fits," he said, interrupting Pierre. "'Every insect should occupy the place nature made for it.' Something like that. It's about a cricket."

"Exactly," said Lagrange. "Although you and I aren't insects, but capitalist sharks, no?" He laughed, pleased with his own joke. "And we'll have to work here according to their rules." He added, sotto voce, "Fucking medieval rules."

"Pierre, look at this airport!" Stanley flung his arms wide. "Does this look fucking medieval to you?"

"What does that have to do with anything? They're barbarians! Barbarians with golden clubs sitting on a huge lake of oil and stinking up the whole world. Just take a look at this character over here. He's waiting for us, in fact. That's the driver from the hotel."

The man failed to make any impression on Stanley. He looked like an ordinary, well-trained driver. Okay, maybe the suit didn't fit him quite right. Maybe his teeth weren't great. And his smile *was* crooked. But he was smiling, wasn't he?

"The funniest thing of all"—Lagrange went on, unable to drop the topic—"is that these Russian barbarians seriously consider themselves the successors of a glorious empire! What nonsense!"

"How's that?"

"The USSR was no great empire."

"What do you mean, it wasn't?" Stanley couldn't hide his surprise.

"It wasn't, because it didn't survive! Great nations don't fall apart on their own." Lagrange stopped halfway to the Mercedes awaiting them and turned to Stanley. "The USSR collapsed on its own, without any war or upheavals. Reagan made a sharp cut to oil prices, and a couple of years later the empire fell. That was it. You Americans could make it happen again, and Russia would fall apart much faster this time. Welcome to *Moskovia*."

The driver greeted the bankers in broken English and asked them to follow him. In the car, he spent some time pressing buttons on his navigational system and warned them that their trip might take longer than usual. Traffic, of course.

"That's why I prefer to fly into Moscow at night, and on a weekend if I can," said Lagrange with a sigh. "But I somehow never remember that until I'm already at the airport."

"I have to disagree with you," Stanley said, going back to their previous conversation with a shake of his head. "Russians have a great nation, culture, science—they put the first man in space. I forget his name."

"Gagarin."

"Whatever...Gagarin."

"Stanley, my friend," said Lagrange and laughed, breathing out a miasma of alcohol fumes. "How can you be so naive! This country has gone through almost a century of negative selection. They've been killing or exiling their best, their most gifted, intelligent, and talented members. Your family is an excellent example. Who are Russians today?" Lagrange cracked his window open and lit up an enormous Cuban cigar. "Degenerates, drunk losers without a chance at success in the world of civilized people. This country has no fucking future, Stanley."

"Well, maybe I'm missing something here, but if you despise them so much, how can you work with them?"

"We're just trying to earn a little money before the music stops and the ship goes down." Lagrange shifted in his seat and closed his eyes, signaling an end to the conversation.

The visitors made it to the beltway around the city center fairly quickly, and traffic was relatively light until they hit Kashirskoye Highway, where everything slowed to a crawl. By the time they turned on Andropov Avenue and traffic eased up again, Lagrange had nodded off, and Stanley was entertaining himself by keeping a count of watermelon stands versus cigarette kiosks.

Watermelons won in a landslide.

The watermelon sellers, all Asians in track suits and baseball hats, sat on wooden boxes under beach umbrellas. Each one they passed was involved in an animated discussion on his mobile phone. Some of them waved their free hands energetically. Stanley only saw one seller actively practicing his trade; he walked along the curb separating him from the flow of traffic, biting into a huge slice of watermelon, and invited the drivers and passengers creeping by to join him. McKnight was astonished to see that this shabbily dressed man had a mouth full of gold teeth. The midday sun filtered down through the lush (if dust-covered) canopy of maple trees lining the road, reflected off his golden smile, and scattered into brilliant specks of light on the windows of the cars.

The exhausted travelers finally made it to the third beltway, where the traffic split into several different streams. Their driver sighed in relief, rolled his shoulders back, and began to maneuver between lanes until he fell in behind a traffic cop in a Mercedes, who everyone yielded to even though the policeman was clearly in no hurry. *It must be that universal instinct for self-preservation*, thought Stanley. *He's in uniform, so he's probably with the authorities. And you should give the authorities right of way.*

When they passed the Ministry of Foreign Affairs, Bernard couldn't restrain himself any longer.

"Why is their architecture full of Soviet symbolism? Just look—the hammer and sickle. Here, there! Everywhere! Germany got rid of the fascist swastika. I don't understand why Russians can stand the hammer and sickle."

"The mysterious Russian soul?" suggested Stanley.

"No one has what it takes to understand the damned Russian soul," muttered Lagrange, slowly opening his eyes. "Believe it or not, ladies, but they still have plenty of streets named after Lenin and other executioners of the Soviet people."

"A paradox!"

"I've got a metaphor for you, Bernard, to help you figure it out." Lagrange blew his nose noisily into a handkerchief. "Imagine a woman keeping a framed photograph of the man who raped her and murdered her children on the wall, and dusting it regularly to keep it looking nice. Is that woman sane or out of her mind? How about a people that tenderly preserve the corpse of a man in the Kremlin who raped and murdered their children—are they sane?"

"A split personality? It sounds like a case of schizophrenia."

"You're absolutely right, Stanley. But there is no 'mysterious Russian soul.' There's only the split personality of the savage, which for some

13

reason rouses the delight and affection of naive Europeans. But these are barbarians. The damned *homo soveticus*! I used to have some illusions too, until Laville said to me: 'Only a Russian man is capable of raping his own fiancée.' That's exactly it! That's their vile nature in a nutshell." Lagrange started trying to relight his cigar. "If it were up to me, I'd surround Russia with another Chinese wall. They don't belong with us."

"I can't understand it, to be honest," Bernard said, thoughtfully examining the next totalitarian socialist realist building.

"That's because you're a naive Swiss village boy," Lagrange replied irritably, yawning. "The Russian people need to wise up, repent, and ask the civilized world for forgiveness. Ask our forgiveness!" He beat his chest with a closed fist. "But they'd probably have to go through even more chaos to get to that point. Either way, it doesn't concern me personally. The world is full of underdeveloped tribes; let them live in their own hell! I don't care—all I want to do is make money off of them."

Bernard sniffed indignantly and continued his perusal of the buildings along Tverskaya Street.

At the Ritz, they were met by a doorman in livery and a top hat, which looked pretty out of place in the summer heat. As did the fact that he was a black man in the middle of Moscow.

"He'd be better off in a loincloth," said Lagrange sympathetically.

"In Africa he'd be fighting his brothers with Kalashnikovs over humanitarian aid from the Red Cross. Here all he has to do is sweat for a couple hours, and then he's free to go have a beer in an air-conditioned bar," remarked Bernard, dropping his bags and with a sigh of relief handing Lagrange's enormous suitcase back to his boss.

McKnight stopped short, taken aback by this unexpected bit of racist banter. At his old job, the two Europeans would have seen some serious consequences from HR if they'd been caught talking like that in the office; it appeared that the Swiss bank's corporate attitudes toward racism and hostile work environments leaned more toward the early twentieth century than the early twenty-first.

He was in a foul mood. The nearly two hours spent in traffic with Lagrange's cigar smoke, after a long flight, had done him in. He was counting on their grim adventures being over for now and having the rest of the day to pull himself together. But Lagrange had other ideas. He checked his Patek Philippe, lips moving as if whispering to himself, and announced,

"We have a little over two hours to recover and get acclimated. I suggest you visit the spa here. But don't go to the Russian *banya*. You'll come out like a wet rag. I'd recommend the massage, though. They have two Chinese girls working here who are simply magical."

The women working the reception desk heard Lagrange's final words and nodded their agreement.

"I'll settle for a hot shower," McKnight replied, hiding his sigh of disappointment. He'd already been picturing a sun lounger by the pool and watching a *Breaking Bad* episode or two. "What are our plans for the evening?"

"Let me check." Pierre got out his mobile and dialed. "Robert, hi! We've arrived. I hope we'll see you tonight? Yes…yes…where?"

The answer made Lagrange burst out laughing so loudly that the porter, who had been about to hand Lagrange the electronic key card to his room, jumped involuntarily and took a step back.

"That was Robert Durand, the lawyer. I can't remember—have I told you about him?"

"You said that he acts as an introducer for our bank and helps bring in clients," Stanley said.

"Exactly, yes, he helps us for a generous commission. Robert has invited us to dinner, a restaurant called Hannibal. Russian cuisine." Pierre finally noticed the porter, took the key, and asked him in labored Russian, slowly and louder than necessary, "Hannibal, it is a ve-ry nice and most tas-tee res-taur-ant?"

The porter, whose excellent posture spoke of a military background, had apparently already realized what kind of person he was dealing with, and spread his arms wide, as if offering Lagrange the entire city, with all its countless restaurants, bars, and clubs.

In his room, Stanley spent a blissful half hour in the shower until he felt his eyelids begin to drift shut from exhaustion and deep relaxation. Wrapping himself in a towel, he made it to the bed, threw back the covers, and collapsed on the sheets before passing out.

He was brought back to consciousness by a quiet but insistent knocking at the door.

"Who is it?" he croaked, his voice hoarse with sleep. He noted with surprise that he was lying naked on the bed, the wet towel around his feet.

15

"Mister McKnight!" a young woman's voice called from the door. "Your colleague said that you needed your shirt and suit ironed before you leave. He's expecting you in the rooftop bar O2 in half an hour."

"One minute!" Stanley muttered, pulling on the hotel bathrobe.

His suit and shirt came back pressed before he'd even finished drinking a can of soda from the minibar.

"You see—that's the efficiency you get in a country advanced enough to compete in the space race! Here, this is for moving so quickly," Stanley said as he handed her a dollar.

He found Lagrange in his usual state; sprawled on a sofa by the bar, sipping Scotch and discussing the morning's murder with the bartender. This seemed to be the major news of the day in Russia. Judging from the bartender's expression of polite boredom, he didn't give a damn about either the deceased champion of a better, democratic future for Russia or this talkative Frenchman.

Pierre saw McKnight and waved him over, pulling himself out of the sofa's embrace.

"You look great, Stan!" bellowed Lagrange. Everyone in the bar turned to see what the fuss was about. Even the bartender woke up a little and gave Stanley a thumbs-up as if to say—looking good.

"Where's Bernard?"

"He's staying here. He needs to finish the presentation on structured products by tomorrow morning."

CHAPTER 3

T HE BANKERS LEFT THE HOTEL and turned onto Tverskaya Street, walking a couple blocks before they hit Tverskoy Boulevard. They found the restaurant, Hannibal, tucked away down a side street, in a building that looked like a big white cake. On the way, Lagrange, bolstered by the several whiskies that he had chased with a pint of unfiltered beer, told the story of how he and Durand had studied together at the Panthéon-Sorbonne University, also known as Paris I.

"He was the only one of our friends who wasn't born with a silver spoon in his mouth. His father was a simple postal worker. His dad went to work every morning, came back home, and drank his wine in front of the television, and all of a sudden it turned out that Robert had gotten the highest grade out of any high school student that year in the entire department of Rhône! His dad had thought his boy would follow in his footsteps, become the head of the post office maybe. But people had already taken notice of Robert; he received personalized letters of admission and guaranteed stipends. His dad couldn't take it. Became a drunk. Imagine: a father jealous of his own son! And Robert became the top student in our class."

Lagrange was eyeing a pretty girl. Sensing something, she turned around, and he winked at her, throwing her a fingertip kiss.

"The law firm Langer & Schwartz took an interest in Robert when he was still at university, and now he's a managing partner. He could have gone further, but he moved to Moscow in the mid-nineties and started learning Russian."

"Just like that?" asked Stanley.

"What, the move?"

"The interest in Russian."

"Well, I'm telling you: he came from a dreary provincial family. A game of ball every Sunday. He wanted more. As for why he started learning Russian, no one knows. Maybe he fell in love with a Russian girl. In any case, he became indispensable to some Russian oligarchs, managing their mergers and acquisitions, their initial public offerings in London and New York. Basically, he helped the Russians neatly package up their stolen—pardon me, privatized—assets at home for sale abroad." He paused again. "Or maybe we should say for legalization by hungry foreign investors." Lagrange chuckled. "Durand consults for us, attracting Russian clients. For example, a rich businessman from Moscow wants to sell his oil business to some Americans, and Durand gives him advice on where to stash the money from the sale. Why not put it in the safest bank in the world at the recommendation of your smart lawyer? Have you guessed that bank, Stanley?"

"I may have an idea."

"Very good. You're a quick one, for an American! We pay Durand fifty percent of the bank's revenue for each client."

"Not bad!" Stanley whistled.

"Not bad at all! My annual bonus is half that. Ah, here we are!"

Robert Durand was waiting for them on the second floor of the restaurant. He was a tall, slightly stooped man of about fifty, with a large, hooked nose. *He looks like a scholarly crow*, thought Stanley as he extended his hand to shake. *The kind that wouldn't hesitate to peck my eyes out.*

He introduced himself to McKnight and then waved his hands like an orchestra conductor, sending off the two waiters standing nearby. He leaned over to his guests and said, "I always reserve the table between the globe and the two bookshelves. It makes me feel like a well-read traveler."

Lagrange let out a loud, forced laughed.

"Robert is quite the comedian," he told Stanley. "But he actually needs the globe to figure out where he is after he drinks his favorite vodka here."

Just then, the waiters set down vodka in potbellied decanters, beaded with perspiration, along with special faceted shot glasses that Durand called *lafitniks*. They were covered with a layer of frost.

"It's a Russian tradition," said Durand. "You have to drink vodka out of frozen glasses. That's the only way!"

Lagrange snorted.

"Don't argue with him, Stanley! He's been hanging around Moscow for over twenty years; he knows all the local ways and customs. Otherwise, we wouldn't have such a stream of Russian clients."

"I hope you're not trying to be sarcastic, old man?" Robert donned a pair of rimless glasses and examined Lagrange through the thin lenses, raising an eyebrow.

"What are you talking about? You're always in our prayers. And so, I propose we drink the first toast to my friend Robert Durand, thanks to whom our bank consistently has one of the largest collections of Russian billionaires." Lagrange raised his glass.

Robert smiled at Stanley, and nodded to Lagrange.

"You can tell right away when someone doesn't spend much time in Russia, right, Stanley? We clink our glasses here. Cli-i-nk!" Robert trilled.

"Not just clink glasses, but give long toasts too," Stanley added.

"I'll pass on that, thanks," Durand replied. "That's an art known only to native Russians. I just can't do it. If worse comes to worse, I can retell a fable by La Fontaine. They have their own favorite writer of fables here, but I can't remember his name...but!" Robert raised his long, knobby finger. "I have a surprise for you! We've got some real Russians coming, and they'll teach us anything we want to know."

"Oh la la! Robert, I've got the feeling you're up to no good," laughed Lagrange.

"What do you mean, dear fellow? I'm not what I used to be. Even if I get up to mischief, I do it quietly and calmly, without scenes or police involvement. Especially since this is a restaurant where you're supposed to be on your best behavior. The Russians consider it a respectable place. They come here to feel like aristocrats." Durand couldn't hold back a smirk, and leaned in for a whispered exchange in French with Lagrange.

Stanley looked around the room. The interior was decorated in a nineteenth-century style: heavy oak furniture, wooden paneling on the walls, cabinets of walnut and rosewood. The faded gold lettering on the spines of old books glittered from bookshelves. Tripods with telescopes and brass navigational instruments stood here and there throughout the room.

He wondered what message the interior decorators had been trying to send with all this.

Durand patted Lagrange on the shoulder, then he seemed to recall something and switched into English, nodding toward Stanley.

"So, my friends, let us raise our glasses to a toast the Russians love—to your health!"

He said the last sentence in Russian, attracting the attention of the waiters, who smiled understandingly. Robert was turning out to be more of a handful than Lagrange. The vodka was spreading pleasantly throughout Stanley's body, and he was laughing a little, watching this duo.

"I always said that Russian vodka is the best drink in the world," pronounced Lagrange, biting into a small pickle.

"Shame on you, Pierre. What about your own Swiss kirsch? Cherry, pear, apple kirsch? Aren't you a true Swiss patriot these days?"

"I don't like the fruity flavors," Lagrange replied.

"And you, young man?" Robert turned to Stanley. "Are you also a fan of Russian vodka?"

"I prefer whiskey."

"That's because he's an American," Lagrange cut in, already quite drunk. "You know how they only drink that bourbon."

"I prefer Scottish malts, actually," said Stanley with a laugh, recalling how much Scotch Lagrange had downed on their journey from Zurich to Moscow.

"How could you spend a semester here in college without anybody teaching you how to drink Russian vodka, Stan?"

"They tried. But not successfully." Stanley gave an apologetic smile. "Vodka can be hard on a man."

He reached for the decanter, but the waiter got there first, filling Stanley's glass with a quick turn of the wrist. He set the decanter down and took a step back from the table, where he froze in place, ready for whatever his foreign guests should require.

"Sorry, what is this vodka?" Stanley turned to ask him.

"Traditional Russian vodka, sir," the waiter said, inclining his head. "We've got two sorts of vodka: rectified and distilled, that is, made according to time-tested Russian techniques."

"And we're drinking…"

"Distilled, of course. You're drinking classic Russian vodka, sir. I recommend it with this beluga sturgeon. Can I serve you some?"

"Please."

After his sixth glass, which Stanley paired with Caspian herring and cold new potatoes, turnovers with viziga, the dried spinal cords of fish, and the traditional Olivier salad, they were served hot appetizers—mushroom julienne and large plates with hot baked potatoes split in half and covered with mounds of beluga caviar.

"I've never seen this much caviar in my life," Stanley admitted and nodded his approval at the hovering waiter, who filled his glass, while the second waiter did the same for Lagrange and Durand. "Do our Russian clients eat like this every day?" Stanley asked Lagrange.

"Ask him," said Lagrange, pointing with his fork at Durand. "He knows them better. We know their banking histories, but he knows their secret lives."

"Not every day, no," Durand replied. "Many of them suffer from some kind of illness, take medication for high cholesterol, get liver or kidney transplants. The majority are in poor health. Making big money in Russia is bad for you. Exciting, though!"

"It requires every ounce of your energy. Emotional and physical." Lagrange relaxed against the high back of his chair. "Our new client…"

"Gagarin." Durand picked up the conversational baton. "Our new client is named Viktor Gagarin. Shares a last name with the first cosmonaut. But the space-traveling Gagarin was from the working class, and this Viktor likes to hint that he is descended from an aristocratic lineage. He adores meat, very rare, very spicy. I have it from trusted sources that if you add vodka to a meal like that, Gagarin often ends up hooked to an IV. The doctors work miracles on him."

"But his wealth grows by the day," said Lagrange, popping a potato half topped with caviar into his mouth.

"Forbes estimates his worth at $12 billion." Durand swallowed a spoonful of the julienne, and wiped his mouth with a napkin.

"I think it's more than that," Lagrange said. "A lot more. I heard that he's got over six billion in UBS alone."

"But how!" Stanley poured himself a glass of the cranberry drink and took a sip, savoring the delicious mix of caviar and cranberry seeds on his tongue. "How do you acquire that kind of wealth?"

Durand and Lagrange exchanged a look.

"Only a private banker who's had a lot of Russian vodka to drink could ask that," Lagrange replied. "A forgivable, one-time mistake."

"He started out like everyone. At a 'scientific-and-technical creative youth association,' I think that's what they were calling them in the late eighties." Durand signaled the waiter to bring the main course. "Under the wing of the Komsomol, the Soviet youth organization under the control of the KGB. Gagarin started out small, grew, developed. He told me about his big business after the fall of the USSR—setting up the delivery of Soviet machine tools to Denmark through Estonia. And he had little trouble getting permission, of course. The people who approved it just couldn't understand what the Danes wanted with old Soviet machine tools? It turns out he wasn't delivering machine tools, but the metal chips filling the containers for the machine tools."

"So, what did the Danes need with metal chips?" asked Stanley.

"Well, first of all, neither the machine tools nor the metal chips reached the Danes. The machine tools were sent off to be scrapped as soon as they crossed the border, but the chips were actually from expensive nonferrous metals. He made his first million on that."

"It's a dangerous business as well," Lagrange added. "Someone once tried to blow Gagarin up, along with his limousine."

"Damn, really?" Stanley drank his vodka, no longer feeling its strength.

"A sniper's shot at him, he almost got stabbed in a resort in Spain, and someone set up a car accident in Italy," Durand listed. "He lost three fingers on his right hand. How it happened, we don't know. Rumor has it that he ran into some trouble while vacationing in Como."

"Our client has a definite tendency towards violence," Lagrange went on. "There was a story in the media that he had been accused of kidnapping two underage models in the early nineties. Allegedly, he kept them locked up in his country house, where he and his buddies spent several days sexually assaulting them."

"I don't believe it!" Stanley exclaimed. "No way is our compliance department going to approve an account for him!"

"They already have," said Lagrange, casting a thoughtful gaze up to the ceiling. "They spent all of one day on KYC."

"Pierre, your new banker is too naive for Russia."

"Give him time, Robert. He'll learn," Lagrange said with a laugh.

"This story never attracted the attention of the police? How did he escape arrest?" Stanley couldn't let it go.

"He who has enough money cannot be punished!" Lagrange was now completely drunk. He raised his pointer finger in the air and began swinging it back and forth in front of Stanley's face. "That's what they said in ancient Rome! And it's even truer in Russia."

"And anyway," Durand interrupted, "it's impossible to live an honest life in Russia. You can't earn money honestly—their damned system of laws is arranged so that you can't avoid breaking them. As a lawyer, trust me. In Russia, where everyone is guilty, the only real crime is getting caught. And a select few don't even have to worry about that!"

"In the world of Russian thieves…" Lagrange paused. "Sorry—in the world of Russian oligarchs, the only mortal sin is stupidity."

"What does stupidity look like to them?" asked Stanley.

"Simple." Lagrange cut off a slice of venison, slathered it with horseradish, and stuffed it into his mouth. "Stupidity is not being a loyal servant to the state or not being ready to give everything up as soon as you're asked. Everything else is permitted."

"That's it?"

"Absolutely."

"Gagarin's first wife, the winner of a national beauty pageant, disappeared without a trace in 1995. She left their son behind; he's now a student in London. Viktor just might have had something to do with her disappearance. His second wife died of a heart attack. At the age of twenty-five. Strange, no?"

"A drug overdose?"

"Possibly. He's a fickle lover. But nothing was ever proven. Speaking of which, a journalist who was investigating Gagarin's personal life also disappeared in the nineties."

"You don't think he could have just gotten tired of his wife?" Durand smiled and peered at Lagrange over the top of his glasses. "Happens to the best of us!"

"La Barbe Bleue." Lagrange shrugged. "His third wife is the daughter of a high-ranking official with close ties to the former prime minister of Russia—a good match. He launched from the planet of millionaires into the orbit of billionaires! All thanks to his marriage."

"And where has the new wife gone? Also to the grave?"

"I told you she has a serious family. If he hurt her, he's the one who could end up in a coffin," Durand said, lighting up a cigarette.

"Get used to it, Stanley. Business is so closely connected with the state here that it can be hard to tell where private interests end and where state interests begin."

"What's hard about it?" Lagrange snorted. "Don't confuse the naive American! Everything in Russia is about private interest. It's just disguised by the state. Very poorly disguised, I have to say."

CHAPTER 4

Dishes began to cover the table before them: rabbit with mushrooms, breaded chicken cutlets, baked grouse, sturgeon, a braised side of lamb. Durand asked the waiters to leave them, and poured the vodka himself.

"I ordered all this ahead of time," he said, looking over the table. "You have to discuss your meal with the chef first, except for the cutlets. They assured me that this rabbit was running through the fields just yesterday."

"Game should hang for a while," Stanley noted.

"That's right," agreed Lagrange. "How do you know that, Stan?"

"I used to hunt with my grandfather. I was a pretty good shot."

"Well, I never did," Durand said. "Killing poor little animals, somehow…"

"Better to bag the poor two-legged ones," Lagrange interrupted. "Metaphorically speaking, of course. Or not the human beings themselves, but the fruits of their labors. Say, for example, some ingenious businessman were to create a manufacturing company in Russia…"

"Making, say, devices for cleaning snow off the streets." Durand picked up his former classmate's train of thought. "That are operated through a complex computer program."

"No, better have this ingenious entrepreneur create some sort of IT business. Maybe a Russian version of Facebook. And he's planning to become a billionaire."

"Like Gagarin?"

"Oh, much richer than that!"

Stanley listened to their joking dialogue with half an ear. He couldn't tell anymore when his new French friends were being serious and when they were making up tall tales to scare him for a laugh.

"But you're advising…" Lagrange slowly cut off a piece of one of the cutlets.

"Gagarin!"

"Exactly! You're advising Viktor to buy the business of this Russian Zuckerberg. He'll listen to your advice, ply this poor businessman with promises of milk and honey, and then—"

"I think in Gagarin's case it wouldn't get too complicated. Shamil would pay this Zuckerberg a visit, and he would hand his business over to Gagarin for a nominal fee." Durand said, proposing a toast to his companions' health.

"Who's Shamil?" asked Stanley, lifting his glass.

"Oh, you'll meet him," Lagrange promised.

"Yes, and no need to rush that," Durand said. He topped off his glass of vodka and bit down on a lamb chop. "For now, there are two things you need to know."

"I'm all ears," said Stanley, chasing the vodka with a sip of the fruit drink.

"First, Shamil is Gagarin's head of security and loyal down to his bones. But also, one investment banker from J. P. Morgan once called him a Russian bear, and Shamil got offended, saying he was neither Russian nor a bear. He threw that clever joker right out the window."

"Don't look so shocked, Stan," Lagrange said, slapping Stanley on the shoulders. "That's normal for them. Russian barbarians. And it was only the third floor. The third floor of a five-star hotel. The guy fell into the awning over the entrance and wasn't hurt at all. Not a bit."

"Of course, we can't deny the investment banker got quite a scare falling into that awning," Durand said, wiping his greasy fingers on a starched, snow-white napkin and gazing attentively at Stanley. "Second, Shamil is gay and closeted. He acts so macho all the time and always talks about how gays are going to burn in hell, that they should be rounded up into special reservations, et cetera. But he also has a friend in a modest neighborhood in southwest Moscow where he goes to relax…"

"After all this throwing of jokers out windows, shooting, and driving 120 miles an hour, and burying people in concrete," said Lagrange. He'd finished the cutlet and was digging around in his teeth with a toothpick.

"I don't know where you're getting such detailed information, but it's not far from the truth," put in Durand.

"You guys have got to be kidding!" said Stanley. What he actually wanted to do was get his hands around Lagrange's neck and shout, "You old son of a bitch! Why the hell didn't you warn me that I'd be dealing with

Russian maniacs!" Good old Goldman Sachs was starting to look like the calmest and safest place on earth. Somewhere to go back to and never leave again.

"That's an American for you! The slightest bit of trouble, and it's 'wait, guys!'" Durand was going after the rabbit now.

For the span of a moment, Stanley felt real fear. Felt it like a little beetle in his stomach was crawling up his esophagus into his throat. He shuddered and downed a glass of vodka straight off. The beetle halted somewhere around his solar plexus, stamped around, and then disappeared, dissolving into its component atoms. *It's probably just the Russian vodka. I drank too much. Or not enough. Yeah, that's it. Not nearly enough. There's no reason to worry. I've just got the jitters before this new stage in my career. That's normal.* Stanley shook his head, smoothed his hair down, and tried to concentrate on the conversation.

"It's not so bad, Stanley," Lagrange said, as if reading his mind. "Russian clients aren't the most dangerous type for a bank."

"Compared to who!" Stanley interrupted. "The Italian mob? A Colombian drug lord?"

Lagrange paused, watching Stanley, his lip curling, slowly tapping an unlit cigarette on the table.

"And who told you, my dear, that it was going to be easy? Life loves those who don't complain." Lagrange lit his cigarette and let out a stream of smoke toward the ceiling. "If you want a million bucks, you have to be prepared to work for it. I've met precious few 'good' clients over the years. In my experience, most of them are trash. Some of them are monsters. The main thing to keep in mind, if you're working for monsters, is not to become a monster yourself in the process. I'm constantly fighting the temptation. As for you, we'll find out soon enough," Lagrange said with a laugh.

"By the way, Stanley, why did you suddenly pick up and leave sunny California for scuzzy old Europe?" asked Durand. "Listen, you don't have to tell me if you don't want. But Pierre told me you were in a big hurry."

Stanley wiped his mouth. *So Lagrange had been discussing him with people, with Durand. Well, it would be strange if he didn't discuss the new employee with his oldest friend. Especially since they'd all be working closely together.*

Stanley decided that it was best to speak plainly. "In something of a hurry, yeah. What happened was my mother, Louisa, was killed in a car accident. I believed then, and still do, that my wife was to blame for her death. My current wife."

26

"I didn't know you were married, Stanley," Lagrange said.

"I haven't divorced her yet. Both of us had nervous breakdowns after my mother's death. My wife recovered first and went about trying to convince me that she wasn't at fault. I might have changed my mind eventually, but she did that every day."

"I'm so sorry!" Durand said sincerely. "I didn't know; Pierre didn't say anything."

"I didn't know the details, either. All Laville said was that our new employee had recently lost a family member." Lagrange's speech had begun to slur from the vodka. "I'm very sorry to hear that as well, Stan!"

"Thank you," Stanley nodded. "Thanks, guys! Let's drink!"

The waiter reappeared at this juncture to refill their glasses, and they drank.

"The thing about Russians," began Durand, turning the conversation from the sad subject, "is that they'll drink vodka anytime, anywhere, for any reason. The appetizers might be long gone, the main course over, dessert on the table, but somebody will decide they have to drink vodka. He might go ahead and chase it with a piece of cake."

"Yes," Lagrange nodded. "That's what they call a St. Petersburg tea: cold vodka, hot, sweet tea, and a cream cake."

"But usually," Durand continued, "they'll bring out the standard snacks for vodka, like herring, and set them down amid the dessert plates."

He turned to the waiter.

"Did you hear what I just said?" asked Durand.

"I never listen to our guests' conversations, sir!"

"Well done! But bring us back our herring."

"And pickles!" Lagrange shouted after the retreating waiter.

The waiter soon returned with a plate of herring, pickles, and a plump cabbage pie.

"What is this?" asked Stanley.

"We have a new pastry chef. He works wonders. This is a real Russian pie, a classic recipe. You'll like it. Shall I cut you a slice?"

"Go ahead!" Stanley sipped his vodka, feeling pleasantly sated and tipsy. The worries that had been tormenting him just minutes ago had retreated. "Hey, this is hot!"

"Of course, sir! It's just out of the oven."

They drank again, and Durand, speaking with his mouth full, told them that Gagarin was planning to buy a new yacht.

"He's tired of the old one?" Lagrange asked in astonishment. "We financed that purchase just two years ago. It was an ocean liner! With a helipad."

"Now he'll have his own submarine built into a yacht. He's already put in an order with the Lürssen shipyard. Right now, it's priced at about 400 million euros, but Gagarin might still order some ivory paneling or what have you."

"The sale of ivory is banned." Lagrange was trying unsuccessfully to catch a bit of herring on his fork, examining the empty fork each time in surprise.

"Ok, fine. Detailing with the hide from a baboon's ass. There's no ban on baboons, is there?"

"No, there's no ban on baboons."

"Thank God for small favors! He could come up with anything, and the price will jump upwards of a billion."

"I get the feeling you're not just making idle chitchat about Gagarin's new yacht," Lagrange said.

"Of course not," Durand agreed. "I might get asked to finance this yacht as well. Anton Biryuza, the head of his family office, who's in charge of all Gagarin's personal expenditures, already asked me about it."

"You can count us in." Lagrange at last managed to spear a piece of herring on his fork. "But at that price, you're going to have to lower your commission."

"Why is that?" Durand flushed in outrage. "You think I make too much in commission?"

"But you really do make a lot. Robert, please understand, I'm happy to pay it, but Laville has given me more than a couple lectures about your retros. He's getting stingier and stingier as the years go by. He made us start keeping a record of how much we spend on paper, pens, and pencils. Can you imagine? The owner of a top bank counting rolls of toilet paper!"

"So how much will I have to cut it?"

"What do you think, Stanley?"

Stanley looked at Durand, who winked at him.

"Don't worry, Stanley. I don't hold a grudge. Speak your mind."

"Twenty percent."

"Go down twenty percent?"

"No, keep twenty percent."

"But Stanley!" they both cried in unison. Durand went white. But he pulled himself together and nodded to Stanley.

"This one's going places!" he said to Lagrange.

"Okay." Durand hit the table. "I've invited some people to join us."

"Who?" asked Lagrange.

"Don't worry, Pierre. You'll like them. They should be here any minute now, and while they're making their way from taxi to table, I'll tell you about our plans for tomorrow. You have three meetings during the day with some difficult Russian fellows. When you see them, you'll understand. Second-tier clients. But we've been working with them for a long time, and they bring in a stable income. So you'll need to treat them with respect. And understanding. Don't pay attention to their exotic upbringing and, if we're speaking plainly, terrible manners. À la guerre comme à la guerre. In the evening, you'll go to see Gagarin. That's serious. I've already reached agreement with him on everything. Before you get anxious, Pierre, he's no problem to work with. I heard today from my experts in *the big house*."

"The big house is the Kremlin," Lagrange explained to Stanley. "I like to call it Ali Baba's cave."

"And here are my guests," Durand pointed toward the stairs, where three girls had just walked into the room.

CHAPTER 5

"THEY'VE GOT THE BRAINS OF a chicken, but lovely legs that go on for days. They may seem like they can't add two and two, but there's nothing wrong with their memories, I assure you. So let's not indulge in stories about our business triumphs in their presence, all right, gentlemen? We don't want some bimbo penning a novel about our adventures."

"Tramps are writing novels in Russia?" asked Stanley in surprise.

"They're trying! That's why I advise against getting into their Instagram photos. There will be stories and compliments and…"

"All that song and dance," Stanley said, smiling.

"Exactly!" Robert got up to meet the girls, blowing them kisses from both hands as they approached.

Lagrange and Stanley also rose as well, giving the waiters space to add chairs for their female companions.

Durand set about introducing his current and new guests.

First, there was a tall blonde named Vera in a short black dress offering a view of her magnificent tanned legs. The second girl, Katya, was a thin brunette with hints of red in her hair, which was twisted into two long, perfectly formed braids. She kept carefully placing them in different positions, now behind her shoulders, now at her front. This process would alternately reveal and conceal the symmetrical tattoos running from her ears to her collarbones—small, interlocking hieroglyphs of some kind. Katya informed them right away that she'd had trouble getting off the set; she had played small roles in various television shows but was waiting for a casting call from Netflix, where they were apparently looking for a classic Russian vamp.

Lagrange told Katya that he could send her portfolio to a producer he knew at Canal+ in France who worked with Luc Besson. Katya, meanwhile, let him know that she couldn't stand French cinema, wasn't interested in Besson, and only wanted to work in Hollywood, with Tarantino.

Stanley was about to butt in and explain that Besson actually worked in Hollywood, but refrained just in time. The rest of them seemed not to understand who they were talking about.

The third girl, Anastasia, caught McKnight's eye right away. With her short haircut, long sharp nose, and dangling half-moon earrings inlaid with tiny tourmalines, she looked like a fairy from a children's cartoon. Unlike her companions, Anastasia was made in miniature, with a small frame and narrow shoulders. Her loose gray dress, caught at the waist with a colorful scarf, made it difficult to guess at her figure. When asked her occupation, she looked up at the ceiling, smoothed her fingers along her thin eyebrows, and proclaimed, "I do nothing," She laughed, her hand over her mouth. "And I'm not ashamed."

Stanley was the only one to hear more details, about how actually Anastasia had a degree as a dog groomer and that she gave haircuts to royal poodles for shows. He wanted to know everything about dog grooming at her salon, which was situated in an exclusive Moscow neighborhood.

The rest of them were busy engaged in what people came to restaurants for—eating, drinking, talking nonsense, and flirting with each other. They topped all this off with light jokes, gastronomic commentary, and appraisals of the fashion choices of the other patrons filling the room.

Stanley, fascinated by his unusual new acquaintance, failed to notice that he was drinking glass after glass of champagne with the girls, on top of the twenty or thirty shots of vodka he had already consumed. That was a strategic mistake. He had little memory of the evening after that, only random snapshots of images here and there.

Here was one with Anastasia and Durand trying to figure out what the stuffing in the poultry was. Or, for that matter, what kind of poultry it was. Anastasia is insisting that they go to her friend the ornithologist, a PhD, who would explain everything. But instead of the ornithologist, they somehow end up traveling to a fashionable bar called Mania Furibunda in the Patriarch's Ponds neighborhood. Then, another snapshot, Lagrange buying vodka for some Russian soccer players and telling them that the World Cup in Moscow was going to get cancelled because of sanctions. The players are getting ready to beat Pierre's face in, but Stanley unexpectedly remembers a great number of Russian words and manages to talk them out of it.

In the next fragment, he and Anastasia are sitting on a bench, still in Patriarch's Ponds, and she is telling him about some kind of talking cat and a tram cutting off someone's head. Then, back on the Garden Ring, Durand is refusing to get into an ordinary taxi, because they should have a limousine; then he shatters an empty bottle of Cristal against a passing tram. The police show up, and Lagrange is trying to buy them off. But it's Vera and Katya who manage to convince them. After some brief negotiations in the police microbus, they are all sent on their merry way.

Sometime later, they all end up on Vosstaniya Square, and Katya is calling three taxis at once, but Durand is again refusing to ride in a taxi, again insisting on a limousine. He soon grows despondent, however, and heads off alone in one of the waiting cabs to parts unknown, explaining on his way out that he knows an underground bar where members of a secret society called "anonymous alcoholics" meets. Lawyers only.

Stanley, Lagrange, and the three girls arrived at the hotel around four AM. Lagrange took Katya and Vera up to the rooftop bar for a nightcap, but Anastasia and Stanley went right to his room. Inside, Stanley found an open bottle of vodka in the pocket of his jacket. He wasn't sure where it had come from, but he took a swig. A wave of nausea rushed over him. He managed to reach the bathroom, but realized that his path to the toilet was blocked by a door locked from the inside.

The next wave of nausea was so intense that Stanley almost lost consciousness. He went out onto the balcony, where he found salvation in the form of a plastic trash bag that the cleaning lady must have left behind.

Stanley stumbled back into the room on wobbly legs, his shirt dripping with sweat, leaving his stained shoes on the balcony behind him.

The headache came on a few minutes later, but brought with it an awareness of the world around him. Time stopped skipping and slipping, and fell back into its usual rhythm.

The bathroom door opened, and a white rectangle of light reached out to touch his feet.

A naked female form stood bathed in that cold, white stream.

At first, he saw only her red-soled shoes. Stanley marveled at the tiny size of the feet.

"Turn on the light. I can't see anything," he asked.

Anastasia obediently moved over to flip the switch, and it was as if the room exploded before his eyes: it was filled with so much light. When he took his hands from his face, her chest was directly in front of him. Stanley was fascinated by the color of her nipples, so dark they were almost blue.

He turned his gaze to her legs. Anastasia might have been small, but her legs were incredibly long. *Beautiful legs, perfect tanned skin*, thought Stanley, looking her over. On the inside of her thigh, almost at the very top, he saw a hidden vein pulsing underneath her translucent skin. Slowly, one-two-three. Above the vein, her mons was shaved completely bare.

"I thought you would have a trim there, but it turns out..." Stanley, trying to be clever, remembered a Russian saying, "A shoemaker without shoes!"

"Don't be crude, handsome. Sweet things should be smooth." Anastasia grabbed his tie and gave it a sharp tug toward her. "Come on. I'll rinse you off."

"You will? What are you going to do to me?"

"Anything you want."

CHAPTER 6

T HE NEXT MORNING, McKNIGHT SPENT a long time soaking in the shower and then chased two Alka-Seltzers with half a liter of lemon club soda. He thought about going for a run, but only got so far as taking his sneakers out of the suitcase before giving it up. There was a fitness center in the hotel, but he didn't really feel like dragging himself down there, either. His last hope of a hangover cure was the man dressed in a fez and satin caftan working over a brazier in the corner of the hotel dining room. The sign on the wall nearby promised "Turkish coffee."

Stanley couldn't remember a thing that happened after Anastasia had dragged him by his tie to the shower. He had the sense that he'd gone under the water still wearing his pants, shirt, and socks, but this morning everything had been laid out neatly on the ottoman by the bed. His wallet sat on top. He checked the contents, and nothing was missing: the three hundred dollars and a couple hundred francs he'd had were still there. Anastasia had disappeared long before his painful awakening, leaving only a business card with the address and telephone number of her elite dog grooming business. On the back, she had written her mobile number, and the message: "You were incredible…" Reading the Russian words, Stanley first experienced a sense of involuntary pride, then concern over the ellipsis. He remembered his Russian professor advising them to avoid the ellipsis in writing—"For us Russians, the ellipsis is a sign of confusion!"

Pierre and Bernard were waiting for him in the hotel lobby. Lagrange looked surprisingly well, considering. He cleared that mystery up right away, though, explaining that after spending the night with the girls, he'd ordered an early-morning massage, and two masseuses had spent an hour setting him to rights.

Bernard, on the other hand, looked concerned. He complained that he had tried to stay up to talk to them, but they'd come in too late, they hadn't been answering his calls, that some kind of terrible machine had been making noise all night right under his windows, and when he complained to the doorman, he was told there was nothing to be done, that they were redoing the sidewalk. So he demanded a new room. While that was being arranged, the sleeping pills he'd taken started to work—the end result was that he'd fallen asleep in the lobby in his suit. He'd woken up, still wearing his suit, in a new room, with no memory of how he'd gotten there. "If you'd drunk a bottle of cognac before bed, like normal people, instead of those pills, you'd have slept happily in your pajamas, and that noise outside wouldn't have bothered you a bit," said Pierre.

"Next you'll tell me that I should have ordered a prostitute for a good night's sleep!" Bernard shot back.

"Of course, you should have! Time spent with hookers is never wasted. Didn't they teach you that in your Swiss village?"

Stanley felt his stomach twist in nausea at the talk of prostitutes. He went over to the bar and returned with a steaming cup of coffee.

"Here, Bernard. This is the first step—hazelnut coffee." He winked at the investment consultant. "Get one for yourself."

"*Il n'y a pas de bonne fête sans lendemain*," said Lagrange. "What's the second step?"

"I have several second steps to recommend," said Stanley. "Let's walk over to the meeting with our first client, Mr. Peshkov. I know how to get there."

Lagrange opened his mouth to object, but Stanley cut him off.

"It's only a ten-minute walk, and it's a lovely morning, still cool. But most importantly"—here, he pointed toward the exit—"the street cleaners have just come through and washed everything down. We all could use some fresh air."

Stanley's estimate was accurate; ten minutes later, they were walking into the Coffeemania on Bolshaya Nikitskaya Street. Peshkov walked in after them and invited the bankers to the table, stumbling and looking around all the while. *He looks like he had a glass of vodka with breakfast*, thought Stanley.

Peshkov waved away Bernard's suggestion of a table outside, shooting Lagrange an irritated look, as if to say, "Where do you find such thoughtless employees?" Peshkov was a tall, well-built man, with an expressive, handsome face. If not for his thin lips, which he was constantly licking, and his darting eyes, he could have been a television presenter or sitcom actor. He had two ancient Nokia mobile phones, twenty years old at least, that he turned over and over in his hands.

"My colleague," began Lagrange, gesturing toward Bernard, "has prepared an offer for you, a plan to rebalance your investment portfolio. We can go over the broad strokes today, and then we'd like to set up a transfer of your funds to us under a discretionary portfolio mandate—"

"Fuck the offer!" Peshkov interrupted. "The situation has changed. We have to take care of something, and quickly."

"What exactly?"

Instead of answering, Peshkov took a napkin and quickly sketched something on it, then pushed it over to Lagrange.

He looked at it and passed the napkin to McKnight. Stanley saw a crossed-out dollar sign, some kind of scribble, and a yuan sign.

"You wouldn't be able to explain this in words, would you?" Stanley asked politely.

Peshkov looked around the café, out the window, and then whispered, "I need all my dollar cash to be transferred over to the yuan."

"Why?" asked Pierre.

"For what purpose?" echoed Stanley.

"Oof," Bernard said on a long exhale.

"No need to make faces," the businessman went on. "Everyone knows that this"—he pointed at the dollar—"is going to turn into toilet paper any day now."

"Where are you getting your information?" asked Lagrange. "Are you absolutely sure about the American dollar? The end is at hand?"

"Okay, I'll give you a different answer," Peshkov said, tapping Bernard's laptop. "Transfer all my dollars to yuans today. I agree to the discretionary portfolio mandate, as long as it's in yuans."

"Our trader will call you in five to do the FX conversion," Pierre said calmly, but Stanley could see the tears welling up in his eyes. He was barely managing to restrain his laughter.

"What will the fee be?"

"A discretionary portfolio in yuans is not a standard service. I think we can offer you…" Lagrange scratched behind his ear, counting something up in his head. "We can offer you an annual management fee of 2.45 percent of the funds in your portfolio plus an annual custody fee of a quarter percent."

"Why so expensive?" Peshkov exclaimed. "I pay your competitors at Julius Baer a half percent, all-in fee for a full-service package."

Lagrange shook his head and said sternly, "Mr. Peshkov, are you aware that there will soon be an automatic international exchange of information in the banking world?"

"Yes, you told me about it at our last meeting in Zurich. New international tax legislation. So?"

"I'm glad that you haven't forgotten." A note of steel appeared in Lagrange's voice, and his eyes narrowed. "Soon, the Russian tax authorities are going to have access to information about all your accounts in Swiss banks."

"You promised that information about me wouldn't reach Russia," said Peshkov, sticking his lower lip out in a childish pout.

"That's right! And we keep our promises. In our bank, you are formally registered as a citizen of Belarus, which hasn't signed the exchange of information agreement, and no one in Russia knows about your accounts." Lagrange paused significantly. "But if you're suddenly concerned about discounts, go ahead and sign with Julius Baer. No one's stopping you."

"All right! To hell with you," Peshkov agreed gloomily. "What's next?"

Lagrange let a satisfied smirk cross his face, and pulled a pack of cigarettes out of his jacket's inside pocket.

"Meet Stanley McKnight, your new private banker. He'll send you the documents to sign."

Stanley nodded to Peshkov and pinched his own leg under the table to keep from laughing. He couldn't believe the bald-faced stupidity he was witnessing. And this was a man who had built a billion-dollar business in the shipping industry and had about $150 million in accounts in their bank.

Peshkov stood, announcing, "I'll expect your call within the hour!" He added, quietly, "Please wait for ten minutes before you leave. Protocol."

"We will be happy to do so," Lagrange replied, all friendly smiles again, holding out his hand to shake.

When Peshkov had gone, Pierre pointed toward the napkin, laughing out loud. "He forgot to burn it! Or eat it! I'm going to save this," he cackled.

Even reserved Bernard allowed himself a smile. But he was smiling for a different reason—he'd done a quick calculation of the approximate amount he'd earned in the last ten minutes.

McKnight, however, had stopped laughing.

"Pierre, I'm not sure he's all there. Maybe someone drugged him? Or he's under hypnosis or something?"

"You're right, Stan, and I've even guessed what the drug was. He's overdosed on Russian news. Apparently, he's been watching too much Russia Today."

"A strange character," Bernard noted. "Why was he using those mobiles? They belong in a museum. He's certainly not suffering for money."

"It's a trend here in Moscow. People think the old phones are harder to listen in on, and now everybody and their mother are walking around with them. Even those who are certainly of no interest to the FSB. Nonsense, of course." Lagrange licked his lips and looked at his watch. "That conspiracy theorist has just handed us two hours of free time before our next appointment. However, I do have a job for you, my dear Stanley. A certain Mr. Natan Grigoryan should be arriving soon, the head of the private banking department for a major Austrian bank in Russia. I've known him for a long time, and I must confess that I just can't stand him. He's such a blatant swindler that he'll recommend clients of his bank to switch to ours—for a nice retro fee, naturally."

"That's a violation of corporate ethics."

"Yes, it's a bit much even for Russia. But he's brought us hundreds of millions of dollars in client money over the last six months, and it doesn't bother us if he's stealing from his employer. Meet with him, discuss, and I'll take a walk and find someplace to have a good cup of coffee. Okay?"

"Okay." Stanley nodded, not a little taken aback. "How will I recognize him?"

"Don't worry about that. He'll find you. I described you to him. You just promise that Grigoryan anything he wants. We'll figure it out later. This is a crook we can't lose. Bernard, you're free until our next meeting. You don't have to drink coffee with me. Take a walk. Go back to the hotel. Take a nap if you can manage it."

Lagrange stuck a cigarette between his lips and left the café with Bernard, a spring in his step. Stanley rubbed his temples and asked for a freshly squeezed juice to help with the hangover. The juice the waiter brought him had clearly just come from a box, but Stanley couldn't find the energy to protest, so he drank it down as quickly as he could, hoping that there was a significant dose of vitamin C in whatever concentrate had gone into making it. He looked up to see a small, pudgy man entering the café. *He looked like a woman; no, wait, was it, a woman who looked like a man?* Stanley thought irritably. The hangover had given him a wicked headache.

The person was short-necked, shaggy, and pigeon-toed. He immediately picked Stanley out from the other patrons, walking straight over to his table. He asked in a contrived baritone, "Mr. McKnight? I'm Natan Grigoryan."

Without waiting for an invitation, he sat down across from Stanley and launched into a narrative about how he'd taught children for years at the embassy in London, had been on many business trips to England, and had a doctorate in psychology.

"I'm very glad for you." McKnight inclined his head. "I always dreamed of an academic career, but I guess it wasn't meant to be."

At that, Grigoryan began to describe his lectures to students at the Higher School of Economics here in Moscow. Lowering his voice, he told Stanley that half the teaching staff of the university had connections to the country's security services, but then switched back to extolling his own accomplishments—his teaching program had been chosen as the best out of anyone's, and he was planning to become a professor.

Stanley felt like he was slowly suffocating under the flow of words—Grigoryan was unstoppable. He chattered on, sprinkling his narrative with little witticisms, bragging about his son studying in a private English school, his wife the lawyer at Credit Suisse, something about a daughter married to an Italian aristocrat who owned one of the world's largest private collections of Renaissance engravings. Grigoryan also touted his Moscow connections, dropping the names of highly placed government officials, almost none of whom Stanley knew, of course, but of whom Grigoryan spoke as if Stanley was on the best of terms with them: "Well you know how Ivan Ivanovich loves to fish, the kind of rods and reels he has. Everything custom-made by the best; you remember that salmon he caught in Alaska—a real beauty, isn't that so, Mr. McKnight?"

But he managed to slip into this veritable flood of words the actual reason for their meeting. Just after his description of a birthday party for yet another official, he told Stanley that he had another three clients ready to switch from his bank to Laville & Cie, with a combined balance of about 200 million, but "No, no, Mr. McKnight, I can't discuss that yet. We're both bankers. You know how it is: ethics are paramount, right, Mr. McKnight? Isn't that right?" He would only set up this transfer under one condition.

"What condition is that?" Stanley asked, feeling like his head was about five seconds from splitting wide open.

"It's nothing, really!"

"I would still like to know." Stanley hailed a waitress and asked for a shot of whiskey, any whiskey, as long as it arrived quickly.

"Isn't it a bit early for whiskey, my friend? Even on Swiss time, it's still morning."

"It's ten PM in San Francisco," said Stanley, like Lagrange before him, beginning to nurse a sincere hatred for this arrogant Armenian. "Everyone's drinking at ten PM in San Francisco."

The waitress set a glass in front of him containing some sort of brown liquid.

"What's this?" asked Stanley.

"Whiskey."

"I've got that. What kind?"

"Hibiki. Japanese whiskey."

"Excellent! So, at ten PM in San Francisco, everyone is drinking Hibiki!" Stanley raised his glass and gulped down its contents.

"To your health, Mr. McKnight, to your health," Grigoryan said with a gap-toothed smile. "So my condition is the following: I want you to raise my commission from 25 percent to 40. Believe me: the bank won't even notice. But I'm getting ready to open a shelter for children. We're getting corporate social responsibility here!"

"Very well, we'll consider it. We will probably be able to accommodate you. If it's a matter of corporate social responsibility, we're ready to do everything we can. We will be happy to support"—Stanley hiccupped—"support children, yes…"

Stanley felt so depleted after the meeting with Grigoryan that he called a taxi to Mario, the restaurant where he was to meet Lagrange. He didn't realize that the restaurant was a ten-minute walk away, or that the taxi driver, grasping quickly that he had a clueless foreigner on his hands, took Stanley for a ride around the city center, choosing a winding route that had Stanley completely turned around by the end.

Lagrange was standing at the edge of the sidewalk and watched in amusement as Stanley got out. He asked how much Stanley had paid.

"Only forty dollars, and not a penny more! And we hit so much traffic. What a mess."

"You could have saved those forty bucks," said Lagrange. "Or donated them to Grigoryan's foundation for children. Did he tell you all about his family?"

"Oh yes, and not just them." Stanley took off his sunglasses, wiped the bridge of his nose, and put them back on. "Why didn't you tell me he was a former psychiatrist? He sucked out all my brains and licked my skull clean."

"Since when was he a psychiatrist?"

"She—I mean he—that's what he told me!"

"And did he tell you about the children's shelter he wants to open?" Lagrange laughed and slapped Stanley on the shoulder. "He was a snitch. He worked at the embassy in London until the fall of the Soviet Union."

"A snitch?"

"Yes, an informant. He reported to the KGB about any suspect behavior by Soviet citizens abroad."

"Wow." Stanley was at a loss. "Well, that was a long time ago."

"Russians have a saying: there's no such thing as a former snitch. So Grigoryan is probably still following someone's orders."

"The thought did cross my mind that he was acting like he was trying to recruit me!" said Stanley.

"Probably not," said Lagrange. "But I know why he left the service."

"Oh?"

"He suddenly developed allergies. To almost everything—just imagine! The London air, their pudding, his morning orange marmalade, to five o'clock tea, roast beef, the English language, and even the way Tottenham was playing. Grigoryan was covered in rashes, wheezing. His limbs were swelling up. So they brought him back to Russia, ran tests, were getting ready to treat him with some kind of special medications, and—poof! Just like that, his allergies disappeared. You could call it the allergy of a Russian patriot."

"More like a Russian thief. He wouldn't be able to set up these kinds of deals in London. Are we really going to give him 40 percent?"

"We are, Stanley. Of course, we are! And here's Bernard! Let's go in. We're a minute and a half late. I hope they'll forgive us."

Waiting for them in a private room of the restaurant was Hadjiyev, who Lagrange called "our Fifty-Seven," though naturally, not to his face. This referred to the oil magnate's ranking on Forbes's Russian list.

Hadjiyev dispensed with any small talk, starting in on Pierre about how the quality of Laville & Cie was getting worse and worse and that his family office was advising him to restructure his financial streams because his investment portfolio had dropped by 15 percent. And now, again, he was going to have to hear about a correction on global markets, as if justifications will change the minus on that 15 percent into a plus. Pierre sighed sympathetically at the oil baron's laments, and when the latter at last paused for breath, introduced him to Stanley.

"Your new relationship manager, Mr. McKnight. He's the one we can both rely on. Your friend in the bank!"

"My friends have become quite expensive lately." Hadjiyev observed Stanley with the same indifferent perusal he had given the dishes waiters put down in front of him and then removed. He had eaten nothing yet.

"We have prepared a special presentation just for you," said Pierre. "Shall we?"

Fifty-Seven nodded.

"Mr. McKnight, please go ahead! Bernard, let's have the copies."

Stanley took a deep breath and opened the first page of the presentation.

"Volatility returned to the markets and dominated headlines early this month as the VIX Index recorded its single largest spike of the last five years."

Hadjiyev yawned and glanced briefly at the graph of prices that Bernard held out to him.

"Unfortunately, after the introduction of sanctions, this was a disastrous year for the Russian securities market. Negative numbers and mistrust from investors pushed Russia into the group of outsiders among emerging markets. This trend is tied to the absence of positive relations between the West and Moscow, the intensification of the sanctions standoff, and the total absence of drivers of growth for the Russian economy. We can see that on the next slide."

Stanley raised his head to see that the beads in Hadjiyev's hand had stilled, and his eyelids were drifting shut. The oligarch had clearly dozed off.

Lagrange, who couldn't help but notice as well, coughed and cut Stanley off.

"The rest from there is clear. Would you agree, Mr. Hadjiyev?"

Fifty-Seven shot up and rubbed his eyes. The beads in his hand resumed their motion.

"Fifty million," he said. "Tomorrow they're going to be transferred from Latvia, from ABLV Bank. But the next time we meet, I better not hear any unpleasant numbers from you, like minus 15 percent. And I better not be saying them myself. You show up with other numbers. Positive numbers."

As they were walking out of the restaurant together, Hadjiyev showed Lagrange his prayer beads and asked, "Do you know how many beads this has?"

"Not sure," answered Pierre.

"There are fifty-seven." For the first time since their meeting, the oligarch became animated. "I don't want there to be, say, one bead. Ten would be too little. But fewer than there are now—twenty/thirty beads, somewhere around there, that would be good." Hadjiyev threw an arm around Lagrange's shoulders and added. "I have faith in you, my friend. If I didn't, well, you know. And tell your boys too. Tell them to work hard for me."

In the car taking them to the office of their next client on Krivokolenny Lane, by Chistye Prudy, or Clean Ponds, Lagrange spent a long time massaging his forehead and face. Interacting with Hadjiyev had clearly taken a lot out of him, although he didn't seem to have done all that much. Stanley and Bernard remained quiet. They waited for their boss to speak first. Finally, Lagrange took a flask out of his jacket, sipped from it, and said, "The first, last, and most important thing to remember about this client, boys, is that we have to treat him like a child. Our only child. Capricious, nasty, ill-mannered—but ours. He's completely uninterested in our nonsense chatter, our graphs, our percentages and forecasts. What we need to do is convince him that we have a personal, almost familial, interest in his well-being. Yes, this will be a lie. But he *has* to believe it. This is a child that wants to be fooled."

"And what if we feel like strangling this child?" Bernard said.

Lagrange took another swig from his flask and shot Bernard an irritated look. "We don't do that. We're bankers." He lit up a cigarette and blew the smoke out in a huff. "And remember, boys: sincerity is key. Learn to imitate it, and your success is assured!"

"Bravo, boss!" Bernard exclaimed, clapping. "You're a genius!"

"That was a poor imitation of admiration, Bernard. Insincere." Lagrange smiled and flicked his ash out the window. "No annual bonus for you."

A narcissistic French windbag and a damn Swiss sycophant. Stanley sighed quietly and pressed his temple against the cool glass of the door, trying to chase away his headache. *What lovely company! Where in the world did I end up? Lagrange's cheap act is only effective on a weak, young mind like Bernard's.*

Stanley was nothing but disgusted with Hadjiyev, a narcoleptic oil bubble. Even the psychopathic Peshkov seemed better in comparison. Stanley was getting ready to tell Lagrange that business in general, and the banking business in particular, was no place for maxims. That it is a cruel world in which the intellect wins. But he didn't say anything. His intuition told him that it was a good idea to keep a low profile for now, and simply observe.

Their third client was a Mr. Puzikov, a modestly dressed, ordinary-looking man. Stanley's eye was drawn to the liberal coating of dandruff on the shoulders of his cheap jacket. Puzikov was carrying an old Motorola mobile phone, and his office looked like nothing so much as a tourist agency for the elderly. They didn't spend long there. Lagrange introduced Stanley, and Bernard then gave Puzikov a briefcase with papers and a flash drive. The client spoke all of two words, in English, "Sorry," and "Thank you."

On their way back to the car, Stanley asked how such a strange character had managed to earn $350 million. Lagrange lit up a cigarette and offered one to Stanley.

"Thanks, I don't smoke."

"Ah, my memory must have failed me. Not in business, though, thankfully. As for our untidy client in desperate need of a hairdresser, it's all quite simple. The Russians call them *frontoviki*—a play on words from the English word *front* and the Russian word for a soldier on the front line. Mr. Puzikov is a front man for a highly placed government official. All his assets are in Puzikov's name—stock, real estate, money, cars, yachts, airplanes. Everything except his women," Lagrange said, laughing. "So all those millions belong to the front man on paper. Meanwhile, the real owner receives a government salary and doesn't have to worry about declaring his income."

In the car again, Lagrange, as if suddenly remembering something, announced,

"Here in Russia almost all our clients are frontoviki in one way or another. It's just not always easy for everyone to see. But you'll catch on, I'm sure."

"What do you mean, all our clients?" Stanley was hit with a strong urge for a cigarette.

Lagrange frowned down at his BlackBerry, ignoring the question.

"Ok, we're heading back to the hotel. Bernard, you go over the documents for Gagarin again, then relax, go over to the Bolshoi Theater if you want. You and I, McKnight, are going to rest for a bit, get prepped for battle, and head out to our most important meeting of the day."

CHAPTER 7

McKnight went downstairs at six that evening and found Lagrange in the bar.

"We're running late. Can you try to talk to that mysterious character over there?" Pierre nodded toward one of the hotel's drivers standing by the revolving door. "He claims to speak three languages, but I can't understand a word he says. Maybe your Russian will help us out here."

"Where do we need to go?" asked Stanley.

"Gagarin's office is on Ostozhenka near the Kremlin," Pierre said, continuing to look the driver over skeptically. "Here's Ostozhenka"—Pierre pointed it out on his smartphone—"from that bridge to that square. Here's where we are. It's about eight hundred meters if we travel there directly, but traffic is jammed up in every direction."

Lagrange dug around in his jacket pocket and pulled out a business card. "Here's the exact address."

Stanley glanced at the card, then examined the map. Both the Garden Ring road and the Boulevard Ring were highlighted in blinking red lights, with the occasional stretch of orange, meaning that the entirety of central Moscow was one big traffic jam. The situation, which was looking highly problematic at the least, if not hopeless, was resolved in the most unexpected of ways.

Two men entered the hotel, immediately drawing every eye in the lobby. The first, wearing a severe black suit and white shirt without a tie, was over six feet and solidly build, speaking to a former career as an athlete or soldier. He reminded Stanley of a Viking; his curly red hair waved around his face as he walked, a short beard framed his massive jaw, and his eyes shone with a mixture of madness and complete confidence in his own superiority over all around him.

"I saw a psycho just like him in a Kubrick movie," Stanley muttered under his breath. "Although I don't think Jack Torrance had a beard."

"He's here for us, actually," Lagrange replied, slapping McKnight on the shoulder. "Relax. That's just Shamil, Gagarin's top security guy."

"He looks pretty dangerous."

"Oh, he is," Lagrange said. "He was in the special forces, back in Afghanistan, and he's been with Gagarin for over twenty-five years. So we'll get there fast. And I wouldn't be surprised if these fine gentlemen coming to pick us up were responsible for some of that traffic."

There was something mechanical in Shamil's movements, his gaze scanning across the people in the lobby, gray eyes slightly narrowed, one hand in his pocket while the other swung in time with the rhythm of his steps. His entire image, especially his lips compressed into a narrow line, testified to power held in check until needed, and an explosive power, at that: if someone got in his way, he would be thrown to the side, if a wall blocked his path, that red-bearded Viking would have simply gone through it, pausing afterward for a moment to brush the brick dust from his shoulders.

Trailing him was a rosy-cheeked man of about thirty in huge Tom Ford glasses, a gray suit and pink shirt, with a pink handkerchief in the jacket's outer pocket, and his full, red lips pulled up in a half smile. A hotel employee hurried over to them, but was stopped in his tracks by a look from Shamil. For a flash of a moment, looking into his eyes was like looking down the barrel of a shotgun, and the employee came no closer.

"Who's the other man?" asked Stanley.

"That's Anton Biryuza, the head of Gagarin's family office, his éminence grise," said Pierre, holding up his handkerchief as if wiping his mouth.

That deliberate gesture wasn't lost on Stanley. He turned his back on the two men and asked in a whisper, "So this gray eminence can read lips?"

Lagrange shrugged and met McKnight's eyes briefly.

"Even in French. He graduated from MGIMO—the Moscow State Institute of International Relations. That's the Harvard of Russia. It puts out spies and diplomats. I'm sure he learned a lot there. Let's go say hello. And smile, McKnight. Smile!"

"I'm trying," Stanley said, automatically straightening his tie.

"Biryuza likes both men and women. So try to get him to like you, darling!"

47

When Gagarin's head of security saw the bankers, he finally let Biryuza walk ahead.

While everyone exchanged the necessary greetings and pleasantries, Stanley studied the secretary discreetly. It looked like Lagrange was right; Biryuza really was gay. In the expression on the secretary's pretty face, or rather, the lack of any particular expression, all he could see was sterile courtesy. And with a bit of imagination, you could read anything you wanted into his hard but impersonal gaze, from secret madness to a boyish innocence.

Meanwhile, Shamil circled the bankers, noting everything of interest for a man of his profession. Everyone in the lobby—the hotel workers, and all the residents and guests—followed his movements, fascinated like cats drawn to sunbeams. From his smooth, mechanical motions, it was clear that Shamil was ready for any threat and would emerge victorious from any conflict. Stanley was surprised that the people closest to Gagarin were of a nontraditional sexual orientation. It seemed like a sign, or a challenge. Especially taking into account the open discrimination against sexual minorities and widespread sexism throughout Russian society.

Biryuza explained that they had come to personally collect their dear guests, as Moscow was experiencing a total breakdown in transportation. When Stanley asked what new invention Russia had devised to combat traffic, Anton showed the first hint of real emotion, something resembling a good-natured smile appearing on his face. "Just a little blue light," he answered, gesturing at McKnight and Lagrange to follow him to the exit, "a flashing light under a blue top."

Lagrange, exiting the Ritz's revolving doors, added that a car's license plate numbers mattered in Moscow as well.

"License plates starting with 'AMR,' for example," Pierre continued, as their armored black Mercedes, siren wailing away at sluggish drivers, began weaving down one-way side streets, heading in the opposite direction of the law-abiding motorists with whom they shared the road. From the passenger's seat, Shamil waved at the oncoming cars as they went, shooing them out of the way.

As they turned from Sechenov Lane onto Ostozhenka Street, near the Galina Vishnevskaya Opera Centre, the Mercedes just missed the bumper of a patrolman's parked Toyota. The officer was startled out of his doze by their screeching brakes, and grabbed for the microphone of his radio, a flush climbing on his frightened face. But he didn't get the chance to report on the incident; Shamil lowered his window and held out some sort of license toward him. Or an all-powerful pass of some kind. Whatever it was, all that mattered was the effect it had on the patrolman. He put the microphone back down in its cradle and gave a salute.

Stanley and Pierre exchanged meaningful glances.

Gagarin's office was located in an old merchant's estate affixed with a plaque reading *Protected by the State*. A two-meter-high, redbrick fence circled the building's perimeter. The fence was topped by several feet of barbed wire and a number of video cameras pointing in various directions.

Stanley read the inscription on the door—"Charitable Foundation for the Support of Entrepreneurship." "I didn't think that entrepreneurship needed charitable aid," he whispered to Lagrange as they ascended the stairs between two stone lions.

"It does in Russia," Lagrange answered quietly.

The old-world merchant style ended just past the engraved wooden doors. The mansion's interior was a huge, open room with glass staircases up to circular mezzanine floors that were intersected by winding waterfalls. Little winter gardens hung on steel cables. All of this crazy splendor was light, quiet, and empty. The only sound was the running water, and the call of a bird somewhere out of sight. They only encountered one person as they crossed the hall to the elevator. Judging from his clothing and the tools in his bag, he was either a gardener or a florist. The elevator took them up to the roof.

"We have a room here for private meetings," said Biryuza, swiping a card through an electronic lock, and they entered a large circular room, its walls and ceiling composed of frosted glass. Bookshelves stood around the perimeter of the room, alternating with aquariums of various sizes. Vases of cut flowers were placed here and there, on the floor, on benches, and on metal stands. The flowers and the vases were illuminated by lights installed in the floor. There were no signs of an office in the room, which looked more like a relaxation room in an expensive private clinic. This impression was intensified by the soft background music; the lazy strumming of an acoustic guitar was occasionally augmented by the sound of either a flute or a pipe.

It was only when they had nearly reached the opposite end of the room that the guests saw several low, wide leather chairs grouped around a black marble pedestal. McKnight went closer and noticed a crystal chest about the size of a shoebox atop the pedestal.

"What's that?" asked Stanley, gazing in astonishment at the chest.

Inside, on a crimson velvet cushion, rested a human skull, yellow with age.

"Scared, McKnight?" Lagrange asked, eyes alight.

"Is that real or fake?"

"Real, of course. Everything in Russia is real!" Lagrange bumped into Stanley with his shoulder, nudging him closer to the chest. "That's the skull of a banker from UBS who sold Gagarin an unprofitable structured note. Do a bad job, and your skull will end up next to his!" Lagrange gave a loud, guffawing laugh.

Stanley failed to appreciate the joke. He continued to stare at the skull, fascinated, and it seemed to him that the empty eye sockets were drawing him in.

"That, my dear friends, is a skull. The skull of a hero," a hoarse voice said from behind Lagrange and McKnight.

Stanley jumped and turned to see a short, stocky man with a mobile, intelligent face and mocking blue eyes. He looked to be about fifty and was wearing a gray suit over a black turtleneck.

It was a mystery where the master of the house had appeared from. He came right up to them for a handshake, watching their faces intently all the while. He offered his hand to Stanley first, and looked inquiringly at Lagrange. Stanley saw the fine lines at the corners of his elongated, impenetrable eyes.

"Viktor, this is Stanley McKnight, who I've told you about. Stanley, this is Viktor Gagarin, our favorite and most valued client," said Lagrange.

"And the owner of this over here," said Gagarin, still gripping Stanley's hand as he picked up the skull to examine it.

"It came to me by chance. I'm not an adventurer or a treasure hunter," Gagarin said with a slight lisp in heavily accented English. "Have a seat. We'll have drinks."

As Stanley and Pierre sat down in the armchairs, the bookshelf behind their backs soundlessly rotated to reveal a bar on the other side.

"Anton, please help our guests," Gagarin said, explaining, "We do without servants here. Security first. Here, we can do our work, completely cut off from the world." He gestured at the high ceiling, and Stanley saw where three fingers were missing on his right hand.

"So who does the vacuuming and changes out the flowers?" asked Pierre. "You do it as your daily workout?"

"Well, and why not? We have a schedule. Today, it's Anton, tomorrow Shamil, and the day after that, me. That kind of work helps put your thoughts in order. And it saves money!"

Gagarin spoke quickly, occasionally switching into Russian, forcing Stanley to focus closely on his words. It was also impossible to tell whether Gagarin was joking or serious.

"Cutting costs is key." Gagarin went on. "I remember one night in 1985, walking outside after another unlucky card game—we were playing in an apartment in Moscow, right by the central telegraph office—and finding one ruble in my pocket. It was a coin with Lenin's face, what we called a *lobanchik* at the time, and I was planning to take it to the only all-night café in Moscow open at that time of night, mostly a hangout for taxi drivers. But I decided to save money on the meal and went back to the card table with my solitary ruble, and I took them for all they were worth!"

Gagarin looked at them proudly and chuckled to himself.

"You were talking about the skull...," began Stanley, still dying of curiosity.

"Oh yes, the skull! This is the skull of a Civil War hero. Vasily Chapayev. A Red Army commander! Have you heard of him? No? There's even a movie about him. A famous Soviet film, directed by the Vasilyev brothers."

"What will you have, gentlemen?" asked Biryuza.

"I'll have a whiskey," said Lagrange, pointing to a Macallan Lalique crystal decanter on the bar.

"Scottish whiskey is old news!" Gagarin declared. "We're going to put Scotland out of business soon! We should be in first place for liquor production. Anton, pour us all *Zvenigorod*! Russian whiskey. Aged fifteen years. I'm the only who has it, everyone else has ten years maximum."

"Really?" Lagrange said doubtfully. "Is there such a thing as Russian whiskey?"

"Twenty years ago, one Russian investment banker decided to set up a business. Now his business is my business, and he's in jail, but that's beside the point." Gagarin smiled dreamily as if remembering something pleasant. "Anyway, he decided to follow the path of the Japanese Suntory whiskey. He gave up his career as a banker, built a distillery here, near Moscow, in a mystical place—it's like the Switzerland of the Moscow region, it's surrounded by churches and monasteries, and the water is pristine, excellent conditions for producing whiskey. Ah, thank you, Anton!"

Gagarin raised his glass.

"To your health!"

Stanley clinked his glass against Gagarin's and, with some trepidation, raised his for a sip. The Russian whiskey was tart, with a distinct taste of vanilla and fruity notes. It made him want to suck his tongue to prolong the pleasure. Stanley immediately tipped his glass for another, deeper mouthful.

"Not bad!" said Lagrange. "Not bad at all! Would you give us a bottle or two, Viktor?"

"Anton, pack up a case of Zvenigorod for our friend Lagrange," said Gagarin.

Lagrange took out a pack of Gitanes and offered them around. Gagarin declined, taking out a pack of unfiltered *Rodina* cigarettes from his breast pocket.

"After these, every other cigarette tastes weak," said Gagarin. He turned and spat through his teeth, right at the marble pedestal holding the skull.

"Now, what was I saying?" Gagarin took a deep drag and exhaled a stream of foul-smelling smoke upward. "Right, everyone still thinks that Chapayev was shot in the stomach by monarchists in 1919 and that he drowned in the Ural River. But that's not how it happened! Not at all! Red Army soldiers fished his body out and informed Stalin, who was the commissar there, and Stalin had the body of the hero transported to Moscow. But it was very hot, and the body began to decompose, so they removed the head, but even that was too far gone for burial by the Kremlin's walls, and Stalin forbade burning it, so KGB decided to preserve the skull in a museum. Long story short, I ended up with the skull. I've had it since the nineties. You could get anything from the archives then if you had a couple thousand bucks. And I liked the skull. Anton! Show our guests the slice of brain!"

Stanley, who had been listening to Gagarin's story in amazement, thought for a second that the ever-loyal Biryuza was about to show them a slice of his own brain, but it turned out to be a much simpler affair.

Anton opened a drawer and pulled out two small pieces of glass, with an object pressed between them; it resembled a piece of paper, grayish, with curving white lines.

"The brain!" Gagarin held up the glass, inserted into a sturdy steel frame. "This is a slice of Lenin's brain. Yes, the very same founder of the Union of Soviet Socialist Republics. The greatest of men, and the greatest of syphilitics." Gagarin chuckled nervously again. "I got it from the Soviet Brain Institute. Do you remember how much it cost us, Anton?"

"It was a gift," said Biryuza with a smile.

"Of course! A gift! From the Minister of Culture on my birthday. In thanks for my support of the Bolshoi Theater…what was I talking about? Oh yes: Lenin's brain has mystical powers. It's a scientific fact. Hitler, when he occupied Moscow during the war…"

Stanley flinched and glanced over at Lagrange, who was listening to Gagarin with his eyes half closed, sipping his whiskey, unperturbed.

"…the first thing he did was order them to find Lenin's brain," Gagarin went on. "Hitler was sure that all the power of Russia was contained in Lenin's brain. He didn't know that it was sent out of Moscow at the start of October in 1941 under the guard of a special division of the NKVD, beyond the Urals to a hiding place in secret salt caves. Hitler was a syphilitic too, you know. But while Lenin got the disease in a Zurich bordello, Hitler got it at about the same time from a Jewish prostitute in Vienna. Syphilis changes a person's outlook. It brings those cannibals, Lenin and Hitler, closer, and explains their bloodlust. You see? After they invented antibiotics, those kinds of maniacs didn't come to power—"

"And what's that old rifle hanging to the right of the bar?" Lagrange waved his glass of whiskey toward the wall.

"That is a Carcano Model 91/38 rifle, 6.5 mm caliber. One of three. Just don't ask me where I got it from."

"But what's so odd about this rifle?" asked the perplexed Lagrange.

"Don't talk about it with an American in the room." Gagarin tossed the rest of his whiskey back and exclaimed, "Hoo! Excellent! By the way, I have a decent collection of rare books. Come take a look."

They all got up and followed Gagarin to one of the large bookcases. The spines of expensive-looking books were visible behind matte glass doors. Stanley saw a book that he had studied at Berkeley, *Daily Life of the Western Wall* by Savvaty Sharkunov.

"Anton!" Gagarin commanded, and Biryuza opened the glass door.

Gagarin pulled on white cotton gloves and selected a large folio. "This is the rarest of the collection, a Torah, the Bologna Pentateuch, including incunabula, from the end of the fifteenth century."

"It probably cost a fortune?" Lagrange asked, shaking his head.

"My mother said that everything you can buy for money is already cheap. This Torah cost me a case of cognac. A bribe, of course." Gagarin spread out his hands apologetically. "From the state archives as well. They had no place to keep such books, you see. The damp, the rot. I signed a pledge to treat it with care, gave the cognac to a certain staff member, and now the book is mine. Why do they need the Torah in their archives? I, meanwhile, read it sometimes when I have a free moment."

"You read Hebrew?" Stanley asked.

"I studied it for just this type of thing," Gagarin said casually and tossed back another glass of whiskey.

Gagarin took a breath and looked at his guests. It was clear that he was prepared to go on talking. Stanley glanced at Lagrange again; his boss was in an excellent mood after his second Zvenigorod and looked as though he could happily go on listening to their client.

Gagarin's mood, however, shifted suddenly. He put the folio back in place and began in a calm, businesslike manner, "I have a suggestion. Let's discuss one matter here, have another drink or two, and get to know each other. Otherwise, it's just me talking. You're already tired of listening to me."

"Oh no, Viktor, of course, we're not!" protested Lagrange. "Not at all!"

"Of course, you are," Gagarin continued. "And I don't want to be a bore. So let's talk, and then I'll invite you to my home. My wife is having a party for Russian Independence Day."

Lagrange and McKnight spent the next half hour discussing Gagarin's plan to buy his new mega-yacht. Laville & Cie wanted to conduct this deal, and provide the loan, and the main issues were keeping the purchaser—i.e. Gagarin—anonymous, and the corresponding legal formalities and details.

It fell to Stanley to explain their plan for minimizing taxes. And it was here that his lack of fluency in Russian began to bother him. Several times, Gagarin couldn't hide a smile at Stanley's clumsy phrasing, which he initially found quite irritating, as he could have had a laugh or two at some of the oligarch's peculiarities of speech in English. But when Gagarin apologized sincerely and tactfully for laughing, he actually began to develop a liking for this unusual person.

From the outside, Gagarin seemed like a devil of demagogy and casuistry. But a completely different man sat before him now, discussing a business matter. Intelligent, and also somehow comfortable to be around, ordinary. As if they had stopped in to see a friend just for fun, to have a couple of drinks and talk about nothing.

It had been a long time since someone had been so happy to listen to Stanley. But their conversation ended as abruptly as it had begun. Biryuza, who had stood like an immobile shadow behind his boss this whole time, shuddered as if chilled by a draft, and lifted his wrist to check his watch.

It must have been an understood signal between them; when Gagarin saw the motion over his shoulder and the shadow of the arm before him, he interrupted Stanley's enthusiastic speech midsentence with a gentle motion of his hand.

"Sorry, McKnight! But I've got the main idea. I like you. We'll work with you. But not today. Now it's time to have some fun. You haven't forgotten the party? Pierre, *na pososhok*? Pierre!"

Lagrange had gone into a state of deep relaxation in the comfortable chair, and was nearly sleeping with his eyes open. He startled, hearing his name, and addressed Gagarin, pointing at McKnight.

"This one, Viktor, is going to buy and sell both of us. But I hope I don't live to see that day." He raised his eyebrows. "What's that Russian expression you're using?"

"One for the road," Stanley translated.

He hoped that his voice didn't betray his frustration that Gagarin hadn't let him explain his financing plan all the way through.

While they exchanged pleasantries and toasts, Biryuza was giving orders into his radio handset. They all went to the main hall a few minutes later, where Shamil waited with an entire team of security guards.

Gagarin underwent an instant transformation. Even his walk changed. He moved like ex-boxers and fighters do, rocking a bit from side to side, shoulders forward, arms held out from his body. And when he spoke, his voice was curt and hard.

"Shamil! Biryuza and Mr. McKnight are in your car. Monsieur Lagrange is with me."

The G-wagen they put Stanley in pulled out onto Ostozhenka and blocked traffic, making way for the Mercedes, siren blaring, containing Gagarin and Lagrange. A second G-wagen pulled up in front of them and a little to the right, flipped on its sirens as well, and the convoy took off toward the Church of Christ the Savior, blue lights flashing.

CHAPTER 8

S TANLEY SAT NEXT TO A guard in the back seat, and examined the large-bore, short automatic weapon the latter held upright. He knew a thing or two about guns; not because he was truly interested, but for the sake of being generally well-rounded. It was useful knowledge to have for conversations in serious company, particularly in Switzerland with its cult of weaponry. But he couldn't determine the brand of this particular gun. It was clear that Gagarin's guards had not only the last word in weapons but also tomorrow's news as well.

The G-wagen was making sharp turns right and left, pressing the flow of traffic away from the Mercedes in which Gagarin rode. Stanley was getting tossed from side to side with the motion of the car, despite being belted in. But Shamil, who was behind the wheel, was clearly having a great time. When some hapless driver tried to amble into their path, Shamil hit the loudspeaker and growled out, "To the right!" Biryuza grinned in appreciation.

When the convoy sped onto Bolshoy Kamneny Bridge, leaving the worst of the traffic behind them to wait for a green light, Biryuza pressed some buttons on the panel in front of him. A harsh guitar riff rang through the speakers, followed by a heavy drumbeat. Next came the bass, sometimes overpowering the guitar, sometimes fading to the background. Keyboards backed up the guitar, and on a powerful sonic wave over them, Stanley heard the singer's voice, high but stressed, cracking. He had a vague recollection of this voice from his time at Moscow University, singing something about blood on a sleeve.

"Wish me luck in battle!" Biryuza sang along in a thin voice against the beat and melody.

"Who's that singing?" asked Stanley. "I know that voice."

"That's the Soviet rock group, Garin and the Hyperboloids."

"I didn't know that the USSR had rock music," Stanley said. "He's a good singer; did he die a long time ago?"

"He's alive! He lives." Biryuza turned toward him and said in a tone of sudden malice, "You're the one who's already dead."

"Leave our American guest alone," Shamil said and laughed, giving Stanley a wink in the rearview mirror.

Stanley shrugged and turned his gaze out the window. He didn't understand what the haughty Biryuza was talking about, and decided not to pay him any mind.

From Lenin Avenue, their motorcade turned on Kosygin. To the right, Luzhniki Stadium rose past the Sparrow Hills and the Moscow River. The cars slowed down and took a sharp left off the road under a barrier gate. The Mercedes in front of them flashed its rear lights. Then they went through yet another barrier gate, this one with a checkpoint booth, staffed by men in camouflage carrying automatic weapons. Shamil leaned out of the window and shouted something to them in an unfamiliar language. They greeted him, flashing a peace sign.

The first G-wagen had already passed through a larger gate beyond. McKnight saw the enormous iron gates and whistled in surprise. It bore a family coat of arms, also forged in iron, made of the interweaving initials of the owner.

"Are you imagining what those gates weigh!" said Shamil with a laugh, seeing Stanley's expression in the rearview mirror.

Stanley wasn't, because he was more struck by what he saw past those gates. The parking space in front of the house was filled with rare Italian and German cars from the '60s and '70s.

Stanley leaned toward Shamil and asked, "Do those all belong to your boss?"

"Of course not," said Shamil in surprise. "He's got all his cars in the garage. And he doesn't like old cars. He likes the latest models. Ones that no one else has but him. And ones that other people get—he wants the next one. He calls Jeremy Clarkson right up, from *Top Gear*, you know the show about cars? You seen it?"

McKnight nodded.

"Clarkson gives Gagarin advice on what new Ferrari models to buy, and our boss sends him the best Russian models to show his gratitude. Our international cultural exchange."

After driving past the rows of parked cars, the G-wagen braked by the porch of a palatial three-story building, parking right behind the Mercedes, from which Gagarin and Lagrange had already emerged. Two young women were approaching, dressed in light cover-ups and straw hats and carrying glasses of champagne. But Stanley didn't have the chance to get a good look at them, because they had already entered the house with Gagarin and Lagrange by the time he was out of the car.

Biryuza approached and invited Stanley to follow him.

He explained that this place had been one of the residences of the first president of the USSR, but after things went badly for him, he had to sell it to a charitable foundation, headed by Gagarin. For a paltry $20 million.

"The boss calls this place his 'backup aerodrome,'" said Anton. "But I call it 'Uncle Tom's Cabin.'"

"Oh? And why is that?" asked Stanley.

Biryuza paused for a moment, looking at Stanley as if seeing him for the first time. He said that he had his reasons, several, in fact, but it was an open question whether their American guest would figure those reasons out.

After hearing these vague explanations, McKnight decided that the secretary was just trying to mess with his head and resolved not to take it seriously. He was well aware of how Russians liked to make mountains out of molehills and to blow smoke.

They went through a long procession of rooms decorated with cheap-looking, tacky furniture. These rooms were obviously not used often.

"We'll stop in the dressing room first." Seeing his guest's confusion, Biryuza explained, "You see, as Viktor told you, his wife Mila is hosting a society party here tonight. She calls these events 'freak parties.' Why freak? I'll explain. Mila has a weakness for unusual, strange, and exotic personalities. If you ask me, they are all foolish, untalented, and egocentric psychopaths. The boss can't stand them. But he must. Those are the rules of our public life. If you don't want to stand out in this motley crowd, I'd recommend changing into something a little more frivolous. In that suit and tie, you're likely to be mistaken for security."

Stanley couldn't tell whether Biryuza was being serious or not. It was abundantly clear, however, that Biryuza's attitude toward him had suddenly soured, and that the secretary was now paying particular attention to him, intentionally noticeable attention. But when their talk turned to business, all his irony and sarcasm disappeared instantly. It took Stanley a bit longer to notice that Biryuza only allowed himself these liberties in the absence of Lagrange or Gagarin. Not that the secretary's behavior bothered him so much or caused him any inconvenience. He had just become accustomed to the strict observance of hierarchies in his (admittedly not lengthy, but still serious) career as a private banker. And while Lagrange, his own boss, was responsible for determining the level of distance between them, which was clear to them both, with Biryuza, there should have been no room for any individual, or personal, emotions between them. He realized, however, that it would be simpler just to ignore the attitude.

"I have two questions," McKnight said.

"I'm listening, my dear," Biryuza replied.

"How soon can I see my boss, Monsieur Lagrange? I have to tell him something, and it is, unfortunately, somewhat urgent. And mobile service is blocked here, I see."

Stanley had zero urgent news. But he was very uninspired by the prospect of participating in some sort of Russian clown show. He was also pretty confident that there was no need to get dressed in carnival gear, either, and that Biryuza was trying to play a prank on him.

Anton glanced at his watch.

"The main show starts in half an hour. I'm sure that your boss won't be late," he said, switching into his official tone again. "Will your urgent news keep for half an hour?"

"Or do you need to tell him over the radio?" a high-pitched voice asked over Stanley's shoulder. "I have a walkie-talkie."

McKnight and Biryuza turned at the same time, nearly banging heads.

There was a young man right behind them, bent toward the ground in a ballet dancer's reverence. Stanley couldn't hold back a smile. Who was this joker, with his heavy makeup, shiny skin-tight suit à la 1970s Freddie Mercury, and the mannered speech of a capricious child? At the same time, the stranger's expression was perfectly serious; his suggestion was clearly meant to be helpful.

"Michel!" Anton said in a scolding tone. "You're sneaking up on me again like a ninja. Just you wait: some jumpy special forces veteran is going to shoot you one of these days. This is Mr. McKnight. McKnight, this is Monsieur Gauthier. He is our head conductor and the director of all our adventures and events. Which you can take part in, if you wish."

"As a matter of fact, I have been asked to escort you, Monsieur McKnight. Come along. I'll show you everything and tell you all about it."

The three of them walked on. While Michel enthusiastically recounted what show business celebrities would be participating in the entertainment that evening, and how much money he had saved in negotiations with their agents, Biryuza quietly told Stanley about Gauthier himself. As it turned out, the Swiss man had originally worked as a doorman in a hotel that Gagarin owned. There was nothing particularly noticeable about him, except that Gagarin happened to strike up a conversation with him the day of his return from an exceptionally successful business trip to Switzerland. That coincidence was enough to spark their acquaintance, and Gauthier turned out to be full of pleasant surprises. He spoke excellent Russian and knew everything, or almost everything, about the Moscow club scene where, thanks to his sociable nature and charm, he knew everyone worth knowing.

Anton began to list all of the doorman's famous friends, but Stanley stopped him.

"I'm afraid it's wasted on me. I'm not going to know any of the names." He paused, adding, "Nor do I want to. In America, stars like yours play dances at roadside bars."

"Oh, and now you'll tell us you don't know the prima donna?" Biryuza asked, offended.

Michel heard that question, and he stopped, interested in McKnight's reply. What would this arrogant man have to say?

"She's still alive?" asked Stanley, his tone surprised.

Biryuza and Gauthier exchanged glances. They couldn't tell whether McKnight was making a bad joke, or whether he was hopelessly ignorant about Russian life.

Stanley's question was intentionally provocative. He knew that the aging singer who rose to fame in the USSR, whom all the Russians called the 'prima donna,' was still alive. That she even had a young husband, with whom she had some children, no less. He was just plain tired of listening to Biryuza's pointless bragging.

The ensuing awkward pause was broken by the arrival of a dwarf, who appeared from out of nowhere. He was wearing a vest and shorts of red leather, decorated all over with an abundance of rivets and spikes. Steel chains shone around his head and neck, fastened with more rivets and bolts. The metal didn't end there: his ears, nose, and eyebrows were adorned with numerous pins, crosses, and bells. Even his shoes appeared to be made out of some kind of foil, with spurs. Despite his militant outfit, the dwarf turned out to be quite a cheerful guy.

"Michel! Just the man I'm looking for," he said to Gauthier. "We're starting soon, and no one can explain to me how I'm supposed to serve cocaine to the guests. I can't get it separated into little packages for everyone in this crowd—we have about a hundred people on the guest list, and then there's another thirty or forty artists. And the girls from the escort service, I can't even count them. So what am I supposed to do?

"Not a problem!" Gauthier pulled a pack of cards from his pocket. He found the one he needed, and Stanley saw that they were electronic key cards. He handed it over to the dwarf: "This is to the basement. There are porcelain bowls on the rack, painted with dragons. Get five; the waiters will help you. You didn't see the pyrotechnics guys arrive, did you?"

"They're in the garden, getting their cannons ready," said the dwarf, and left.

Stanley and his companions continued on.

They came to an interior courtyard, and stepped into a human whirlpool. Gauthier excused himself to go prepare for the show, and Biryuza led McKnight over to a small fountain. Guests wandered around with glasses of champagne, many of whom Stanley recognized: Russian oligarchs, members of parliament, and several ministers. And here was Lagrange in a group of bank clients, Durand, and several women. Even from a distance, you could tell he was perfectly at ease in this atmosphere.

He paused and raised his glass, about to make a toast, it seemed, and all heads turned in his direction. Just then, Pierre noticed Stanley and gestured him over with a nod.

While McKnight maneuvered through the crowd toward Lagrange, he had time to observe that only the performers and the models were in circus costumes. All the other guests were dressed in clothes appropriate for this type of gathering; the men were in tuxedos or suits, and the women wore evening gowns. So why had Biryuza tried to get him to change into a circus outfit? Was he upset about the attention Gagarin, his boss, had paid McKnight? Work jealousy? Ridiculous. It should have been clear that Stanley was just a promising specialist in a private bank. Tomorrow he would return to Switzerland, and this might be the last time he saw these Russian businessmen in his entire life.

A familiar face flashed in the crowd and was gone just as quickly. Anastasia? What was she doing here! Actually, why wouldn't she be? But then Pierre threw an arm around his shoulder.

"Where have you been, Stanley?" Lagrange waved a waiter over and grabbed a champagne flute from his tray. "I've already solved the problem of the yacht for our dear friend Gagarin. He, of course, shares a name with the first cosmonaut, but we'll fly higher. You'll be in charge of the deal. So tonight, you have more than enough reason to get blind drunk."

Stanley shrugged. It was odd; in considering this problem, he had prepared himself for lengthy, involved discussions, multiple clarifications and revisions of fees and interest rates, the involvement of outside experts on all types of technical issues—and all of a sudden the decision was made, in no more than half an hour. Maybe this was the Russian way, to get things done with a handshake behind the scenes, and let the assistants figure out the rest. He started to express his concerns to Pierre about this manner of handling serious matters, but the sky above grew dark, and the guests shouted and clapped.

"Maybe I should try and talk to him? There are several key points that I'd like to resolve in a private conversation." McKnight had to shout over the din so Lagrange could hear him.

"Assume that the answer to all of your questions is yes," Pierre said, closing his eyes firmly. "And anyway, he's gone. Somebody important called. From the Kremlin, I believe. The minister of extremely important and extremely urgent affairs. So he said. But I have a sneaking suspicion that he simply didn't want to waste his time on all this nonsense. Ah, it's starting."

CHAPTER 9

S TANLEY LOOKED AROUND. GIGANTIC FIGURES stalked about the courtyard, stilts peeking through their long robes. Their convulsive motions made them resemble mannequins come to life. They wore hoods over their heads, with slits for eyes and painted mouths, and their robes were covered in crudely drawn circles and broken lines. Someone in a chicken costume was leading this procession. Every few steps, people in multicolored tights would approach the chicken, carrying an egg. The chicken would leap onto the egg, clucking loudly. Each time, the egg split open, and doves came flying out, accompanied by the shouting of the crowd nearby. The performers on stilts added to the cacophony, frightening the birds with their whooping and whistling.

"These *performances* in the French manner are all the rage here in Russia," Lagrange explained to McKnight. "They're considered a very sophisticated kind of entertainment. This guy on stilts in the chicken costume has managed to convince his rich friends that they get a glimpse of high culture with these intricate and expensive shows. These poor Russians, so lacking in culture," he sneered.

The dove-filled eggs ran out, and the chicken began to mime an attempt at flight, surrounded by the figures on stilts.

Enormous inflatable red hammers and sickles flew down from the roof onto them. New performers descended on trapezes among the balloons, dressed as characters from the Soviet period—miners, steelworkers, milkmaids, sailors, and other members of the working class, as if the statues in the Moscow metro had come to life. When the first of them had reached the ground, the Russian anthem began to play, and pairs of singers, women and men, emerged onto the balconies overlooking the courtyard to join in. They were also dressed in costumes; Stanley's best guess was that these were the national costumes of the former Soviet republics.

When they had finished the second verse of the anthem, another singer came out of the fountain, dressed as a diver. The song's melody switched to a lively disco rhythm. To Stanley's amazement, most of the Russians around him started to sing along, as they had not been doing when the anthem was playing. Or at least, not that he'd noticed.

The performers who'd come down from the roof split into several groups and began to dance, fanning out between the guests and coming back to the fountain. Light from spotlights raced around the courtyard, and confetti in the shape of red stars rained down from above, followed by streamers. A new, slower song came on; from what Stanley could make out, it was about intoxicating Russian evenings. The lead singer was now an exceedingly tall, curly-haired man with white wings spreading out behind his back.

While he sang, waiters began to wheel carts carrying appetizers and drinks onto the lawn. The guests, along with the crowd of performers, continued to sing along and dance as they began to eat and drink.

The wild scene left Stanley a bit stunned.

"I guess I'm behind the times," he told Lagrange. "But it's over my head, I have to say."

"That means your head is in good order," Pierre answered impassively, lighting up a Cuban cigar.

They walked over to one of the bars set up under a balcony. It was so noisy that there was no point in trying to talk.

At that moment, someone fired the cannons on the roof. They looked quite real, but were loaded with some sort of fluorescent powder. This, it turned out, was a prearranged signal. The singer with the angel wings passed the microphone to the chicken.

"Comrades! Dear comrades!" he pronounced enthusiastically. His voice trembled with nerves and soared into the evening sky, multiplied by the many speaker columns around him into an electronic echo.

"We are gathered here today to celebrate Independence Day. Our great Russian independence." He paused and continued louder, "Independence from the rest of the world."

"Down with sanctions! Down with America!" the crowd shouted, and McKnight caught Lagrange watching him with laughing eyes.

"The world isn't always fair to us," continued the chicken. "Although the only thing we bring into this world is love." He lowered his voice to murmur. "Well, and a little oil and gas."

This was met with friendly laughter.

"And after you have a little refreshment, you'll have as much independence from everything in the world as you can handle."

He waved his hands, and the cannons on the roof fired once more into the sky.

A drum roll began, and the dwarf appeared in the spotlight, carrying cups. Four waiters walked ceremoniously behind him, carrying the same cups.

Stanley had been prepared for anything, he thought, but not this.

"Pierre!" He turned to Lagrange. "Is that what I think it is?"

But it was Biryuza who answered him, approaching from behind.

"You thought, right, my dear! It's coke. High-quality cocaine. The people love it."

Lagrange laughed slyly and slapped Stanley on the back.

"I warned you, my friend. Russia is a country of big surprises. Don't worry about your reputation; everything that happens here is strictly confidential. No photos, no blackmail. It's a celebration of independence, just like they said."

"If you don't like it, you can go up to the second floor," said Biryuza. "For your enjoyment, we have a cigar room, bar, billiards room, private rooms with women. Private rooms with men." Biryuza paused, looking at McKnight with interest for the first time that day.

"Really? Stanley, my dear, looks like there's a good time waiting for you!" Lagrange exhaled a stream of smoke and smiled broadly.

Stanley just shook his head, but Biryuza went on.

"I'm afraid that you won't be able to leave the grounds until midnight. Security rules. Shall I take you anywhere?"

"Thanks, no need," Stanley replied. "I'll manage on my own somehow."

Biryuza left.

"Ok, Stanley, I'm not your babysitter, either," said Lagrange. "There's nothing a young man needs as much as the company of a beautiful women. And don't play the virgin. Moscow is sin city! You never know when you'll get the next chance to really let go. Especially in that damn village they call Zurich. The business part of our schedule is concluded. Now we celebrate independence!" At that, he clapped loudly and beckoned a waitress over.

McKnight circled the perimeter of the courtyard, keeping to the shadow of the balconies. The spotlight roved over the crowd, highlighting scenes of revelry here and there. The dwarf appeared in each scene, as if scripted, with his cup full of cocaine, which he now carried on a tray, along with everything necessary for a quick mood booster. Stanley watched a man approach, grab a straw, and place one end at the line already set for him and the other end in his nose. He inhaled, and his head jerked back sharply—another traveler off on the night's journey.

A trio of well-dressed men rolled up hundred-dollar bills, took the cocaine from the dwarf, and stood on the edge of the fountain. One of the girls with them waved her hand, and they followed her command, sniffing once, twice, and then loudly shouted at the same time "Hui!" before toppling face up into the water. The girl dove in after them, and several more guests followed their example.

The dwarf disappeared from the spotlight and reappeared at the other end of the lawn, where a large group of men were entertaining themselves by spraying jets of champagne onto the dancers on stage. The idea was that if they hit their target, the girl would take off the item of clothing where the champagne landed. The performers on stage were joined by several women who were clearly guests at the party. The dwarf decided to liven up the game with his magical chalice. He began to weave among the dancers, tossing handfuls of cocaine into their faces from below, causing a panic, the girls squealing in fear. The men below let out a defensive volley of champagne, and the dwarf, protecting his cocaine, dove back into the darkness.

Stanley saw him again a minute or two later. A waiter was carrying a tray with glasses in front of him, and the entertainer was smearing the edges of the glasses with powder.

At the same time, however, Stanley noticed various people in elegant suits and evening gowns conversing quietly. Light sparkled on diamond necklaces and flashed off the gold frames of glasses, shining in the ripples of silk dresses. It was like watching two different, completely separate, realities, intermingled on the same screen.

But McKnight walked past them both; neither was his reality.

He seemed to be in some kind of third dimension where only snatches of strangers' conversations and the polite, inquiring glances of waiters reached him. Several times, Stanley automatically took strange drinks from their trays before setting them down again without a sip the first place he could find.

I need to find somewhere to take a break from this hurricane, he thought. *Or maybe it's time for me to get so drunk this craziness starts to make sense. Then we'll see what happens.*

Remembering Biryuza's mention of a cigar room, Stanley decided to seek it out. Maybe the guests snorting coke and diving into fountains hadn't made it there yet.

He got stopped twice on his way. The first time, he ran into Peshkov, who was thoroughly drunk, and supported by twin girls dressed as rocket ships. One of them was labeled *Soyuz*, and the other *Apollon*. From the looks of the girls' eyes, they had recently met with the ubiquitous dwarf. Maybe not for the first time, either.

"You have to come fly with us!" Peshkov cried. "Look what excellent rockets I have. If you come, we'll have a truly international crew. This guy"—he turned to the girls—"is an American, and a Swiss banker. Have you ever heard a thing like that?"

The twins liked the idea of taking another pilot on board.

"We have enough fuel!" said one of them with a laugh.

"Just don't knock us out of orbit!" added the other.

He was finally able to get away only after they talked him into having a drink. By the time they released him, McKnight felt that the smile on his face had turned into a grimace—he didn't recognize himself in the mirror behind the waiter who was serving them.

But the tests to his willpower didn't end there.

Robert Durand was the next to grab him—he couldn't find the bathroom, where, he was certain, the woman of his dreams was waiting for him.

"Or man?" he interrupted himself. "Doesn't matter. Gotta end up on the toilet either way. Can you take me there?"

He was so drunk it took him three tries to get the last word out. Robert latched onto him, and McKnight was too cautious to knock him off like he wanted to. There were definitely security cameras all around. In the end, he had a drink with Durand as well. That was the only way to get rid of him.

McKnight set off toward his destination once again, but fate had other ideas.

"I know my man by the way he walks!" a voice sang out behind him. Stanley turned slowly; Anastasia stood in the doorway, listing slightly to one side from the weight she was carrying. An enormous bottle of champagne rested on one shoulder, and her short dress was embossed with a Veuve Clicquot label.

"Hey!" called Stanley. "Are you part of the masquerade?"

"I am."

"How much does one of those 'widows' cost?"

"Are you asking about me or about the bottle? Either way, they're not going for cheap!"

"How much?"

"I am not on sale today, noncommercial days, you know, but I can share the champagne," she said, nodding her head toward the bottle. "Can you give me a hand? This bottle's too heavy, just like my life."

McKnight sighed, trying again, without success, to remember the unpleasant circumstances of their night in the hotel room, and took the bottle from her.

"What's eating you, Stanley? Don't sigh like a lonely orphan, please," said Anastasia with a grateful smile.

"Me? Ah, nothing serious—I just can't remember anything from last night. I remember you pulling me towards the shower and then—it's a blank." Stanley cradled the bottle in his arms as if he was rocking a baby.

"You're right. That's not serious. I know an excellent way to restore your memory." Anastasia pulled her dress back into place. "Follow me! I'll show you the master's mansion. I know everything from top to bottom here. Not my first time." She took off her shoes and started up the staircase.

Anastasia pressed some numbers on the code lock leading to the third floor, and they passed down a long hallway into a spacious room with high ceilings and a balcony overlooking the park.

"We won't turn on lights or music, and no one will know that we're here," Anastasia said as they entered.

"Who's looking for us?" McKnight asked in surprise. "And anyway, it's Independence Day today."

"Forget it. Let's open up the champagne. Just be careful. There's some glasses on the table. See them?"

"Yes, and don't worry. I'm pretty much the world's best champagne opener."

Stanley didn't hold onto the cork, and it shot up to the ceiling, the stream of champagne just missing Anastasia. They could barely see to fill their glasses.

"Now we just have to avoid stepping in that puddle," said Anastasia, drinking from her glass. "Or we'll get stuck for good. Champagne makes the best glue, and I hate getting stuck to someone more than anything else in the world."

While she was talking, she reached down with one hand and deftly unzipped Stanley's pants, then pushed him down into a soft chair.

"This is how you recover memories." Anastasia took a little champagne into her mouth and got onto her knees in front of Stanley, pulling his zipper down further. Her agile tongue and the champagne bubbles quickly did the trick—he closed his eyes and began to remember.

At some point, Stanley's member was so far down Anastasia's throat that he couldn't hold back a shout.

"Did you remember?" asked Anastasia, raising her head.

"Not entirely," whispered Stanley, "but that's really helping, what you're doing…"

"Then we'll continue!" Anastasia took another sip of champagne, but just then, they heard the door creak, and a cold draft blew into the room. The curtains at the balcony fluttered in the breeze, their shadows snaking across the floor.

"Who's there?" a sharp female voice called out.

Their uninvited guest searched around and found the switch of a large floor lamp. Stanley squinted. The intruder was a young woman—tall, slender, with a proud bearing and black hair flowing down to her shoulders.

"What is going on in this house!" she said. "There's a blowjob in every room. It's not Independence Day. It's Blowjob Day. May I ask why you're doing this in an area closed to guests?"

"Damn!" said Anastasia, quickly gulping down her champagne and leaning down to whisper in Stanley's ear. "Sorry, honey, I have to run!" She kissed his cheek, her lips sweet from the champagne. "Till next time!"

Anastasia grabbed her shoes, and with the parting words, "Sorry, girl!" ran past the woman standing in the doorway and down the dark hallway. The woman walked further into the room, and Stanley quickly covered himself with his hand. Her silhouette was familiar to him, as if he'd seen it already today.

"Who are you?" she asked.

McKnight could tell from her voice that she was very high. The lamplight fell on the girl's long legs, illuminating the thin fabric of her dress, and Stanley thought she might not be wearing any underwear.

"Guard? Dancer? Guest?" she continued, flipping her long back curls behind her back.

"Guest," replied Stanley. "I was invited…I'm a financial consultant… at your service!"

"I hear an accent. You're not Russian. Definitely not Russian."

"The accent gave me away?"

"You're too handsome for a Russian."

"You don't like Russian men?"

"They're boring. And usually ugly. They don't like good-looking men like you in Russia. Suspicious. Except if you're gay, or a lowly physical trainer at the gym." The girl laughed. "A Russian man should be fat, with a potbelly, and a second chin."

"Like a penguin?" Stanley recalled the appearance of the party guests down below.

"Exactly. An emperor penguin." The girl walked closer, wiping the palm of her hand across her nose. "Where are you from?"

"California. A small town called Carmel. Do you know it?"

"Yes, I've played golf there. You look like their famous mayor, but shorter." She fell silent, studying him intently. "Are you married, financial consultant?"

"I'm getting divorced." Stanley came to a full realization of the foolishness of his situation. He awkwardly felt around for the edge of his pants, stood partway, and pulled them back up. Then he located the bottle of champagne and lifted it up with two hands to take a sip.

"That's what you all say. Champagne? Excellent. I've got coke. Not the stuff that everyone's been using tonight. This is high quality, from Argentina, the purest you can find in Moscow. Here, try some."

"I don't do coke," Stanley answered gloomily. "I don't like drugs; I'd rather drink."

"You're boring."

"I'm an alcoholic. And proud of it."

"I'm going to call security now," she threatened and sat down on the wide arm of the chair, leaning against the back so closely that Stanley could feel the heat of her body.

Suddenly Stanley realized where he knew her from. He'd only seen her from behind—when he got out of the car after Biryuza. Why had he remembered her? Ah, definitely her height. The woman walking next to her had been in six-inch spike heels. But this girl had been half a head taller nonetheless. And it was all in the legs. They were nothing short of breathtaking. The stranger threw one leg over the other, bringing her knee just inches from Stanley's lips.

"Come on, handsome stranger with the mysterious accent. Let's do it!" She held the packet out to Stanley. "Let's go!"

"What's so mysterious about my accent? And I'm surely not handsome," Stanley protested, but the woman spilled a mound of cocaine onto the arm of the chair, cut two lines with her credit card (J. P. Morgan Reserve card, Stanley noted automatically) and pulled out a silver tube.

"Ok," she agreed. "Not as handsome as a fairy-tale prince. And your accent isn't mysterious, my American friend. But you have a nice look about you. I can tell you're a good guy. Otherwise, that slut wouldn't have been on her knees in front of you. How did she do it?"

"Do what?"

"You know what."

"She had champagne in her mouth and…"

"What a pro! Here, have some!"

Stanley could see there was no getting out of it. He couldn't see what he was doing in the dim light, and inhaled more than he meant to. Stanley hadn't touched coke since he'd been a student at Berkeley. The icy cold burned down his throat, and the chill hit his temples. In an instant, he felt wild energy flood down his arms and legs, a rainbow of colors appeared before his eyes, and, almost unconscious, McKnight heard a woman's voice from a neighboring universe.

"You spilled! There's a little left…on my leg."

Stanley leaned over again and licked the remainder of the powder of her tanned skin, rubbing a little over his gums.

"Oh wow!" she said. "You're sweet, American."

Ten minutes later, she pulled out yet another packet. She inhaled its contents, switching between nostrils.

"Don't worry. I don't do this often," she said, catching Stanley's eye on her. "I mean, I'm not like these sluts they rounded up for the party. But it's so fun with you!"

"With me or with the coke?"

"With you, dummy, with you. A chance meeting with a handsome stranger…"

She looked past Stanley, reaching for the neck of the champagne bottle. Stanley moved to help her, and they ended up in an accidental embrace.

"Sorry," said Stanley, pulling back a little.

"No problem," she said, taking a sip from the bottle.

"Those legs are works of art," Stanley said, surprising himself. "They belong in a museum, a Botticelli painting, maybe. But I always thought that romantic Italian was exaggerating, making things up. Or that he had something wrong with his eyes. Because legs like that just don't exist in nature. But you look like his *Spring*. Except that one was a redhead, if I'm remembering correctly."

"Oh my god! What is this? I've never heard such compliments! Are you saying I'm the *Spring*?"

"Long legs aren't that rare," Stanley went on, still with no idea why he was speaking so openly. "That's not it. But there are certain rules of harmony. No, not rules. Laws. And there are exceptions to the rules. Violating those laws. But with you it's the other way around."

Stanley thought that the cocaine had done a good job of loosening his tongue. *This drug is the best thing in the world*, he thought. An entirely different thing than the cocaine he'd tried as a student. It was as if, after long years of blindness, someone had handed him magical glasses, and the world was filled with marvelous colors. His senses were heightened, and he could smell every cell of this woman's body.

"Are you still talking about my legs?"

"No, not just your legs. Now I can see that it's not just your legs."

"And what do you see? It's pretty dark here, with just this lamp." She reached out and ran her fingers over McKnight's face. "But to the touch, you're not bad, either. And you smell like champagne."

She tried to continue the conversation in a mocking, independent tone, but she was doing worse and worse at it.

"We don't know each other," said Stanley. "And we probably won't get to know each other. Ever. So there's no point in pretending to be someone else, given our situation."

"Okay, then! Carry on about Botticelli. I liked that. I will just suffer from my curiosity about the sophisticated romantic who ended up here. We mostly have penguins here."

She shivered a little and smoothed her curls across her forehead.

"I just have one personal question. It's important to me."

Stanley nodded. He was ready to answer all her questions, but he couldn't let go of the fear that everything he was experiencing was just the effect of the drug.

"You said you were getting divorced? I know it's stupid to ask. It's just that I'm married, myself. But free to do what I like. If you see what I mean."

"Legally, yes, I'm also married, but practically single. You could say that it's an open marriage. My wife lives in San Francisco, and I live in Zurich. We see each other twice a year, and haven't had time to get divorced."

"It doesn't matter how often you meet; what those meetings mean to you—that's what matters. And by the way, if the spouses do not live together, good marriages are more frequent."

"But you have a different situation, I think? Married for money?"

"All marriages are a calculation," she answered. "Everyone counts on finding happiness, after all."

Stanley decided that he didn't care what she said, because all he needed to do was watch and remember. Remember that profile. And how she ran her little finger over the corner of her mouth. How her eyelashes fluttered, and how the moonlight caught on them.

She leaned forward slightly, and her breasts brushed against his face.

"Let's not get into details about me." Her voice seemed to be fading. "I'm just officially someone's wife. Everything else is just details."

For the first time in a long time, there was a break in their conversation.

"That's it? No more Botticelli?" she asked, interrupting the silence.

Now she was peering through the moonlit dark, trying to make out the face of her unknown companion.

"I saw you, you and your girlfriend. I saw you from below, from the courtyard, when you were coming here. I thought it was Polina. My friend Polina. Although she's in another city now. But that's what I saw, what I imagined I saw. I thought something stupid and came here. And it was Anastasia. I know girls like her. A model from the escort service, but she had the nerve to act like I was her friend!"

"Sorry, weren't you saying something about Botticelli?" Stanley returned to the conversation with some difficulty. The cocaine made him feel like his eyes had frozen in place, that he'd never be able to blink again. His new acquaintance had been telling the truth—either this was very pure cocaine, or someone had added a hallucinogen.

"Too bad that you're done with the compliments. I liked those."

"To be honest, I just started thinking out loud. Because it was so strange—when I got here today, I saw you from a distance. For only a matter of seconds. And I didn't even see your face. But it left a mark on me, somehow. You know how it is, some insignificant moment from

73

childhood gets stuck in your memory forever, down to the smallest detail. And for some reason, your figure, your walk, how you climbed the stairs, all of it was stamped in my mind. I'm looking at you now, and it's as if I'm remembering all of you."

His companion produced another packet out of thin air.

"Have you ever tried writing poetry? But maybe you better not. How about I give you more food for thought. Want some?"

The packet slipped from her fingers.

Stanley wanted to answer yes, but his mouth was too dry. She threw her leg over his, and then she was on top of him.

"Scared?" she asked Stanley, running her hand down his cheek. "Everything you're dreaming about now is on the other side of that fear."

Stanley felt her hand moving down his pants.

"Get up!" she commanded, wrapping one arm around Stanley's neck, and lifting her dress with the other. Stanley's pants ended up around his ankles once again.

"Like that! Just like that!" she whispered, "I'm the *Spring*! You'll have to remember that as well. Like that! Yes!"

When she left the room, she told him not to follow for at least ten more minutes. Stanley spent the time pulling himself together. He found the packet of cocaine on the floor and finished the remaining half a gram. He took a sip of warm, nasty champagne, grimaced, and glanced at his watch.

He felt empty inside, but at the same time, thoughts whirled through his mind, his heart beating even faster. He felt stronger than he ever had, energy bursting to get out of him. Goddamned cocaine.

Stanley crossed the room to the window.

Two men in black suits were trying to pull a third out of the fountain by the main entrance. The man in the water was wearing only a shirt, high black socks, and shoes, and was fighting as hard as he could, threatening to chase everyone out, castrate, and kill them.

"Comrade, Konstantin, you'll catch cold! It's late! Your family is waiting for you at home. And you have to be at the ministry in the morning!"

said the men in black suits surrounding him. Stanley drank more champagne from the bottle and looked at his watch. Exactly ten minutes had gone by. He left the room.

When Stanley found Lagrange in a bar on the first floor, his boss looked him over with an experienced eye, assessing Stanley's condition.

"Excellent! I hope the reputation of our bank is not in danger," said Lagrange. "Your eyes are shiny from cocaine."

"It just happened," answered Stanley.

"Hm, what do we have here," Lagrange pulled Stanley's collar to the side. "One woman with nearly colorless lipstick, and another"—he took a half step back and pointed to the waist of Stanley's pants—"with a bright-red shade!"

In the corner of the bar, a thin musician with a wide smile played the guitar and sang a song about a maniac in the alley. The sparse crowd of remaining guests sang along with him discordantly.

"I'm proud of you, Stanley!" said Lagrange. "Ah, to be thirty-three again! Where is that happy, young Pierre Lagrange? I'm proud of you, and envious. Now you just have to finish with what you started."

"What's that?"

"Whiskey! And then we'll head right to the hotel. We have a plane in three hours." Lagrange pointed a bottle of whiskey out to the bartender and put up two fingers. "But we'll have one for the road!"

Stanley smoothed the hair over his head and tried to slow down the rhythm of his heart.

"I could use a cigarette," he asked Lagrange.

"Take one, and some good advice for free." Lagrange dug around in his pack, took out the last cigarette, and handed it to Stanley. "Remember the prime commandment of the private banker."

"I'm all ears," said Stanley, lighting his cigarette with a trembling hand.

"Never do cocaine with Russian clients!"

"Why not?"

"It's dangerous. You'll get chatty, and they'll definitely use it against you."

"Don't worry. I wasn't with a client."

"Who knows what the future holds and who will be a client one day?" Lagrange drank his whiskey down, shook himself, and looked at his watch. "Still, there's nothing better in the world than drinking whiskey at six AM!"

"I agree," said McKnight, and tossed his glass back. "It's even better than doing coke at five AM."

"You're a quick learner," said Lagrange, pulling Stanley toward the exit. "It's time to go."

That morning, Stanley, Lagrange, and Bernard flew back to Zurich. To McKnight, it felt as though he'd been thrown into a different dimension for a couple of days, and now he was back in his own.

PART TWO: PRIVATE BANKER

CHAPTER 10

I T ONLY TOOK A COUPLE of days in Zurich for McKnight's time in Moscow to recede into the distance, his adventures there taking on the quality of some art house film. Or a nightmare, drug-induced hallucination. If it had all really happened, where was that shirt with the traces of lipstick on the collar? But he couldn't find it anywhere. He didn't recall throwing it away upon returning to the hotel that morning.

One week went by, and then another, without any word from Gagarin, no references to their Moscow trip. Neither Lagrange nor Bernard were to be found at the bank, spending entire days away at client meetings and on trips. And so the frightening memories seemed to melt away in the languid, serene warmth of the Swiss summer.

In the mornings, Stanley rode his bike past the University of Zurich on his way to work. He liked to look at the open faces of the young students, concerned about ordinary things like classes, exams, first loves. There was no place in this simple word for the crazy Russian nouveau riche, who drank like it was their last day on earth, and could buy most human beings like any other product. *Or maybe I'm underestimating modern students*, thought Stanley.

In addition to everything else, he was tormented by feelings of guilt. He and Christine weren't divorced; they may have seen each other infrequently, but they had agreed before Stanley's move to Europe to try to revive their marriage. To give it a shot, at least. And now he had cheated on his wife with two Russian whores, two days in a row. What a bastard he was. There was no excuse for it.

The memories of those nights filled him with heat, and shame: both for his actions and for how much he had enjoyed them. Then the shame was replaced by vague feelings of guilt that he tried to repress as best he could. He told himself that Christine was probably not living the life of a nun, either. A beautiful young woman in San Francisco, all alone? Wait, that was absurd. Would Christine really cheat on him? No, it wasn't possible. Why would she cling to the marriage so tightly, then? She could just tell him it was all over, and start a new life. Christine, unlike him, had the guts to make a change. She had been engaged to an L.A. lawyer when she met Stanley. The lawyer was unceremoniously dismissed, even though the wedding was only two months away. As soon as Christine realized where her relationship with McKnight was going, she moved on decisively.

McKnight buried himself at work, and it was a refuge from the unwanted memories. He began to think that it might be time to actually divorce his wife and find a new girlfriend. It would be simpler, and he could get rid of this guilt.

Thoughts of this imagined girlfriend began to nag at him, but the girls he met in Zurich didn't do anything for him, especially when he started to compare them with the exquisite beauties of Moscow. The local Swiss girls were a little too masculine for Stanley, a little unkempt, with gray faces, bad skin, and an eternal cigarette in the mouth. It seemed as though every damn woman in Zurich smoked like a chimney.

The only woman Stanley spent any time with, now, was his assistant, Barbara Zika. But their relationship was strictly business; she was old enough to be his grandmother.

Barbara's communications with him were motivated more by curiosity than sociability.

It sometimes seemed to Stanley that he spent his entire working day giving her a test on managing securities. To be fair, Barbara had warned him from the start that she planned to complete her education and get a degree in finance—she didn't want to be an assistant forever.

Stanley even began to enjoy his role as guru. Sometimes, if Barbara asked him a particularly difficult question, he asked for a little time to prepare his answer, paying no mind to the fact that his actual business affairs sat idle while he did research on the internet or the bank's extensive online library. Meanwhile, Barbara's secretarial work was exemplary. Her most fabulous talent, bordering on the mystical, was her intuition. All McKnight had to do, for example, was think about a nice cup of coffee, and Barbara was already walking into his office with coffee on a tray. Swiss foresight.

Work sucked Stanley in, and he started to like that more and more. In addition to a girlfriend, he thought about buying a car, one that would be practical for city driving, but that would also telegraph that its owner was no stingy German, but a successful man who had achieved a lot and planned to achieve much more in the near future. For now, Stanley tried to switch up his bike routes as much as possible on the way to the bank and back home. That meant he had to map out his trip ahead of time, and he made a rule for himself that he had to pass at least one new site or point of interest each day.

While he studied the map, Stanley also read up on the history of the city, its buildings, and all the famous and not-so-famous people who had lived in it. In a couple months, he was going to know this city better than any tour guide. After a couple weeks of this, Stanley made the surprising discovery that the majority of Zurich's statues were dedicated to the naked female form.

When he shared this with Barbara, she confirmed his observation.

"This city only pretends to be boring," she said. "Monsieur Lagrange can tell you that—he's expecting you in his office in half an hour."

This was unexpected. Stanley had grown accustomed to his boss operating in some other dimension, only communicating through emails and couriered documents.

"Did something happen?" asked McKnight in concern.

"I don't know what, exactly, but all my colleagues from Paradeplatz and Bahnofstrasse are expecting big news," Barbara said, with a significantly raised eyebrow.

Lagrange greeted him with an unusual expression of concern, one McKnight had never seen before.

"Sit down and listen carefully," Pierre said over his shoulder, pacing around the office. "First, Gagarin is going to buy that yacht. Second, he's traveling here to discuss financing the buy. Got it?"

"Yes, but what's got you so worried? Gagarin already told us in Moscow that the deal was ours."

"He can say anything he wants," interrupted Lagrange. "That doesn't mean anything. That damned Biryuza suggested he set up a tender for all the banks. Asshole!"

"So Gagarin's word isn't good?"

"The word of a Russian doesn't mean anything in this world. Gagarin will come, yes. And we'll discuss, yes. But there's one detail that he won't mention." Lagrange went over to the shelf, picked up a crystal decanter of whiskey, looked at it, then sighed, and put it back down. "Which is the following: while Viktor is making nice with us, and we walk around on eggshells, Biryuza is going to be in talks with our competitors. That sly little shit is probably getting kickbacks and is looking for the bank that will give him the best one."

"So what's the problem? Why don't we offer him a percentage of the deal?"

"Ah, aren't you the clever one. Except we're already paying Durand, and if we start sharing with someone else, there won't be any annual bonuses. Let's see how well-informed you are. Tell me, what other banks will Anton be meeting with?"

"UBS, Credit Suisse, and Deutsche Bank," said Stanley without pausing to think.

"Excellent! Good thing you're working for us and not them." Pierre even smiled. "And you, McKnight, need to outdo them. Not because we are going to offer Gagarin some special perks. We can't afford to. Besides, we don't even know what those three banks will offer Biryuza. Even if we try to find out, they'll spread fake numbers around to trick us."

Lagrange began to pace back and forth directly past McKnight, stamping down with each step as if grinding some thought down into the carpet that he couldn't say out loud. He stopped suddenly right in front of Stanley and looked him over attentively, as if taking his measurements for a new suit, and trying to decide what style would fit him best. Then he continued, his tone now calm and even, as if dictating a tedious office memo.

"As you can imagine, your career depends on the results of this deal. What's on the table is the financing of $500 million for a boat. We're also going to ask him to deposit $450 million in discretionary portfolio management with us. I want that money! I want this deal, Stanley. If Gagarin goes to another bank, no, no one will penalize you. And the bank won't go under. We'll focus our efforts in other areas. In hindsight, it will look like nothing more than an unpleasant episode. But this *must not happen*. And you have to understand that with every fiber of your being. This isn't a matter of career or self-esteem, no. This is your life. Up until this point, your life has been a certain way; and now it will change. But the nature of that change depends on your results." Pierre stopped to take a breath. "All the papers are with your secretary. Durand prepared them, and you need to review them all. Go and prepare. We leave for Geneva at seven AM tomorrow."

McKnight stood and walked to the door. Behind him, he heard Lagrange impatiently snap his fingers, and turned.

Pierre was already holding the potbellied bottle of Zvenigorod whiskey.

81

"I have faith in you," he said, his friendly tone restored. And winked.

McKnight nodded and went out.

Barbara was waiting for him with coffee and a packet of chocolate cookies from the Sprüngli pastry shop near their bank.

"I already looked over the documents. They are almost all in order. You'll just need to clarify a few points and rewrite some figures, and the rest will take about two hours. Okay?"

McKnight took a sip of coffee, pulled the cookies toward him, and said, "We'll manage. We don't even have to rush. The meeting isn't till tomorrow."

As soon as Barbara heard they didn't have to rush off anywhere, she poured her own cup of coffee and began to question McKnight like a strict teacher giving a test, as was her wont.

"Why does he need financing from us?" she began. "He could buy three of those yachts with the snap of a finger. I know he isn't going to read this mountain of paperwork." She prodded the stack of documents in front of her. "And that he'll pay this loan off without even thinking about it. So why all these trips, meetings, signings, trust management? Doesn't he have anything better to do with his time?"

"Because that's how rich he is," answered Stanley. "Because billionaires prefer to do major transactions, like the purchase of a yacht, plane, or house in London, on credit."

McKnight shook all the cookies out of the package and arranged them neatly into identical stacks. Barbara watched the process with growing interest.

"Firstly, it cuts tax costs," Stanley said, taking two cookie stacks and moving them toward his secretary. "That's the tax money he won't have to pay. A nice benefit, you'll have to agree. Secondly, it's going to be a low-cost loan for him, maybe 2 percent annual interest, unless, of course, the Federal Reserve suddenly raises the rate. At the same time, he'll invest in bonds in different countries, and get a coupon rate of 7 percent. Or he could deposit some of those bonds in our bank at 2 percent and use them as collateral for a mortgage on a little house in Belgravia. So he makes the buy and nets 5 percent."

The stacks of cookies, having moved all around the table, returned to their package. McKnight used a napkin to wipe up the crumbs.

"That's the general idea, anyway. Make sense?"

Barbara shrugged.

"Hopefully, I'll understand better as we go along." She gulped down the rest of her coffee in one go and opened her laptop. "It's good to be rich. Move your millions around from one basket to the other, and everyone bows to you and thanks you for your efforts with a bunch of dividends."

"It's not that simple," said McKnight. "You have to understand the baskets better than anybody else. And if you get greedy and overleverage, you can get hit with a margin call, the bank demanding additional payment to cover the loans, or the sale of existing assets."

"And you and Monsieur Lagrange are going to convince him tomorrow that our basket is the best basket on the planet," Barbara said, placing her fingers on the keys. "Shall we begin?"

Stanley opened the first folder, and picked up his pen.

CHAPTER 11

I T WAS ONLY WHEN HE was approaching the Zurich train station that McKnight realized it would be his first visit to Geneva. He tried to remember the last time he traveled by train, and came up empty. Nor did he have any idea who was memorialized in the monument by the train station, but he didn't walk over to read the plaque. For some reason, the thought of being taken for a tourist embarrassed him.

Lagrange sent him a message on Telegram, saying that he was already on the train. The train was two-storied, but only the second story had unobstructed access along the entire length of the train. Stanley walked down the platform, looking in the windows of the first-class cars, but Pierre was nowhere in sight. Stanley found him in the café car just before the train departed, where he was, for a change, drinking Evian.

"Here's my buddy McKnight!" Lagrange told the elderly bartender, pointing as Stanley approached. "Make him a real cup of good coffee. Coffee machines at home, at work, and coffee in restaurants. And so the younger generation loses its taste for the beautiful. Then they're surprised they have problems in their personal life. What kind of feelings are you capable of if you can't even enjoy a cup of coffee?"

The bartender nodded approvingly.

"Are we going to ride in the café car?" Stanley asked, looking around. Aside from him and Pierre, there was a large group of Asian tourists. The neatly dressed, elderly Japanese crowd looked at their tablets and out the windows as directed by their guide. The leader of the group was a young woman with European features, and McKnight was impressed at her command of the Japanese language. He had looked into studying an Asian language in college, but hadn't had the patience.

"No," answered Lagrange. "We'll go to the car once you get your coffee. We don't have far to go, but the scenery along the way is unique." He smiled at the bartender, and added in a whisper, "I'm already sick to death of it, myself. I prefer a clear maritime horizon…and the Caribbean Sea… preferably without yachts, which are going to ruin our whole day today."

The conversation naturally turned to their upcoming meeting.

They headed to one of the first-class cars, where no tourist groups were to be found, and McKnight and Lagrange sat down to continue their conversation. The train began to pick up speed, and the promised scenery merged into a flickering, multicolored blur.

"I'll tell you what distinguishes Swiss banks from other banks," began Pierre, filling his glass of mineral water with ice. The attentive bartender had given him a separate glass of ice cubes to take along. "Despite their many similarities. Privacy, for example."

"Isn't privacy good in our business?" asked McKnight.

"Privacy is great," confirmed Lagrange, and looked down at his glass in surprise. It was clear he had expected, out of habit, to find an entirely different liquid there. "I wanted to say something else. Each bank has their own specialty. What do you think Laville & Cie's is?"

Laundering dirty money, thought Stanley to himself, but instead said, "Confidentiality and a special relationship with clients."

"Hm, let's say a certain flexibility of thought in our leadership. What has made Swiss banks so famous?"

"Bank secrecy, of course."

"Right. But there are many other banking institutions that will hide your money and keep your secrets. In Latin America, for example, or the Caribbean islands, particularly the Caymans and Belize."

"Perhaps, but it's more difficult these days. I think the Chinese banks are gaining power, and they don't care about the US Department of Justice!"

"You're thinking along the right lines, my cunning American friend. Switzerland's uniqueness lies in the fact that while they operate like every other offshore jurisdiction, the country has a stable economy. Where else in the world can you hide your money in the twenty-first century, and be completely confident that your bank won't go bankrupt one fine day? Plus, the Swiss are good marketers—they know how to create a national brand. Although I have to say that the talk about Swiss quality is highly exaggerated. Their chocolate is shit, and their watches break!" Lagrange said, angrily tapping at his wristwatch.

"I do agree that Sprüngli has the worst chocolate I've ever had."

"Excellent, Stanley, you see where I'm going. PR is more important than anything else. The truth is, Swiss banks ceased to be of interest when they lost the right to bank secrecy. Look around you—all these countries have signed an agreement to exchange information about bank deposits. The world is growing ever more transparent, so where is the advantage of Swiss banks? There isn't one!"

"But our bank is still going strong, no?"

"Answer me one question, Stanley: What advantage does a Swiss bank have, if clients don't have a reliable way to hide their money from prying eyes? Why bother depositing your money in Zurich, where bankers take two-hour lunches and write letters in German full of typos? A potential client from Germany could cross the street from his house in his home country and open an account in Deutsche Bank there; it would be a lot simpler and at half the cost. The gnomes of Zurich are just going along, thinking that their century-long banking party will just continue forever. But no! The party has been over for a long time, and nobody wants Switzerland without bank secrecy."

"So maybe I made a bad move, joining this bank?" Stanley said with a laugh.

"I think this fairy tale of the mighty Swiss banks has about ten years left to live. Twenty, maximum. By the way, it's clients from Russia and the former USSR who believe in this lovely fairy tale most of all. To them, the name of Laville is a symbol of the right kind of European life. A synonym of capitalism. The roots of that idea probably go back to the Soviet Union, when they told everybody that the Rothschilds, Rockefellers, and Lavilles were the main enemies of communism, about the same as Coca-Cola," Lagrange said with a laugh. "Well, that kind of propaganda is the best advertising! It's embedded deep in the Russian brain that Laville equals capitalism, equals money. Imagine a slow-witted, fat bureaucrat in Moscow or a high-ranking manager from Gazprom who stole a billion dollars from the Russian state budget—where is he going to take that money? Where will he hide it? Only with Laville."

"But according to your pessimistic outlook, Swiss banks are doomed."

Lagrange paused and loosened his tie a touch.

"Of course, they're doomed. Sooner or later, the clients will realize that either American, German, or Singaporean banks, or, like you suggested, Chinese banks, are no worse than the Swiss. But as I said, my friend, we have time to squeeze as much money as possible from these stupid wooden Pinocchios."

"And how much time do we have?"

"At least five years; time to earn enough for retirement." Lagrange smiled and tightened his tie back into place.

"Not that much time."

"Enough to put together a nice little nest egg and enjoy life. You just have to listen to everything I tell you. So says Lagrange!"

McKnight shrugged and nodded his head in acceptance.

"You're going to meet Laville today. It just so happened that you were hired while he was recovering after a series of surgeries. It may have looked like I was the one who hired you, but I think you know that isn't so. Laville chose you and approved you."

And blessed me on his way down to the grave, thought Stanley, remembering a stray line from some Russian poem.

"Sure," he said aloud, "I know that."

"Hush! Laville, you understand, knows more about you than you do. And he could tell you a great many of our bank's dirty secrets. But the average citizen, i.e., client, doesn't doubt for a second that our financial specialists are the purest and most law-abiding bankers in the world. Purer than a child's tears." Lagrange squared his shoulders and smiled. "But I'm not particularly outraged about this large-scale hypocrisy. I'm the same. I didn't make up the rules of this game, and it's not for me to change them. Not that anyone else is trying to, either. For what? The current situation suits everyone just fine. It's like the Swiss railways. Everything operates in accordance with a timetable, which everyone can read up on the board. Everything is clean and smells good. The staff smile at you and are ready to help. Even if you're a brainless idiot who can't figure out what track your train is leaving from, they'll take you by the arm and lead you to the right window. I'm talking about our clients, our average, everyday clients."

At that, Lagrange paused, pressing his mouth into a thin line. He clearly had more to say on this topic, but it looked like he wasn't going to share those thoughts.

"Pierre," began McKnight cautiously, "that's all clear. But why are you telling me all this? The less you know, the better you sleep. I stay within my sphere, doing the job I am assigned. And I'm just as aware of my career prospects as you are. I don't believe in lotteries or lucky tickets. I'm a gloomy realist."

Lagrange didn't answer right away. As if just noticing the bright sunshine outside, he pulled the curtain across the window. The features of his face, now in shadow, looked rougher, the dark circles under his eyes more pronounced. He opened his briefcase and dug around, pulling out a pair of sunglasses. He put them on and asked McKnight, "Do you think it looks foolish when aging playboys try to dress young?"

"Only if they feel that way themselves. But if they're confident, it works fine."

"You're wise, Stanley," Pierre smiled broadly, and his face looked younger again. "And that can't be taught. So thank God that he gave you the talent of perception. But not everybody likes that. Gagarin does, because you see the person behind all of his masks. While Biryuza, as far as I could tell, would cheerfully murder you. Just because you saw him for who he is, a hypocrite and opportunist. After all of ten minutes. That's a valuable skill. So my advice to you—do a better job hiding your emotions. Keep a modest, reserved smile on your face and an eye on the sleeping dog."

Stanley had been listening to Pierre's thoughts on life with half an ear, but the last phrase brought him up short.

"What dog?"

"It's a psychological trick. Popular with poker players. If you want to maintain a calm facial expression, watch a sleeping dog in your head while you're playing. Observe carefully whether it is getting ready to wake up. It doesn't have to be a dog, though. You can come up with something else"

"The corpse of an enemy floating past me down the river?" McKnight suggested gloomily. "But I don't have any enemies."

"You're living a boring life, friend!" replied Lagrange. "It's high time you got some. The world will come alive for you. As a matter of fact, if we talk Gagarin into choosing us today, you'll be in disfavor with a couple of people right away. And they'll be easy to turn into enemies. They'll do it on their own."

A voice announced in French over the loudspeaker that they were approaching Geneva.

"That's the main benefit of living in a tiny country," said Pierre, taking off his glasses and examining his face carefully in the glass of the window. "You get to where you're going before a pleasant and meaningful conversation has time to descend into dull, empty chatter."

McKnight nodded. He didn't find his boss's quips funny; he was sure this wasn't the first time they'd been told.

CHAPTER 12

T HE HEADQUARTERS OF THE BANK were situated in a mansion in a quiet, respectable district of Geneva, on the Rue de la Corraterie.

On the way, Lagrange asked the taxi driver to make a short loop around so that he could show McKnight the Cathedral of the Exaltation of the Holy Cross, a Russian Orthodox church.

"Do you see that Mercedes escort out front? That's Gagarin and his retinue buying candles," said Lagrange. "Our client is a very pious man, has his own personal confessor, donates millions of dollars to Orthodox churches. I've noticed that the more people steal from Russia, the more they pray. You're not Russian Orthodox, are you?"

"No. My father's side of the family was all Presbyterian, but I'm not very religious."

"You've got the right idea! Our religion is money," Lagrange said with a laugh and folded his hands into a gesture of prayer. "That place of worship there"—Lagrange pointed out the window—"is St. Peter's Cathedral. The locals like to listen to the chimes playing the anthem of Geneva at midnight. At least they don't play at six in the morning."

When Pierre and Stanley arrived, they had half an hour before lunch. Both Laville and Gagarin were expected to arrive on time.

Laville & Cie was tucked away inside the neighborhood, next to fashionable shops and famous watch workshops. The bank sat a bit back from the street itself, hidden behind a large front garden. There were no plaques or signs, just a grand mansion, concealed from prying eyes by the leaves of plane trees, a colonnade, and a pediment with a bas-relief depicting the rape of the Sabine women. Stanley recognized the scene immediately.

"Don't tell me you studied art history? And classical mythology?" asked Lagrange in surprise. "You're the first educated American I've ever met."

"I did. My head is full of all kinds of information, Pierre, if you can believe it."

"And so?"

"I'll tell you, without false modesty, I can even sort through it and apply it as needed."

"I could give you a little tour of our headquarters, Stan," said Lagrange. "It's both an office and something of a museum. Pretty much nothing has changed since the end of the nineteenth century. But we'd be dying of boredom before we even got off the second floor. And I have to admit that I got all these endless architects, sculptors, and artists mixed up in my head a long time ago. However, I *can* tell you about the casino fire on Lake Geneva in December 1971 in Montreux. Yes, that fire. The one they wrote that great song about. I was there at that crazy guy's concert. So let's go into the garden. There's a rose garden, a bunch of gazebos. A good place to have a quiet cigarette. I could use a drink, of course. But we'll have to wait on that."

The garden was, indeed, lovely. The sounds of the city were muted here, and unseen birds sang in the honeysuckle bushes. They found wicker chairs in a gazebo so covered with climbing roses that it was indistinguishable from a distance. Holding out his pack of cigarettes to Stanley, Pierre said, "It's good that no one passing by can see this little paradise. It would be one more reason for people to envy 'those shady bankers.' And they don't have much love for us as it is."

McKnight pondered for a moment, taking the proffered cigarette automatically. The upcoming negotiations didn't worry him too much. He was sure that he was perfectly prepared. Moreover, he and Barbara had put together two backup proposals to regulate interest on the loan, so they had room to maneuver if Gagarin dug in his heels.

Lagrange flicked his lighter, and Stanley drew in the aromatic smoke, feeling briefly dizzy. He hadn't smoked since Moscow.

"Won't they be wondering where we are?" he asked.

"With the staff they have here? They know every move you make."

As if in confirmation of his words, a young blond woman in a severe pantsuit appeared on the threshold of the gazebo. Murmuring an apology in barely audible French, she put two crystal ashtrays bearing the bank's logo on the table in front of them.

"Can I bring you anything?" she asked. Then, turning to McKnight, she repeated the question in English. "They will be expecting you in twelve minutes in the main reception room on the top floor."

"No, thank you, we're fine," Lagrange said.

When she was gone, he went on, "Your last name threw her off, so she spoke to you in English just to make sure. They earn good money here and value their jobs. But every couple of years someone gets tempted into spying for our competitors. Which, you understand, is completely pointless with our current methods of electronic security."

A young man came out onto a third-floor balcony and rang a bell.

"Hear that, Stan? That's our invitation to join the meeting. How do you feel? Ready for battle?"

"Are we expecting a battle?" asked McKnight. "I was expecting a nice lunch."

"In these kinds of meetings, the situation can turn on a dime, and you'll be left choking on the bite you just took," said Pierre as they ascended the stairs. "But for now, I'll acquaint you with another of our local attractions. We're going to the fifth floor, and we'll be taking the elevator, which is almost a hundred years old. I think it's the only thing in the building that's been modernized at all. It was initially hand-operated—so they say."

The first person Stanley and Pierre saw when they got off the elevator on the fifth floor was Jean-Michel Laville, owner of Laville & Cie.

No clue as to his identity was needed. Lagrange cut quite an impressive and dignified figure, it was true, but Laville far outstripped him in respectability and stateliness.

He stood in the hall, adjusting his bow tie in front of a mirror. Even his gray hair and elegant mustache seemed to possess a special silver sheen. The outer corners of his blue eyes were significantly lower than the inner ones, giving a slightly melancholy cast to his long, noble face. Stanley wondered what illness could be troubling this aristocrat, whose family had founded Laville & Cie nearly a hundred and forty years ago. Cancer? He recalled Barbara telling him that the sixty-five-year-old Laville had recently left his former wife, twenty-five years his junior, and married a nineteen-year-old beauty. She wasn't a model or pop singer, however, but an archaeology student. Jean-Michel Laville received rejuvenating treatments from the best doctors—he wanted to make his young wife a mother, and probably more than once (he had at least two children with each of his former wives). This time, however, things apparently hadn't worked out for him, and the archaeology student hadn't yet managed to conceive. But the bank owner had an athletic figure, and certainly didn't look his age, with his broad shoulders and straight back. He saw Stanley and Pierre in the mirror and turned, greeting them with a barely perceptible nod. With another, similar nod, he invited them to follow.

"I've heard good things about you, young man," he said to McKnight. "Let us see how you do in action. I would like you to handle the business part of the conversation with our Russian client. Pierre is an excellent negotiator, but for some reason he and Gagarin seem to get sidetracked on irrelevant topics, and then it seems like we're on a golf course instead of at a business meeting." He looked over to Lagrange. "No offense, Pierre. You know how much I value you. But I want to let our colleague try his hand today."

They entered a high-ceilinged room, where waiters moved soundlessly around a table laid out for lunch. The moment they came in, another set of doors at the other end of the room swung open, and their guests entered the room.

Viktor Gagarin entered first, with a young woman on his arm. She was carrying a bouquet of tall yellow flowers, hiding her face from view.

But Stanley recognized her by her walk alone. And those hands! Sensitive, restless, with delicate wrists. He remembered those hands as well. How deftly they had handled the packets of cocaine. And other things.

Gagarin's companion wore a long silk dress. Similar to the dress she had on when they had merged into one, the hem of which she gathered up in one swift, graceful motion.

McKnight's hands seemed to have acquired their own particular memories. A traitorous drop of sweat slipped down his forehead. Luckily, Laville and Lagrange were standing in front of him, and he managed to quickly find his handkerchief and dry his face before anyone saw.

For the next few minutes, as the guests exchanged the necessary pleasantries, Stanley focused all his attention on maintaining a polite smile. This woman was Gagarin's wife! She extended her narrow, perfumed hand to McKnight with a polite, distant smile.

"Pleased to meet you, Mr. McKnight," she said, her voice absent any of its former huskiness or playful tone.

Stanley shook her hand and handed her his business card. By the time they sat down, he had finally pulled himself together. Gagarin cast a mocking eye around him at the antique furniture of carved mahogany, the starched tablecloths, crystal, and silver flatware. Then he slapped the table with his palms and invited everyone to drink vodka.

Mila, as Gagarin had introduced his wife, sat directly across from McKnight. The topic of yachts hadn't yet been introduced. The documents were handed over to Biryuza; Stanley hadn't noticed his arrival.

He decided that his only path to salvation here was to focus on the food, which was certainly worthy of his attention.

Mila watched Stanley's methodical consumption of the meal surreptitiously, but only drank champagne, herself. There was a spark of mischief and amusement in her gaze. She had obviously recognized the man across from her.

Meanwhile, Gagarin continued to discuss abstract topics, despite the best efforts of Lagrange and Laville to turn the conversation toward the subject of this meeting. When lobster carpaccio was served, the oligarch brought up the price of oil and his friends among the sheiks in the UAE.

After the carpaccio was replaced by foie gras prepared three different ways with goat's cheese, Gagarin lectured his companions about the bridge being built in the Crimea, and why the government hadn't let him participate in the project.

When they served Sanda beef with Spanish artichokes and crispy perch with saffron cooked over charcoal, which McKnight couldn't even look at by this point, their Russian guest had moved on to explaining in detail why he no longer invested in the gold market.

Stanley was impressed by Laville's patience and restraint, as he listened to all this useless and unasked-for information about the Russian business world with an imperturbable expression.

And then Gagarin, as if just noticing McKnight despite shaking his hand before lunch, began speaking directly to him. Lagrange, who had long since lost control of the situation, gave Stanley an approving nod.

Stanley began giving unexpectedly clear and meaningful responses to their guest.

With each of his rejoinders Viktor grew more and more animated.

But things took a new turn at the table. When the waiters replaced their plates once again to serve pumpkin pie and ginger ice cream, Mila joined the conversation. She had by then consumed quite a few glasses of champagne, and was in an excellent mood. She spoke Russian, so of the Swiss side, only Stanley understood her.

"You're all so self-important and boring!" she said loudly. "What am I doing here? I can drink champagne at home."

Out of the corner of his eye, Stanley saw Biryuza jump and throw his boss a worried look. Gagarin seemed to wake up as well, and wagged his finger at Mila.

"Gentlemen, I believe our meal has come to an end," Gagarin announced. "As for the main purpose of our meeting, I will say the following. I've already had the pleasure of listening to the arguments of your young banker." He nodded toward Stanley. "They seemed clearly reasoned and convincing at the time. I don't have any reason to believe his work has declined in quality since then!" He turned to Laville. "He was the one who put together the packet of documents, was he not?"

Stanley tensed, unsure of how to react. Their Russian client was behaving unpredictably.

And then McKnight felt someone stroke his leg. He flinched and looked at Mila. There was no question—her tipsy gaze was focused directly on Stanley's face, direct and challenging. He could have fainted from terror. Any second now Gagarin would see, smash the neck off a bottle of vodka, and leap over the table to gut him.

But nothing happened. Viktor went on telling Laville and Lagrange that their points had convinced him, and that only the formalities remained.

"Biryuza is also a specialist in these matters, you know," said the oligarch. "He'll check everything over and give you a call. But for today, I suggest we just relax. I always enjoy seeing you, and I rarely get the chance to talk with decent people."

He looked over at McKnight, and said in Russian, "In Moscow, you were drinking like a real Russian. Today I've only seen you take a couple sips. Holding back?"

"There's still time to catch up, right, Viktor?" said Stanley.

Gagarin clearly liked Stanley's tone.

"There is, indeed, McKnight! But," he said, finally looking at his wife, "someone has managed to drink enough for all of us. How do you do it, my dear? It must be magic, even I haven't had the time. Something went wrong. Anton!"

"Yes, boss!" answered Biryuza.

"Do you know where they smoke around here? I could use a cigarette."

Lagrange guessed what he was asking, and stood up to point toward the gallery leading out onto a balcony over the garden.

"Come, Mila," Gagarin ordered, bowing to Laville. "We'll be back shortly."

Biryuza hurried after his boss.

"Go ahead. I'll be right there," Mila replied, but Gagarin didn't hear her.

"You never know what you're going to get into with these Russians," Lagrange remarked quietly to Laville in French.

"I think he may have had a bit too much drink before he even arrived," Laville replied, not a muscle on his face moving. "McKnight, you take the lady to the balcony. I think she has something important to tell you. Pierre and I have something to discuss. Given the, ahem, informality of our dinner."

Stanley rose from the table and offered his arm to Mila. She got up, stumbling a bit.

"Your husband is waiting."

"Let's go! Let's go, my friend! I'm delighted by this gift."

"What gift?"

"The gift of fate." Mila laughed. "Botticelli says hi. Okay, let's have a smoke. Otherwise, my husband might lose it. Start smashing the furniture."

As they walked along the gallery, she whispered to Stanley, "You don't have to worry about the yacht contract. Consider it yours." She squeezed Stanley's hand so tightly he nearly cried out. "You'll owe me a favor."

"What will I owe you?" asked Stanley.

"Three wishes," Mila whispered, running her moist fingers over his lips. "Do you know that old song, 'I have three wishes but no golden fish'? You're going to be my gold fish."

"I don't understand."

"You haven't read Pushkin? And here I thought you were a man of culture."

"I've read Pushkin. I even remember some lines...wait, isn't this Pushkin—'and blessed me on his way down to the grave'?"

"It is, it is, but let's not talk about the grave and nonsense like that. Don't you worry. They will be pleasant wishes. You'll like them. Sorry, I really did overdo it on the champagne. But I didn't like the meal. You need a new chef. Only the ice cream was good."

Biryuza approached, his manner businesslike, with a message from Gagarin that Mila was to leave for their villa immediately.

"He couldn't tell me himself?" Mila smiled crookedly. "Okay, then. Let's go! Anton, you take me. Goodbye, Mr. McKnight, it was nice to meet you. Very, very nice."

Stanley returned to the dining room to find both Laville and Lagrange missing. He asked the waiter where Lagrange had gone, and learned that his boss was in the garden with the blonde in the pantsuit and a bottle of cognac. Stanley had to start drinking with Gagarin, who demanded vodka and the usual accompanying small plates. The waiter raised his eyebrows, but rushed off to fulfill the demands of the important guest.

Gagarin followed shots of vodka with bites of spicy sausage and tiny pickles, but Stanley declined any food, sipping the vodka like tea, instead, which made Gagarin laugh at him, but didn't get him drunk. It only made his head feel heavy. Gagarin talked nonstop—on the political situation before the Russian parliamentary elections, about what a high-ranking official did in his free time, about his hobbies—fishing, which he never had time for; soccer, and how he would like to buy a European soccer club, not as famous as the club one of Russia's richest men had bought, but a modest one, one that would gradually become successful and win the Champions League; how back in the era of cooperatives, competitors hadn't stopped at killing his partner, but had even cut a diamond ring off his hand, together with the finger it was on.

"The era of what?"

"Cooperatives! You don't know what that is?"

"I know about agricultural cooperatives—here, in Switzerland—"

"All right, hush, my ignorant friend. Cooperatives are…actually, to hell with them! Waiter! Bring another bottle. And pickles! Don't forget the pickles!"

Stanley lost his grip on reality.

He came to when they were back on the train. Evening lights flashed past outside the windows. Lagrange was dozing across from him.

"Where are we?" McKnight asked through dry lips.

"We just passed Bern," Pierre answered without opening his eyes.

The next day, as Stanley was getting ready to drop his suit off at the cleaners, he found his own business card in the jacket pocket, with a handwritten note: "You owe me three wishes!"

Thinking that fulfilling any of Mila's wishes could be a death sentence for him, Stanley tore the card up into little pieces. Then he flushed them down the toilet. And when it was done flushing, he double-checked to make sure that no paper remained to be seen.

CHAPTER 13

WHEN MCKNIGHT WAS BACK AT work in Zurich, he was troubled by a sense of internal division that was new to him. On the one hand, he was drawn to Mila. On the other hand, he realized that nothing good could come of a relationship with her. So he tried to bury himself in work, hoping to get rid of this craving for a woman who was, to all intents and purposes, a stranger. And a dangerous one, at that.

True, he did feel a certain sense of pride—*Look at me, I picked up the wife of an oligarch, who, while he might not have personally poured concrete over the bodies of his enemies, definitely gave direct orders for it to be done.* Stanley was aware that Mila had chosen well with him—in her narrow circle of acquaintances, under the constant watch of her husband and the vicious Shamil, she didn't have the slightest chance of carrying on even an innocent flirtation. But there was also the possibility that everything hidden could come to light: Stanley recalled Laville saying something like "The lady wants to tell you something important." His face had been impassive, but Stanley realized that Jean-Michel must have intuitively sensed a connection between him and Mila. And if Laville had sensed it, then others would too, soon enough.

Meanwhile, June was drawing to a close, and all of his colleagues, as well as the bank's clients, were gearing up for the summer holiday. All ongoing transactions had to be put in order, or completed, or scheduled for continuation in the fall. That was for management to decide.

On top of his usual concerns, Stanley had to deal with family business as well. *Although it might be a stretch to call it 'family,'* he thought. Christine called him from San Francisco every other day, and sometimes daily. The worst part was, she always seemed to catch him at the most inconvenient moments. She could never get the time difference straight. That's what she said, at any rate. No, actually, that wasn't the most unpleasant part. The worst part was that when he heard his wife speak, he thought of Mila's voice. How different they were. And how distant, in all ways, Christine's voice now seemed to him.

The circumstances of his first chance encounter with Mila, and that crazy lunch in Geneva, seemed to McKnight like a trap laid by fate. This would be the snare into which he would stumble, never to right himself again.

There was no rational explanation for this feeling. And there is only one tried and true way to deal with that kind of obsession—to dive into your work. All the way in. Not bad for your career, either, or your reputation. When Stanley's mind refused to take in new information, and the numbers and graphs started to waver in front of his eyes, he would go to the lake for a swim or for a ride at the Oerlikon velodrome.

The other employees at the bank still treated him like any other outsider. To his Swiss colleagues, he was just a cog in the machine. They would probably have preferred another PC over an American. But as they didn't have that computer yet, okay, let McKnight do the work.

On top of that, his loyal assistant Barbara was sent to an economic summit in Paris. Not as an authorized representative of the bank, of course. She was plucked from the Zurich office at the request of Laville himself to be his errand girl for the event. It seemed that Laville's young wife had managed to get pregnant after all, and was overcome with jealousy at the idea of her husband being gone for an entire week. The rumor was she had personally selected his assistant for the trip by looking through photographs of all the bank's employees, and found one to her taste in the Zurich office.

Lagrange, who also didn't think much of Barbara's appearance, told Stanley the whole story.

"She's not a good-looking woman, it's true," he said, "but she's elegant, and has a nice figure, eh, Stanley? She's got that mixed look, I love ethnic-looking women."

"Yes, she has a nice figure."

"It's a good thing the photos that girl, Jean-Michel's wife, was looking through are only head shots," Lagrange interrupted. "By the way, Barbara was a swimmer and a diver. She was a candidate for the national team. I saw a photo of her at a competition, in a swimsuit, and let me tell you, Stan: it was something, all right."

He and Lagrange were sitting in his car in the bank's underground parking garage. Lagrange had called Stanley with the unusual command,

"I'm waiting for you in the car!" and Stanley hadn't the faintest idea of the reason behind it. They had to hide from the rest of the staff and Lagrange's own secretary just to gossip about Laville's jealous wife and how Barbara looked in a swimsuit? As Pierre described Barbara's figure, he flipped through a Ferrari promotional magazine. Tapping on one of the photos, he exclaimed, "Rosso Fiorano! Rosso Rubino! Who comes up with the names of these car colors!"

"Advertisers," said Stanley. "Not too many clients are going to be interested in a 'bright-red' car, so they get fancy."

"Which one do you like?" Lagrange asked, passing the magazine to McKnight.

"I prefer the darker and subtler shades." Stanley turned a page. "Here, the Grigio Ferro, for example. The Ferrari California looks like the right amount of aggressive to me with this color."

"'The right amount of aggressive,'" repeated Lagrange. "I like it. Aggressiveness is never a bad thing to have. In reasonable doses." He went on, the tone of his voice unchanged. "You're flying to Milan tomorrow. From there you'll take a car to the coast. Rent a Grigio Ferro, if you want. The entire Russian establishment heads there for vacation. There's a resort, Forte dei Marmi, not far from Florence. Somebody told those Russian savages that it's paradise down there, that the crème de la crème of European society goes there. So the Russians started going. Which is why that European elite won't set foot there these days. Besides, the prices have gone sky-high after the Russian invasion. Gagarin and his whole entourage arrived yesterday. I just spoke to him. You'll take him the documents to sign there."

Lagrange pulled a folder from his briefcase and handed it to McKnight.

"Our contract with him is a major breakthrough, my friend. I want you to get closer to him. He likes you, and he doesn't trust many people. Here's the thing—when he stops trusting his friends and family, and that'll happen soon, believe me, he'll need a capable person on our side. It seems like that person, as of now, is you."

"I'm afraid Biryuza, for one, is not going to like that at all," Stanley replied thoughtfully.

"Well, don't be afraid. That one's got a sharp bite, agreed. And a good eye. But guard dogs are there as protection for their owner, not as allies. But they don't understand that. Questions?"

"I couldn't get a more modest car?" asked Stanley. "I'd choose a Mercedes AMG, myself."

"No! You have to be on the same level as them," Lagrange said. "After Fidenza, you should turn off for La Spezia before you get to Parma. The road goes along the coast from there, beautiful views. But you'll figure it out. Put all the expenses on our corporate card."

———————

McKnight spent the night at a karaoke bar, then a strip club, entertaining new clients from Kazakhstan, and was flying into the Milanese airport of Malpensa at 6:00 AM the next morning. A half hour later, he was behind the wheel of a new Ferrari California, heading toward the city. His eyes were burning from lack of sleep, and "Strangers in the Night" was playing on a continuous loop in his head after the Kazakhs' five (at least) renditions of it the night before.

———————

The early summer Italian sun had already heated up the motorway, and the scorching air shimmered in a haze above the tarmac. Far off to the right, the mountains were already in sight past the Ticino Valley.

Stanley took the A50 around Milan onto the A1 Milan-Naples, the A35 off of there, and then he could relax. Until the turn toward La Spezia, it was a straight road along the valley. The square vineyards were interrupted by small hills covered in olive groves, and from time to time, old farmhouses would appear, surrounded by small islands of trees. They were mostly abandoned, but retained a certain cozy charm, nevertheless. Stanley picked out the presence of towns by the bell towers of churches, and the occasional castle flashed past like a ghost in the mountains. They looked like chess figurines forgotten by some careless player. What was going on in them now?

He thought that if he could pick anywhere to live, he would buy an old farmhouse, like the ones he was passing. He couldn't afford a castle in the mountains, and despite property taxes being cheaper in Italy than Switzerland, they were still quite high. He could fix up one of these houses; his father and uncle had taught him a fair number of practical skills, after all. What he couldn't handle himself, he'd hire someone to do. He'd buy a little vineyard. Olive trees. Take classes on agriculture. Who would live with him in this house? Christine? Not likely. Mila? He'd have to buy an entire arsenal, practice shooting every day, and spend all his time waiting for Gagarin's people to attack.

Suddenly, he saw an image of Barbara Zika—she was walking down the side of the road in a red swimsuit and sticking out her thumb for a ride. Stanley decided to stop for her—and woke up, just before hitting the metal guardrail. He yanked the wheel sharply in the opposite direction and blew out a breath, as a car flew by, honking wildly. A Maserati!

He parked on the side of the road, just where dream Barbara had been walking. He got out, poured some water from a plastic bottle onto his head, sighed deeply, and got back into the car.

Stanley drove, thinking how much he was enjoying this place, its peace and tranquility. It seemed to pass from the ancient natural surroundings to the Italians themselves. Even the rivers were sleepy here; you couldn't tell what direction they were flowing in. That is, if you could even pick the river out through the coastal thickets of willow trees and reeds.

So Stanley didn't get a look at the famous River Po. It was only when he passed the outskirts of Piacenza that he realized he's missed it.

The road began to wind into the mountains, and he had to pay more attention to his driving, and less to the scenery.

The closer McKnight got to the sea, the lusher the groves around him were. The wind blew through verdant meadows, and even the houses grew prettier. Suddenly, he saw stone gates, standing right in the middle of a field, with a cross above the arch. About a hundred meters behind them, under a hill, the wheel of a water mill stood still. There was no sign of any water that could have powered it.

After La Spezia, Stanley turned onto a seaside highway. He switched the air conditioner off, opened the roof, and continued along at a leisurely pace. The breeze from the sea dispersed the heat and brought the occasional delicious smell from one of the coastal hotels. It was nearing siesta time, and McKnight was thinking about stopping somewhere for a bite to eat. According to the internet, there were more restaurants around here than fish in the sea. One for every palate. Stanley finally chose a trattoria that promised the best steaks. The meal was simple, but made with love and skill, and it was fabulous.

He checked into the hotel where Barbara had reserved him a room, and crashed immediately, sleeping deeply until five in the afternoon.

He had dinner plans with Gagarin at eight.

McKnight spent a couple of hours swimming in the sea, walking around the local shops, where he bought guillotine cigar cutter for Lagrange, and drank a tall glass of slightly sour rosé with some olives. At seven, he returned to the hotel, dressed in a light-gray suit, and drove over to Riccardo, the restaurant. He had the folder with the documents for Gagarin in a safe metal attaché case inscribed with the bank's emblem and logo.

CHAPTER 14

S HAMIL MET MCKNIGHT AT THE restaurant. The security chief stood at
the top step by the entrance, rocking on his feet from heel to toe, looking
off to the side somewhere. There was no easy way around him; Stanley
had to either ask him to move aside or risk falling off the side of the stairs
into the barberry thickets by trying to inch around him along the edge of the
entryway. Stanley chose the second option, but when he had made it almost
all the way around Shamil, purely by accident, he hit the head of Gagarin's
security squarely in the kneecap with the corner of the metal attaché case.

Shamil swore. For a moment, his face twisted up in irritation, but then
he regained control of himself.

They went up to the second floor, which had a panoramic view of the
sea. Besides Gagarin, his guests and their companions, there were no other
diners on the large veranda, surrounded by a living fence of juniper as tall
as a man. Stanley found out later that Gagarin had rented this place as his
own personal banquet hall for the week, and no outsiders were permitted.

In addition to Viktor and Biryuza, who lifted their glasses to him in
greeting, there were some new faces.

"You just got here, and you're already tanned!" said Gagarin, and turned
to a tall brunette who was carefully brushing her Pekinese. The dog was
agitated and trying to escape. "Polina, meet Stanley. I already told your
husband about him. He's a private banker from Switzerland."

The brunette glanced at McKnight without any particular interest and
nodded.

"You shouldn't be so quick to dismiss him, my dear! This clever guy
can rewrite your taxes in half an hour so the government will be paying *you*.
He's some kind of wizard."

Stanley bowed politely.

"Polina is my wife's best friend. You didn't meet at our party on Independence Day? No?"

McKnight shrugged. He, of course, remembered what Mila had said about her best friend.

"You'll meet the other guests later. They are busy at the moment, as you can see," said Gagarin.

The others, several older men, were grouped around a monitor at the other end of the long table and talking animatedly into their mobile phones. Three young women stood nearby, chatting. It was too far away to hear what they were saying.

"Christie's is auctioning off some more antique junk of Petrov-Vodkin's," Gagarin explained. "I try to avoid the art world as much as possible. Too many conmen. I know a guy who bought up a whole bunch of works by old masters from a dishonest art dealer and overpaid by about a billion dollars. He's suing him now. Have a seat, McKnight."

Stanley sat down and put the case in front of him, as if to signal he was here for work.

"No, no! Anything but that. I'll lose my appetite from those damned papers. Anton!" Viktor waved his hand at Biryuza. "Take all this away, and bring it to the villa later."

Stanley had hoped up until the last possible moment that this trip would be all business. That he would bring the documents, Gagarin would sign them, they would discuss the prospects of the oligarch's other financial deals, identify opportunities—and there were some—to minimize taxes when registering the yacht (after all, if the yacht sailed under the flag of Belize, Liberia, or Myanmar, it would be subject to the laws of those wonderful countries), and that would be the end of his mission. But now it turned out that Polina was here, and he knew what that meant.

Another meeting with Mila was not in his plans.

In fact, he had planned to never see that woman again. He realized that any relationship, even the most innocent flirtation, with the wife of a monster like Gagarin could end very badly for him. Remembering her three wishes, how she sang a line from a Russian song, Stanley wondered what she would come up with next time.

McKnight lifted a glass of champagne and drank it down without realizing what he was doing.

Viktor laughed and applauded.

"That's the Russian way. They all think that if a bottle of champagne in this place costs a thousand euros you have to spend an hour savoring each sip. Bravo, Stan! Hey, waiter! Stand by this American guy over here. And fill up his glass as soon as it's empty. And, Stan, don't be shy—the way we do it here is everybody orders whatever they want, whenever they want. Polina and her dog over here, for example, are waiting for some kind of fancy desert, something sweet with caramel, yuck, while I'd like...I'd like...Anton! Biryuza! Shit! What did I want? Come on! Remember! If you don't remember, I'm going to send you back to Moscow and the rain, traffic, the fight against corruption..."

It took McKnight that long to realize how drunk Gagarin was.

The group that had been busy with the auction approached their side of the table. Biryuza, unable to remember what his boss had wanted, and apparently not too concerned about the threat to send him to Moscow, stood and introduced them to Stanley. When they heard he was just a private banker, here from Zurich on financial business, they immediately lost interest. The women started to tell Polina about what they bought in the auction. The men turned their attention to the champagne and wine. It soon became clear from their conversation that one of them, Polina's husband, Anton Krapiva, was a very influential official in the administration of the Russian president. Stanley realized that he had seen the man's face before on CNN. Something to do with rigging an election. Either the Russian presidential or parliamentary election.

"Stanley! Stanley, my friend!" said Gagarin loudly. "We have to eat, you and me. ASAP! Let's have something to eat, and have a drink together. Not this champagne, not this crap wine. Waiter! Bring us vodka and—Stanley, what will you have?"

"Pasta...yes, pasta, please," Stanley said.

"I said don't be shy!" Gagarin banged his fist on the table, and Polina's dog howled. "They've got oysters, every kind of crustacean thing and fish you can think of. *Bistecca alla fiorentina*," Gagarin read slowly from the menu. "What is that, anyway? Waiter! Hey, bring me a menu in Russian. Waiter! Two dozen oysters, *speciale de claire*, they're good with vodka! And risotto, the risotto here is excellent, I'm telling you, Stanley..."

"Viktor, I'm sorry, but you already had risotto today," laughed Krapiva. "Order the steak Florentine instead. What is this American doing here?"

"He's my friend. You can tell people what's best for them back at the Kremlin," interrupted Gagarin. "Here, thank God, there's freedom. I'll eat risotto twenty times a day if I want to."

"Of course, of course, sorry." Krapiva acted afraid, but his gaze behind the smoky lenses of his thin-framed glasses was hard and mocking.

"There—the littlest thing, and—sorry! Children were taken hostage at school—sorry, the submarine sank—sorry," Gagarin took the frost-covered bottle of vodka from the waiter, and filled his glass almost halfway. "You're always apologizing. But our people don't like apologies."

"I'm apologizing to you, not the people." Krapiva looked around and winked at another man over his glasses, a burly guy whose face looked familiar to Stanley.

"I'm the best representative of the people!" announced Gagarin, pouring vodka into Stanley's champagne glass. "And the people won't make it without me...McKnight! Come here! Come here, I said!"

Stanley got up, walked around the table, and came over to Gagarin.

"This is how we do it, you damned Yankee. Brüderschaft!" Gagarin said, putting his hand with the glass under McKnight's arm, and, lifting Stanley's arm with his elbow, drank his whole glass in one go and made Stanley do the same. After that, he let out a heavy breath, tossed his glass onto the floor where it shattered, grabbed Stanley by the forehead, and kissed him on the mouth. "That's how it's done! Brüderschaft! Now we're friends, Stanley, and you can use the informal pronoun with me and call me *ti*, okay?"

Stanley nodded, afraid that if he moved that vodka would come right back out, and slowly swallowed an oyster. His mouth was on fire with vodka and Tabasco sauce.

"You have to answer!"

"Okay, Viktor! We're friends, and I'll be informal."

"That's why I love Americans," he said to Krapiva, releasing Stanley. "They learn fast. You show them something once, and they can do it themselves the next time. But Russians, Russians are thick idiots."

"For the best representative of your people, you don't have a very high opinion of them," said the burly man.

"Not a good opinion?" Gagarin asked in horror, picking up an oyster from the plate. "I despise them!" He sucked the oyster down. "Anyone who's spent some time alive and thinking has to despise people in his heart!"

"Our people are decent. They just don't understand much." said Krapiva.

"The people are stupid and uneducated, and they need to be governed harshly, and you're acting like you're all so soft. McKnight! Let's have something, some tartare, it's delicious."

"And you propose..." Krapiva paused significantly.

"There are always simple answers to complicated questions," said Gagarin, thoughtfully chewing away on a chunk of lobster. "And vice versa. The answer to all problems is a strong hand at the reins, even more centralization of power...all for the most important objective of all...safety."

"I learned in school," McKnight broke in, unable to hold back, "that those who are willing to trade liberty for safety deserve neither."

Gagarin gave Stanley a contemptuous glance and snorted.

"The Russian people don't need liberty. They need an idea! If you manage to gain all their attention, nobody will bother asking for liberty. The government must keep the Russian people in a constant state of amazement! When you surprise Russians, it stuns them, and they'll be submissive and obedient until the end of their lives."

"How much further do you want to go, Viktor? The people have already turned into putty—you can do what you want with them!" said Krapiva.

"And why do we need even more centralization in Russia?" added the burly man.

"To smother any protest before it takes off! To sweep dissent out of this country. To crush any who disagree!" Gagarin banged a fist on the table as he spoke.

"Aren't you afraid that, sooner or later, you'll tighten the screws too far and the people will revolt?" asked McKnight, putting on an expression of faint concern.

"Ooh, I'm so scared...oh, I'm frightened," whispered Gagarin, and then burst out laughing. "Russians love to revolt. It happens once a century, but usually they just kneel in front of their master's house.'"

Gagarin stopped laughing, and he frowned slightly, gazing intently at Stanley.

"In the future, we'll need a monarchy. One that's organic, not an absolute monarchy to start, but with a tendency toward that, that ends up absolute. Only one person making the decisions. Everyone else—out you go."

Stanley decided that it was time for him to silently study the tablecloth, but Gagarin looked around him and banged on the table.

"All of you—out!"

"Viktor, Viktor, calm down," hissed one of his guests. "Don't make a scene here."

"Not now, not now, we still have to eat and drink, but in the future—none of you will be necessary!"

"And the monarch will be..." Now it was the burly man's turn to pause significantly.

"We all know his name," answered Gagarin, and poured himself more vodka. "Tell me, Krapiva: Why do you all pretend so stubbornly to be a democracy? What's the point? Nobody believes it any more. Okay, we don't believe it. We've seen worse. I get cold sweats thinking about the nineties. It's all plywood scenery on a stage. Reality is simpler. The country has a master. The master has servants. Everyone else are his subjects. Half of Europe lives that way."

"But European monarchies are restricted by constitutions," Stanley objected. "And the countries with the oldest systems of monarchy are the most democratic countries. The UK, for example."

"Oh great, your opinion is just what we all needed!" barked Gagarin. "The UK! We're going to buy the UK soon enough! My Russia won't stand for another victory of democracy. The benefits of dictatorships over democracies are obvious to everyone. It's better to deal with one swindler than with many. And anyway, why should we live under other people's rules? We are who we are. We are Russians! It's fabulous! The vodka is tasting good tonight."

"No need to get so worked up, Viktor," Stanley said, hearing the words coming out of his own mouth in surprise. "You're presenting your daydream as if it's reality, but in actuality, you want Russia to be like…"

Stanley realized that everyone was looking at him in astonishment. Biryuza's face was particularly noticeable—his mouth hung open, and a thin line of saliva was coming out of his mouth onto his cleanly shaven chin.

"…like Saudi Arabia!" finished Stanley, and thought that if Shamil didn't come running in right now, limping on the leg that Stanley had bruised, and shoot him with a gold pistol (Stanley had heard that Russian gangsters loved gold pistols), if that didn't happen, he would live a long and happy life.

Shamil didn't come. The silence was broken by an eruption of laugher. Gagarin started it, then Krapiva began to laugh, and finally everyone else joined in. Biryuza wiped off his chin and laughed along with them. Even Polina managed a crooked smile.

"Stanley, my boy, you're really something!" Gagarin said, wiping the tears from his eyes. "Saudi Arabia! No, thank you! See, Krapiva, it's all the same to Americans—either you follow their way, or you're Saudi Arabia! Who are their allies, by the way? Friends can do whatever they want. The rules apply to everybody else? Oh, Stanley, Stanley…"

"By the way, Polina, where has Mila gone off to? Our Viktor is going to get out of hand now, and who will calm him down?" Krapiva asked his wife with a strained smile.

McKnight tensed. That Mila was somewhere nearby. He imagined it and broke out into a cold sweat. He downed another glass of vodka. This would be worse than any bullet from Shamil.

Polina looked up at her husband, barely concealed contempt in her gaze.

An awkward pause fell over the table. They could hear the Pekinese grumbling and the crackling of melting ice in the champagne buckets. Biryuza bit his lip and watched his boss, ready to come to his aid, to stop this risky conversation from going any further.

Polina got up and walked over to the table, picking a piece of cheese off a plate and giving it to her dog. She began speaking, but to Gagarin, not to her husband.

"We were already on our way back from Viareggio. Of course, everything those people promised us over the phone, they didn't deliver. No vintage, just ordinary modern stuff. We were coming back, and then of course, just like always."

"What happened?" mumbled Gagarin.

For the second time, it seemed to Stanley that for the fraction of a second there was something hard, mocking, and absolutely sober, in his gaze—it wasn't an expression, exactly, not a feeling, but a shadow, or a flash of light. And then his face went slack again, his mouth parted slightly, and his eyes dimmed.

"Mila left her purse in that stupid salon. I said, let's send Shamil. He can get it. No, she said, I'll go myself. And she went. And there's traffic. So she's on her way. And there's no mobile connection here."

All Stanley understood from this confusing tale was that there was some kind of complicated family fight going on here.

But Gagarin put it all to rest.

"She's a big girl. She'll figure it out," he said.

Everyone sighed in relief, and Viktor went on sharing his thoughts.

"So they go…"

"Who goes, Viktor?" sighed Polina.

"The Russian people!" Gagarin barked irritably. "Damned zombies go, heads held high, to their voting booths and vote for our president, the scumbag. What's the point? We need a monarch. Most Russians are too stupid to know how stupid they are. That's what holds our society together."

Stanley wanted to interject that he had recently wanted the guy he was now calling a scumbag to be an absolute monarch, but he refrained.

"Here's what you need to do with these people, to make them more obedient. I'll tell you what you need." Gagarin looked around the table again. "Russians are slaves at heart. And it is the nature of a slave to always test others, for example, his superior—is he a slave too? The first thing a Russian will do is try to hurt you, humiliate you, and if you manage to stop him, if you show strength, he'll immediately grow docile. There are only two possible realities in his head: either you're a slave, or I'm a slave."

"And what are you, Viktor?" Krapiva asked indifferently, smoking a cigar.

"I'm somewhere in the middle. Me and you, Krapiva, need a kind and just master, but one who shows the rest"—Gagarin waved in the direction of the outside world—"the crude, worthless, and lazy people, that he's keeping everyone in check. Chekhov put the pathos on a bit thick here."

At that, Gagarin shook his head, as shaking off unwanted thoughts, and commanded, "All of you look too sober. Everybody have a drink!"

The waiters hurried around the table bringing small plates, and bottles of vodka and cognac appeared.

"Stan!" called Gagarin. "Come with me. There's a little balcony over here, I'll show you the harbor. My yacht's there as well, but I'm sick of it, to be honest. I'll build a new one with your help. The size of a football field. Or bigger. Wouldn't be a bad idea to get a football team to go with it."

Gagarin got up, stumbling a bit, and waved McKnight along. There was, indeed, a small balcony in a corner of the veranda with a view of the sea. Gagarin leaned heavily on the railing, took out a pack of Rodina cigarettes, and offered one to Stanley.

"Have a smoke!"

Stanley hesitated, but didn't want to refuse, seeing the condition his client was in. He lit up the filterless cigarette and felt his head spin as he pulled the minty smoke into his lungs.

"Don't mind the fact that I've had a bit to drink," Viktor said, drawing out the word. "The situation is under control. I just like to wake them up, keep everyone on their toes. You're on your toes, I can see." He smiled. "You're always focused, like the sights of a gun. But Biryuza is also focused. On something else, though. He's building a career. He'll follow me through fire and water, no questions. The only thing is, at the end of the tunnel, he sees himself in my position. I won't live forever, and all that. You're different. You're more interested in the process than the goal. That's an entirely different characteristic. That's why I like you. But business is for tomorrow. Now let's finish our cigarettes, have another drink, and relax. Just don't drive after drinking. They're strict about that here. One of the guards will take you back."

But Stanley wasn't listening closely to the drunk oligarch. He had one thought running through his mind—would he still be here when Mila returned?

"You're a little distracted, McKnight!" Viktor said. "Are you worried about the contract? No need. Tomorrow, ten AM, it'll be right here," he said, pointing at the table. "Signed and confirmed by me personally. Biryuza!"

Anton approached.

"Yes, boss?"

"Get a driver to take our guest to his hotel."

"Done."

Biryuza led Stanley to his car, where a young man was already sitting behind the wheel, a local Italian from the restaurant staff.

"Come to the villa tomorrow, you know the time," Biryuza told Stanley. "You'll get your papers and go back to Zurich. And try not to come around again. I don't know why he likes to talk to you. Not my business. But I know something else. If he doesn't meet you tomorrow morning, there'll be one less reason to continue drinking. Got it?"

McKnight tiredly nodded and mumbled in Russian.

"Didn't really want to."

"What was that?" Biryuza snapped.

"Why won't you all just let me be!" asked Stanley. "I'm here for work. And I hope this is the last time I ever see your crooked face. Have a nice life! Let's go, *guidatore!*"

Biryuza spit on the ground, turned on his heel like a soldier in a parade march, and headed back.

On the road heading into the center of town, the driver slowed down and said to Stanley in broken English,

"A woman named Polina came to me. She gives you words of her *amica* Emila."

"Mila?" cried Stanley.

"Si!" the Italian smiled broadly. "She said that tomorrow at the villa she wants her first wish."

"God damn it!" Stanley swore in Russian.

He was in trouble. And the harder he tried to avoid dangerous adventures, the faster they came at him. As if a current had picked him up and was taking him, against his will, out into the open sea.

The Italian driver saw the expression on his passenger's face, and his smile slowly disappeared. He whispered quietly, "Oh mio Dio."

CHAPTER 15

THE NEXT MORNING, McKNIGHT WAS just about to run down to the beach and have a swim to clear his head when the telephone calls began. A worried Lagrange called first, asking him in detail about his meeting with Gagarin. Biryuza was next; he was expected at the villa at noon. He apologized on behalf of Gagarin, explaining that he had been called away on an urgent matter, and it wasn't clear when he'd be back. Stanley was happy to hear it. Things would be straightforward with Biryuza—he could go, get the briefcase, and goodbye.

He decided then that he would make no attempt to see Mila. No sense in risking his entire career, which was just starting to take an upward trajectory. He would let his fantasies remain just that.

If he was expected at noon, Mila was probably aware of the appointment, McKnight thought. If he arrived half an hour early, she would, like any other woman, be busy getting her appearance "combat ready." In her absence, he would get the documents, apologize for being so unforgivably early, and leave Milan as soon as possible for the airport. It would be nice to take advantage of the trip and go on a leisurely drive up the coast in his Ferrari, but no matter. Life was long, and there would be another time.

There was still plenty of time before noon, and McKnight took a slow drive all around the resort town to plan his exit after visiting the villa.

Despite it's being peak tourist season, and yesterday's talk of traffic jams, Forte dei Marmi looked deserted to Stanley. Waiters loitered on the verandas of restaurants, waving hopefully as the Ferrari motored by. There were few guests.

Only after parking at one of the cafés did Stanley realize why the streets were so empty—the sun beat down on him mercilessly when he emerged from his car. He felt the asphalt gently spring beneath his feet, and the cicadas made a deafening chorus in the pines and fir trees all around.

He had a double espresso in the café and devoured a plate of scrambled eggs, two sausages, and crisp bacon. He checked his watch: time to go.

As planned, Stanley pulled up to the villa half an hour before noon.

Past the automatic gate, he was met by a guard, who glanced at his license plate, said something into his radio, and directed Stanley toward the parking area, where several cars were already lined up under a tent.

McKnight parked and got out of the Ferrari to see an electric car approaching. Yet another guard was behind the wheel of the toy-sized vehicle. Stanley recognized this one from Moscow, from his first meeting with Gagarin.

"It's good you're here early," the guard said, deftly turning the small wheel. "Biryuza's in a rush to get somewhere. Everybody's been stressed all morning. Our boss's wife, Mila, you've probably met her, she got into some kind of fight with the police. We went there to figure it out, and there were already a crowd of reporters by the time we got there. So there's a scandal for the TV today. They watch the Russians closely here; the political situation is complicated," the guard said officiously, raising his finger. "Get in. Let's get going."

"We can't walk there?" Stanley asked out of curiosity.

"That's not how we do things here," the guard answered. "And Biryuza's waiting."

The electric car turned soundlessly into the park, down a lane lined with palm trees, made a wide circle around a rose garden, and stopped in front of a pool, past which, behind a screen of tall pines, stood the villa.

"We're here," said the guard, pointing. "See those tables under the tent? I'll tell Anton you're here."

Stanley walked the length of the pool to the villa. A dog was barking somewhere inside.

The main building was almost entirely hidden behind trees. The only visible part was a second-floor balcony, with elaborately decorative stucco. He could make out statues on the parapet of the roof. It was hard to guess at the age of the building; for one thing, he saw a blue glass cube behind the statues, which could have been the roof of a winter garden or greenhouse, or an indoor pool. When he grew closer, Stanley saw, through an opening in one of the tree-lined lanes, another building, or a continuation of the first, with interweaving staircases in front of its façade. Then, suddenly, the mountains behind both buildings came into view in the distance, rising above the low clouds.

McKnight realized that the sea was now behind him. A quiet rushing sound accompanied his progress as sprays of water arced over the green grass around the pool—someone had turned on the sprinkler system. Dozens of streams of water poured from a fountain just over a hedge of azaleas to his right, and a cool breeze washed over him. A rainbow flashed and trembled over the pool.

And there was Biryuza, walking right through the rainbow toward Stanley. Despite the heat, he was dressed in a dark business suit and a pink tie with a gold pin. His hair was carefully arranged. He was clearly not planning an afternoon of lounging by the pool; he was carrying the briefcase with documents, and he looked exceedingly concerned.

"My apologies again. For my rudeness yesterday as well. Sometimes the stress gets the better of me. The boss just called again—it's not clear when he'll be free. He just took a helicopter to Monaco." Anton held out the briefcase to McKnight. "All signed, everyone is notified. So you're free to get back to your regular affairs. Congratulation."

Biryuza was in such a rush that he slipped on the poolside tile, nearly falling.

While he caught his balance, briefcase in his outstretched hand, the sound of women's voices carried to them from the pavilion concealing the entrance to the villa.

Stanley recognized one of those voices immediately. And realized that now he would be able to recognize that voice in any crowd without hesitation.

"Looks like I didn't make it," sighed Anton, seeming to go limp. "Bad timing," he added under his breath. "I meant to catch you right at the entrance."

"Biryuza!" Mila's voice called. "I just saw him? Where did he get off to?"

"I'm over here," said the secretary quietly, handing the briefcase to Stanley. "Take this. Go. Meeting's over."

But Mila's voice seemed to have a hypnotic effect on McKnight, and he made no move to leave.

Mila came into view and clapped her hands.

"There you are!"

Biryuza straightened his shoulders, pasted a smile on his face, and turned around.

"And where was I supposed to be?" he asked

"What do you mean?" Mila said, approaching Stanley and Anton. "The plan was quite clear: a bike ride before lunch. Were you planning to ride in your suit and tie? An original choice."

"No, I wasn't," answered Biryuza. "I'm afraid that I won't be able to join you. I have a conference call with Credit Suisse that I can't put off."

"Well, good," Mila sad and laughed, "I'll get a little break from you." She looked over to Stanley. "I hope the financial genius doesn't have any calls he needs to get to?"

McKnight was scrambling for an excuse he could give, but didn't manage to get a word out.

"My spies tell me, Stanley, that you spend all your free time in Zurich on a bike. That you even ride to work on your bike. Is that true?"

McKnight nodded.

"Excellent. My fitness instructor, a boring character like our Anton, here, recommended bike riding. And I haven't been on a bike since I was a child. So you can be my trainer today." She turned to Anton again. "Anton, go arrange for some bikes. And get someone to find clothes and sneakers for Stanley. He'll tell you his size."

"But I have a plane to catch," Stanley protested, seeing that he was on the verge of that very adventure he had been trying to avoid. The road to hell, paved with his good intentions. He pointed to the watch on his wrist.

"Don't worry about it!" Mila interrupted, "It won't take long. We won't want to go for a long ride in this heat. I want to ride down Michelangelo Street." She added a meaningful glance. "It's not Botticelli, of course, but it's something. That's my first wish."

Biryuza turned back to the villa. McKnight lifted the briefcase in his hand.

"Someone will bring you clothes and take your case with all its treasures," said Mila, adding confidentially, "Relax, Stanley! You see my word is good—your bank got its golden fish, and now you owe me three wishes."

They left the villa through the main gates. The guard with the radio smiled, recognizing the man in tight bicycle shorts, mirrored glasses, and helmet as the one who had just come by car.

115

Mila had clearly been playing games with her claim of inexperience; she switched gears and rounded the curves of the road with easy skill, and her calves (Stanley remembered the feel of their smooth skin beneath his fingers) were perfectly muscled.

They rode for a short time on the bicycle path beside the highway, and then Mila turned sharply onto a narrow asphalt road going downhill and picked up speed. Stanley could barely keep up. The road went through a field, then turned, and a railway embankment appeared before them.

They traveled through a narrow tunnel under the railroad, which smelled of cats and bore the inscription *Francesco Totti forever* on its brick wall, and emerged on the other side into the shade of wide chestnut trees. Mila stopped, turned to Stanley, and said, "I can just about smell the smoke from the hole your eyes have been burning in my shorts."

Stanley could only lift his shoulders in helpless acknowledgement. He picked up the bottle of water from its holder in the bicycle's frame and took a few swallows. Yes, he'd been watching the whole ride, entranced by the way her body moved under those spandex shorts.

He felt almost as if he had stepped onto the set of a porn film. His imagination ran wild, and he began to picture her naked body with perfect clarity. And now, when she spoke, half-turned toward him, he couldn't take his eyes from the small, raised point her nipple made in her T-shirt.

Mila followed his gaze and beckoned Stanley over. He pedaled closer, so that the front wheel of his bike rested against her leg.

She glanced around quickly, then tore off her shirt with her right hand, while her left unsnapped the helmet and let it drop. She grabbed the back of Stanley's head and brought it to her chest, and he wrapped his lips around her nipple, his tongue circling the tender red circle around it.

Mila jerked his head closer, freeing her other breast at the same time. Stanley finally had the sense to let go of the bike, pulling her to his face with both hands, biting each nipple gently in turn. Mila moaned quietly and arched against the bicycle seat.

Noise thundered above them and they jumped apart.

It took only a few seconds for the train to pass. Stanley and Mila stared into each other's eyes the entire time—they both knew what they wanted, and that there was no turning back from it now.

"There's a small grove just ahead, before the vineyards," Mila said hoarsely. "It's not quite an impassible thicket, but it's all we have. And if I don't take these shorts off as soon as possible I'll die from the heat."

Then they were in the grove.

And then their clothes were scattered on the grass around them.

Mila turned to Stanley, grabbing on to two slender trunks in front of her, and lowered herself slightly. McKnight lifted her hips, shifted her slightly to the side, and drove all the way into her.

Mila stumbled on her tensed legs, then leaned back and down, adapting to Stanley's thrusts, and when she felt him moving in and out without any barrier, she screamed. It was hard to tell what that passionate cry held more of, triumph or pleasure.

The next sound she made was a long, drawn-out animal moan, and the slim trees she gripped trembled in her grasp.

Suddenly, coming from the direction they'd been heading, a hunched figure in an angled bicycle helmet flashed into view and passed through the air next to them, metal rim shining.

On his way down, the rider's rear wheel slammed into Stanley's handlebars, and the iron rattle reverberated in the air. The rider landed, righted himself, and was gone in an instant, barking an inaudible curse as he went. Even if he had gotten off his bike and come over to them, Stanley couldn't have stopped; he came just as the bike flew by in the air.

"The stupidest thing about it," said Mila, gasping for air, "is that bicyclist is Russian too. Like us." She finally managed to catch her breath and laughed a little nervously. "Italy is a wild country. Three Russians in one square meter. And all three on bikes."

"You know him?" asked Stanley in surprise, pulling on his shorts.

"Yes. Unfortunately. A crazy Russian banker who thinks he's the next Richard Branson. He used to be a professional cyclist." Mila pulled Stanley close and kissed him with unexpected tenderness. "It's a funny story, all right."

"Do you think he saw you and recognized you?" asked McKnight.

"If he did, we'll have to stop by the church on the way back and light a candle for our funerals. If that psycho recognized me and wants to tell Viktor, there's only one thing I can say." Mila fell silent and smoothed her hand along Stanley's head, as if straightening his hair.

"What can you say?"

"That we lived for nothing. But let's not panic. It's just a possibility at the moment."

"What should we do then?" McKnight asked.

"Find a more hidden place on the way back," Mila said with a smile. "Where Russian bicyclists won't jump over us." Lowering her eyes, she whispered, "I was just on my second round when he interrupted us. And I need to have at least three orgasms a day. For my nerves. That's my second wish."

CHAPTER 16

T HE WINTER HOLIDAYS AND ALL the accompanying rituals were difficult
for Stanley. He kept thinking about that last Christmas he had spent
with his mother, Louisa.

He had gone to her house in Berkeley the day before Christmas Eve.
Before dinner that evening, Christine realized she was out of cigarettes and
had to go to the store right away. Louisa decided to ride along to keep her
company, despite Stanley's protests. Christine was already pretty drunk.

The car slid off the road on a curve and hit a telephone pole. There were
no serious injuries, but Louisa hit her head against the window. They came
back home, drank some more Basil Haydens, and the next day Louisa fell
into a coma and died from internal bleeding. There was nothing the doctors
could do.

So when Stanley saw a crowd gathered in front of Zurich Central Station,
his mood fell. They were putting up a Christmas tree, decorated with stars
of Swarovski crystal. It shone brightly the next evening, one of Zurich's
main holiday sights, and it was, indeed, something to see. They opened the
Christmas market then as well.

A few days later, Stanley came to visit the train station along with
everyone else, drawn by the excitement of the crowd. He saw rows of
small wooden pavilions, styled to look like Alpine cottages, where they
were selling anything you could imagine. Local cosmetics, cheeses, richly
aromatic sausages, Indian incense for some reason, floor lamps in the local
ethnic style, cheap jewelry, Santa Claus figurines, including ones made out
of sugar, pasta produced by local businesses, and sweets of all kinds.

Stanley drank a glass of mulled wine and ate crepes with Alpine honey. The honey was a little bitter, and Stanley bought another glass of the wine, only this second glass was too sweet.

Stanley walked the market from end to end and then went over to the shopping center on Bahnhofstrasse, which also had a Christmas market, albeit a more modest one. It was quieter here. He sat down at a table in a small café, and ordered sausages, stewed cabbage, and beer. The sausages were too greasy, and the cabbage too sour. The food in Zurich was the worst Stanley had ever encountered. He took out a pack of cigarettes, but the waiter ran over to tell him anxiously that the fine for smoking was nearly 300 francs.

Stanley almost lit it up anyway; but they wouldn't take the fine right there—he would have to go to the police station, the local police would be sarcastic and pedantic, and they would find out where he worked, and probably send the bank a message to inform them that their employee scoffed at the laws and public health. Let him ruin his own, fine, but not those around him, the respectable burghers. Smoking therefore became a serious crime against the person.

Stanley ordered a second beer. Beer was good. He thought that if it tasted bad, he would buy a ticket and fly back to San Francisco. And then he thought that the honey had been good, as had the wine, sausages, and cabbage; he simply couldn't stop thinking about the mother he had lost.

Stanley paid on his way out, and rode the escalator to the first floor. He bought a sugar Santa and then went outside to smoke, standing to the side of the entrance near a tall urn, watching the people going to the market. Young people in red Christmas hats shouted and laughed. A tall man led a girl in a fur coat by the hand. On closer inspection, Stanley thought it might be real fur. The girl was whining about a special toy she wanted. The man nodded absently and then suddenly leaned down and barked, in Russian: "I've had enough of your damned complaints! Shut up!"

The shocked girl looked ready to cry, but then looked around her. When she met Stanley's gaze, she gave him a gap-toothed smile.

"Excuse me, sir, but you can't smoke here," Stanley heard behind him. It was a policeman, in a jacket with reflective stripes and a peaked cap with plastic brim.

"Oh? But I'm standing by the urn. I thought—" Stanley began.

"You're a foreigner? Tourist?"

"A foreigner, but I live and work in Zurich."

"You're an American, no?"

"That's right."

"If you look at the urn, here, you'll see a circle, with a cigarette crossed out inside. This tells you you're in a nonsmoking area. Please put out your cigarette."

Stanley did as he was asked and threw the butt into the urn.

"I could write you a ticket," the policeman went on, "but I'll let this go with a warning. And smoking is harmful to your health, I might add."

"Fuck right off, you Swiss moron," said Stanley in Russian.

"Is everything all right, sir?" asked the officer, moving closer. After the beer and mulled wine, Stanley smelled strongly of alcohol.

"Everything's great, officer, just great."

Stanley decided to walk along Bahnhofstrasse. The streetlamps were decorated with Christmas wreaths. He turned into a small side street leading upward, Rennweg, and bought some fried chestnuts. Then he ducked into a small jewelry store, and, surprising even himself, bought a woman's watch on a soft leather band. He didn't even look at the price, just pointed at the case. The salesman suggested buying a gift box, and now Stanley did ask the price, wondering aloud if a hundred francs was reasonable, but paid in the end and went back out onto the street.

He went along Bahnhofstrasse again and turned onto the narrow Augustinergasse, admiring the twinkling Christmas stars, and stopped into a little basement bar, where he had a brandy. Then another. And a third. He decided to give the watch to Elise, a pretty German girl from the European client department.

They'd gone out a few times. Elise had been open about recently splitting with her fiancé, and told him that she believed deeply in marriage, but that Stanley had nothing to worry about with her—yes, she knew he was married, and yes, yes, she knew he'd been trying to get divorced for a couple years, but Stanley, no matter how good he was in bed, did not meet her requirements for a good husband.

When Stanley asked what these requirements were, Elise started to talk about children, common interests, dependability, mutual understanding, and kindred spirits. Stanley grew bored. He listened a little longer, and was getting ready to head home, when Elise asked him to spend the night. They'd only seen each other at work since then, in the hallways of the bank, but they'd had lunch together once. Stanley had been planning to invite her to his place, but Lagrange had called while they were having dessert and asked him to come back to work.

"Is it urgent, Pierre? I, I mean we, just started dessert."

"And then you'll go fuck," laughed Lagrange. "Who are you with? Do I know her? Is it—yes, Elise? You'll have to disappoint her. Reschedule the sex. I need you."

In reality, Lagrange could have waited till the next day. When Stanley came to the bank, Lagrange told him that the client funds under his, Stanley's, management had grown to $1.5 billion, one billion coming from Gagarin, which was primarily due to Stanley's efforts. Stanley shrugged—none of this was news to him. But Lagrange went on. The bank's management, and Laville in particular, had decided to give Stanley a bonus of 850,000 francs. Not only that, but also the bank would pay the taxes on it. That was certainly the most generous gift of Stanley's life.

"When that yacht hits the water," said Lagrange, "which will happen at the start of summer, I think you'll get another bonus like this one. Stick with me, kid. You'll go far!" Lagrange clapped him on the shoulder.

Stanley called a taxi after the brandies. In the taxi, he realized he didn't know Elise's exact address. He remembered that she lived outside the city in Rapperswil, in a long apartment building. She had a nice apartment, but someone next door was constantly torturing Beethoven. He found Elise's name in his list of contacts. She picked up right away.

"Are you home?" asked Stanley.

"I am," she answered simply, not at all surprised to hear from him.

"What's your building number, floor, and apartment?"

"Are you...but..."

"Building number! Floor!"

"Stanley! Are you okay?"

"Everything's great, honey. I just need to know."

Elise gave him her address, Stanley repeated it after her and forgot it immediately. Luckily, he was in a taxi with an attentive driver. He helped Stanley find the right entrance, and Stanley went on by himself after that, asking the driver to wait.

Elise met him in the stairwell: it seemed that her sister and brother-in-law had come to visit unexpectedly. They were more upset over the end of her engagement than Elise was, and had come to talk her into reconciling with her ex.

"I won't keep you long," said Stanley, and took out the watch box. "It's not a ring. I'm not planning to get down on one knee. It's a present. For Christmas!" He bent to kiss her on the lips, but missed, and kissed her neck instead.

"Stanley!" cried Elisa, opening the box, "Oh, how lovely! For me? Oh, Stanley! It's so expensive!"

Stanley was bored again. If a woman this beautiful could bore him, any kind of spiritual kinship had to be impossible. There was no such thing. Connection, thought Stanley as he went back downstairs and into the waiting taxi, only happened between bodies; the incorporeal couldn't bond.

He told the taxi driver his address and sat back, sticking his hands into the pockets of his jacket, only to find that his candy Santa had lost his head.

In the morning, Stanley got yet another SMS from Mila. "Good morning, handsome," she wrote. "Hurry back! They're waiting for you at the bank. And remember: you owe me another wish. Your *Spring*."

They had been corresponding for a while now; after their meeting in the vineyard near Forte dei Marmi, Mila bombarded him with passionate messages. She only asked that he not write her first, as she could always get away for a moment, but an unexpected message from him could catch her at the wrong time.

Stanley also spoke with Biryuza nearly every day, over Telegram or by email. Sometimes he thought that clients like Gagarin were clinically paranoid, and all their employees were infected with the disease too, if such a thing could be contagious. In conversation with Biryuza, Stanley did begin to believe in its infectious capabilities and that he should take steps to protect himself.

Biryuza asked so many questions on behalf of Gagarin, that Stanley had to set aside time in his day to answer them all. Their main concern was some kind of conspiracy, some kind of outside influence, or the completely impossible collapse of Laville & Cie.

At his boss's behest, Biryuza even asked Stanley to have some trusted associates placed at the shipyard where the yacht was being built to ensure that no bugs were being planted in the vessel or explosives that could be detonated after its launch.

When Stanley said that Gagarin surely had his own spies, Biryuza replied that, of course, they had their own, but if Stanley sent his as well, they would have more reliable oversight. He insisted on it, promising that the bank's management should know nothing about it, and that Gagarin would certainly compensate him for his troubles.

He had to discuss these conversations with Lagrange, who laughed them off, as was his wont.

"What idiots!" Lagrange nodded in the direction of the cognac, indicating that Stanley should pour them both another round. "They really don't know how the game is played, do they? Seeing conspiracies everywhere. Russian nonsense. If someone was trying to kill Gagarin, it would be done with approval from on high, and Gagarin would have no chance of escaping his fate. You think he's the only one with observers there? He's valuable to the top players in Moscow, and there are probably FSB agents at the shipyard, or their foreign intelligence officers, or somebody else. They watch over Gagarin like one of their best-kept secrets. Anyway"—Lagrange tipped his glass back for a long swallow—"we'll think of something."

Several days later, Lagrange set up a meeting with a short, dark-haired man. They met in a noisy bar, rare for quiet Zurich, near an industrial part of the city. The man arrived precisely at the appointed time. Like Shamil, he exuded menace. Unlike Shamil, however, who grew more frightening when he smiled—or rather, bared his teeth—when this man smiled, it was as if a light shone from within him.

"Avi," he said in introduction as he sat down, nodded to Lagrange, and asked the waiter for mineral water, still.

Avi, Lagrange later explained, had worked in some branch of the Israeli special forces. After retiring, he had opened a security service in Switzerland.

He sat with them for the exact amount of time required for him to drink his glass of water in small sips. He agreed to do the job, but suggested it was better for them not to inform their client that the observation had already begun, in fact, it was better to keep any details of his work from their client. Avi promised that he would monitor the other observers as well as the process of construction. Finishing his water, he rose.

"You'll receive weekly reports." Avi said with a nod, and disappeared.

"We didn't agree on payment," Stanley said, ready to run after him.

"Don't worry," said Lagrange, sipping from his beer with evident enjoyment. "He'll send you an invoice along with his reports. His prices are modest, and his results are the best. Send Biryuza the invoices. It'll calm him down."

But Stanley traveled to Moscow again long before the Christmas season. He was hoping to see Mila, but she and Gagarin were vacationing in St. Barts.

Stanley, who had been working for as long as he could remember, starting with collecting bottles, mowing lawns, and bringing groceries to his elderly neighbors, then moving on to restaurants and bars, could never understand what made rich people so tired. He had even tried to set up a mathematical correlation between fatigue and the size of one's annual income. Moreover, these people always saw the worst side of things, barely dragging their feet through life.

He spent most of his time in Moscow with Biryuza, meeting with his other clients only once. Peshkov, who had previously transferred all his assets into yuan, now wanted those yuan invested in bitcoin. Glancing nervously over his shoulder, he asked Stanley why profit from his investments had dropped so drastically.

"We told you that you would lose out in the transfer from dollar to yuan. Also—" began Stanley.

"If this happens again with bitcoin," Peshkov interrupted him," I'm going to withdraw my assets from your bank."

"That's up to you, of course, but permit me to remind you that our contract includes a fee for premature withdrawal."

"A fee?" Peshkov's eyebrows shot up. "I don't know anything about that!"

"It's in the contract, nonetheless. You'd do better to wait until the end of the period specified in the contract."

"My lawyer checked that contract."

"But it's your signature on the document. You can fine your lawyer for it, if you like."

"I can't," said Peshkov sadly, "he died. Well, he had some help, but that doesn't concern you. How much is the fee?"

Stanley named a figure, but then remembered Peshkov's order to transfer everything to the yuan, and wrote several numbers on his napkin.

"What currency is that?" asked Peshkov, looking down at the napkin.

"Still the most reliable and desirable currency for now, the dollar," answered Stanley.

"You're a bunch of crooks!" Peshkov pronounced dramatically.

"First of all, I'm here alone, and second of all, our bank is a dependable and well-respected institution, and the contract you signed is largely to your benefit."

"You're going to answer for this!" Peshkov stood abruptly, but before he left, he leaned close to Stanley and said, "Transfer it all to bitcoin!"

As if repeating the schedule of meetings from his first Moscow visit, Stanley met up with Grigoryan as well. Grigoryan asked for a higher percentage, promising Laville & Cie another five depositors. Stanley nodded

125

dutifully and promised to discuss the rate increase with his management. He looked at Grigoryan's smug face and wondered what new information this traitor would reveal about their allegedly common acquaintances.

Grigoryan proved to be more astute than Stanley had given him credit for.

"You don't think particularly well of me, Mr. McKnight," he said, "but I need money for the shelter. Orphans! They need help!"

"Yes, of course, I understand. Our bank—"

"What about your bank!" Grigoryan slapped his knee. "I'm talking about the orphans!"

As Stanley watched Grigoryan walk out of the café, he thought that those poor orphans would be lucky to see one red cent of his money.

Mila called him that evening, very upset that they hadn't been able to meet. When he asked how her trip was going, she told him that she was exhausted and sick of everything there. And so she called him.

"You—we—are taking a risk," said Stanley.

"I thought you'd be happy to hear my voice, handsome."

"Please don't call me that."

"All right, all right, don't be a bore. Everyone here is drunk. Viktor got in a fight with someone. Can you imagine?"

Stanley had never seen a fistfight between billionaires. He actually couldn't imagine.

"He did. He did. They argued about their visions for Russia's future. I don't give a shit about the future. I'm worried about waking up with a headache tomorrow. My only medicine for that is far away. Bye, handsome!"

Just before Christmas, Lagrange told him that Gagarin was back in Europe, skiing in Lech.

"At Princess Diana's favorite ski resort, and mine too," Lagrange went on. "It's in Austria, about two hundred miles from Zurich. He's invited us to join him. Want to go?"

"Do I have a choice?" Stanley asked.

"That's the thing, not really. I was planning to go to Cuba for New Year's, but I'll have to skip it. I reserved us a corporate car."

"Cancel it, Pierre. We'll go in my car."

"You bought a car? And you didn't tell me? No bragging? What's the model?"

"You'll see. When are we leaving?"

"That Russian is expecting us tonight."

"I'll pick you up," said Stanley, and left Lagrange alone in his office with his glass of whiskey.

CHAPTER 17

STANLEY HAD BOUGHT HIMSELF A Tesla electric car, becoming the first in Zurich to own this miracle of modern engineering. He'd put in an order as soon as Tesla opened a dealership in the city.

As for why, he wasn't exactly sure. Not because he wanted to stand out—there were a million other ways to do that, especially after that bonus from the bank. He would have had his favorite car shipped to Zurich, an old Ford Bronco—a huge vehicle with the stick shift by the steering wheel—if it wouldn't have made him look like an oddball. And he might not have been able to squeeze it into several of Zurich's narrow streets. At one point, he was even thinking about buying an Aston Martin, but realized it was a bit above his current station.

They didn't manage to leave on time—Lagrange called and said he'd been detained by some business. Stanley came to get him in the afternoon, and Lagrange was delighted by the Tesla. Not because he particularly liked the car, but because Stanley had, in his opinion, completed his 'coming out' by buying the car.

"What are you talking about?" exclaimed Stanley, heading down Gessnerallee toward the A3.

"This is a gay car!" Lagrange declared authoritatively. "The great gay division will head to battle in a fleet of these cars. To attack the poor asses of the hetero population. Say you'll have mercy on me?"

"Give it a rest, Pierre! This is the first absolutely unmotivated decision I've ever made. I even thought about seeing a psychologist. To ask, 'Doctor, if I buy a Tesla, what's wrong with me?'"

"Funny, Stan, but you can't justify this one. At least the villa Gagarin has rented can't be reached by car. In this one or any other. We'll have to leave your effeminate car in a parking lot and take a lift. But this car can move; I'll give you that."

"Zero to a hundred in five seconds," boasted Stanley, and pressed down a little more on the accelerator.

"Engine in the back?" asked Lagrange.

"Even if you looked for it back there, you wouldn't find it," answered Stanley. "There are four of them, if I'm not mistaken."

With an eye on the huge display mounted on the car's central console, Stanley easily overtook every other car on the road. The mirrored surface of lake Obersee appeared on his left, and the high fences of a manufacturing zone extended along his right.

"So how far can you go on one charge?"

"It'll get us to Gagarin's."

"But how far in general?"

"About five hundred kilometers."

"Wow!" Pierre whistled.

"That's not even the most impressive part, Pierre. The main battery is composed of about seven thousand AA battery cells, arranged in a particular pattern of positive and negative contacts. And that pattern is the big secret!"

"I see, Stan—if you're not ready to raise the rainbow flag just yet, at least you'll be a healthy-eating environmentalist. You'll give up meat, start eating nuts and berries. Do you meditate yet? Time to start!" Lagrange pulled out a cigar, lit it, and lowered the window after unsuccessfully searching for an ashtray.

Brisk air streamed in from the open window, and Stanley turned the heat up. After Obersee they came upon another lake, Walensee, with low hills rising behind it. The mountains of Liechtenstein emerged and disappeared again into the fog as they drove.

"At least you didn't buy a pink or purple car. With a black one, you still have a chance."

"A chance at what, Pierre?"

"At not turning into that kind of European asshole. Care for the environment! Give water to the Africans! Feed the Indians! Protect the whales! Aid the refugees! Goddamned Merkel!" Lagrange accompanied his words with energetic gestures, as if he was speaking to a crowded rally. "You know, I hate the liberals, always feeling bad about everything in the world. The left is more obsessed with power than the right."

"Why is that?" Stanley checked the display, glanced up at the road sign, and turned off the A3 by Sennwald, heading toward Rheinstrasse.

"Because they're more certain than the right about how you should live. Their favorite word is 'social justice.' Not equality, not freedom, but justice. Justice, fairness. Have you seen fairness anywhere in this world, Stanley?"

The Rhine appeared on their right. The river was narrow here, but even a quick glance at high speed was enough to see how powerful its current was.

"Probably not," said Stanley after a brief pause. He drove onto the Feldkirch bridge, and they entered Liechtenstein.

"Our work is based on unfairness, as you have probably guessed," said Lagrange. "If the world was fair, we'd be out of work. That doesn't mean that I wouldn't like fairness and justice everywhere. It's just impossible to achieve. Only in small doses. Pull over by that stand—it would be an injustice for me to piss my pants!"

Lagrange returned with a small bottle of wormwood-infused vodka and a can of tonic water.

"Like with like," he said. He had obviously already sampled some of the drink. "Let's roll! But just to finish my point—Gagarin loves to talk about fairness. Have you had that talk yet? No? You will. But his idea of fairness is really something, just wait. What's good for Gagarin is what is fair, and vice versa. He's sure that he is just a font of fairness, himself. For everyone. Those who can't, or won't, accept his fairness are enemies to him. And he chews them up. Mostly using Shamil's teeth. Are we already in Austria?"

Stanley looked at the display.

"We'll get past Sebastian Kneipp Strasse and...forget the details! When we get to the A14, we'll be in Austria. Why did Gagarin invite us? To talk about fairness?"

"Uh-huh." Lagrange nodded, and took another large swallow of the vodka, chasing it with a sip of tonic. "He wants to work with us more. He likes us. Thanks to you. Laville, by the way, asked me to pass on his best wishes for the holidays. As far as I can recall, you are only the second employee of this bank whom Laville has ever sent an individual holiday greeting, even if it is through a third party."

"And who was the other employee?"

"Me, naturally." Lagrange took another pull on his bottle.

Stanley loved how the Tesla handled. The powerful electric engines gave the two-ton car an agile and elastic acceleration over a range of speeds. The car started fast and picked up speed at a rate that put actual sports cars to shame. Stanley remembered the more measured pace of his old Bronco. If it hadn't entirely disintegrated into rust, it was still parked at a relative's house in Oregon. The Tesla also had superb brakes—a Brembo brake system, as they told Stanley at the dealership, could stop a two-ton car short even at a decent speed. And, of course, it handled magnificently, particularly on the winding roads after Langen.

Then the road straightened out and grew steeper. They came out onto the Arlbergstrasse, entered the Arlberg valley, and took the B197 and Lechtalstrasse into Lech.

Stanley turned sharply into a small parking lot in front of a restaurant named Hus Nr. 8, and found a spot.

"Why are we parking here, exactly?" asked Lagrange suspiciously.

"Because I saw an open parking spot," answered Stanley.

"I thought you must have found out somehow." Lagrange fell silent.

"Found out what?"

"That I already reserved a table here. In this restaurant. There will be food at Gagarin's of course, but they start with the vodka first, and I can't take that. I'm French. What's in first place for the French? Dinner! A scarf and a lover too, of course, but dinner above all else. Let's go!"

They went in, sat down, and ten minutes later the waiter began to bring them their food. Meat on hot rocks, fondue, melted raclette cheese. There was also soup with liver meatballs and a stewed leg of lamb. Lagrange partook heavily of the plum schnapps and unfiltered beer, and he ate as if he'd been starving for days, demanding that Stanley keep up with him in the drinking. They paid with a corporate card and left.

"That was excellent!" said Lagrange, zipping up his coat and pulling on a knit cap. "Now we just need to walk over to the lift. I'm not exactly sure where it is. We still have two hundred meters further up to go. The village is called Oberlech. And let's not forget our bags!"

Stanley pulled both their bags out of the trunk. Lagrange, in a friendly mood and tipsy from the liquor and huge meal, asked, "Do you know how to ski, Stanley?"

"Well, it's been ten years since I last went."

"Where was that?"

"In the US, Mammoth Mountain."

Lagrange's good mood disappeared.

"I'm sick of hearing about your America. Heaven on earth! You live *here* now. They'll be happy to see you, Tesla owner. Everyone's an environmentalist here. Look around you—not one smoking chimney. A single boiler heats all the hotels and houses here, and only wood for fuel. They don't even have satellite television—antennas would spoil the view, you see. Pardon me, monsieur. Where can we find the lift to Oberlech?"

The man wearing a jacket bearing the inscription *The White Ring* just looked at Lagrange before slowly turning his wrist to look at the time.

"You're late. The lift is already closed," he said, and walked off.

"Oh ho!" laughed Lagrange. "I'm not going to call Gagarin. You do it, Stan. You're his favorite new drinking buddy, I heard. I know everything," He wagged his finger at Stanley warningly. "Go ahead and call. He'll think of something."

Gagarin did: he told them to go to the lift and wait. Five, seven minutes, tops. That was how long it took for the lift to start up again as a special favor to Viktor Gagarin. At his very persuasive request.

CHAPTER 18

I N OBERLECH, SEVENTEEN HUNDRED METERS above sea level, Gagarin
and his guests occupied one of the ski resort's most expensive chalets.
So it was really no surprise that he could insist that the staff turn the lift
back on.

Oberlech's wooden houses fitted beautifully into the landscape of the
Arlberg massif, and the chalet Gagarin had rented didn't stand out from
the others. From afar, it might have been a home for some of the resort's
ski instructors, who made up about a fifth of Oberlech's fifteen hundred
residents. The building's modest exterior, however, marked only by the
letter *N* on a plaque and several balconies and terraces, concealed a seriously
luxurious interior.

Against the traditional Alpine frame of wooden beams and walls the
décor of the chalet included black granite, shining chrome surfaces, and
Swarovski crystal, while the windows were made of bulletproof glass.

Guests usually rented these chalets for a week, but Gagarin had taken
this one for two, at a cost of nearly 600,000 euros. Twenty staff members
had their hands full providing services to the temporary residents: in the
kitchen, in the spa, maintaining the enormous pool, the waters of which
were changed in accordance with the wishes of each new group of guests,
while tennis instructors waited to assist anyone who wished to play on the
court located in the basement. A butler was available at any time of day or
night to pour a glass of champagne, while the steward of the wine cellar
could offer wine from any country to match any dish.

Stanley emerged from his room before Lagrange and found a number of
familiar faces in the main hall downstairs.

Gagarin, Biryuza, Durand, and Krapiva sat in armchairs around an oval table laid with small plates and bottles. Gauthier hovered around the table and, while Gagarin was distracted by something, invited the other guests to have some cocaine.

Shamil sat on a low chair, legs stretched out, warming himself in front of an enormous fireplace. The ladies were gathered around a different table, on low, cushioned sofas. Their table was spread with sweets, chocolate, and several silver buckets with bottles of brut and rosé champagne.

Mila and Polina were there with two unfamiliar women: Yulia, a blonde with a triangular face, pointed chin, and full lips, and a young girl no older than sixteen or seventeen. This, he learned later, was Durand's new love interest, a top model despite her young age, and already the face of several popular brands.

Gagarin leaped up as soon as he noticed Stanley, knocking over a bottle of vodka on the table in front of him.

"Stanley, my friend! I'm delighted to see you! Your boss told us you bought a Tesla? Switching your sexual orientation, eh? You're probably sick of that question—I'd kill anyone who asked me!"

Gagarin managed to say all this as he walked over to Stanley, then embraced his guest, and, to the surprise of Stanley and everyone else, kissed him three times.

"That's the Russian way, my friend!" Gagarin explained. "When we drank to our friendship, we didn't forget to kiss! And so there's the continuation!"

"Yes, I remember," muttered the stunned Stanley, searching for something to say.

"Lighten up, Stanley! Make yourself at home! Hey, Biryuza! Pour Stanley a glass. Here, come sit with us!"

"No," protested Mila, watching with interest as her husband kissed her lover, "come sit with us—we need an arbiter. We have an important disagreement, and Stanley can be our judge."

"Okay, okay," Gagarin agreed. "But he has to drink vodka. Followed with some real herring and onions."

Biryuza handed Stanley a glass of chilled vodka and a piece of black bread with herring.

"I had this brought specially from Moscow," said Gagarin, pointing at the fish. "I've seen what they call herring here. They pour vinegar into the brine, sprinkle it with spices, do God knows what to it. This is our good Russian recipe! Here, to your health!"

Stanley, mentally thanking Lagrange for making sure they'd had a real dinner, drank the vodka and took a bite of the sandwich.

"That's the way! Have a rest, Stanley! He's all yours, girls," he said, turning to Mila.

When he sat down with the women, it quickly became apparent that they had indulged quite heavily in the cocaine on offer, including the young model. The topic of their argument was about the power of masculine beauty and charm, and French actors.

Mila asserted that the epitome of male beauty was and forever would be the French actor Maurice Ronet, because that was what her mother and grandmother had believed before her. Stanley didn't recognize the name—film wasn't really his subject, and he readily admitted to both facts.

The blonde with the sharp chin, Yulia, who turned out to be Krapiva's daughter from his first marriage, tapped away at her tablet with a manicured nail and handed it to Stanley. The man on the screen had piercing blue eyes and a wary smile.

Polina, meanwhile, was certain that Alain Delon was the handsomest man. This actor, at least, was a familiar name to Stanley. In fact, he'd seen him in person once, at restaurant in London, but couldn't remember a single one of his films.

"Yes, he's handsome," agreed Stanley. "Interesting that they're both blue-eyed."

"Just like you, Mr. McKnight," said Polina with a crooked smile. "Has anyone ever told you that you could practically be his twin brother? Delon, I mean. Only you look a bit rougher. Did you serve in the army? The marines?"

"The marines?" Out of the corner of his eye, Stanley saw Gagarin get up and approach their group, listening intently. "No, I never did. I went to college."

"They aren't mutually exclusive," replied Polina. "You could serve first, then enroll. But anyway, Delon is sexier than Ronet, and you're sexier than Delon. You've never heard that before, either?"

"I'm a private banker," said Stanley with a smile. "In my business, sexiness is probably more of a minus than a plus."

"Sexy, indeed," agreed Gagarin. "That can be a real help sometimes."

"Let's ask Biryuza," suggested Mila. "He clearly knows more than Stanley about film and men."

Everyone laughed. Biryuza snorted, wiped the coke off his nose, and came over as well.

"Anton, tell me, who do you like better? Delon or Ronet? And which film of theirs?"

"Well, then we have to consider the movies they were both in. They were competitors, in life and film, and—"

Biryuza spoke in affected tone, imitating the style of a film critic being interviewed.

"Get to the point, Biryuza," Gagarin said.

"Okay, okay, the best are *Purple Noon* and *Swimming Pool*. Even Stanley's probably seen the first—well, it's remake, anyway, *The Talented Mr. Ripley*, made much later than the first, based on the novel by Patricia Highsmith. You Americans always co-opt everything you can. Matt Damon plays in the remake and—"

"Leave our Stanley alone," said Gagarin. "Go on!"

"All right, fine, so Ronet is better in *Purple Noon*, but Delon steals the show in *Swimming Pool*. I would happily sleep with either or both of them," Biryuza ended unexpectedly.

"Ugh, Biryuza!" objected Gagarin.

"It's not the time for your confessions, Anton," Mila said. "But we would sleep with them too. Right, girls? Except Alain is an old man now, and Ronet died some time ago. I'm not a necrophiliac. How about you, honey?" she asked the model.

"Me neither," said the latter.

"Neither what?"

"I'm not a necrophiliac. That's disgusting. Anyway, I don't know those singers. I'm into Alex Turner—he's so cute!"

"Hear that, Durand?" Gagarin shouted over. "That's who you have to live up to."

"Oh, Robert! You don't have to live up to anyone. You're sweet just the way you are!"

"Well, then you have a fondness for monkeys," said Biryuza, and everyone laughed.

Stanley laughed along with everyone else, although he had no idea who Alex Turner was or what monkeys had to do with anything. He could feel that something wasn't quite right, that this conversation about sexiness, with himself as the prime example, had been brought up intentionally, and that it could lead to very unfortunate consequences. An awkward pause was broken by the appearance of a drowsy Lagrange, who, he recounted, had intended to lie down for just a minute, but ended up falling into a deep sleep.

"And here I am! What a lovely group! What are you all up to?" asked Lagrange.

"Like usual," Gagarin answered. "Figuring out who has the biggest dick."

"Viktor! Don't be nasty!" said Mila.

"Come on, dear. That's what all conversations really boil down to," Gagarin replied.

"Exactly!" Polina agreed. "I'm with Viktor. Pierre, you have to agree that whatever men are talking about, advanced calculus or opera, they're all, in the end—"

"Comparing the size of their wieners!" Krapiva finished, to general laughter.

"Papa!" cried the blonde. "Shame on you!"

"Can't argue with that," replied Lagrange. "So, who won?"

"Stanley!" Gagarin suddenly pointed at him. "It's Stanley!"

After an instant of confusion, everyone laughed again.

"Ladies and gentlemen," Stanley began, starting to rise. He wasn't quite as amused as the others, and was getting ready to tell them to knock it off. But Gagarin came over and threw an arm across his shoulders.

"We're just kidding, Stanley. We're all friends here. Don't be offended! If you want, we can test everyone." His voice dropped to a loud whisper. "But I'm afraid that if we include Shamil, you're going to lose your top spot. So just enjoy your victory and don't tell anyone about it!"

"No one will ever find out, anyway!" retorted Polina, and the burst of laughter ended their discussion of French actors and male sexuality.

The evening ended with a light dinner, at which Gagarin poured Stanley another glass of vodka, and insisted he follow it with herring and onion on black bread, and then called for strong tea.

"You know that's not good for you, Viktor," Mila said.

"Shut up!" Gagarin hissed and went off to the kitchen to instruct the chef how to properly steep the tea.

Stanley, trying to stay out of the conversation, wandered around the room. When he approached the fire, Shamil opened his eyes, looked at Stanley blearily, nodded, and went back to sleep. At some point in his perambulation, he looked up to find Yulia's eyes on him. She gave him an inviting look, eyes half closed, and ran the tip of her tongue along the edge of her lower lip. Stanley turned away and poured himself a shot of vodka. As he was putting a sandwich together, Biryuza appeared beside him.

"Can I give you some advice, Stanley?" he said very quietly.

"Go ahead," Stanley nodded.

"Lock your door tight tonight, and don't open it for anyone. Unless it's Shamil about an emergency evacuation."

"Oh? Why's that?"

"That Yulia has her eye on you. She goes after all the men and then makes scenes. And her father deals with the men after that. Be careful. She's also a liar and a gossip. Don't give her any material to work with. You get me?"

"Got it. Thank you." And Stanley tossed back the shot of vodka.

He did, in fact, hear someone knocking and scratching at his door almost right after he locked it that evening. But if there were any other attempts to get in his room after that, Stanley knew nothing about them—he fell onto his soft bed and passed out with all his clothes on.

CHAPTER 19

T HE NEXT MORNING, STANLEY GINGERLY made his way downstairs tormented by a hangover. Everyone was already seated at a single, long table, and waiters were passing out dishes.

"Ah, I have a feeling someone isn't too happy with us this morning!" Gagarin said in greeting.

Stanley said hello to everyone, with the unhappy premonition that yesterday's jokes were going to continue this morning. The waiter leaned over to take his order.

"Juice, coffee, toast, and strawberry jam," said Stanley, "and Alka-Seltzer, please."

The waiter poured him a tall glass of orange juice, and set a steaming cup of aromatic coffee in front of him. Stanley looked up to find Mila and Julia sitting across from him.

"So Stanley, are you going to give us a hard time?" said Gagarin.

"It depends," Stanley replied, accepting a glass of water with a fizzing Alka-Seltzer tablet from the waiter. "About some things, maybe."

"The thing is, we've got a strange group here," said Gagarin, gesturing at his assembled guests with an ironic smile. "They all want to sit inside, smoke weed, and drink champagne. I promised them that anyone who didn't provide me with documented proof that they'd gone down one, at least one, slope today wouldn't get any dinner. These people immediately chose the smallest, easiest trails so they could get back here sooner to start getting wasted. So then I raised the stakes to two descents, then three."

"Do I need to choose a trail?" Stanley asked, spreading jam over his hot toast. "I'd be happy to! But I don't have any equipment."

"What are you on about, Stanley? Where do you think you are?" Gagarin lit up one of his smelly Rodina cigarettes. "Why am I paying for this fucking chalet, huh? They'll give you any gear you want, Porsche skis, goggles—but who cares about the brand? You'll get the best! You don't have to choose a trail, either. You and me are going together. Finish your coffee, and we're off."

Stanley bit into his toast, trying not to look at Mila, and met Julia's gaze. She gave him a malicious, vindictive little smile. Apparently, they'd already heard about his solo outing with Gagarin, and it didn't bode well for Stanley.

As soon as Stanley finished his coffee, Gagarin rose from the table and left the dining room, gesturing for Stanley to follow him. A ski instructor was already waiting for them in a special equipment room.

"We're going to fly, Stanley!" Gagarin announced. "We'll fly up to the top of the mountain, and go down pristine, untouched snow from there, risking our lives. Do you like risk? I love it! Do you know how much it cost me to get permission to heli ski?"

"Permission to what?" asked Stanley.

"To ski using a helicopter instead of a ski lift! It's banned in Austria, but money, as you well know, works wonders. They made an exception for us. Have you ever skied on virgin snow?"

"I never have," admitted Stanley. "Couldn't we do without that? If you want, I'll go down four trails? How about five?"

"Just one descent, Stanley! But we're getting there by helicopter, and then we're skiing down. Chased by an avalanche. Kidding!"

Gagarin was in a state of high excitement. His equipment was already prepared, and he bothered the instructor with advice while he chose gear for Stanley. This took much longer than Stanley would have thought. Stanley tried to catch everything the instructor was saying, and to ignore Gagarin's chatter. His clothing was selected for its membrane structure, and then he was given thermal underwear, a helmet, goggles, and gloves. The instructor spent a particularly long time on the skis, boots, and bindings. They then proceeded into a different room, where a safety instructor gave Stanley an avalanche airbag backpack with a first-aid kit, beeper, probe, and shovel as well as a Swiss army knife, and explained how to use it all.

Stanley felt a strange indifference settle on him. He realized that there was no way out of this, that Gagarin had chosen him as a victim. He either suspected, or knew, what had been going on with Stanley and Mila.

Stanley knew that this might be the last day of his life, and of Gagarin's as well, for that matter. Once he hit upon the thought that this was Gagarin's way of going out in style, he couldn't get it out of his head.

They left the chalet and walked to the helipad. The helicopter looked small to Stanley, not like a serious aircraft at all. There was just one pilot, and only space for four passengers.

He forgot to breathe for a moment when the helicopter made a sharp ascent. As it circled over Oberlech, Stanley saw the largest peaks of the Alps in the distance, and then they flew off in a northeasterly direction before landing on a level area high up in the mountains. He could no longer see Oberlech from here, or any other human dwelling.

The steep slope before them was covered in virgin snow and flanked by gray-brown cliffs on either side, with tall spruce trees sticking out of the snow here and there.

"Do you remember everything I told you?" asked the instructor, shouting over the noise of the rotors. "Just don't make too much noise—chances of an avalanche are low, but better safe than sorry."

Stanley nodded.

"I'll go first. Try to follow in my tracks, or as close to them as you can get."

"No!" shouted Gagarin. "We're going down together. Side by side! You wait down below, there, in that valley." He pointed somewhere further down the slope.

"Herr Gagarin, my instructions are..."

"Back to the helicopter, Herr instructor. Go on!" Gagarin was in a rage, so much so that he added in German, "Get the hell away from me!"

"But you can't—"

"Hey!" Stanley shouted at the instructor. "You heard the man! Everything's paid for, no? So wait down there!"

The instructor shrugged, threw his skis and poles back into the helicopter, and told the pilot to take off. Stanley and Gagarin squatted down while the helicopter took off, showering them with snow, then stood up on their skis, took their poles, and pushed off toward the edge of the slope. The helicopter was gone, and the world was completely silent.

"I thought you'd get scared," Gagarin said with a laugh.

"And I thought you would," answered Stanley.

Gagarin slowly took off his gloves and, squinting in the sun, looked around.

"A beautiful day. A beautiful day, but too quiet, don't you think, Yankee?"

"Who's going first?" asked Stanley, lowering the ski mask over his eyes.

Gagarin silently unbuttoned his jacket and pulled a 9 mm Smith & Wesson out of his inside pocket.

He pulled back the bolt, took out the clip, and then snapped it back in place before Stanley's astonished eyes.

So he does know about Mila and has decided to leave me here. Not a bad plan, actually. I wonder what he'll tell the others? Stanley fell into a ravine? Poor guy, I really liked him. Lagrange, who's going to be my private banker now?

"'The moon comes out across the land, with a sharp knife in his hand,'" Gagarin began reciting a Russian nursery rhyme. "'Come to cut you, come to beat you, come to guide you through the land.'"

The gun was pointed right at Stanley.

Unable to speak, Stanley watched the barrel of the gun, spellbound. After a few seconds that seemed like an eternity, the gun moved to the side and began to turn toward the mountain.

"It's too quiet here," Gagarin said. Then he aimed at the sun and fired the gun three times. "I'll go first."

And then he was off, down the hill.

"Catch me if you can!"

Stanley pushed off after him, without preparation or hesitation; he knew that falling behind was simply not an option.

The slope down which they both flew seemed to come to life under their skis. It was as if Gagarin had challenged the mountain to give them an avalanche with his shots, and the slope turned into a game of life or death with each new curve.

Gagarin, clearly the more experienced skier, instigated small avalanches and sped away with skillful maneuvers—Stanley raced after him, imitating his turns.

They came down from a jump onto a small area of springy snow, and Gagarin made a sharp turn, sending an avalanche down in front of him, and after that they chased the avalanche downhill, with other avalanches coming after them from above.

But then the small avalanches began to come together, forming into one powerful, menacing movement of snow. It was catching up on them. Stanley glanced back: a high white wall followed them, emitting a low, heavy roar.

Gagarin took a turn to the right. Stanley did the same. Then Gagarin took a sharp left turn. Stanley followed him. The avalanche hit a large black rock, split in two, froze for a moment, and then roared downhill again, gaining speed. Gagarin veered further left and then quickly turned right, sliding through a gap between the cliff and a spruce tree growing on the very edge of the ravine.

When Stanley had slipped between cliff and tree after Gagarin, he saw another cliff ahead of him, from which he could see a smooth descent down to where the helicopter should be waiting. But Gagarin wasn't on that slope. It was as if he'd fallen through the snow.

Stanley managed to brake at the very edge of the cliff. A bit to the right, he saw a crevice that one could ski down as well without having to jump off the cliff. To get into it, you'd have to ski between two spruce trees standing close together. Gagarin had almost done it, but had hit one of the trees. The binding had come loose, and he'd lost his right ski.

Gagarin was down on one knee in front of the crevice, looking at Stanley; looking at what was happening behind him. The wall was coming toward them.

Stanley didn't bother looking back. He knew what was happening. He sped over, threw his arm around Gagarin, gripping him tightly, and for a moment they were at the edge of the crevice, and then they were flying down into it, away from the wall of snow, now caught between the cliffs. He'd done it. Straining with all his strength, he was dragging Gagarin by the collar of his jacket while the other man balanced on one ski.

They approached another small jump, and at last, the slope began to flatten out, while the snow grew thicker and denser. Stanley pulled Gagarin down, forcing him to bend his knees, and squatted lower himself. They flew over the jump, landed on a large, even surface, and came to a stop.

The helicopter circled overhead.

"I owe you one," said Gagarin, taking off his glasses.

"It's my job," said Stanley, unclenching his fingers and releasing the collar of Gagarin's jacket. "The welfare of my clients is everything to me."

Stanley didn't come down for lunch, ordering beer and a decanter of Zvenigorod whiskey to his room. The fingers of his left hand would occasionally clench together frantically of their own volition.

He took a shower and didn't bother getting dressed afterward. Instead, he sat down in an armchair, naked, and poured himself a full glass from the decanter. He drank the whiskey and ate olives and jamón. He felt like he'd been born again.

McKnight drank all the beer and finished the decanter of whiskey without feeling the slightest bit of intoxication.

When he entered the dining room for dinner, everyone acted as if nothing out of the ordinary had occurred. Lagrange gave him a wave, and Gagarin didn't even look his way.

Stanley snagged a dish with black caviar and scooped a big spoonful onto his plate. The waiter asked what he would like.

"Steak," said Stanley. "Bison steak, bloody, and French fries, make them like McDonald's fries. And beer. But first, pour me some vodka."

"What kind of vodka, sir?"

"Your preference."

He had to wait a bit for the steak; he had time for more than one vodka.

Everyone else finished eating. The women went out onto an enclosed veranda to watch skiers descend the slopes of Oberlech with flashlights, and the men went into the cigar room.

Stanley worked his way through the steak, slowly and thoroughly, and mopped up the juices with a piece of bread, then washed it down with a swig from his second bottle of beer.

The cigar room smelled of cognac and coffee, and smoke clung to the candelabra by the fireplace.

Gagarin was, as usual, talking about democracy and how democracy in Russia was a path to fascism. Krapiva objected without much energy. Then Krapiva got tired of arguing, put his cigar in a silver ashtray, and left to join the women.

"He's afraid that Polina is going to lose her patience and slap Yulia across her face," said Gagarin. "Or that Yulia is going to scratch out Polina's eyes. Women are a curse! Right, Durand?"

"Of course. A woman is a failed man."

"Agreed!" shouted Biryuza.

"And you, Stanley?"

"A curse. Most definitely," said Stanley, sitting down and accepting a cigar from the specially trained cigar room attendant, wearing a tailcoat.

"A curse!" he repeated, lighting a cigar and gesturing at the waiter to pour him a drink as well.

The room swam before his eyes, and the buzz in his head grew from the cigar smoke.

"Why with such conviction?" asked Durand, and Gagarin stared at Stanley with open interest.

"I've always believed in the power of banal truths," Stanley said, blowing out a series of smoke rings. He didn't like cigars; they always made his mouth fill with viscous saliva.

"The banal truth is that it's become difficult to work with Swiss banks. Everything else is not banal," said Gagarin, shifting the conversation back to business. "They're always throwing a spoke in the wheel, want to be holier than the Pope, always asking for new confirmations about the cleanliness of your money, refusing to take cash."

"Yes," said Durand, pursing his lips thoughtfully, "that's true. Compliance is going after the Russians more and more all the time. It's politics. It's a prejudice that is only growing stronger."

"UBS and Credit Suisse don't know how to work individually with VIP clients. Well, they never did; that's not why they were founded," said Lagrange. "They're like those French fries that Stanley gobbled up tonight."

Stanley wanted to say that he actually liked those fries, but decided against it.

"There won't be any such problems with Laville & Cie," Lagrange said.

"I'm thinking about transferring additional funds to Laville & Cie. But you've got compliance as well," said Gagarin.

"The head of that department reports to the owner of the bank," said Lagrange, taking a drink of cognac, "and I'll take care of it."

"That makes working with you an even more attractive proposition," Gagarin said with a wide smile. "I could increase my portfolio in your bank to four billion. Stanley, how much of my money do you have now?"

"You have about 600 million in your investment portfolio in trust management, and a credit line for the yacht which is currently at 400 million," said Stanley, spitting out a stray piece of tobacco. "If your portfolio goes over four billion, your discounts for our services will rise significantly."

"Is that so?" Gagarin asked Lagrange.

The latter nodded in reply.

"So we have another reason to be grateful to Stanley," laughed Gagarin. "Thanks, Stanley!"

Stanley lay awake for a long time that night, kept up by all the alcohol and the tension of the day. When he heard a knock at the door, he opened without hesitation.

Mila slipped into his room. She took his hand silently, led him over to the bed, and fell back onto it. Stanley wondered what was more dangerous: the avalanche or the woman lying beneath him with her legs spread. He frowned, pushing the thought away, and settled heavily on top of her.

"Why did you save him?" she asked, after their sex ended in intense simultaneous orgasms and they lay there, smoking cigarettes.

"Did he tell you all the details?"

"He said that he owes you now. That's very bad. No one he feels obligated to, in any way, even the smallest thing, lives very long."

"Then so be it." Stanley put out his cigarette and poured himself a splash of whiskey. He rinsed his mouth with it and swallowed.

"There, now I believe you have Russian roots. You want to trust in fate?" Mila kissed Stanley's neck. "Try it. It won't go well for you. I asked him to leave you alone."

"And what did he say?"

"He smacked me. He knows how to hit you in the face without leaving any marks, with an open palm. Not that painful, but I hate it so much. I want to leave him."

Stanley took out a new cigarette and lit it.

"Is that possible? Will he let you?"

"If there's no threat to him. He sometimes likes to do things for those he loves. But that doesn't really apply to me! Do you know that his name's not really Gagarin?"

"What? But I saw a scan of his passport. Viktor Pavlovich Gagarin…"

"He changed his patronymic and his last name. He was born Viktor Kaganovich, in a modest Jewish family. His father was an engineer, and his mother was a doctor. He was a bright child, but nothing extraordinary. He wanted to go to college, to study physics, but there was a quota for how many Jews they would take per year. His father died, and someone fixed up all their documents for them. I don't know how much they paid him, but I do know he was one of the first to whom Viktor owed a debt. Back before computers were widespread, in the Soviet Union, when I was in seventh grade, Viktor came up with a data processing system for some kind of classified research. Then some other programs. He did that himself, his ideas. He's smart. Very smart. And I hate him! Come here, handsome."

Lagrange and Stanley left Oberlech in the morning. Everyone came out to see them off. Gagarin was the soul of courtesy, presenting them each with a bottle of some kind of unique liquor and walking them to the ski lift himself.

Yulia embraced Stanley, slipping a card with her number into his pocket as she let go. Polina and Mila gave him air kisses on both sides of his face. Even Shamil came out of the chalet and gave him a thumbs-up.

Stanley and Lagrange came down the mountain and found the Tesla waiting for them in good shape. Lagrange was excited about their new business prospects, saying that he'd never have expected this in his wildest dreams.

If Gagarin made Laville & Cie his main bank—which Pierre believed to be his intention—it would bring in even more Russian clients. They took the B197 and turned left at the Langen-Klosterle exit.

"At the moment, we're all in your debt, Stanley," said Lagrange. "Try not to ruin it."

"And how could I ruin it, Pierre?" asked Stanley, fiddling with the defrost button on the dash.

"There's something going on with you and the wife. If I've noticed, others will too. If you don't cut it out."

"There's nothing going on between us!" Stanley said, all the while remembering when he had bent to kiss Mila's breasts. "Where did you get that idea? When? How?"

"Of course, you'll deny it." Lagrange lit up a cigarette, but then immediately tossed it out the window. "I would do the same in your place. But it would be better to tell me the truth—we can discuss how to get you out of this without any lasting damage. To you or to the bank."

"Believe me: there's nothing between us!" said Stanley. "She's not even my type; I liked Yulia, look—she gave me her number. We're planning to meet up."

"It's too bad you don't trust me, McKnight. Too bad you're denying everything. Yulia crawled into bed with me after you didn't let her into your room. She's an insatiable nymphomaniac, totally nuts. Don't lie, Stan! You have to end it with her. You already saved his life; sleeping with his wife will be your death sentence!"

"You've got to be kidding me!" It seemed to Stanley that a shadow had fallen over them, despite the sunny day. "What is this, the Middle Ages?"

"It's too dangerous. Think about what I told you, McKnight, really think about it."

PART THREE: RUSSIAN DESK

CHAPTER 20

T HE RUSSIAN DESK HELD WEEKLY meetings at 8:00 AM on Monday mornings. Stanley had always been an early bird, so it wouldn't, in theory, have been painful for him to start his working week so early, even if he had spent the weekend at parties or patronizing some of Zurich's many watering holes. But it was one thing to simply sit down at his desk and accept a cup of coffee from Barbara, invite her to pour a cup for herself, and have a nice chat about the latest news in the world of finance. Then they would gradually move on to politics, international relations, and end with sports—Barbara was a serious soccer fan who adored Messi. She'd even gone to Barcelona one weekend to visit Camp Nou to see them play a home game. They'd get back to finance after their third cup. But it was quite another thing entirely to come in on Monday morning knowing that you were expected shortly in the meeting room, where Lagrange had assembled the entire team.

He had to spend the entire second half of his Fridays preparing for the meeting, and ask Barbara to be at work no later than 7:00 AM Monday to enter any significant edits and additions into the already prepared material.

Stanley himself showed up at about seven forty, and they managed to gulp down some coffee while he reviewed the materials. His contributions at these meetings were always detailed, precise, and well-founded. This had made a big impression on his colleagues from the very start. But when Lagrange asked him where he got his information from and how he prepared for these meetings, he asked Stanley to take it down a notch.

"This is not a weekly report, my dear Stanley," he said. "You report only to me, one-on-one. If you show off like this, your colleagues might start thinking that you're an American striver only interested in making an impression on the bosses. Our meetings are just a general get-together after the weekend, to bolster team spirit. If someone comes in acting like a super banker, king of investment and prince of derivatives, he might get a dagger in the back. Don't stress out. I'm joking. But, you know, keep it simple, Stanley. Our Russian bankers like to say that. Total stupidity, but there is a grain of truth in it."

Their meetings were held in the main room on the first floor. Actually, not quite a room, more of a small, gloomy hall that reminded Stanley of a medieval knight's castle.

The room had a low ceiling, the dim light of matte lamps, oak paneling on the walls, bronze figures, a long table, and enormous, high-backed leather chairs. The walls were hung with paintings by the Old Masters, each of which was illuminated by its own small lamp. One painting depicted one of Laville's paternal ancestors.

One table usually held a coffeepot, teapot, and croissants. There were notebooks and vases with pencils arranged around the main table. They were expected to leave their mobile phones with Lagrange's secretary, who came to the meeting along with her boss, but remained just outside the door on a low sofa with her laptop on her knees.

Stanley asked Lagrange once if the paintings on the walls were authentic, and his boss raised one eyebrow meaningfully.

"What do you think, Stan?"

"To be honest, I doubt they are. Bruegel the Elder, Rogier van der Weyden. This collection would be the envy of any museum."

"Well, well, I didn't know you were knowledgeable about art, my American friend. Bruegel! How about that! Everything in this bank is authentic. Laville's family has been investing in items of lasting value for a long time now. If you only knew what Jean-Michel has hanging in the guest bathroom of his country house, across the wall from the sink. If you only knew!"

"So what is it?"

"If you ever get an invitation, you can go wash your hands there and see for yourself. They keep their most valuable items in a safe in some other bank—nobody knows which one, except Jean-Michel himself, naturally. I've heard that it's either in New York or in Singapore."

It had, indeed, caused some tension with Stanley's colleagues initially when he had performed so well at their first meetings. But they'd gradually gotten used to him, seeming to make some allowances for his American ways.

Eight people total attended the meeting, including Lagrange and Stanley. There were two men named Muller—Gustav and Mario, as well as Frank Adler, Dino Bernasconi, Theo Schneider, and the only woman, Andrea Kovalevich, who spoke decent Russian.

There wasn't a single Russian working for the Russian desk. Lagrange didn't care for Russian specialists; he thought their education too superficial for the job, for one. But his main objection was that a Russian bank manager, regardless of his education, position, or knowledge would, even if subconsciously, kowtow to wealthy Russian clients.

"Russians are simply in awe of serious wealth. They immediately fall over for the rich or crawl over like dogs to lick their hands," Lagrange would say.

Both Mullers were blond, but Mario was the youngest member of Lagrange's team, and Gustav, the oldest; Mario was balding and rosy-cheeked, while Gustav sported a lush head of hair that Stanley suspected might have been aided by expensive hair implants and dye. He liked to peer critically at his colleagues through a lock of hair that had fallen over his eye.

Adler was low to the ground and bug-eyed, and when it was his turn to report on the week, he drew an enormous, monogrammed handkerchief out of his pocket and continuously wiped the perspiration from his prominent forehead as he talked.

Bernasconi, in contrast, was very tall, and held his Russian clients in even greater contempt than Lagrange did, but still managed sell their investment products aggressively, and had the best numbers.

Schneider joined Laville & Cie after Stanley, also adhered to the practice of the hard sell, and was the most envious, particularly of Stanley. When Lagrange joked about how Stanley was drinking buddies with a top client and how he'd even saved Gagarin's life during a descent down an untouched ski slope, Schneider's envy grew to previously unseen proportions.

Andrea had a narrow, cold face and disproportionately large, gray eyes. She always sat at an angle to the table, crossing and uncrossing her long legs.

She had once seen Stanley and Elise in a small bar, around Christmas time, and watched them for a long time, unaware that Stanley had already noticed her. She had been there with a tall black guy with the walk of a professional dancer. Her companion, Stanley saw from the corner of his eye, took advantage of her distraction and slipped a hand beneath her blouse to passionately stroke her flat chest. So as not to disappoint Andrea, Stanley leaned across the table and kissed the shocked Elise on the mouth. Andrea now watched Stanley from time to time at their meetings with greater interest.

Everyone spoke in turn, Lagrange directing them to go around the table clockwise, starting with Gustav Muller.

On this occasion, Stanley entered the room a little behind schedule, just as Lagrange was saying, "Let's get started!" and sat where Lagrange pointed, making him the last to speak.

The subject was the same as always—how much client money they had each brought in the previous week, which investment products they had sold, and what sales they were expecting in the coming week.

As the reports went on, Lagrange's expression grew increasingly displeased.

He made indecipherable notes as they each talked, broke off his pencil lead, and tossed the pencil down with such force that it rolled onto the floor.

"This won't do!" he finally said. "This. Will. Not. Do. Where has all your aggression gone? Where is your fire? You've got to keep your hands wrapped around your client's necks. That's what our clients need. Russians *admire* strength. They *like* to obey. Remember: I'm going to calculate the annual results this week and work out your bonuses. I'm afraid that there are going to be some sad members of this team walking around the office. So…ah! Stanley! We'll wait for Stanley to finish his croissant. Ready? The floor is yours!"

Stanley wiped his mouth.

"Please excuse me," he said, looking around the room. "I was hoping you'd forget about me. By the way, these croissants are fabulous! How do they get them so crisp?"

"McKnight, this is a bank, not *The Martha Stewart Show*," Lagrange said, tapping his new pencil on the table. "Please go on!"

"I've been lucky with my clients. I don't have that many, but they are quite active and quite aggressive—I just do my best to keep up with them. Mr. Peshkov is a major depositor, and constantly asks me to shift the strategy for the deposits and the development of investment products, which he wants our bank to handle. Currently," Stanley continued, pulling a sheet of paper out of a folder and sliding it over to Lagrange, "on my recommendation, Mr. Peshkov has given up his plan to transfer all his assets into bitcoins, but he has decided to create a portfolio of short-term bonds. This client's particular characteristic—and the psychological characteristics of our Russian clients is, in my opinion, the most important factor in their business decisions, even more than market conditions or any other market data—this client's peculiarity is his suspicious nature, bordering on mental illness."

"Do you have a background in psychology, Mr. Freud?" Lagrange interrupted. "I think not! Let's stick to the subject at hand. Please, we're not interested in wandering into off-topic discussions."

"I beg your pardon."

"Although," Lagrange interrupted him again, "I'm in complete agreement with you. I know Mr. Peshkov as well, and support your diagnosis."

Lagrange glanced down at the sheet of paper Stanley had passed him, and underlined several numbers in pencil.

"Okay, we're clear on Peshkov. Next!"

"I'm afraid I will have to resort to imagery and associations a bit distant from our everyday work," said Stanley.

Lagrange's employees relaxed and began to exchange smiles.

Some thought that Stanley was trying to relieve the tension in the room after Lagrange's promise to distress them with the size of their bonuses.

"Damn it, Mr. McKnight." Lagrange broke his pencil in half. "If you're talking about Mr. Grigoryan, I'll have to agree with you again. Gentlemen, Mr. McKnight is dealing with quite a guy here, not just a cunning agent of the FSB or some other special service, but also a blatant crook prepared to betray everyone he knows just to raise his referral fee. He wanted our bank to raise his commission to 40 percent. The bank management has decided to agree to his terms. You're displeased?"

"To be honest, I was hoping the bank would turn him down, and I wouldn't have to experience the dubious pleasure of his company anymore."

"He's very beneficial to the bank."

"I know. It's just a matter of morality and corporate ethics."

"We're making money here, Mr. McKnight."

"I was joking," said Stanley, and his colleagues all laughed in unison. "So, we come to Gagarin. Comrade Gagarin thinks that our bank offers successful investment portfolio management services; his assets have grown 30 percent with our assistance."

"And?" Lagrange was clearly interested.

"So he wants to increase the amount of his assets in the bank."

"Didn't he already do that?"

"Yes, sir, he has. He transferred an additional $500 million to us last week. But our compliance department has raised some questions. The transfer came from a third party. They don't know the company that transferred the money to Gagarin's account."

Lagrange wrote something down in his notebook.

"We'll work on that. So how much more does he want to deposit?"

"Just over 1.5 billion. Euros."

"Oho!" Schneider exclaimed.

"And what else does he want?" asked Lagrange.

"He wants us to set up a diversified, aggressive, high-risk, high-return investment portfolio."

"Discuss that with Bernard, he'll put a proposal together." Lagrange made some more notes, and looked up at his employees.

"I would tell you, gentlemen, to follow McKnight's example, but you already understand that," he said. "In closing, an administrative announcement: the bank management has decided to stop reimbursing corporate expenses on prostitutes and strippers."

"What!" Schneider burst out. "They can't do that! How else are we going to entertain our clients!"

"Cost-cutting," said Lagrange, raising his hands in the air. "Our department alone spent 75,000 francs on hookers using corporate cards. You're responsible for half of that, Schneider, and you brought in zero new client money!"

"How am I supposed to work now? You know how my Kazakhs love the girls."

"Pull yourself together, Schneider. Otherwise, Laville will deal with you personally. Take your lecherous Kazakh clients to the opera. The variety will do them good."

"Come on, boss. That's a bit too much!"

"Enough, Schneider, the matter is closed. Thank you, everyone! Stanley, you stay!"

Once he and Stanley were alone, Lagrange said, "I think we should make Gagarin a separate case. The rest of our colleagues, aside from management, don't need to know all the details. It's not even the size of his portfolio in comparison with the clients our colleagues manage. For that matter, it's not even the unhealthy attention and envy it will draw—*look, he just got here yesterday, and he's already managing the money of a client like that.* The issue is, the sources of Gagarin's funds are extremely dubious. Not to us—we understand each other, and we couldn't care less about whether

155

these sources are questionable or not, but who knows what bright idea those Mullers or our dear Andrea might come up with? Rumors will start. They might start circulating anyway. Agreed?"

"I'm with you," said Stanley.

"And another thing: find a reliable IT guy and ask him how to keep as little information as possible on your computer about Gagarin."

"What do you mean?"

"We need to have only front data on there. Clean, without any references or links to anything that could be followed up later."

"I'm sorry, Pierre. Are you suggesting I keep what accountants call double books?" Stanley felt an unpleasant chill in his chest, and his mouth went dry.

"No, no, of course not, but we need to hide any questionable operations, find some way to secure—"

"That's a crime!"

"No, we don't need any crimes. None. No crimes and no official misconduct. But we need to somehow split Gagarin's business into two, or even better, three lines. Just think about it. If you decide not to, I won't push it, but my advice is to take that route. Okay"—Lagrange slapped the table—"now let's go visit Monsieur Poiccard. I'll try to talk some sense into him!"

The head of their compliance department, Michel Poiccard, was an enormous man with a large nose and a magnificent head of salt-and-pepper hair reaching his shoulders. He looked more like a rock star than a bank employee, but Poiccard could take more liberties than the rest of the staff.

He never met with clients; moreover, he and his staff usually came in the back entrance, from a quiet side street and through the garden.

Michel occupied a tiny office, but his desktop was covered with several different monitors, his thick fingers jumping from one keyboard to another. He was—not without reason!—considered one of the bank's most meticulous and perceptive analysts, capable of finding the criminal element in even the most outwardly aboveboard and trustworthy operations. His self-regard was correspondingly high: Poiccard saw himself as the most important employee in the whole bank, or at least the most indispensable.

Lagrange burst into his office; just a moment before, he had seemed calm and relaxed. Now, all of a sudden, he was acting out an extreme degree of irritation, he was flushed red, and he'd even, shockingly, loosened the knot of his tie.

"What happened? Did the Russians invade somewhere else? Have they taken my homeland of Normandy? Are they getting drunk on Calvados as we speak?"

"Pierre!" said Poiccard in greeting, looking over the rims of the glasses perched on the edge of his nose, but regarding Stanley, not Lagrange, with great interest.

"This is no time for jokes, Michel!" Lagrange plopped down into the chair in front of Poiccard's desk, banged his knee on the corner of the desk, and let out a quite natural-sounding groan. "Not time for jokes, damn it!"

"Yes? Problems? Can I help?" Poiccard took the glasses of his nose and settled back in his chair. "Mr. McKnight! Very nice to see you. We usually only talk over email. And now here you are in the holy of holies of banking integrity and purity."

"Michel," Lagrange interrupted, "you're going to ruin us! You'll leave us with only poor, honest clients, weak impotent men who barely have enough money for the cheapest Ferrari."

"You can stop right there!" Poiccard put his glasses back on and grabbed a mouse, moving it over one of his monitors. "I can guess why you came, or rather, rushed over. It's that Russian, who shares the name of the first cosmonaut, Gagarin. Or wait…it's not a coincidence? Could it be? He's the son of the first cosmonaut! And that's why he can do whatever he wants. Get hundreds of millions of dollars transferred to his account from a company that probably doesn't even exist. Well, of course, he is the son of the first cosmonaut! Or maybe the grandson? Well in that case…"

"Enough, Michel! Enough! Gagarin isn't the son, or the grandson, of a cosmonaut. He's a very, very wealthy businessman. With connections to the very Russian politicians that are about to invade your Normandy. Talking seriously—the barriers you put between us and his money have already cost the bank millions and will cost even more going forward." Lagrange crossed his legs, banging his knee again as he did. "If you don't loosen your grip, I'll have to complain to Laville about you. He's not in the best mood at the very end of the financial year, believe me."

"I'm sure." Poiccard nodded. "But I don't have any special grip here. I'm prepared to approve the transfer on two conditions. First—I get the documents for that company. Second—the transfer comes another way. It would be better for it to come from the client's own funds instead of some third party! I'm not telling you anything you don't know, Pierre. And, yes, I know Laville will be upset if I don't approve that transfer, but he'll be even more upset—enraged, even—if he hears that we missed something this big at the end of the financial year. Would you agree, McKnight?"

"But why didn't you say anything to me about this?" asked Stanley. "I would have resolved these issues with my client instead of complaining to my manager about you. By the way, I suggested something similar, but you said that you wouldn't approve the transfer in any event. That it was a matter of principle for you."

"Well, now I have a different one. It's immoral not to change your opinions, as Talleyrand said."

"He actually said: it's immoral never to change your convictions," said Stanley, his irritation reaching a boiling point.

"Ah yes, I think you're right," said Poiccard, "but it's the same thing, isn't it?"

"No, I don't think so," said Stanley sharply, still standing. "I will discuss this with my client and inform you of our decision. Thank you!"

He flung open the door to Poiccard's office, walked down the hallway between the large rooms occupied by the staff of this department, and began to climb the stairs. Lagrange caught up with him one floor up.

"You got him, Stan," Lagrange said breathlessly. "He nearly shat himself! He asked me where you'd come from. He thinks Americans are stupid and limited, and here you are, quoting Talleyrand at him, correcting him. But you've made yourself a bad enemy. I'm technically his manager, but he could go directly to Laville."

"He can go to hell!" said Stanley. "I don't give a shit!"

Gagarin was most displeased at having to do the transfer again, but then relaxed a bit.

He joked that Laville & Cie were clearly a solid bank if they were so attentive to the sources of money, which meant the money itself would be completely secure there.

Gagarin also said that he and all his friends, especially his friend's daughter Yulia, were hoping that Stanley could join them on vacation again. He asked if Stanley would come if he were invited, after all, he, Gagarin, would always know that he'd have a brave companion on hand in a crisis, who would risk his own life to save him.

"You'll save me, won't you, Stanley?"

"Of course, Viktor!"

"Lovely to hear it! By the way, Mila says hi! She misses you too."

"Thank you!"

"Shall I tell her you say hello?"

"If it's no trouble."

"Of course not, Stan! No trouble!"

"Then please pass on my kind regards to your wife."

"So formal, Stanley! You're not saying a toast at a ceremony. How many times do I have to tell you that you're among friends with us?"

Close to the beginning of spring, Gagarin transferred all the new funds he had promised.

CHAPTER 21

O N THE DAY THE NOTIFICATION of the transfer arrived, showing that Gagarin had deposited an additional four billion euros, Stanley accepted a lunch invitation from Bernasconi. They decided to go to Cantinetta Antinori. Andrea and Schneider joined them.

They chose a table on the outdoor terrace to take advantage of the warm weather. Ever since Stanley found out about Gagarin's transfer that morning, he'd been racked with a fierce hunger. He ordered carpaccio, soup with *fregola* and mussels, and baked halibut served with salmoriglio sauce.

"And we'll all have risotto with truffles," said Andrea.

"Then I'll have the risotto as well. Give me a half portion, please," Stanley said to the waiter.

"Wow, have you been starving yourself, Mr. McKnight?" Schneider asked, lighting up a cigarette and gesturing to the waiter for an ashtray.

"It's past time for us to drop the 'mister,'" said Stanley.

"Works for me! Rumor has it you've gotten pretty informal with your biggest client as well. I also heard you nearly saved his life?"

"I wonder who's starting those rumors?" said Stanley, and lit his own cigarette. Bernasconi poured him a glass of white wine.

"That's what makes a rumor, a rumor, Stanley, the fact that you don't know who started it. If you discover the source, the rumor dies."

"Sometimes, together with the source," said Stanley.

"You're right out of the Wild West, aren't you?" chuckled Andrea. "The littlest thing and you reach for your revolver."

"Poiccard hinted at it," admitted Schneider. "He didn't go into details, but he said it was true."

"As for saving the client..." Stanley took a sip of the wine. "Ah, this is excellent! Sicilian?"

"Tuscan," answered Bernasconi.

"It's the duty of every banker to save his clients. Even at the cost of his own life. And our relationship grew more informal after I told him about my Russian heritage. My great-grandfather was Russian. You seem not to care for the Russians," Stanley said, looking at Bernasconi.

"Heaven forbid! I love everyone." Bernasconi waved away the streams of tobacco smoke. "I don't care much for the nouveau riche, however, regardless of nationality or race. I have a deep personal preference for old money. For the carved banisters of Europe. But the nouveau riche keep a roof over our heads. You can't make much from old money."

"Some are doing better than others in our bank," said Schneider. "They'll announce the bonuses tomorrow. Then we'll see what's what."

"But they won't mean anything," said Stanley. "Our numbers, I mean the bank's numbers, are really good. You'd never know there was a banking crisis going on."

"Exactly," said Andrea. "We're over here eating truffles. What crisis? To be sure, the European Clients department is not looking forward to seeing what their bonuses are. They haven't been doing so well."

"Yes," said Bernasconi with a nod, "we're pulling everyone."

"To be precise"—Stanley smiled—"it's Russia pulling everyone."

"That's fucking everyone," said Schneider, and then apologized to Andrea.

During lunch, Stanley kept getting the feeling that someone was watching him. He tried to figure out which of the other diners on the terrace was looking at him. Or rather, observing him.

He thought at first that it might be Avi wanting to tell him something important but waiting for the right moment. But then he realized that Avi would be unlikely to come to Cantinetta Antinori for that.

It turned out to be a blond man sitting one table over.

The first time their gazes met, Stanley experienced a certain anxiety. He thought he'd seen this man before. *But where? Where?* thought Stanley. *Maybe in Lech? In that restaurant up the mountain? If so, he's just a skier who lives in Zurich.*

He looked over at the blond again. The man ordered dessert and watched the waiter fill his shot glass with liqueur. *No, he doesn't look like a resident of Zurich. But what do I really know about Zurich, anyway?*

When they'd paid and were walking down Bahnhofstrasse back to the office, Stanley noticed that the man from the restaurant was walking behind them. Stanley looked back a couple times, and Andrea said, "Is someone following you, Stanley? You keep looking behind you."

"Ha, of course not! I just thought I saw someone I know from London."

He still looked around again, but this time, the blond man was nowhere to be seen.

Back in the office, Stanley went out onto the balcony for a cigarette. He glanced down, almost hoping to see the man standing beneath a tree, watching the bank.

Nothing of the sort was going on, naturally. *You're just paranoid!* Stanley told himself, and put out the cigarette he'd just lit.

Lagrange summoned him in the late afternoon. He'd found out about the transfer and kicked up a fuss: Why hadn't Stanley told him right away? Why did he have to wait the entire working day to find out? Stanley protested weakly, all the while wondering whether to tell Lagrange about the blond man from lunch.

Lagrange finally calmed down and forgot his irritation, and got out a bottle of Zvenigorod. He filled two glasses, and told Stanley to open a letter on the desk containing the amount of his bonus.

Stanley had barely touched it when Lagrange began telling him its contents.

It turned out that Stanley had the new title of executive director, and his annual bonus was two million francs.

"Are you happy?" asked Lagrange.

"Do you even need to ask?"

"Just don't start crying out of gratitude, my friend. Everyone is very pleased with you. You are the best acquisition we've made in many years. And your bonus is at least double everyone else's. And that's just the start. I think your bonus will be much bigger next year."

"Thank you, Pierre."

"Don't thank me just yet. You'll only get 50,000 in Zurich. In taxable income. The rest will go to your account at a branch of our bank in the Bahamas. Bonuses like yours, for the select few, get sent there, where they're not taxed."

"I'm one of the select few?"

"What do you think?" Lagrange smiled widely. "Welcome to the club!"

CHAPTER 22

I T WAS AS IF SOMEONE had flipped a switch in the opposite direction, and everything changed in an instant. Even the colors of the world around him looked different.

If it hadn't been for the flip of that switch, he would be passing Hardturmstrasse and turning onto the A1H in his Tesla, the car that he had loved so much so recently. Instead, Stanley moved into the left lane, cutting off a gray Mercedes, heading toward Basel. And he did that in a black Porsche 911 S Turbo convertible.

It all started after lunch on Thursday. McKnight stepped out of his office to make coffee and noticed the screensaver on Barbara's computer: a winding mountain road, and on it, a car he recognized by its familiar soft contours and large headlights. He asked her what model Porsche that was.

Barbara chuckled, thinking that her boss was just joking around. But Stanley repeated the question. Barbara apologized for not knowing exactly—all she knew was that it was a Porsche, the legendary car of her dreams that she knew would never come true.

Stanley went back into his office without listening to the rest of Barbara's revelations about her automotive dreams. He hadn't been joking; sipping his coffee, he sat down and googled "Porsche, buy." He remembered how long he had waited for his Tesla, and added, "In Zurich." And then, "Today."

Stanley clicked on the company website and read: *Efficiency is the ratio of results to expenditures. High efficiency keeps expenditure low while maximizing results. This principle applies to any Porsche 911 when taking into account that Porsche spared no expense in the development of this magnificent automobile.*

"A bit banal, but it makes its point," Stanley muttered to himself.

Barbara was a bit surprised to see Stanley leaving his office soon thereafter in his jacket, with his tie already loosened, his soft leather briefcase tucked loosely under his arm.

"I'll be out for the rest of the day," he said as he walked away.

"Okay, boss," said Barbara. "But you have a meeting at three forty-five with…"

Stanley didn't hear the rest—who? Didn't matter! As he stepped into the elevator, he called out: "Cancel it."

———————— •••• ————————

The salesman at the Porsche dealership in Dufourstrasse saw Stanley approaching the glass doors of the entrance, and realized immediately that his day was about to improve dramatically.

Everything about Stanley radiated determination. The salesman's assistant snorted, asking his boss if he'd seen what car that guy was driving. A Tesla!

"So he has money," said the salesman, and got his best smile ready.

The salesman had some trouble talking his customer out of buying a car with a manual transmission.

The client insisted, until the salesman introduced two convincing points: he would have to wait at least a week, if not longer, for a totally manual car, and he would really have to spend some time driving a new manual car on a racetrack, until driver and car fully adjust to each other.

Stanley gave in. Especially since the salesman explained that the Porsche Doppelkupplung transmission came standard with the 911 Turbo S.

"You're kidding!" Stanley stood next to one of the cars, elevated slightly on a podium. It looked so small, or at least smaller than a Tesla. He had never heard of that transmission in his life, and had no idea what it could do.

"Really?" said Stanley, doing his best to look like a connoisseur.

"That's right!" The salesman was fully engaged in the process of hooking his wealthy customer. "The PDK transmission, with manual and automatic modes, is essentially composed of two gearboxes built into one frame, seven gears, and two clutches. It shifts gears in a matter of milliseconds. With only the slightest effort. And, by the way, compared to a manual, the PDK gives you higher acceleration rates with lower fuel consumption. There are special paddles on the steering wheel for when you want to switch to manual. They work on the right or left, so you can switch gears with either hand. If you're operating the car in automatic, there's a mode switch with four positions: Normal, Sport, Sport Plus, and Individual. With the last mode, you can customize your active suspension, Auto Start-Stop function, and sports exhaust system. And in the center of the switch, you'll find the Sport Response button. When you press it, for twenty seconds, the car will have maximum acceleration capabilities. To be honest, the only time you'll need it is to overtake another Porsche. You'll already be faster than other cars without any special effects."

"I see. I see," Stanley replied, loosening his tie. "I'll take it."

"I'm sorry?"

"'I'll take it.' I'll take a Porsche! Wrap it up! That one! I want it!"

The salesman studied Stanley's face.

"Are you Russian?"

"Not exactly. I'm an American, with a little bit of Russian blood," Stanley said, showing the slim percentage in the slim gap between thumb and pointer finger. "I want to drive this car out of your showroom today, this car right here, and I'd like you to take the one I arrived in back to the Tesla dealership."

"But Herr…"

"McKnight."

"But Herr McKnight, we can offer you a number of different options, some amazing additions. For example, this car has a Bose sound system, but if you wait a couple days, we'll put in a Burmester, which has some advantages in—"

"I want to drive out of here today. Right now. In this car. I'm quite satisfied with Bose. Is that going to cause a problem?"

"Not at all, Herr McKnight. Please, have a seat. Coffee? Tea? It will take just a couple minutes to draw up the documents. We do the registration for you, and we'll have your license within the hour. Insurance—"

"I understand," said Stanley, relaxing into his chair, and accepting a cup of coffee from a long-legged girl in a tight gray dress. She had a scarf with the Porsche logo wrapped around her neck, the long tip of which was tucked into the collar of her dress. She smelled like the perfume that Mila wore, a jasmine and bergamot scent with a hint of cinnamon.

To his surprise, Stanley felt a pleasant warmth spreading through his groin. He realized that if he got hard now, it would be immediately obvious to all the Porsche staff.

"I can wait for a little while. But not too long," said Stanley.

"We're already working on it, Herr McKnight!"

165

On the way to the dealership, Stanley had felt as if some kind of beast were controlling his actions. Capable of any kind of insanity. Ready to bare its fangs, to attack. Finger on the trigger.

Driving the new Porsche, Stanley was in the same kind of mood. A stray scent, a look of invitation in a woman's eye, the allure of her walk, and his erection immediately returned. He was full of desire. It helped him operate his new car.

At first it was unusual, how low it sat on the road, the stiffness of the driver's seat in comparison with the Tesla, and the need to lean forward to make out the traffic lights. But Stanley adapted quickly.

He suddenly—perhaps with the aid of that same switch—ceased to hear the inner voice that asked: What will people think? Am I disturbing anyone, causing trouble? He just kept his eyes on the road in front of him, and pulled smoothly ahead of the other cars.

But still, switch or no, he was driving in a city. A ticket would be unfortunate, not so much because of the fine, but because his name would go on the list of traffic law violators, which would probably displease Laville, who received weekly reports on events related to his bank and his employees.

Lagrange had warned Stanley that the bank's security service was omniscient. They wouldn't interfere in your private life, but they knew where you went, what you bought, how much you spent, what wine you liked, what condoms you bought, and if you visited prostitutes.

"But since you don't go to whores, your condoms won't be in the report," said Lagrange with a laugh. "You're practically a monk here. Laville loves that kind of employee. He's got some Calvinist preachers in his family tree. All in black. Back in those days, condoms were made out of pig bladders, you know."

Stanley entered the underground parking garage. His spot was located against the far wall. To his left was his neighbor, a lean, fair-skinned frau.

Her husband, a lawyer, was always away on business trips.

She always gave Stanley a friendly smile, and they exchanged pleasantries, but there was nevertheless a touch of condescension in her gaze.

It was obvious that she was sick to death of all the good, dependable men in business suits surrounding her.

She was taking a grocery bag out of her car, and already carrying another, when Stanley pulled up. She was bent over, her breasts nearly spilling out of her partially fastened blouse.

She stared openly as Stanley climbed out of the Porsche.

His jacket lay on the passenger seat. His shirt sleeves were rolled up, his eyes concealed behind dark sunglasses, and his usually neat hair was disheveled, even though he'd been riding with the top up.

Stanley had had to rev the engine a bit as he turned in to alert her of his presence; the warmed-up tires moved almost soundlessly over the road, and at low speeds, the engine was almost as quiet as the Tesla's.

"Good evening," said Stanley. "Can I give you a hand?"

"I wouldn't say no, Mr. McKnight," she said, stepping back from the trunk and fixing her hair. When she raised her arm, Stanley caught the scent of her perfume. That was enough.

He tried to remember her name, or her last name. Hasselbrink? Husselbrink? Something like that. Or maybe simpler? Could it really be Schmidt?

"I didn't recognize you," his neighbor said. "Something's different."

"Something good?"

"Unexpected." Her nostrils trembled slightly as she drew in breath. "You don't look like you usually do. I'd never have thought…"

"Never have thought—what?"

They were already in the elevator. In the bright overhead light, he could see the fine lines at the corners of her eyes and clumps of mascara on her eyelashes. The small space was filled with the scent of her perfume, tempting Stanley.

How old was she? She looked to be about thirty-five, but she was probably pushing forty. *She's a bit older, no big deal*, said Stanley's inner voice. He spoke sternly to himself—*No matter how turned on you are, nothing's going to come of it. You're going to help her carry her bags to the door of her apartment and say goodbye.*

But it was not to be. The neighbor said that whenever she saw Stanley in his conservative business attire, she'd always been surprised at the narrow frame this handsome, powerful man had squeezed himself into. They had reached her apartment. She said that her husband was the same way; he had become a dried-up husk of his former self. He was on one of his trips, her husband. In Norway. Or Denmark. It didn't really matter.

She opened the door, asked Stanley to bring the bags into the kitchen, and followed him inside.

McKnight set the bags down on the wide countertop next to the sink.

She offered him something to drink. Wine? She had a fabulous Chablis. Her favorite. Without waiting for an answer she passed by him, their hips almost touching, to the wall cupboard, taking down two glasses.

Stanley felt as if a thick veil was falling over him. This Frau Schmidt—or was it Hasselbrink?—stood in front of him, holding the glasses, her arms spread, offering herself openly to him. He put his hands on her hips. Her eyes were so close to his that he saw her pupils contract. McKnight's hand began to travel upward, her skirt rising with it. Stanley kissed her dry lips, feeling them grow instantly moist and warm.

"I need to take a shower," she said, gasping from the long kiss.

"No," said Stanley pulling down her panties, and lifting her onto the kitchen table. "No need for a shower." He tugged his pants down, bent his knees slightly, and entered her easily.

She was still holding her hands out to either side. Her breathing grew rapid.

"To hell with the shower!" she said in a surprisingly low voice in Stanley's ear. "Just don't stop!"

She dropped the glass in her left hand, wrapped her legs around Stanley's waist, and drew him down toward her, dropping the second glass.

"Don't stop!"

Luckily, he hadn't been planning to.

CHAPTER 23

S TANLEY SAW THE SPOILER SLIDE out automatically in his rearview mirror.

So he was already going faster than eighty miles an hour.

The road moved smoothly to the right, skirting Bern. The glass of the city's windows sparkled far below.

Stanley reached for a pack of Parliament on the passenger seat, starting to turn the wheel to follow the turn of the road, and saw on the display that his rear wheels were also deviating from the axis.

He pressed down on the gas, and the spoiler moved a little more. Stanley flipped the lid of his lighter open, noticed he was almost in the oncoming lane, flicked the wheel of the lighter, and touched the flame to the end of his cigarette. He saw a bus coming toward him. Stanley calmly adjusted his wheel slightly and slipped back into his lane. The bus flew past, the driver leaning on the horn in panic. Stanley raised his hand and gave him the finger. The poor guy probably didn't even see it; the bus had already transformed into a dot far behind him.

Down the E27, Stanley dove under an overpass, hugged the curve of the road, and flew onto the A9, where he saw Lake Geneva spreading out before him.

Two hours on the road felt like five minutes to Stanley. He saw the exit sign on Rue Chailly, poked at the display, and heard a voice advising him to slow down and prepare for a right turn. He accelerated and turned off the GPS. He turned, the lake still visible, and began his descent, turned left onto Rue du Lac, and found himself in Clarens.

Stanley saw a sign for the Cave du Chateau de Glerolles winery and headed there. He parked in the lot and got out—he liked the idea of picking up a couple bottles of wine. A little while later, he was driving through Clarens again.

In a few minutes, Stanley was in Montreux, where he switched the GPS back on. The voice suggested he turn off Avenue Casino and onto Rue de Bon Port.

The road took Stanley out of Montreux, toward Durand's home high on a hill overlooking the lake. Behind it, distant mountains were half visible in the twilight, their peaks covered in snow. He took a deep breath.

The GPS announced that he had reached his destination. His car came to a stop, its shiny black hood kissing the gate.

The gate slid to the side, and Stanley drove up to the house, where Durand stood waiting on the steps. He held an unlit cigar in the corner of his mouth.

"Now that's what I'm talking about!" exclaimed Durand, coming down to meet him. He bent down and slapped his palm lightly against the Porsche's spoiler. "What about protecting the environment? Where's your Tesla?"

"Fuck the environment!"

"You've changed, Stanley old pal!" he held out his hand, and they shook.

"For the better or worse?" asked Stanley.

"The important thing is change itself," said Durand. "There are two kinds of people—those who change and those who remain the same. Those who change are the masters, and those who can't are the slaves. Where did you buy all that?" he asked, pointing to the bag with the wine bottles.

"In Clarens. We'll have to give them a try."

"Well, let's risk it. Although the only interesting thing about Clarens is that a Russian writer is buried there—I can't remember his name. He wrote a novel about some old goat who lusted after his wife's daughter. Have you read it?"

"I don't think so. It doesn't ring a bell. So? Did the old man get what he wanted?"

"I forgot. I read it a long time ago. Probably. I think I have it in the library. I'll give it to you. I hardly read anything these days. I've changed, you see. Come on, follow me. I'll show you the house. Ah, I remember! Nabokov is his name. Or Nabokoff. Doesn't matter. He wrote in English. Can you believe that? A Russian writing in English, and now here you are, a Russian speaking English, dealing with Russian money."

"Robert, how many times do I have to tell you—I'm not Russian. It's my great-grandfather who was Russian. Speaking a little Russian doesn't make me Russian."

"Get over it, Stanley! Why so defensive? What matters is that you're a good guy and a skilled professional. And here's Tina," Durand said, nodding toward a pretty girl headed their way with an Asian tilt to her eyes and smooth, dark hair. "She runs the place."

Tina smiled and bent at the knees, pretending to curtsey.

"A very ceremonious person, I have to tell you, Stanley," said Durand.

They walked through a hallway and back out of the house onto an enormous panoramic balcony.

The lake glittered far below them. A tourist bus trundled across the bridge over the railway, and a train with bright-red cars moved beneath it.

Not a sound reached Stanley and Durand. A small bird with a red breast sat in the laurel bush next to them.

"Is that real?" asked Stanley, pointing to the bird.

Durand raised his eyebrows in bewilderment.

"When I was in Moscow, Gagarin had artificial birds singing in his garden."

Durand laughed so hard he began to cough. "Everything our dear Russian friend has is fake—that's just between us, mind you. The only real thing about him is his money. He has quite a lot of that. You can feel it, count it all up. And you can do it in such a way that part of it becomes ours. He won't even notice."

"You're unusually candid today," said Stanley, lighting a cigarette.

"First, you buy all this crap Swiss wine, and now you're smoking this garbage." Durand practically snatched the cigarette out of Stanley's mouth. "Tina's going to bring us a drink and some cigars right away."

Durand drew back from the balustrade, invited Stanley to sit on a wicker chair at a low table, and sat down himself. Tina appeared with a tray and set the table with a bottle of wine, glasses, a plate of tartlets, a box of cigars, and an ashtray.

"This is the Sancerre Cuvée La Grange Dîmière 2010," Durand said, filling their glasses. "You're not supposed to smoke cigars with it. A connoisseur would be opposed. But I enjoy the combination. To your health! Try this one, with the pâté. Tina makes her own pâté; she doesn't trust my chef to get it right."

"You have your own chef?"

"Why the surprise, Stanley? Not just a chef. I also have a gardener and a chauffeur. I need one sometimes, especially when I go into town. It makes an impression—you're sitting in a low-class tavern with some easy local girl on your knees, you get drunk, and when you stumble out with your arm around the girl, there's your chauffeur waiting for you, who takes off his hat as he opens the door of your Rolls-Royce."

"And you leave the girl standing on the sidewalk?"

"Sometimes I take them with me. But Tina doesn't like that, the stupid woman gets a little jealous. She's the only permanent resident here. My people only come here when I do. This house cost me 4.5 million francs way back in 2000. Now its price, along with that bird in the laurel bush who has already flown away, is nearly four times higher. Property is a responsibility."

Durand drained his glass. After enjoying the aroma of the wine, Stanley took a few sips. The wine was moderately tart, with surprising fruity notes. Its taste reminded him of Mila. Just then Stanley remembered the lawyer's wife. Yes, something was, indeed, going on with him. How could he have done such a thing? It would have seemed completely impossible mere days ago.

Durand opened a box of cigars and selected one. A guillotine was on the table by the ashtray, but he bit off the end instead, and spat it onto the balcony floor. Stanley realized that Durand must have had quite a time the night before.

"And your family?"

"They live in a different house. In France. We're citizens of the world, right?" Durand poured himself more wine, and drained his glass again.

"You, for example," Durand said, gesturing toward Stanley with his glass, "are an American living in Switzerland and working with Russians. People like us change the world. By the way, congratulations on your promotion."

"Thank you."

"Don't be modest, Stanley. Modesty isn't flattering. I like you. You're capable of change. When people like you buy a Porsche, it seems natural. Changeable people have the right."

Durand poured wine into his glass. Something beeped in the pocket of his loose-fitting pants. He took a small remote out.

"For the gate," he explained. "When I'm here, I like to run everything myself. It's Biryuza. We'll wait for him here."

Tina brought in another bottle and a third glass. She wanted to bring over a third chair, but Durand waved her off and asked her to go greet the new guest.

"Let Biryuza do it himself," he said quietly to Stanley, drinking the rest of his wine.

Biryuza, accompanied by Tina, appeared on the balcony. He was wearing loafers, wrinkled pants, a loud, untucked shirt, and a good haircut. Despite the apparent carelessness of his attire, it was clear that his entire look had been carefully designed. Stanley noticed something he hadn't before—the expensive watch that Biryuza wore on the wrist of his right hand.

"I'm not trying to imitate the Russian president," said Biryuza, noticing Stanley's glance. "I really am a lefty."

"I actually didn't know that the president wore his watch on his right hand," said Stanley, exchanging a handshake with Biryuza.

"There's a lot you don't know about him," said Biryuza, shaking Durand's hand. "Very few know much about him, in fact."

Biryuza looked around and walked over to the chair intended for him, getting ready to pull it over. A satisfied Durand jumped up, and they carried the chair over to the table together.

"People want to know what our president likes to eat for breakfast and for dinner, what books he's reading, what movies he's watching." Biryuza sat, nodding to thank Durand for the proffered glass of wine. "I don't care about any of that. For me"—he paused—"for us, all that matters is how to do business under him. Let him sit in his Kremlin another hundred years if he wants."

"I'm sorry, but what about the change in leadership?" asked Stanley.

"Oh, come on!" laughed Biryuza.

"Don't disappoint me, Stanley!" put in Durand.

"But for state institutions to work, you have to…"

"You're thinking like a true American," said Biryuza. "That's strange, and harmful, to us Russians, real Russians. And you're repeating yourself, anyway—I think you were saying something like that in Italy."

"Well, what would be useful to you, then?" asked Stanley, washing down a bite of tartlet with pâté with a sip of wine.

The pâté was excellent. In Stanley's experience, women capable of culinary delights were capable of many other kinds as well. There were exceptions to this rule, of course, but as soon as Stanley laid eyes on Tina, he was sure that there was a little devil concealed beneath the demure exterior. She definitely kept Durand on a tight leash. When she approached the table, his hand shook involuntarily—he wanted to stroke her hip—but Tina stopped him with a slight narrowing of her exquisite eyes.

"I'll ask you a different way," said Stanley, when he saw that Biryuza was having difficulty providing an answer. "What's not harmful for Russians like you and Viktor? So you don't have to answer for everyone."

"We need to be left alone," answered Biryuza readily. "We're beneficial to the country. We're the support structure. Everything would fall apart without us."

Stanley looked over at Durand, who smiled beatifically after several glasses of wine.

"Who's bothering you?" asked Stanley. "You seem to be doing just fine. You're keeping your money in the bank where I have the honor to work. You have very healthy assets. You've got property all over Europe—and probably not Europe alone."

"Sanctions!" Durand slapped his hand on the table with such force that the bottle jumped up. "The Russian authorities are to blame for the introduction of these sanctions, but they won't accept the blame, so businessmen like Gagarin have to bear the costs. Right, Anton?"

"Precisely. We're the first on the list of those the state will come after. Our businesses will be under threat. They'll ask us to hand over a third, then a half, then two-thirds of our business to some newcomers. Practically all of whom are from the security forces or are the children or relatives of people working in them." Anton opened a cigarette case and pulled out a hand-rolled cigarette.

"This isn't pot," he said to Durand, who was watching the process with great attention. "I roll my own cigarettes. It's a bit healthier than all the rest."

"In addition," continued Biryuza, inhaling and letting out a cloud of thick gray smoke. "In addition, the number of Western investors was decreasing dramatically even before sanctions. Nobody wants to bring money to us. Even with the most beneficial offers. And past investors are now working on one thing only—how to get their money out of Russia as fast as possible with the minimum of losses. Only the international monsters are left— Coca-Cola, McDonald's, et cetera. We had a promising business in Siberia. Geological exploration. Exploratory drilling. Oil and gas. Our Western partner was a leader in the field, with the most cutting-edge technology, and had worked with us for many years."

"I didn't know that Gagarin was involved in oil and gas," said Stanley, and glanced over at Durand, who was examining the smoking end of his cigar with an innocent expression on his face.

"It's our friends who are involved in oil and gas, and they ask Viktor for help distributing assets, and ensuring that they are completely secure. And these friends invited him to participate—"

"So what about the partner?" Durand interrupted.

"What partner? Oh, yes, so they suddenly announce that they won't be extending their contract for another five years. How do you like that? Six months before they were supposed to sign a new contract, they decide to drop everything and leave Russia. We asked them—what's going on? And they said—we can leave you all the equipment, at a depreciated cost, but as for the personnel—Russian engineers, mind you!—we're taking them with us, together with their families. We offered them work in the US, in South America, Australia, who knows where else, and they said yes. They said yes, dammit. And what are we going to do with their equipment without personnel to run it?"

"You should have asked them that," said Durand.

"Of course, Robert, no one else thought of that." Biryuza crushed his cigarette out in the ashtray. "We asked. They offered to train new staff, at our expense, naturally. The training would take several years. And all that time their equipment will be standing unused, gradually sinking into the Siberian swamps."

"With real Russian bears running around nearby!" Durand rose and made a gesture of invitation. "I can't offer you bear meat, but I do have something for you to try. Follow me, please. Let us have some dinner!"

Stanley and Biryuza rose and followed him into the house.

"And what does Gagarin think about it?" McKnight asked Biryuza.

"He knew that something had to be done. And made a decision."

Stanley wouldn't find out what decision Viktor Gagarin had made until later. That evening, Durand interrupted their conversation, and, grabbing both of them by the elbow, jokingly tapped both of them behind the knee, leading them through the hallway to the dining room. Both Stanley and Biryuza took up the game, pretending to protest, Stanley arguing that the officer should read him his rights first, and Biryuza repeating, in a high, nasal voice in Russian, "Why did you pick me up, boss?"

Despite the jokes, Stanley understood that his visit here was no social call, that a very serious conversation was coming and that a lot would depend on what decision Viktor Gagarin had made. And even more depended on the extent to which Stanley and his bank could implement Gagarin's decision.

Tina met them in the dining rom. She offered each of them a shot glass of vodka from a silver tray covered in crushed ice and plates of warm crepes topped with heaping mounds of large beluga caviar from another tray covered in parchment paper. This was the same appetizer they'd had when he met Durand in the restaurant in Moscow, Stanley recalled. McKnight winked at the lawyer, who nodded in answer.

"Ah!" exclaimed Biryuza. "That's what I like. Simple, no frills. That's the Russian way!"

"I don't know. I'd say this is pretty fancy," said Durand with mock offense, and added with a smile, "One appetizer, one soup, one main dish. That's my system."

"I've heard something similar somewhere. One people, one country." Biryuza drank his vodka and took a bite of crepe.

"Don't joke like that!" Durand laughed, shaking his finger at Biryuza. "But in all seriousness, that's how my chef cooks. For me, the main thing is a variety of beverages."

Stanley slowly poured the vodka down his throat, waited a beat, and took a crepe from the tray. The caviar burst in his mouth. It was fabulous.

The oak-paneled walls of the dining room were hung with portraits of men in frock coats and lace collars, and ladies with fans and elaborate hairstyles.

The huge mouth of the fireplace was fenced off by a screen painted with brightly colored birds. In the center was a coat of arms including a small crown from which a knight's hand bearing a sword emerged.

"Are those your ancestors?" asked Biryuza, finishing his second glass and licking caviar off his fingers.

"Uh-huh." Durand drank without eating. He didn't grow any drunker, only redder. "And that's my coat of arms. Didn't you say, Anton, that your great-grandfather was nobility, and your grandfather served in the secret police?"

"In the NKVD," corrected Biryuza.

"Yes, well, my grandfather was a butcher who was almost ruined by his proclivities for young girls, and my father was quite intelligent, but was a simple postal employee."

"Why are you telling me all this?"

"I bought the portraits with the house. The coat of arms belongs to the former owner. He was a baron, I think. And his barony, for that matter, was fake—one of his ancestors bought it from someone."

Tina carried in an enormous soup tureen; Stanley was impressed by her strength. She placed it easily on the table.

"Gentlemen," she said in a low-pitched voice, and lifted the ladle.

"Yes, yes, my dear," Durand gestured them toward the table, and they all sat down around a low, round table. Tina began to serve the soup.

"Give it a try—it's real Russian solyanka, which means 'hodgepodge,' Stanley, just in case you didn't know. Sturgeon and the rest are very expensive fish. Anyone who tries it has to agree: it's the best there is."

Stanley tasted it; Durand was right—this oddly named soup may have been the best he ever had. But then he saw Durand and Biryuza exchange glances out of the corner of his eye, and mentally prepared himself.

"Here's the thing, Stanley," Biryuza began. He ate several spoonfuls of soup and pushed his bowl away.

"Thank you, Tina," said Durand, "I'll call you."

Biryuza waited until Tina left the room, and continued.

"So, Viktor has accumulated a great deal of money in several Russian banks as well as banks in Latvia and Lithuania. This is completely legal, clean money, but, as you know, Swiss banks are more rigorous than most in verifying sources of money."

"And they don't trust anyone, except..." Durand added, wiping a napkin across his greasy lips.

"Except other, smaller, Swiss banks. You get me?"

"Banks like mine?"

"Excellent, Stanley," said Biryuza, watching him without blinking, his lips curved upward in a half smile. "We need to transfer these funds from these worthless Russian and Baltic banks to your bank. That's a simple operation, no?"

Stanley felt Durand watching him with the same intensity of attention. To give himself time to think, Stanley dipped his spoon back into the solyanka and came up with a piece of lemon and an olive.

Rolling the olive pit around in his mouth, he thought that sooner or later he would have to cross the line. Do something that could send him off to jail for many, many years.

"Yes, quite a simple transaction. But what amount of money are we talking?" he asked, looking first at Durand, then Biryuza. They both looked down, avoiding his gaze.

"Not so much," said Durand, watching the wind outside shake the branches of a dark-purple spirea. "About $4 billion."

Tina came in, pushing a cart carrying a platter covered with a gleaming metal cover and champagne in a bucket. The men fell silent.

Durand stood and lifted the cover, and Tina began to serve the guests. Stanley examined the portraits on the wall, trying to conceal his anxiety.

"The Russian part of our meal has come to an end—now begins the European section."

"Just like Gagarin's funds," said Biryuza.

"Well spotted, Anton! Now, we've got lobster in a cream truffle sauce and black caviar."

"Caviar again?"

"The caviar is Russian, though, isn't it?" Stanley felt increasingly unsettled. He poured water from a carafe into the tall glass by his plate and took a small sip.

"Well, not quite," Durand replied. "The chef used Iranian caviar. Now, for the lobster…"

Tina drew the champagne from the bucket and wrapped a towel around it.

"For the lobster, we have Cristal Rosé."

"A marvelous pairing," said Biryuza.

Durand tore off the foil, twisted off the wire hood, and pointed the bottle to the side. The cork popped out and hit the high ceiling.

"Not much at all," repeated Durand as Tina left the room, filling Stanley's glass again. "Only four billion. Maybe a bit more."

Stanley had no doubt that this money was dirty, blacker than Tina's hair, blacker than Biryuza's soul—if he even had one. He raised the glass to his lips and took a sip. The bubbles sparked against the roof of his mouth. He speared a piece of lobster with his fork. The lobster melted in his mouth, the magical wine washing away the slight bite of the spice.

"Not much, no," nodded Stanley, amazed at his own self-restraint. "A small sum, but I'll have to get permission from management, wait and see and what Lagrange has to say. And, of course, get approval from Laville."

"My friend, for us, your opinion is the most important one," said Durand, filling Biryuza's glass, then his own. "After all, you're the one who will be in charge of the whole transaction. What if, say, they agree to it, but you don't. What would we do then?"

"Especially because that's not all," said Biryuza, taking several more swallows and clucking his tongue.

"I don't believe you!" Stanley tried to laugh it off.

"Believe it!" Biryuza set his glass down and began to twirl it by its stem, looking off to the side. "Viktor has accumulated quite a bit of cash in Russia."

"In rubles?"

"Good lord, no! Dollars, euro, some pounds. In addition to, naturally, the gold, diamonds, and paintings—lower quality than what Robert acquired from the previous owner here, but not bad at all."

"Rubens? Cranach? The Elder, I mean..."

"Ah, so you know something about art? I had no idea." Durand extended his glass across the table, and he and Stanley clinked rims.

"Actually, Stanley guessed right," said Biryuza. "Viktor does have a Lucas Cranach the Elder in his possession. A portrait of Henry VIII, I think. But forget about that! What we're working on now is getting the cash, the gems and gold, and the paintings over to Switzerland. If it works out—and it will, everything always works out for Viktor—we'll have to deposit the cash in Viktor's account in the bank and arrange for the storage of the rest."

Biryuza stopped, worn out by his long explanation, and dug into the food on his plate with enthusiasm.

"How much?" Stanley asked Durand, girding himself for a very unpleasant reply.

Durand picked up a napkin and drew a pen from his pocket. Stanley was half expecting a gold fountain pen studded with diamonds, but Durand quickly scribbled a series of numbers on the napkin with a yellow Bic. He pushed the napkin over to Stanley, who looked down to see the number 6 followed by nine zeros. So, with the four, that was ten billion all together. Ten billion! If he were sentenced to a year for each billion—not an unlikely prospect—that would be ten years in jail. And that was a best-case scenario.

"Well, as I said, if management approves it, and you can get the Cranach delivered, I'll be glad to assist." Stanley pushed his plate away and drained his glass.

"I knew it," Durand said to Biryuza. "Stanley's our guy. You know what he did, Anton? He got rid of his shitty Tesla and showed up here in a Porsche! That's our kind of man. Am I right?"

For the first time in their acquaintance, Biryuza looked at Stanley with some sympathy.

Just then, they all heard the distinctive sound of a helicopter engine.

Durand checked his watch.

"Like usual—here for dessert. That's our resident sweet tooth, your boss, Stanley…"

Stanley walked over to the panoramic window. The white-and-blue Augusta AW109 hovered lightly over the house, blades spinning lazily.

The setting sun had turned Lake Geneva into a mirror, the dark tops of the pines overlapping against the sky, the sun's rays shining between their slender trunks one more time before the end of day. The helicopter descended out of view, and Stanley realized that the Durand's villa must have a helipad. He turned around, and Durand went out to meet Lagrange.

Biryuza had pushed back from the table and sat with his legs stretched out. He smoked, not looking at Stanley, but Stanley could feel his attention, his consideration of the main question—could Stanley be trusted. Biryuza looked up suddenly.

"So, you're our guy, right, Stanley?" he asked quietly.

"I work for Laville & Cie," said Stanley, surprising himself. "What's good for the bank is good for me. Serving the bank's clients is a sacred duty to me. Viktor Gagarin is a client of our bank. So I'll do whatever is necessary to…"

Stanley didn't get a chance to finish; Lagrange entered the room, followed by Durand and Tina.

"What's with the long face, Biryuza?" asked Lagrange, exchanging a handshake with the younger man who hadn't bothered to rise from his seat, and turned to Stanley without waiting for an answer.

"You drove, right? Is your Tesla charging? Charged up? Can I tell the pilot he's free to go? Laville held me up with an endless discussion about all our business, and we came to the best possible decision. Jean-Michel sent me over in his helicopter to make up the time. So, should I let him go?"

"Go ahead. The Tesla's all charged up," said Stanley with a wink to Durand.

"I'll put the cost of the electricity your employee here used to fuel up his Tesla in my fee," Durand added with another wink.

Dessert was a traditional crème brûlée and vanilla ice cream, served with cognac. But when Lagrange heard what they'd had earlier, he ordered several crepes with caviar and vodka for himself.

Tina brought in a tray with glasses of vodka on ice, and the reheated crepes with caviar. Lagrange took care of most of the shots and crepes in a matter of minutes, only then proceeding to dig into the crème brûlée.

"The more I travel to Russia, the more I start to pick up Russian habits. How many times have I seen that herring dish return to the table after the end of a hearty meal, when the coffee and tea have already been drunk?"

"Herring under a fur coat," Biryuza reminded him. "Any good news?"

"Ah yes! That piece of herring drowning under mayonnaise, potatoes, beets, and who knows what else. It's awful! Or pickled mushrooms. They put them all on the table next to the cake and start pouring vodka. And everything starts all over again. Pretty much like Russian life and Russian history, for that matter. Everything goes in a circle."

"Is there any news?" Biryuza asked again.

"Laville approved it. If that's what you're asking about. I'd like to see who wouldn't."

Biryuza exhaled in relief, rose, and prepared to leave, explaining that he had business to attend to. He shook Stanley's hand briefly, giving him a searching look. Stanley smiled widely in reply. Durand, who had been applying himself to the cognac, had grown even redder, and started to yawn, his head tipping forward on his chest.

"Well, then!" Lagrange said with a laugh, puffing on a Cuban cigar he'd taken from the box Tina brought in. "And Robert is one of our strongest lawyers. In all senses of the word. I think it's time for us to depart as well, Stanley. Is your Tesla charged up?"

"You asked me that already, Pierre. It's charged to the max. Tina, please pass on my thanks for a lovely evening. And to the chef as well. That *solyanka* was superb."

The hint of a smile flickered over Tina's impassive face, and her eyes narrowed slightly. She nodded and gestured for them to follow her.

Stanley and Lagrange left through a side entrance, and a servant brought the Porsche around. A glass of water and a box with two small pills appeared in Tina's hands as if by magic.

"This will take away all the effects and the smell of alcohol," she said, in a strong Brooklyn accent. "I highly recommend it."

Lagrange was still staring at the Porsche after Stanley had taken the pills and the water.

"That's what you're driving? Where's your Tesla? I've been looking forward to riding in an electric car once more, with a real eco-warrior and healthy lifestyle activist at the wheel, and this is what I see? Tina, honey, maybe you can explain?"

"Have a nice trip!" Tina said to Stanley, then turned on her heel, and headed back up the spiral staircase leading to the first floor.

"Where did Durand find that bitch, anyway?" Lagrange muttered under his breath, but loud enough for Tina to overhear.

"Get in, Pierre, and don't forget to buckle up," said Stanley.

"I hate seatbelts!"

"Otherwise, it won't go faster than twenty-five miles an hour. Buckle up!"

Stanley turned on the GPS and headed out, relying solely on its instructions. He drove very carefully, slowing down and turning at its advice.

"Pierre," Stanley began, braking at the intersection of Avenue Casino. He passed a bright-red Mercedes, its color even more brilliant in the twilight, turned right, and right again, as the GPS commanded, getting on the A9 before hitting Clarens. "Pierre, you understand that what we're planning to do is completely illegal."

"Stanley," broke in Lagrange, "shut up. You've already bought yourself a nice little house in Küsnacht and a Porsche. That's just the start. It's time to take the next steps. This transaction? Nothing out of the ordinary. Everybody does it. If we say no, Gagarin will just find another bank, we'll lose a ton of money, and you'll have to sell your Porsche."

"Why is that?"

"Because Laville will get rid of both of us. He'll give us good severance packages, of course, but nobody will hire us. Especially me. You'll have to start practically from scratch. Go back to the States, start handing out your résumé."

"Okay, I agree on the transfer of funds from Russia and Baltic banks, but how will the cash be sent? Are you aware that he also wants to send gems, paintings, and gold?"

"Of course, I am. As is Laville. It's none of our business, or yours, how it all gets here. Our job is to deposit the money in the account and take our percentage. Can you imagine what that's going to be? Laville put you in charge of the transfer to bank storage once it's all in Switzerland. Everything has to be done through third parties. Tenth parties would be better."

"And where am I supposed to find these parties?"

"That, my friend, is your problem. You're a big boy, Stanley. If you back out, no problem. Well, neither Laville or I will have any problems with you. Biryuza, on the other hand…"

"What about Biryuza?"

"He won't even say anything to Gagarin. He'll just whisper to Shamil, and…"

"Are you trying to scare me?"

"I'm kidding! I'm kidding! What is this, kindergarten? I'm giving you a warning. You're a great guy, and I really like you. You just have to make a choice. It's difficult, I know—principles, ideals, I know. You don't have anything to drink in here, do you?"

"There's a Christmas present from Gagarin in there."

Lagrange, already quite drunk, dug around in the glove box and found a bottle.

"What is it?"

"Macallan, 1947."

"Can you drink that from the bottle?"

"However you want, Pierre!"

Lagrange took a drink and nodded in appreciation.

"We do this deal, and we're set for retirement. Me, for sure." Lagrange yawned and closed his eyes. "There's been a cozy little shack waiting for me a long time now, near where they roll the world's best cigars, pour the best rum, and have the loveliest hookers."

"Where's that?" asked Stanley. "You have a backup aerodrome in Cuba?"

Lagrange shifted, opened his eyes to take another drink from the bottle, and, after a satisfied burp, mumbled something else about hookers before falling asleep.

Stanley mulled over the choice facing him the rest of the trip. The car ran smoothly mile after mile. It was approaching midnight when Stanley entered Zurich. He parked in front of Lagrange's house. His boss woke up as suddenly as if he'd been shocked, opened the bottle for a farewell sip, and shoved it back in the glove box.

"I have faith in you, McKnight," said Lagrange. "I know you'll do the right thing. See you tomorrow!"

"Tomorrow's Sunday."

"Really? So I won't see you then, oh, alas!"

Lagrange undid his seatbelt and pulled himself out of the car with some difficulty.

When Stanley pulled into his own parking lot, he saw the lawyer's wife in an evening gown, also just returning home.

"Hi," she said. "I was with some girlfriends at the opera. Something Russian—it was boring, something about a king and a beggar. Ugh. I've just remembered that I have a dozen oysters and two bottles of Chablis. Care to join me?"

"I'd love to."

CHAPTER 24

T HE STATUE OF THE SOVIET marshal Zhukov on horseback looked even more ungainly from the wide, clear window of the Four Seasons than it did on the ground.

Stanley had circled this statue several times on his first day in Moscow, right after checking in to the hotel.

He had strolled around Manege Square, noticing that Zhukov was too big and too heavy for his narrow-backed horse.

Stanley remembered seeing an old film reel in which the marshal observed a parade in Red Square. That Zhukov was rather short, and sat solidly on a powerful white stallion that was always sidling about as if wanting to break into a gallop.

This one, the bronze savior of Russia, looked like he would fall off the second his pacing horse decided to speed up. He had a long body, like the horse on which he sat, for the proportions of the statue. His bronze uniform was adorned with a medal.

Stanley had flown into Moscow late in the evening. At the airport he found a short, thin girl wearing all black—black pants and jacket—with delicate facial features and a piercing gaze. She was holding a sign with his last name on it.

Stanley approached and pointed his thumb toward his chest, saying, "I'm McKnight."

"Gala," she said by way of introduction and lifted his suitcase with ease.

She set a brisk pace; Stanley could barely keep up with her. A gauntlet of heavy-faced taxi drivers offered their services as he passed.

Dusk was gathering outside the large window of the airport. Gala went outside, toward a black car parked in a no-waiting zone. A flashing blue light sat atop its roof.

The policeman standing next to the car saluted when he saw Gala. She pressed the button on the remote, making all the car's lights flash. The trunk opened, and Gala tossed his suitcase in and settled into the driver's seat. Stanley moved to sit in the passenger seat, but she shook her head.

"In the back, please! And buckle up. We'll be going fast."

She operated the car as if it were part of her. Remembering the Moscow traffic jams, Stanley asked how long they would be on the road. Gala smiled. "Not long." Once the car joined the highway, she hit the sirens and moved into the far left lane, almost pushing the other cars off the road as she went.

Now Stanley was standing in front of the window in his room, looking down at the square packed with people, and that awkward statue.

Russian flags flew over the crowd, the banners snapping in the wind.

The waiter who brought him breakfast lowered his eyes gratefully as Stanley tucked fifty euros into his pocket. Stanley would never normally give a tip of that size, in the Four Seasons or any other hotel. A ten would be enough, with the prices in this hotel. But the waiter was highly trained. He probably prepared a daily report on the visitors he served, for the FSB or some other agency. But Lagrange had told him to get an expensive room, and to forget about his American ways.

"No percentages, no calculations!" he ordered. "You have to be impulsive. You can decide not to tip one person, but then you have to give the next one double. Act more capricious. Start a big fuss over nothing. Russians will respect you for that…"

"What's going on down there?" Stanley asked the waiter.

"It's an opposition rally, sir," the waiter answered in serviceable English. "They were only given permission to hold a rally on Mayakovsky Square, but they've gone down Tverskaya. There might be some trouble with the police now. If I could offer some advice, it would be better not to leave the hotel for the next hour or two. Can I pour you a cup of coffee?"

"No, thanks, I'll do it," Stanley said, finishing his orange juice. "And what does the opposition want?"

"They're protesting against corruption." Stanley watched the waiter's white-gloved hand adjust a fragrant pale-pink rose in a tall, thin vase. "There's an anecdote about that, if you'd like to hear it?"

"Go ahead!" Stanley moved away from the window and sat in armchair by the table. He pulled the egg cup over—just as he'd asked, the yolk was hot and runny, perfect for dipping cheese sticks in.

"It's from the time of the 1917 revolution. An aristocratic woman, a descendant of the Decembrists…I'm sorry, sir, do you know who the Decembrists were?"

"I do. Go on." Stanley nodded. His egg was perfectly cooked.

"So an aristocratic woman, a descendant of Decembrists, asked her maid what the demonstrators with red flags in the streets wanted. The maid replied: they want there to be no more rich people. Strange, said the aristocratic woman, my grandfather wanted there to be no more poor people."

"Not bad!" Stanley said, biting into his cheese stick. "Not bad. And neither was your anecdote. Thank you!"

The waiter bowed, and exited the room soundlessly.

Stanley could not, of course, wait in his room until the end of this opposition rally, as the waiter had called it.

Yesterday, dehydrated and suffering from a headache after his flight, he'd dined alone in one of the hotel's restaurants, which he'd chosen for its dark interior. After a couple of phone calls, though, Biryuza had set up a meeting, telling Stanley to expect him, along with a surprise.

A business meeting with Gagarin's partners was scheduled; Biryuza did not explain what kind of surprise could possibly accompany such a gathering.

Stanley didn't like surprises. Especially since they'd been growing more frequent lately. He didn't ask Biryuza what this surprise was, but did think to himself that maybe it was time for some surprises of his own. *There are two types of people: those who get surprises and those…* Stanley gave it up, realizing once again that the creation of aphorisms was not his strong suit.

After Gala had delivered him to the hotel, Stanley decided to have dinner. He ordered golden mackerel stewed with tomatoes and fried peppers, and a bottle of Chablis.

In addition to the razor from his great-grandfather, Stanley had also inherited an obscene ditty from the Russian side of his family. He'd memorized it, and then written it down.

His grandfather had often sung the verse to himself, certain that neither his daughter nor his grandson could understand him: "In the vineyards of Chablis/ the pages entertained the countess/ First they read her poetry/ Then they fucked her merrily."

187

When Stanley started studying Russian, he remembered his grandfather's little song, and showed it to his university teacher.

His teacher, an emigrant from the USSR with a slim waist and wide hips, smoothed down the folded and worn page, read its contents, and chuckled to herself. "The poem is about courtly love between a lady and her servant. An untranslatable play on words," she had said, handing the paper back to Stanley.

But a girlfriend of his, a Russian girl working as a bartender in a little place on Forty-Second Street in New York, laughed for a long time when Stanley read her the poem, after telling her in advance that he was going to read her something in Russian.

"You're so funny," said the bartender, who married some film producer shortly thereafter and moved from the Bronx to the Hollywood hills. "Remember this, Stanley: you have to start the study of any language, especially Russian, with an overview of its obscenities. If you don't know the plural past tense of the verb *fuck* from the infinitive *to fuck*, then your being able to read Dostoyevsky without a dictionary isn't worth a thing."

Stanley had objected that he was still far from Dostoyevsky, and his bartender taught him as much as she could about Russian cursing. Most importantly, though, in large part thanks to his grandfather's poem, Stanley learned to love Chablis.

He drank the wine down to the last drop, but didn't finish the fish, even though he'd been waiting to try it ever since he'd read a travelogue as a child in which the author wrote that golden mackerel was the tastiest fish he'd ever had. It was worth coming to Moscow just to order it!

Stanley walked out of the hotel. He was in a dark-blue suit and a fitted, pure-white shirt, all custom-made in Florence. He liked the raised Australian mother-of-pearl buttons on these shirts, thick and hand-sewn.

Stanley had no briefcase or shoulder bag; all he had was his passport, wallet, smartphone, and a flat leather cigarette case. He'd started carrying a case ever since they'd started printing terrible pictures showing the medical effects of smoking on packs of cigarettes. He took out a cigarette, and the porter in livery was by his side with a lighter.

Stanley thanked him and then looked around. The entrance to the hotel was blocked off by two rows of policemen in helmets with their visors lowered, standing shoulder to shoulder, shields resting on the ground. The street past them was filled with a turbulent human sea.

One of the protesters approached the line of policemen and began shouting into a megaphone. Stanley couldn't make out what he was saying, amid the general noise and the rasp of the megaphone.

"What is he saying?" Stanley asked the porter.

"That corruption is evil," the porter replied.

"And that draws a crowd here?" snorted Stanley. "Why does he need a megaphone to tell us something everybody knows?"

Like Stanley's waiter, the porter spoke good English, but was clearly reluctant to give an exact translation of the slogans distorted by the megaphone.

"Well, to be precise, sir, he says that planes are not for corgis," the porter said.

"Not for corgis? What does that mean?"

"The wife of a high-ranking official recently flew to a dog show on a private plane, at government expense, so her corgis could participate."

"Like the queen of England?"

"Yes, sir. And she says her corgis are better than the queen's, so her participation will enhance Russia's prestige."

"Really? An interesting argument." Stanley stood up on his toes, trying to see the signs the protesters were carrying.

"What's written on that sign over there?" he asked.

"We won't forgive! We won't forget!"

"Yeah, that sounds pretty Russian. What about that one?"

"Which one, sir?"

"The one the girl is holding, that one with freckles."

"Ah! Hospitals, not ducks!"

"I don't get it."

"One very, very high-up government official built himself an enormous country mansion with an artificial pond for ducks, where the ducks have a special little house."

"So?"

"You could build two rural hospitals for the cost of that duck house."

"Nice! How about that one? The one the guy is holding, under the red-and-black banner."

"Those are anarchists, if I'm not mistaken. And the sign says: 'War on the palaces!'"

"I see. Well, I liked the ones about the dogs and the ducks." Stanley tossed his cigarette butt and ground it out with the toe of his shoe. "The rest are so-so."

A member of the hotel staff came up to the porter and whispered something in his ear.

"Sir," the porter said, turning to Stanley, "They're about to start clearing the square. I strongly advise you to return to the hotel."

"How do you know?"

"Our security service is in contact with the police. And we listen to their radio, so our information is good, sir."

"I'd be happy to, but unfortunately, I can't today!" Stanley got a fresh cigarette out of his case. "Someone's coming for me shortly. Should be here in about a minute and a half."

"But, sir, how do you expect them to get here? You see what's going on. I'm afraid it will be impossible."

"You don't know who's coming, my friend. But I do. Nothing is impossible for them! They'll be here in a minute and a half, well, forty seconds now."

Stanley was bluffing a little. He did have some pretty serious doubts as to whether Biryuza would be able to get through that crowd and the heavy police presence. He expected that Biryuza would call him and set a meeting point within a walking distance from the hotel.

But his doubts were dispelled by the quacking sound and flashing lights of a siren as a huge black Audi pulled up in front of the building.

It was able to get through thanks to four big brutes hanging off of the spotlessly clean sides, two on each side, and another two ruthlessly clearing the way in front of the car. The nerve and tenacity of this team stunned the police as well as the protesters: their human wall parted, and the car's rear window, its thick, tinted glass clearly designed to withstand a round from an assault rifle, lowered, and Biryuza's pale face emerged from the dim interior of the car.

"Ready, McKnight?"

"Of course, Biryuza!"

"Then come on in!"

Biryuza opened the door and shifted deeper into the interior, and Stanley, winking at the porter frozen in astonishment on the sidewalk, threw his newly lit cigarette on the ground and slid into the car.

"Reverse, Gala!" ordered Biryuza. "We have to return our fighters here to the Jeep escort, and then…"

Biryuza paused, and put a finger to his lips.

"Where are we headed, Anton?" asked Stanley, seeing the miniature girl from the evening before behind the wheel in large mirrored sunglasses.

"I promised you a surprise, didn't I? Didn't I? I did! So shut up and enjoy it."

"Ok, then. Hi, Gala!"

Gala nodded, turned the wheel, dispersing the crowd, and they were moving. The tinted rear windows kept Stanley from seeing what was going on to their right and left, but he could see through the windshield as the hulking men running in front of their car casually knocked anyone in their path out of the way. When the car turned onto the road passing between the hotel and the long-shuttered building of the Lenin Museum, they knocked the police officer rushing toward them aside with the same indifference.

"Anton! They just pushed a police officer!" Stanley said.

"What! You can't be serious! Did you see that, Gala?" Biryuza exclaimed in mock astonishment.

"I didn't see anything," said Gala in a hoarse, low voice. The men running in front moved aside, Gala hit the gas pedal, and the car took off, siren quacking away.

Moments later, they passed Lubyanka Square, flew by the Polytechnic Museum, and passed through Staraya Square. Biryuza took the time to point out the gray building that once housed the Central Committee of the Communist Party, and was now the headquarters of the Russian president's administration.

"Anywhere you spit in this town, it lands on a friend of my boss. They all owe him. Some for a house in London, some for still holding on to their jobs," said Biryuza. "Viktor has an amazing, rare quality—he ensures that people are obligated to him wherever he goes. Even those with whom he's had no dealings. Although I can't think of who that might be."

The car moved downhill toward the river, then turned right onto the embankment. It was a picturesque view: the Kremlin with the gold domes of Christ the Savior rising behind it.

"You're not taking me to meet the patriarch of Russia, are you?" asked Stanley.

"No, not today. We try not to interact too much with spiritual figures. Although that field is looking more and more promising these days. Thanks for the idea, Stanley."

Gala drove past the Prechistenskaya Embankment and made a sharp right turn under the overpass, forcing the flow of traffic to brake suddenly to let her pass, before turning left and then right again and flying onto the Garden Ring.

The cars ahead slowed for a red traffic light, but Gala hit a button on her display panel, the quacking of the siren turned into a wail, and a traffic cop emerged out of nowhere to block off oncoming traffic and let Biryuza's car through. In no time, they were pulling up to the entrance of a tall building topped with a high spire. Its windows looked narrow, and the lower section of its walls were covered in red granite.

"We're here!" Biryuza announced.

"Where are we?" asked Stanley.

"This is the Ministry of Foreign Affairs. I'm going to introduce you to someone."

"This is your surprise?"

"You're a quick one, McKnight! Just pick things up, don't you? Look up, Stanley. You see that spire? According to legend, when they were finishing construction on the building, Stalin happened to drive by. He noted that Russian buildings usually had pointed tops. So they immediately drew up plans for a spire. They made it out of metal for ease of construction, and painted it the color of the building. The spire might have been added to give the building a more unique appearance. Otherwise, it's a bit too much like US government buildings from the first half of the twentieth century, which was unacceptable, of course. Got it?"

"I see." Stanley laughed. "As per usual, the Americans are to blame for everything. What else is new?"

CHAPTER 25

T HEY WERE MET AT THE vast front door by a tall, narrow-shouldered man in a Zegna suit. His tie was tied in a thin, tight knot, and the grip of his slender hand was unusually strong when they shook.

"Zaitsev sent me," the narrow-shouldered man said. "He couldn't meet you himself, as the minister called him in. I'm Igor Novichok, Zaitsev's aide."

Biryuza, who had been tensing up, relaxed and nodded.

To Stanley's surprise, Novichok easily opened the door behind them—then saw that there was a smaller, ordinary door within the enormous one.

Stanley was momentarily blinded by the soft gloom of the entrance hall after the bright sunlight, but recovered quickly to see that they were being waved over to a counter manned by an armed policeman in full uniform. The officer didn't ask for any identification, simply nodded politely and asked them to step through a metal detector.

Once through the metal detector, they crossed the vestibule with its marble columns, reflected in the polished black granite of the floor, and came to a carved wooden stand, where they did have to show their documents.

"We're happy to see you, Mr. McKnight," said the auburn-haired girl as she handed back his passport.

They walked toward the elevators but passed by the main ones where a small cluster of people waited, heading instead to a small corner. Novichok took a card out of his pocket and placed it against a keypad in the wall, and elevator doors opened soundlessly. Stanley noticed that there were only four buttons in this elevator. Novichok pressed the red one.

"Time for takeoff!" Biryuza laughed—and they shot upward as soon as the doors closed.

"Follow me, please!" Novichok said when the elevator stopped and the doors opened. He let Stanley and Biryuza out first, then quickly moved ahead of them, his steps quiet on the hallway carpet.

The hallway was lined with wooden paneling, and dimly lit. The doors they passed were set back in the wall, and each had keypad locks. It seemed to go on forever.

Finally, they came to a tall door without a keypad lock. Novichok pulled a bunch of keys out of his pocket and flipped through them with his slim fingers to find the right one. He opened the door wide, saying, "Please come in, gentlemen!"

They entered an enormous office. Its thick, dark-green curtains were closed tightly, and a large carpet covered the floor. The wooden paneling on the wall reached up to eye level, but wasn't as dark as that in the hallway. They were covered in lacquer, which gleamed under the light of a large chandelier.

"That's Karelian birch. A nice look!" Novichok told Stanley, noticing his glance. "Sit down. Sit down. Zaitsev will be here any minute. Tea? Of course you want tea! One moment!"

Novichok went over to the desk, on which sat two old-fashioned telephones—a black one with a rotary dial and a white one that had a golden USSR emblem in place of a dial. He sat behind it in a high-backed chair, which creaked slightly under his weight. Stanley wondered what would happen to that chair if the corpulent Lagrange sat on it. Novichok picked up the black telephone's receiver and dialed one number.

"Tea. Cookies. Mishka," Novichok said into the receiver. "For three." And hung up.

There was a portrait on the wall above the desk of a man with a large forehead wearing a pince-nez, coat, and hat.

"Is that Beria?" Stanley asked.

"Hah!" Biryuza and Novichok exclaimed in unison.

"You know who Beria is?" Novichok asked, taking out a pack of Parliament and lighting one.

"Stanley! You've already shocked me with the Porsche," said Biryuza. "Now—Beria? Not many Swiss bankers know that Lavrentiy Beria was the last head of Stalin's secret service, that even Stalin was wary of him, and that he was shot shortly after Stalin's death."

"Yes, I know who Beria was," said Stanley. "He also ran the Soviet nuclear project. And he loved young girls. He drove around Moscow collecting them, like butterflies. Then he raped them. I've seen the office where he did it—it's a restaurant now. I also know who the Decembrists were, what year the revolution was, that Stalin wanted to make peace with Hitler, and that they signed a secret agreement, but Hitler managed—how do you say it in Russian? He managed to screw Stalin, and there was a long war, in which Stalin finally managed to screw Hitler. I know a lot. What are you laughing about?"

Biryuza and Novichok were roaring with laughter. Biryuza was doubled over with laughter, slapping his thick thighs, squatting down as if he was preparing to jump into a dance around the room.

"What are you laughing at? What's so funny?"

"Mr. McKnight!" Novichok stopped laughing finally and grew serious. "As a matter of fact, this isn't Beria, although there are some similarities, I agree. This is Vyacheslav Molotov, the longtime Minister of Foreign Affairs in the USSR, the very man who Stalin sent to sign a secret agreement with Hitler."

"Not with Hitler," said Biryuza, wiping tears away.

"Well, of course, not with Hitler himself, but with his minister, Ribbentrop. No offense, it was very funny."

"Don't be mad, Stanley!" Biryuza took a package of tissues and blew his nose noisily, then tossed the crumpled-up tissue into the wastebasket with an accuracy that any pro basketball player would envy.

Deep leather chairs stood around a low table covered with watermarks from glasses and almost burned through in places from cigarettes. Stanley sank into one of them and ran a hand over the table. Whoever usually sat here loved his cigars—there were several deep marks from cigar burns here and there. The scent of old tobacco filled the room. There was a carafe of water on the table, and several glasses on a crystal tray.

The office doors swung open to admit a fat woman in a short dress, white apron, and white cap over straw-yellow hair. She was pushing a trolley that held a small samovar with a teapot, a dish with sweets labeled *Mishka in the North*, another dish with cookies, a plate with lemon slices, a sugar bowl, and three glasses in silver tea-glass holders bearing the USSR emblem.

A chubby redheaded man followed her into the room, a jacket over his arm. His tie lay over his shoulder, and thin-framed glasses sat on the tip of his meaty nose. As he passed the woman, he moved his jacket from one arm to the other and gave her a hearty smack on her substantial behind. She, unconcerned, began to transfer the contents of her trolley onto the table, and the man extended his hand to Stanley.

"Alexey Zaitsev! Classmate and practically brother to this," he said, pointing at Biryuza, "great man."

"Stanley," replied McKnight, half rising to shake the newcomer's hand. "Stanley McKnight, from Laville & Cie. His partner," he added, nodding at Biryuza.

"We know. We know," Zaitsev said, plopping down into an empty chair. "Thank you, Katerina Matfeevna, that will be all! Igor will finish everything and will also be free to go. You can meet in some corner and spend a lovely ten minutes together. To be sure, Igor only needs half a minute, am I right? Kidding, kidding, no offense, Igor!"

The woman left the room without a single word. Novichok, who had somehow grown even thinner and smaller with the arrival of Zaitsev, arranged the glasses and dishes around the table. He then bowed to each of the others in turn, and said to Stanley, "Very nice to meet you!" and left as well.

"Have some tea and chocolate!" Zaitsev invited, pushing an empty glass over to Stanley. "We do things the traditional way around here. Indian tea, with the elephant on the cover..."

"This tea was sold in the Soviet Union as well," explained Biryuza.

"Lemons from Abkhazia..."

"That's an autonomous region in Georgia," Biryuza continued his explanations. "Georgia's independent now, but Abkhazia..."

"I'm aware," said Stanley, looking down at his empty glass.

"Your banker knows everything, Biryuza!"

"Well, maybe not everything," said Biryuza, unwrapping a chocolate and popping it into his mouth. "You've got real Mishka in the North here, my favorite candy. Even Gagarin couldn't get the kind of Mishka they sold thirty years ago. They swore to him it was authentic! Completely authentic! But it wasn't. But as for Stanley, he mistook Molotov for Beria."

"Well, we can forgive him for that. Both of them, let's be honest, were real pieces of shit, although it is, once again, no longer quite safe to say that. Especially about Molotov. His grandson is a combative, rich political player, a political prostitute, if you will. But forget that," Zaitsev said with a frown. "By the way, it turns out they're not going to move the Moscow State Institute of Foreign Relations into the city center. Turns out the rumors weren't true. One simple reason—parking. Now each idiot whose father sends him to study at our alma mater has his own car, usually a Jeep, for that matter. They drive, suck dicks, smoke, talk on the phone, and play games all at the same time. That's the new generation for you!"

"Is that even possible?" asked Stanley.

"What—suck dick, eat, and smoke?" Alexey gave Stanley an ironic once-over. "You just haven't met enough Russian girls yet. I had one student—eat some candy, have a cookie. If they're too hard, dunk them in the tea to soften them up. So this student was on her knees on a chair, typing while I dictated a crappy course paper to her, fucking her from behind at the same time, and she managed to have conversations with her mother, her friend, and her man."

"Her man?" Stanley coughed. "You mean her boyfriend?"

"Yes, her boyfriend. She apologized, told him she was running late for their date. That's the new generation for you. No longer the Pepsi generation, or even the iPhone generation."

"Who knows what the hell kind of generation it is!" said Biryuza. "Anyway, friends, let's talk business."

"Okay, then," Zaitsev said. He fished a lemon out of his glass and ate it, wincing.

"So, here it is." Zaitsev leaned over and spat lemon seeds on the floor. *An unexpected move for a diplomat*, thought Stanley. "I have a 100 percent guarantee that you can send your boss's cash through the Russian post. Diplomatic mail. That means no inspections, no delay."

Stanley was so astonished at the ease with which Zaitsev described transferring Gagarin's enormous cash reserves that he even dropped his teaspoon.

"The amounts are just a bit much. So we'll break them down into batches. About one ton per batch." Zaitsev bent down and retrieved Stanley's spoon from the floor.

Stanley did some mental calculations; one batch would comprise about $100 million in hundred-dollar bills.

"It would be better if you could transfer some of that cash, as much as you can, into diamonds and gold. Otherwise the delivery will take too long."

"It's already in the works. We're going to buy diamonds from Alrosa."

"That's a Yakutia-based company," Zaitsev told Stanley. "They mine diamonds, send them to De Beers to be cut, get back perfect diamonds, and De Beers makes a real profit on that..."

"That's all illegal," Stanley said, shaking his head, "I mean..."

"Stanley is an honest man," Biryuza interrupted, winking at Zaitsev.

"Ah, I could see that right away!" Zaitsev nodded approvingly. "I can always tell when I meet someone. The minister taught me how. As soon as I came in, I got the feeling that there was an honest man here. Not you, Biryuza, naturally. There's no hope left for you!"

"And proud of it!" Biryuza exclaimed, straightening his shoulders.

"The diplomatic mail will be sent to different countries within continental Europe. We can't send it all to Switzerland alone. We'll need armored trucks."

"From your bank," Biryuza said to Stanley.

"We'll do it," nodded Stanley.

"But it's illegal," Biryuza teased, mimicking Stanley.

"Forget about it, my friend. Just forget about it. When I talk about illegality, I'm just telling you what the framework is, and frames are made to be broken." Stanley took out a cigarette, and Zaitsev lit it with a gold lighter.

"There you go. At last, his level of honesty is diminishing a bit," the diplomat said.

"You'll need to personally ensure that everything is delivered to the bank," Biryuza told Stanley. "Personally!"

"I understand. Everything will be taken care of."

"Okay!" Biryuza slapped his hands down on his knees. "We've eaten all the candy. What's next?"

Zaitsev rose and dialed one number on the black telephone.

He was a bit more democratic than his aide. "Katerina Matfeevna, please bring…yes, yes, you know already! We'll be here, my lovely!"

Zaitsev returned to the table and took a bag of white powder out of his pocket. *Are they really going to snort cocaine right in the ministry?* Stanley wondered.

"I've got this while we wait for her to drag her fat ass and our candy over here."

"Coke, excellent!" Biryuza clapped his hands.

"Better than cocaine," Zaitsev replied. "This is *Mielofon*."

"Mielofon?" asked Biryuza and Stanley simultaneously.

"It's made from the same base as cocaine, plus a magical chemical cocktail that will relax your overexcited brains and help you read other people's minds. New nanotechnology from the decadent West. A bourgeois chemist by the name of Charles Dodgson came up with it."

"Alisa, I've got the Mielofon!" Biryuza giggled, making the connection between the name of the product and a children's movie.

"Just not right under Molotov's portrait. That's a bit much. Here's a secluded nook," said Zaitsev, opening the curtains.

Daylight burst into the room. Zaitsev opened the balcony door, and they all went out onto an enormous balcony, invisible from the street below.

Smolenskaya Square bustled noisily beneath them. A police siren sounded somewhere nearby. There was a small table on the balcony and a mirror on the table.

"Everything we need," Zaitsev said and poured the contents of the packet onto the mirror, dividing the pile into three lines with a credit card. He rolled a bill up into a tube and handed it to Stanley first.

"Do it all in one go!" said Zaitsev. "That's how we do it, comrade!"

Stanley inhaled deeply, exhaled, and sucked up an entire line of the Mielofon—he'd chosen the one in the middle. Biryuza and Zaitsev followed his example.

"Good lord!" moaned Zaitsev. "That's amazing!"

"Alisa, I've got the Mielofon!" Biryuza rubbed his nose roughly. "I've got the Mielofon," he said, repeating the nonsensical words as if in a trance.

"He's fine, just caught up in some childhood memories," Zaitsan said and laughed, seeing how Stanley was watching Biryuza with some concern. "Ah, and here are our candies."

They returned to the office. The woman in the apron had already placed a full dish of Mishka in the North candies and was preparing to leave, but she didn't manage to get out before getting another smack from Zaitsev.

"You can't hide from me, honey!" he said, sat down, and began unwrapping one of the candies.

Biryuza and Stanley sat as well. Biryuza's eyes darkened, his pupils narrowed, his bright lips were moist, and he sniffled constantly.

"Take some more tea," Zaitsev offered, leaning over to Stanley.

"More?" Stanley said, his suddenly capricious voice sounding odd to him. "I've had nothing yet."

"He doesn't want any more tea," pronounced Zaitsev, looking off into the distance, and crossed one leg over the other.

"I miss our university time a lot, you know?" interrupted Biryuza.

"Yes! Me too." Zaitsev lit a thin cigar and exhaled a line of gray smoke up to the ceiling. "Do you remember that night club, Ptuch?"

"How could I forget?" Biryuza smiled. "Where I spent all my scholarship money on a pitiful gram of heavily adulterated cocaine. Well, with enough left over for a nonalcoholic cocktail."

"Are you trying to say we're doing better for ourselves now?"

"Well, now we can afford five grams, ten grams, and much more! And even if the stinking Moscow wind blew it away, someone would bring us more, and we wouldn't even notice the loss."

"What does 'adulterated' mean?" asked Stanley, sounding out the unfamiliar Russian word and trying to come to his senses.

"Diluted. With other drugs added in. If you were lucky. If not, it was detergent," explained Zaitsev. "You Americans wouldn't know anything about it."

"We sure would," objected Stanley. "They sold all kinds of drugs on campus at Berkeley, pure and adulterated. One dealer even got killed for cutting his wares."

"So you're trying to say that we're not so different after all?" snorted Zaitsev. "Maybe there are some similarities. But the main difference between us is that America has always been an enemy of Russia, and Russia has always wanted to be your friend. We want friendship, and you want war. You're always sticking your nose into our business."

Stanley struggled to adjust to this quick change in topic. He was also amazed by the fervor with which Zaitsev spoke. He looked at him, then at Biryuza, who was in clear agreement with everything his friend said. How could these two crooks, who would do absolutely anything for money, including busily robbing their own country, pose as superpatriots?

"Okay," nodded Stanley, "I also dislike the way my country tries to impose its own model of government everywhere. But America has done so much for Russia! We helped you in the war..."

"Are you talking about lend-lease?" Biryuza brought out a baggie of marijuana and tossed it onto the table. "You sent us junk, and our soldiers died!"

"Junk?" Stanley almost choked on his own indignation. "What about the planes? The trucks? The steel? Bearings? Junk! We gave you billions of dollars' worth of goods, and forgave a lot. And your soldiers died because of military leaders like that marshal out there on the square, on the horse..."

"Zhukov?"

"Yeah, Zhukov. And because you don't value human life. You never have. You sent people up against machine guns."

Biryuza and Zaitsev exchanged glances. Biryuza got out cigarette papers and rolled a fat joint, lit it, and passed it to Zaitsev.

"Stanley, my friend!" Biryuza tried to put on a friendly smile, but his eyes were cold. "Don't get so worked up! People against machine guns, where did you hear that?"

Stanley took the joint from Zaitsev's extended hand, took a deep drag, and then another. His head buzzed. A million little needles poked at his muscles. All his senses were heightened.

"I read a lot. No time for it now. But I used to read a lot. And I took a special modern history course. I had some decent professors."

"Enough!" Biryuza raised his hands. "We surrender! You win! America is our friend. She'll wipe our snot, wipe our ass. Hit this!"

Stanley hadn't noticed the joint go around the circle again. Another drag—Biryuza must have cut the marijuana with something—and he leaped up and started pacing around the room.

He got thirsty after a while. Stanley walked over to the table, poured himself a glass of cold tea, and drank it down in one gulp. He was hungry.

He'd had a similar experience once before, a long time ago, after graduation.

He'd tried to avoid a repeat, but he was enjoying his current state. The weed was saturated with something, either coke or some kind of synthetic chemical.

"Should we get something to eat?" Zaitsev suggested, also jumping up. "But a word of warning—the dining hall where I'm taking you is only for the minister, his deputies, and scumbags like me. You need to behave there. Otherwise, they might kick me out, ha ha! Give me the boot!"

Biryuza also rose.

"Right, Stanley, if you pass by the minister of foreign affairs of our great nation, try not to spit in his soup. No matter how much you want to. Promise?"

"Nope, I'm going to have to spit!" said Stanley.

"Well, Anton, I can see that Stanley is our kind of guy!" Zaitsev laughed, leading them out of his office.

CHAPTER 26

T HE DINING HALL FOR THE ministry's senior staff was a fairly small room, with the wooden paneling on the wall that Stanley had come to expect. The walls above the wood were painted a dark green.

"Dark green is the color of death." Stanley remembered the line from some novel, and it seemed suddenly hilarious to him.

He tried to suppress his fit of laughter as he followed Biryuza to a free table, but couldn't restrain it once they were sitting.

Covering his mouth with his hand, Stanley started to laugh, and he infected Zaitsev and Biryuza with it, then the people sitting at the tables nearby, and finally even their waitress, who came over to take their order.

The waitress, who looked a lot like the fat woman who had brought them tea and chocolates, tried not to laugh, which made her flushed face even redder.

"We have two set menus for lunch—beet salad, borscht, beef stroganoff, and juice, or potato salad, fish soup, chicken Kiev, and juice. You'll have to wait a bit, hee! for any à la carte dishes."

"What will you have?"

Zaitsev pointed at Biryuza, Stanley, and himself, and repeated the nursery rhyme that Stanley had already heard from Gagarin: "The moon comes out across the land, with a sharp knife in his hand," then added, "I'll have the lunch with borscht!" and laughed heartily. Biryuza wiped his tears away and chose the lunch with fish soup.

"What à la carte dishes do you have?" asked Stanley.

A chorus of laughter burst out from the neighboring tables.

"Oh, ha ha ha," Zaitsev pulled out a handkerchief and blew his nose with gusto. "Mr. McKnight! Take what you're offered!"

"But I wanted…"

"Stanley! Have the juice!" said Biryuza through his laughter. "We've got juice for every kind of condition here in Russia."

"Excellent!" agreed Stanley. "I'll take the one with juice."

"They both, hee hee, both have juice."

"I'll take both!"

"Stanley!" they cried in unison, and Stanley chose the lunch with borscht.

They were already on their second course when a tall, balding man came in. He had close-set eyes, glasses, and full lips.

He looked familiar to Stanley. So much so, that he was ready to go over and shake his hand. Zaitsev, sensing his intent, kicked Stanley's leg under the table, bringing on another fit of laughter.

The tall man looked their way in surprise and sat at a nearby table. Biryuza, wolfing down his beef stroganoff, gave him a casual nod.

"That," whispered Zaitsev, "is the minister of foreign affairs. I'll introduce you!"

"Why?" Stanley whispered back, scared. "Me…I…"

"I see a new face." The deep, smoky baritone made all three sit up straight and pull themselves together. "Who is our guest, Zaitsev?"

"This…this…" Zaitsev swallowed his laughter. "This is Mr. McKnight, an economic adviser at the US State Department. He's here to discuss support for…"

"No business in the dining hall!" the minister interrupted and rose, extending his hand to Stanley. "Happy to see you in our lair!"

"Your lair?" Stanley shook his hand. "Yes, I do see some big animals here. Pleased to meet you as well."

"I hope our menagerie doesn't make you stew?"

"My Russian isn't what it could be. How do you mean 'stew'?"

"The great Dostoyevsky introduced the word to us. To stew, as in, to feel uncomfortable, try to go unnoticed." The minister sniffed loudly, and Stanley wondered if the minister had also been sampling a line of Mielofon before coming down to lunch.

"It's an honor for me. And this might be the best beef stroganoff I've ever had."

"Indeed! We have the best beef stroganoff. And the rest as well, for that matter…"

Further conversation was interrupted by the appearance of a young man very similar in appearance to Novichok. He rushed over to the minister and whispered something in his ear.

"Please excuse me," the minister said, bowing to Stanley, and followed the anxious young man out of the room.

"What happened?" Stanley asked Zaitsev.

"Oh, nothing! The US just kicked out another group of our diplomats," he replied.

"Yes, I saw that on the morning news," Biryuza said with a chuckle.

"Ah, apparently our minister doesn't watch the news."

"His television is broken!" said Biryuza, and all three broke into laughter.

"Okay, I think it's time for us to get going," Zaitsev said. All laughed out.

"Gala will be here for us in half an hour," agreed Biryuza.

"Let's go!"

Under the puzzled glances of the other diners, they headed toward the exit. Stanley turned back, picked his glass of juice up from the table, said, "Cheers!" loudly to the room at large, and drained it in one gulp.

Zaitsev walked Stanley and Biryuza to their car. Gala was at the wheel as before, but this time, Shamil sat next to her in the passenger seat, wearing narrow, mirrored sunglasses, a short haircut, and a week's beard. His lips were compressed into a thin line, the traditional Russian shirt he was wearing, this one with a gold embroidered collar, was buttoned all the way up, and a holster was visible against the red-silk lining of his jacket.

Shamil jumped out of the car and opened the rear door. Alexey said his goodbyes as soon as he saw Shamil, quickly handing Stanley his business card as he left.

"You're fucking late," rasped Shamil.

"We were having lunch with the minister," Biryuza replied.

"Don't lie!" Shamil's entire appearance and voice inspired terror; he didn't even need to curse at you. He could have spoken in Old English, quoted Chaucer, and any rational person would still want to run or hide as soon as they saw him. "What the fuck would the minister want with you? Get in. Gagarin's been expecting Anton for a while."

Stanley wanted to put this thug in his place, but then just laughed and got into the back next to Biryuza. His tongue was sticking to the roof of his mouth after the sweet juice.

He was going to ask Gala if she happened to have any cold water, but then he discovered a bottle of mineral water in the bar. He twisted the cap off and tossed it onto the floor. Shamil's rudeness made him want to respond in kind. *It's too bad I'm not sick to my stomach*, thought Stanley. *I'd puke all over his expensive leather.* He took a few sips and handed the bottle to Biryuza.

"Thank you," murmured Biryuza.

Gala was less bold and independent with Shamil next to her. She didn't turn on the quacking siren, but she did pull quickly away from the ministry and move over into the left lane. A Jeep escort followed her. They passed through the tunnel under Novy Arbat.

"That's your consulate, Stanley. Did you know?" Shamil rasped, pointing out the building.

Stanley didn't answer. He was studying the contents of the bar. There was another bottle of mineral water, an orange juice, and small bottles of vodka. Stanley took two out, kept the juice for himself, and gave Biryuza the mineral water. They twisted open their vodkas simultaneously, clinked the rims, and drank, chasing it with juice and water.

Gala had to go down Brestskaya and take the first right to get onto Tverskaya, which was empty, but they only managed to go about three hundred feet: the street was closed off by a row of closely parked police trucks. Gala hit the brakes. A police officer accompanied by two riot police approached the car.

"Road's closed," the first man said.

Shamil rolled down his window. "We've got a VIP, captain, a guest of the minister of foreign affairs. He's going to the Four Seasons."

"You can try from Volkhonka. No, it's closed off everywhere. There's unrest. I'd advise against it."

"Okay, I'll get there myself!" said Stanley, throwing open his door. "This way? Down this street? Bye-bye!"

And he walked quickly away from the car without looking back.

After a dozen steps Stanley found himself in a dense crowd, then was pulled along by the flow of foot traffic moving along the sidewalk.

They were mostly young people, many girls, some of whom were carrying rubber ducks on the ends of plastic sticks. Stanley guessed it was a symbol of the fight against corruption.

"A house for ducks!" he said to one of the girls, a pretty blonde. "Corruption is evil!"

"Are you an American?" she replied, smiling.

"Yep!" Stanley nodded.

They passed several side streets together, all of which, like the street they were on, were bordered by heavy trucks.

A group of grim-looking young people next to McKnight were carrying an enormous tape recorder, which was playing "Children of the Revolution."

The T. Rex song was drowned out by the rotors of the helicopters flying low overhead.

When they reached the square with a statue of a famous Russian poet, they heard shouting ahead.

Police, in helmets with visors down and raised shields, were attacking the marchers. They cut through the crowd, and used their batons on those who were separated from the main group.

Marchers to the right and left of Stanley were roughly grabbed by other police officers without helmets and shields, and dragged to police buses parked along the boulevard. Two approached Stanley, but he pulled his American passport out of his pocket.

"I'm a diplomat!"

They exchanged glances, and then grabbed the girl with the duck. Stanley didn't have time to think. He stuffed his passport back in his pocket, and whacked the nearest policeman across the head. The officer let the girl go, Stanley dodged his hands, and gave the other one a good kick. The second policeman released his hold on her as well, and now they were both coming after Stanley.

"Run!" he shouted to the girl, raising his hands to get into a fighting stance.

But he didn't have a chance. The policeman rushing him got him with the baton across his back and then slammed his shield into Stanley's face.

Stanley thought his nose might be broken. He could barely see through his tears.

Stanley threw his right hand forward, hitting something. But that "something" turned out to be a police helmet, and he heard his joints crunch against the metal. The second blow of the baton caught Stanley on the back of the head, and two other police officers got him into a stranglehold. He tried to twist out of their grip, but they pulled his arms back tighter, and more police rushed up to help drag him into the bus for detained marchers.

They literally threw him inside. It was a small, rickety bus with curtains over its windows, a dirty floor, torn upholstery on the seats, and an abrasive odor of chlorine permeating the interior. He hit his shoulder painfully on the chrome handrail as he fell in, and slammed his knee into the steps. The doors shut behind him.

Everyone inside had seen Stanley's fight with the policemen and greeted him with shouts of praise and applause.

Stanley struggled to stand and looked around for an empty seat. He found one next to a tall, blue-eyed, fair-haired man in jeans and a colorful shirt with the sleeves rolled up.

"I'm Alexey," said the man, offering Stanley a firm handshake. "You're a hero. But what you did, that's resisting the police. You hit two of them. There might be some serious trouble. If you don't have a lawyer, our foundation can help you."

"Alexey is the director of an anticorruption foundation," explained another man with a neat black beard.

"Thanks, I'm represented by a firm from Zurich," replied Stanley, "Raphael, Raphael und Raphael. One of the oldest firms in Europe. The first Raphael founded it back in the sixteenth century." Stanley couldn't shake his narcotic high.

"So you're Swiss?" Alexey asked enthusiastically. "You're with us?"

"No, American," said Stanley, examining his throbbing nose and the thick bump on the back of his head. "Do you need foreigners that badly?"

"No, I'm sure we'll manage on our own. The main thing for you is not to do business with our corrupt officials."

Stanley snorted.

"I'm afraid we'll have to agree to disagree on that one—I am, actually."

"So then why did you…"

"I don't like watching girls get their arms broken. Or anyone else, for that matter. But I may have gone a little far."

"Russia will be free!" Alexey said in a quiet voice, but everyone in the bus, which was already moving, making frequent turns, repeated after him: "Russia will be free!"

"Who has the power?" the fair-haired leader shouted.

"We have the power!" the rest of the detainees responded.

"What do you do?" Alexey asked him.

"Private banking." Stanley imagined the results if he were to tell the other passengers about the plan to send billions of dollars out of Russia via diplomatic mail. The idea was so funny that he forgot all about his nose, his head, and his bruised knee.

"What's funny?" asked Alexey. "You don't believe that Russia will be free?"

"The thing is," Stanley began, settling into his seat, "freedom is a constant value. It's just the number of people who have access to it that changes. In Russia, the US, Burkina Faso, even the Hebrides, wherever the hell they are. The measurement of freedom is the same. Not many people have freedom in Russia at the moment, and I doubt something will change to dramatically increase the number that possess it. Maybe there's not enough freedom for everyone, and I'm afraid that may only get worse."

"I don't agree with you!" Alexey was close to outrage. "And I'm prepared to argue that—"

But he didn't have the chance. The bus stopped at a police station, the doors opened, and they were ordered to get out.

"Where are we?" Stanley asked Alexey in a whisper.

"The Basmanny District police station. They usually bring protesters here. If they have room. They can take you anywhere, as far up as Khoroshevo-Mnevniki."

Stanley pulled out his smartphone, and Biryuza answered his call right away. Stanley told him that he would be in a common cell with the rest of the temporary detainees, and told him the name of the police station.

"Stop messing around, Stanley!" Biryuza exclaimed, taking it for a joke. "Are you still high or something? Do you want more coke? I'll have it sent over!"

"I'm going to get some more cops in a minute," said Stanley. "I got into a fight with them. I might…"

The duty officer saw Stanley talking on the phone.

"Put that one in a separate cell!" he ordered. "Resisting arrest, violence against law enforcement officers. You're doing time for this!" and the officer told him to surrender his phone.

Stanley complied without any resistance. He was led down a hallway and locked in a narrow, high-ceilinged cell. Stanley lowered himself onto the hard boards of the trestle bed, then lay down, and closed his eyes.

The world spun continuously, and he was desperately thirsty. On top of everything else, the pain in the hand he'd smashed into the policeman's helmet grew worse by the minute.

Stanley thought that this was an excellent chance for Biryuza, who didn't like him very much, and thought he was too soft for serious business, to get rid of Stanley for good. All he'd have to do is wait for them to type up their report—policemen work the same all over the world—and at that point, it would be very difficult to undo.

But Biryuza didn't use his chance. No more than fifteen minutes later, the door to his cell opened wide. A police colonel stood on the threshold, holding Stanley's smartphone, an ingratiating smile on his face.

"Mr. McKnight!" said the colonel. "There has been a terrible mistake! A misunderstanding. Please accept our deepest apologies. You're free to go. Officers will take you to your hotel. I hope you don't have any complaints."

"No, no," Stanley said, standing. "Not at all! On the contrary, I'm happy to pass on my recommendation of your department as an example of courteous and proper police officers."

The colonel's smile turned sour.

"That won't be necessary," he said. "We'll get along, somehow, on our own, without recommendations."

"As you say!"

Stanley got his smartphone back, and when he passed the bars of the common cell, he saw Alexey again. The other man waved to him, and the rest of the detainees joined in.

"Come again!" said Alexey. "You may not believe it, but soon all the crooks and thieves in Russia will end up in jail. Not us, but them!"

"I believe it!" Stanley waved goodbye and thought that he could give this activist, right here in this police station, the names of several crooks that would take his breath away. "I'm sure of it!"

He walked out of the police station and lit a cigarette. A police car was parked in front of him, its lights flashing. He got in, the car switched into drive, the gates opened, and the car drove onto the street. On that side of the gate, he saw a shiny Gelendvagen SUV. Shamil was sitting next to the driver, and saluted Stanley when their gazes met.

CHAPTER 27

McKNIGHT DIDN'T REALIZE JUST HOW tired he was until he reached his room.

When he walked in he kicked off his shoes, threw his jacket onto the banquette, and unbuttoned the cuffs of his shirt. He opened the minibar in the living room.

The first thing he saw was a small bottle of Russian vodka. Stanley unscrewed the top and sniffed the contents, but his broken, cocaine-ravaged nose failed to distinguish any scents.

He tossed a couple cubes of ice into a glass, poured three fingers of vodka, shook the ice around, and took a healthy sip.

Blood from his split lip dripped into the glass while he drank. Stanley twirled the glass in the light, watching the blood mix slowly with the vodka. "Not bad. A real Bloody Mary."

Just then, he sensed the presence of someone else in his room. He looked around and picked up a tall, heavy vase by the neck, dumping out a whimsical bouquet of wildflowers.

Walking quietly, Stanley moved toward the bedroom, but something stopped him. It was the sound of running water from the bathroom.

Was he in the wrong room? Had someone broken in here to take a shower? Stanley had heard of hot water being turned off in Moscow for infrastructure repairs. Maybe they were doing that in expensive hotels now too?

After the day he'd had, nothing would surprise him, but it wouldn't make sense for his room to have water, if another room didn't.

He gripped the vase tighter, and pushed the bathroom door open. In the white tub with clawed lion's paws for feet, a woman sat in a mound of bubbles.

A beautiful woman. Her hair was gathered into a bun, and she held a wine glass in one hand, a long, thin cigarette in the other.

"Don't just stand there staring, Stanley!" the woman said, taking a sip of wine. "I've been waiting an hour for someone to come and give me a towel. Yes, it's me, your wife, Christine."

Stanley couldn't believe his own eyes. Was this still an effect of the drugs, from the blow to the head he'd taken? Christine? Here? How?

Christine seemed to read his mind.

"I got a check from you. You're so old-fashioned. A check! But it was a bit larger than the previous one. So, you're moving up in the world. I called you at the bank to thank you, but your secretary Barbara, she has such a raspy voice, said that you were on a business trip in Moscow. I bought a ticket and got a visa the same day with the help of your bank, and then I was on the plane."

"That simple?"

"Well, yes, I am your wife, if you recall? Hand me a towel!"

Stanley's hands felt clumsy as he picked a towel from the top of the stack.

"That's too little, my love. But it'll do! I got a taxi, and they checked my passport at reception. They were hesitant at first. They were worried that I would make a scene if you brought some Russian hooker home. Were you planning on bringing a Russian hooker here? Admit it, Stan!"

Christine rose from the foam. Stanley had always found his wife's figure amazing. How could she stay in such fantastic shape without ever going to the gym or doing any sports? Christine got out of the tub and came close to him, leaving a wet trail on the dark-blue floor.

"So, were you planning on bringing back a hooker, after all? Or are you involved in a serious affair with some Russia banker? I saw a beautiful Russian woman on the news, a member of parliament, with a slender neck and full lips."

"No, I had no such plans."

"Oh, Stan, you've always been such a nerd! 'I had no such plans.'" Christine mimicked his voice very well. "I wouldn't have caused a scene. I would just have knocked her teeth out; that's all."

211

The towel's knot loosened, and it slipped to the floor. His wife's stiff pink nipples pressed into Stanley's chest. Christine wrapped her arm around his neck, running her hands through his hair. Her other hand went to the zipper of his pants.

"What's this on your head?"

"That's from a police baton."

"And is that what's got you so turned on?" Christine kissed him, her tongue slipping into his mouth.

Stanley felt Christine's hand reach its goal. He was full of desire.

"Stan! I need you!"

"Wait," he said. "Let me take a shower, I got so sweaty today."

"You've always been an idiot, Stan! There's nothing a woman likes better than the smell of her man."

Christine pulled down his underwear with his pants.

"Oh my! As if I'd let any Russian whores get their hands on this! Come here!"

The ringing phone woke him the next morning. The caller was tenacious. Stanley opened his eyes and looked around. He was in bed alone—the night before, Christine, her appearance in the bath, their night—it must all have been a dream.

"Yes," he finally answered. "McKnight."

"Stanley, my dear, why haven't you been answering? Is everything okay?" Lagrange was clearly concerned, if he was calling this early. Stanley looked at the clock—it was only 9:00 AM in Moscow.

"Oh, hi, Pierre. Everything's fine."

"You were supposed to call yesterday. We were worried—how did everything go?"

"Everything went perfectly. We're in complete agreement. All that's left are some technical details."

"Who did you meet with?"

"A girl with a duck…"

"I don't get it! Stanley! Hello?"

"Just a joke, never mind. I met with very high-level people. The highest. I'll be back in Zurich today. I'll give you the details in person."

"So I can tell Jean-Michel that everything's going smoothly?"

"You can and you should. Sorry for not calling."

"No worries, it happens. We'll see you soon!"

Stanley hung up and got out of bed. He didn't see any of Christine's things in the room. He looked at the pillow—she always left strands of her hair behind. The pillowcase was clean. Had it really been just a dream? Or was it someone else who he imagined was Christine? Maybe it had been Mila? Yes, Mila was that persistent, stubborn, and insatiable. Stanley thought again that Mila would only bring him trouble. She was a threat in and of herself.

He got a bottle of Coke from the minibar, and downed it all. Breakfast of champions.

Through the half-open door, he saw the curtain on the balcony waving. Still naked, Stanley walked out. Christine was there, reclining in a low chair, a sheet draped over her, with a glass of juice and a cigarette.

"Did you think you'd dreamed me?" she asked.

"Good morning," McKnight said, lowering himself into the chair next to her.

"Good morning, Stan. You have a lovely waiter—he brought coffee and croissants without me even asking. Shall I pour you a cup?"

"No, thank you. I did think I'd dreamed you. I never thought you were so impulsive."

"I seemed too ordinary for that? Boring?"

"Not boring. It's just…you've gradually become—how should I put it? Do you remember, years ago, you said that we would be different. We would break free from the routine?"

"I remember."

"And then you started to get stuck in that routine yourself. I know, my mom." He paused when he saw Christine's face darken. "But we only talked about why that happened to her, where all our money had gone and how to pay our student loans. About where we should move and how to get a good mortgage."

"I remember that, yes."

"I'm serious…I love you, Christine, but I can't live like that, the way we were living in San Francisco. That's why I went to London, then Zurich. I miss you, but…"

"You always have a 'but'! It makes me crazy! Any conversation with you, there's a 'but'!"

"Don't get angry, Christine," Stanley asked. "Let's get cleaned up, have some breakfast, and go take a walk. I have a flight to Zurich this evening."

"Is Zurich really more fun than San Francisco?"

"No, Zurich is as boring as plain oatmeal, but I've got a very interesting job. I didn't have that at home."

"I thought we would spend a couple of days together."

"I can't, honey. I've got a really important deal going on. I'm sorry! Next week you're going to get a check double the one before…"

"You think I'm here because of money?"

"Of course not." Stanley rose and lit a cigarette. The Kremlin was in front of him, covered in light fog. Cars flew down Okhotny Ryad.

"When's your flight?"

"We have time to take a walk and have lunch," said Stanley. "But let's not order golden mackerel. My childhood dreams have let me down."

PART FOUR:
THE MAGNIFICENT FIVE

CHAPTER 28

S TANLEY STOOD ON THE SCORCHING runway in the suburbs of East Berlin.

The airfield was previously run by the Soviet army, which left enormous hangars and ugly outbuildings when they withdrew after the reunification of Germany.

Several years ago, some crazy rich people bought the airfield to host raves and dance music festivals. They set up a stage on the runway, then immediately went bankrupt, and a group of serious businessmen bought it from them. Now it was an airfield for private planes, with a glass air traffic control tower rising above the old Soviet structures that may have retained their former, unappealing exterior, but had been completely renovated within.

McKnight was in a light-gray suit and old-fashioned straw hat with a wide band, which he had discovered by chance in one of the hangars, and was now wearing for some relief from the heat.

He rocked back and forth from heel to toe, sipping occasionally from a water bottle.

The dispatcher had already told him that the plane from Moscow was delayed, and suggested he wait in the shade or relax in the bar, but McKnight stubbornly remained in the hot sun.

Not so long ago, Stanley had waited for this same plane from Moscow in a Zurich airfield. That plane had been carrying bags with $200 million in cash, and plastic bins filled with gold bars.

McKnight had tried to remind Lagrange that he, McKnight, held a fairly high position at the bank, that he had a great deal of other responsibilities, that someone else, someone with more experience in this type of work, could handle cash transit services to the bank vault. But Lagrange had growled suddenly.

"There's a Russian expression I've heard—'If you like to go sledding, learn to like pulling the sled back uphill!' You get me, McKnight? You like your nice tax-free bonuses and an unrestricted corporate credit card. But other things, like transferring money in person and the like, which ensures your financial well-being, you see as beneath your dignity. Is that right?"

"No, that's not right. Not beneath my dignity at all, but you could have replaced me with someone else for this job. I had some documents I needed to prepare for other Russian clients."

"We don't have any clients more important than Gagarin now. What are you talking about, McKnight? Your other clients have a pitiful few million dollars, and this is billions on the table. Come on, McKnight! Who would you suggest take your place? Bernard? He'd shit himself out of panic. Someone from our team? They'd cut you out of the relationship with Gagarin, while informing on us to the authorities at the same time. So shut up and get your ass over to the airfield!"

Lagrange was more or less correct, of course, but Stanley didn't like his tone. He'd cast suspicious glances at Stanley the whole time, gesticulated too wildly.

They had decided to send the diplomatic postal shipments to different European cities so as not to arouse suspicion. Everything had gone smoothly in Zurich. Here in Berlin, they had three armored trucks waiting for the cargo.

Stanley had had to travel with this convoy the whole way from Zurich to Berlin, in one of the escort cars instead of his own. The driver, the director of the bank's armored transport service, didn't say a single word the entire way. This suited Stanley quite well, actually, and he spent the trip dozing in the back seat.

McKnight finally received word that the plane from Moscow was preparing to land. He tossed the empty water bottle into the yellowed grass and stepped into the shade by the hangar, while the trucks and escort vehicles emerged to meet the plane. The transport director silently opened the back door of his car, and Stanley jumped in.

The plane appeared in the sky and began to descend, its outline shimmering in the hot sky. When the plane's wheels touched down onto tarmac a helicopter appeared over the airfield, and gradually, as if unwillingly, lowered its height, and landed at the far end of the runway, where the plane was now heading.

The plane stopped and lowered a ramp; several guards ran down, carrying machine guns.

Biryuza stepped out of the helicopter, and ran, bent over, to the escort car that had also just come to a full stop.

"Hi." Biryuza nodded to McKnight. "How was the trip?"

"Forget the pleasantries, Anton!" Stanley said, settling his sunglasses on his nose. "Where do you need me to sign?"

Biryuza took out a leather folder containing several sheets of paper.

"Here, here, and here. And on this page as well. I'd wait till my people have transferred the cargo to yours."

"Okay, I'll wait. Why didn't you come on the plane? Or did you come all the way from Moscow like this, plane and helicopter flying together?"

"You know a helicopter couldn't match the speed of a plane. I'm coming from Berlin. I had some business here to attend to."

One of the guards who had flown in with the cargo walked over to McKnight and Biryuza. He unlocked the handcuff on his wrist and handed Biryuza a flat, narrow, briefcase together with the handcuff key. Biryuza signed a form and gave it back to the guard, then passed the briefcase over to Stanley, handing over another form as well.

"Diamonds. Worth about 250 million. Shall I open it?"

"I can't tell a real diamond from a fake," said McKnight. "But we trust each other, don't we? Give it to me. I'll sign."

"First, the handcuff." Biryuza snapped it on Stanley's left wrist. It was wet on the inside, and Stanley shuddered in disgust—the guard could have wiped his sweat off, at least.

McKnight signed the form, and Biryuza carelessly stuffed it into the inside pocket of his jacket.

"Let's not forget about the key," Biryuza said, giving it to Stanley, "And don't lose it!"

"Even if I did, I have to believe that one of the guards at the bank could open it."

The head of the bank's transport service came over to McKnight and Biryuza, and told them that everything was ready, and that he was to collect some important documents in Berlin at Laville's request. There were a lot of these documents, so, first of all, he was taking two armored trucks, and second of all, Stanley would have to travel in the cab of one of the trucks.

"I don't know anything about that," Stanley said. "I'll have to call for confirmation."

"I doubt you'll be able to get through to Monsieur Laville," the director said, frowning, "But if you insist…"

"Come on, Stanley!" Biryuza said, clapping a hand on McKnight's shoulder. "Take a ride in the truck. It's no less comfortable, and a lot safer. If someone does decide to attack, however…"

"I hope you're joking," said Stanley.

"Of course, of course! Go with God." Biryuza made the sign of the cross over Stanley. "Don't worry about a thing. Especially since you're riding with our guys, in two Mercedes G-Class escorts."

McKnight looked around, and saw Gagarin's guards standing next to two Jeeps, all ready to go.

Biryuza shook Stanley's hand and walked briskly back to the helicopter.

McKnight walked over to the truck loaded with money and gold. The weapons-laden guards were already in the back with the doors locked.

McKnight opened the heavy door of the cab and buckled himself in next to the driver.

The whole time, the sharp corner of the briefcase full of diamonds was digging into his chest. The driver opened the compartment between their two seats and pulled out a gun in a holster. The holster was on a shoulder strap that could be worn under a jacket.

"This a Glock 22," said the driver. "Fifteen-round magazine. Do you know how to use it?" He asked the question with a bit of a smirk.

"I could teach you a thing or two," Stanley replied coldly, checking the clip and cocking the hammer before putting the safety on. "I went to shooting courses by Blackwater, pretty much military training."

"Good for you!" the driver snorted.

McKnight stepped out of the vehicle and tried to take his jacket off, but the briefcase got in the way. He had to take off the handcuff, and he spent a panicked ten minutes searching for the key until he remembered sticking it in his shirt pocket. Then he put on the shoulder holster, refastened the handcuff, and got back in, placing his jacket over his knees. Throughout this process, he couldn't help noticing how, after all the alcohol and cocaine, his hands shook badly. He would more than likely miss a target a dozen steps away now. And he'd never shot at a person before, but he knew they hadn't given him a Glock to go after some rabbits.

"Let's go!" he said to the driver.

They didn't run into any difficulties leaving the airfield. Gagarin's guards in the Mercedes G-wagons kept a little behind them, but when the armored truck merged onto the highway, first one, then the other, caught up, one pulling ahead of their truck, one falling into position behind, continually rotating positions, and thereby cutting off access to their truck for any cars moving in the same direction. The driver noticed their maneuvering before Stanley did, and pursed his lips approvingly, giving Stanley the thumbs-up.

"These guys know what they're doing," he said.

"How about you watch the road, instead?" muttered Stanley in English.

"I'm sorry, Herr McKnight. What was that?"

"Yes, they do, indeed," said Stanley in German.

He closed his eyes. This hangover was killing him. Without opening them again, he asked if there was any water.

"Of course, Herr McKnight! Under your seat."

Stanley fumbled with the cap of the bottle and greedily drank about half of it in one go. Then he remembered that he was supposed to send Lagrange a message on Telegram that they had left.

His boss was not happy with the delayed reply. Stanley got a lot of irritated comments and instructions, and then Lagrange asked for a general report.

"What exactly do you want to know?" asked Stanley.

"Did you notice anything suspicious? That's what I want to know!"

"We're driving down the autobahn. We have a drive of about fifteen hours. I'm with one of the three trucks. I'm sitting in the cab, wearing my seatbelt, and I have a suitcase full of diamonds handcuffed to my wrist. A gun under my arm. Nothing suspicious here, boss!"

"Where are the other trucks?"

"They went on to Berlin."

"What the hell? You should have stopped them! They should have come with you, as potential cover!"

"They were following Laville's orders."

"Laville? Well, then…okay, Stanley, I'll be waiting for your next update!"

Stanley hung up and put the telephone in his pocket, suddenly drowsy.

He fell asleep, and dreamed that he was walking down Bahnofstrasse. A tall, gray-haired man walked toward him, his coat buttoned all the way up to his neck despite the warm, sunny day. The man was pale, wearing tinted glasses and carrying his hat in his hand, showing off his perfectly coiffed hair. Stanley's neighbor was walking next to him, her hand under his arm, from which he gathered that this was her boring husband. Just then, he finally remembered their last name, a terribly long German name that meant something, he was sure, but it was beyond his rudimentary grasp of the language—Himmelstossel.

When he woke, he recalled with regret that his neighbor had been avoiding him ever since their night of Chablis and oysters. At first he had wondered why—maybe it had been his suggestion that they eat their seafood in the nude, or the way that he had placed the oysters on her stomach, dressing their delicious flesh with lemon juice and licking it all up before moving on to every intimate part of her body.

The real explanation was more banal: her lawyer husband had found Stanley's lighter, which had fallen out of his pocket, in a fold of their carpet. She had tried to justify herself, come up with some kind of explanation, but Herr Himmelstossel saw right through her.

She admitted the truth, and he made her promise that this was the last time. She told Stanley, when they encountered each other in the underground parking garage, that she meant to keep her word. When he asked how many times she had made similar promises, she blushed and admitted that she had lost count herself. They even had grandchildren, it turned out.

McKnight fell back to sleep and went back into the same dream. The couple had passed him and were entering a restaurant. Stanley turned back one last time, and his neighbor looked up, right at him. Her gaze steady on his, she grinned and gave him a wink.

McKnight woke up. The road ahead of him was straight and smooth. The driver sat, staring straight ahead, with two hands on the wheel.

"What does Himmelstossel mean in German?" Stanley asked.

"I'm sorry?"

"How would you translate the last name Himmelstossel into English?"

"That's what it would be, Himmelstossel."

"Okay, but it's made up of two words. What does *himmel* mean?"

"Sky, Herr McKnight."

"Excellent. And *stossel*?"

"A lever. No…hm, ah, a pistil! You know, like in a flower."

"Sky pistil! Nice."

"But there's no such thing, Herr McKnight."

"Yes, well—never mind about that."

Their trip in the cab of the truck was unbearably exhausting. McKnight drowsed several more times, but would wake up in a cold sweat with a stiff neck, tormented by thirst. He would drink the warm water, look out at the road, adjust his shoulder holster, and fall asleep again.

While he was officially in charge of this operation, Gagarin's people were running it in practice. When Stanley asked the driver to stop at the next gas station, for example, he got on the radio to ask the guard in charge of their convoy. He then told Stanley that they weren't planning to stop for another forty-five minutes.

"Tell him I won't last that long," Stanley replied.

The driver passed on his message, then relayed the reply, that Stanley would have to wait.

"These Russians are such pigs," the driver said after switching off his radio. "He said I should tell you to go ahead and piss yourself! This isn't the first time I've transported their valuables, and they always act like they're the masters of everything. Where does that come from, anyway?"

"It's a common phenomenon when people start off poor and begin to get rich," answered Stanley.

"You think so? It's a rule of life?" The driver was clearly ready to philosophize.

McKnight shrugged. He didn't want to have a conversation with the driver. He wanted a bathroom, a cup of coffee, and something to eat.

They finally pulled into a big rest stop with a gas station on one end and a small shopping center with several fast-food restaurants.

Gagarin's people wouldn't let Stanley get out of the car at the gas station. He only managed to jump out after the armored car had parked in the far corner of the lot next to one of their escort Jeeps. Two guards waited outside his door with expressionless faces. One sat in his seat and slammed the door shut behind him, and another, wearing all black, followed Stanley toward the shopping center.

But they'd only gone a couple dozen feet when the guard's radio beeped.

"Yes, sir!" the guard answered, falling a step back. "What? A permit? I'll ask!"

He ran up to McKnight, who was pretending not to have understood the conversation, and tapped him on the shoulder.

"Mister, do you have permit to carry gun?" the guard asked in broken English. "Permit?"

"Permit? Permit for what? To go to the bathroom? To drink coffee?"

He intentionally answered in a slight Texan drawl, the hardest accent for foreigners to understand, imitating Christine's uncle.

The guard unexpectedly managed to understand him.

"To carry gun, mister!" he said to Stanley, and cursed into the radio: "Goddamn it, this shithead doesn't even speak English, he sounds like a barking dog, Vlad."

Stanley realized he'd forgotten about the gun tucked under his arm. He'd have to go back to the truck. He took off his jacket, unbuttoned the holster, and gave it to the guard who'd been sitting in his seat a moment ago.

"Stay right on him, Alexey," said Vlad, the second guard. "He's either hungover, or he's on something. Keep an eye on him!"

"Understood!" the first guard said. He put his hand on Stanley's shoulder and said, "Come with me, mister. Let's go!"

They walked toward the shopping center, Alexey several steps behind him the whole way. Stanley's immediate destination was the toilet. Alexey followed. Stanley was about to enter a stall, but Alexey gestured for him to wait. He examined every stall, but the bathroom was empty except for them, and gestured again for Stanley to go ahead.

"Are you coming in there with me?" asked Stanley.

Alexey pretended not to understand and turned away, leaning against the wall.

Stanley sat down and got out his smartphone, calling Lagrange.

"Pierre," Stanley began as soon as Lagrange answered. "This is completely out of control! First, they give me a gun, and now Gagarin's thug is following me everywhere. He's dressed like a commando. Everyone is staring at us! You should have at least warned me!"

"Calm down. Calm down, McKnight." Lagrange's voice was even, unperturbed. "What would be different if I had warned you? You would still have resented someone telling you what to do. Please, relax. Where are you now?"

"I have no idea." Stanley thought that Lagrange might be right. Maybe he should accept the situation and not try to throw his weight around. "We're at some rest stop. I'm sitting on the toilet, with a bodyguard right outside. I slept most of the way so far."

"Excellent! Have a drink, maybe a beer, eat some greasy German sausage, and sleep some more. We're all waiting for you here! Call in an hour, unless you're sleeping—then I'll call you. Bye, Stanley!"

McKnight left the stall. Alexey was talking on his mobile phone, explaining to some girl why it would be impossible to buy her what she wanted, since they were traveling through Germany without stopping, and the prices were nearly two times higher in Switzerland. Every other word was a curse, but he wasn't, to Stanley's surprise, using them to hurt or attack the girl. He simply added swear words into his speech as logical connections or to express emotions—surprise or happiness.

Stanley dried his hands and pushed the door open with his shoulder. Alexey followed, and Stanley strolled down the main corridor of the building, which was lined with small shops. At the far end, he saw the signs of fast-food restaurants and stalls, but just as he was getting ready to order from a Nordsee, Alexey's radio came to life.

The guard answered. "Yes. Well, he sat on the damned toilet for twenty minutes. Okay, okay, we're on our way."

"Mister," he said, elbowing Stanley. "Hustle! Got to go! It's time!"

"Okay, sure." Stanley nodded.

He ordered fish and chips and a Coke. The girl smiled at him and started putting together his order.

"You want anything?" Stanley asked Alexey. "I'm buying."

Alexey just swallowed and shook his head.

"Up to you," said Stanley, but asked the girl to double his order anyway.

The fish was a bit dry and oversalted to Stanley's taste. The driver of the armored truck, though, was touched by Stanley's gesture, and had devoured most of his food by the time they were back on the autobahn. Stanley finished his Coke and realized that he was sitting on the holster with the gun inside. He tossed it onto the floor at his feet; the driver shook his head in disapproval. Stanley tipped the hat down over his face and fell asleep. Lagrange called him every hour, and each time that Stanley answered, he told his boss he was sleeping, even if he wasn't, that everything was fine, and that there was nothing to worry about.

CHAPTER 29

S TANLEY LOOKED OUT THE WINDOW groggily to see that they must have passed the border into Switzerland some time ago. When he woke again, it was evening, and they were entering Geneva.

Biryuza was waiting for them at the entrance to the bank vault. He got out of a black Mercedes and shook Stanley's hand.

"Everything okay?" Biryuza asked in Russian. "How was the drive?"

"Everything's great, Anton!" Stanley answered, also in Russian. "It's been a while since I slept for so long in such an uncomfortable position."

"Well, we've got something here worth a little discomfort," Biryuza said with a nod to the armored truck. The bank guards were climbing out, rubbing their stiff legs.

Alexey was listening to their conversation, staring at Stanley in open astonishment.

"Excuse me, Anton," said Stanley, enjoying the expression on the guard's face, "we need to get this unloaded as fast as we can. I'll call Lagrange!"

But Lagrange appeared in person, without any advance notice. He exuded an air of deep satisfaction. He was literally beaming. Instead of their usual handshake, he embraced Stanley, slapping him on the back.

"I'm proud of you, McKnight! Excellent work!" Lagrange exclaimed. "I couldn't have handled it—fifteen hours in a truck! You're a hero! Right, Anton?"

"Yes, indeed!" agreed Biryuza.

The transport driver in charge asked Stanley to sign a special form. Stanley's hands shook a little.

"Do you still need me for anything?" Stanley asked him. "If not, I'd like to get going."

"No, we've got it from here," the other man replied.

"Stanley, I'm eating at Brasserie Lipp tonight. I hope you'll join me. Anton, what about you?"

Biryuza shook his head, explaining that he was flying back to Moscow that night, in about two and a half hours. Stanley also declined—what he wanted more than anything in the word was to take a bath, and then have a real sleep, in a good bed and clean sheets.

"Which hotel did you put me in?" he asked Lagrange.

"The Beau-Rivage," Lagrange said, clearly disappointed to lose his dining companion. "It's at 13 Quai du Mont-Blanc. It's not far from here, but I'll call a car for you."

"Thank you, Pierre! That's all right, I'll walk." Stanley shook hands with both men. "I feel like I've forgotten how to. See you, Alexey! Don't be cheap. Get something nice for your girl!" Pulling his hat further down on his head, Stanley headed toward the exit.

The façade of the hotel was extraordinary, richly decorated with graceful columns and elaborate fluting, miniature balconies, delicately crafted bay windows, and numerous other adornments.

The tall doors opened as Stanley approached, and he found himself in the cozy interior of the lobby. Water burbled in a fountain, and a fire blazed in a fireplace at the far end, despite the warm summer evening. Stanley went over to the desk.

"I believe you have a room for..."

"For Mr. McKnight, sir?" The clerk was lean and dark-skinned, with brilliant white teeth.

"How did you guess? I had no idea I was so famous," Stanley joked.

"I received a call from a Mr. Lagrange just before you arrived," the clerk answered with a smile. "Here is your card. You're in room 404. Would you like anything sent up? Dinner? We could also reserve a table for you in our French restaurant. Perhaps you prefer Thai food? Or—"

"Thank you, you're very kind," Stanley retrieved the card from the polished surface of the desk with some difficulty. "I'll call you if I need anything."

"Anytime, sir! Anything you need, anything at all!"

The lift moved swiftly and soundlessly upward. The carpet in the corridor muffled the sounds of his steps. Stanley slid the card into the reader at his door and turned the handle to enter.

He came in, took off his hat, and hung it at the corner of the door, and only then noticed the man stretched out on a couch in front of the fireplace.

The man's pose was languid, entirely at ease, his feet resting on one soft armrest of the couch, and a large pillow under his head. The knot of his tie had been loosened, and his jacket hung over the back of a chair. Narrow glasses rested on the tip of his nose, and he was reading some papers. He looked up at Stanley with a smile, tapping the end of a pencil against his teeth.

"Don't be frightened, McKnight," he said, without moving. "Although this is, I suppose, breaking and entering, you're in no danger. No need to call the staff for help."

He tossed his papers and pencil onto the floor and rose lightly, holding out his hand.

McKnight recognized him. It was the blond man who he'd thought was following him in Zurich. So, he'd been right about that, after all.

"Who are you, and what do you want?" Stanley asked, his voice loud in the quiet room.

"I'll tell you everything, McKnight. Don't rush, and don't make a scene. There's no need."

"I'll decide what I need," replied Stanley. "Answer my question, or..."

"Or you'll call for help? I wouldn't advise it." The other man let his hand fall back.

"Why should I call for help?" Stanley shifted position slightly to one side. "I'll throw you out myself."

"You're simply tired and irritated," the blond said peacefully. "Unsurprising after such a long drive, all the way from Berlin, let alone in the cab of an armored truck. And under the watchful eye of some Russian morons."

"How did you...damn it! Listen..."

"You can call me Frank. I just happened to have a second key to your room and decided to have a talk with you. Especially since you want to talk to someone yourself, don't you, Stanley? Can I call you Stanley?"

Stanley took a deep breath, held the air in his lungs, and let it out in one rush. Then he walked around the blonde, almost knocking his shoulder into him, heading toward the minibar.

"Sure," said Stanley, debating between vodka and whiskey. "Just not Stan, okay?"

He unscrewed the cap from the vodka bottle and drank down the contents in one gulp.

"Bravo, Stanley," said Frank. "You've learned a lot from your Russian friends. And not just how to drink vodka, I think."

"Who are you?"

"You're not going to offer me a drink?" asked Frank.

Stanley tossed him the bottle of Macallan, and Frank caught it in the air. Stanley took out his cigarette case and lit a cigarette.

"I won't offer you one," he said. "You're clearly an American, with a healthy lifestyle, gym membership, some kind of special diet? So. Who are you, Frankie, and what are you doing in my goddamn hotel room?"

Frank, in an obvious parody of Stanley, also emptied his minibar bottle in one go. Then he walked over to where his briefcase rested against the couch, and pulled out a full bottle of Macallan.

"I brought a gift. I know you like good scotch. How about we continue this conversation on the balcony?"

"Continue?" Stanley snorted. "We haven't even begun. Is Frank your real name?"

"We have already begun, Stanley, long ago. Grab some glasses, if you would. You have such a lovely view from your balcony! Some people sure do have it good. I usually get a room overlooking the alley."

Stanley picked up two glasses and followed Frank onto the balcony. He placed them on the railing, and Frank filled both, handing one to Stanley and keeping one for himself.

"My name really is Frank. Frank Dillon. I work for the US government." Frank took a drink. "I'm an expert in bank transactions and money laundering."

"The US government is in the money-laundering business? How about that!" Stanley took a drag on his cigarette, exhaling a thick stream that Frank had to wave away from his face.

"You can joke all you want, Stanley, but you know I didn't break into your hotel room just to say hi."

"Yeah, no kidding."

"No kidding, indeed, Stanley. This is quite serious. They only call me in for cases involving very, very large sums of money. Of very doubtful provenance. Such as the ones Viktor Gagarin is depositing in your bank. You're familiar with Gagarin. Are you not?"

"Hmm, it's not ringing a bell. I know there was a Russian cosmonaut by the name Gagarin, and there were some Russian princes with that name as well. What did you say his first name was again?"

Stanley took a drink from his glass. He was experiencing two conflicting states of consciousness simultaneously—on the one hand, an unusual lightness and clarity of mind, and on the other, a paralyzing fear. Terror, to be precise.

Who was this cold-eyed man standing next to him, pretending to enjoy the view of Lake Geneva? Who was he, really? Someone sent by Gagarin to test him, or maybe on the orders of his bank's security service? Or, the least pleasant option, was he actually from a government agency?

"Are you in the CIA?" asked Stanley, flicking his cigarette toward the night sky.

"Right away, he goes for the CIA!" Dillon laughed briefly. "A fine organization, with…"

"Excellent people, true professionals, patriots, and faithful democrats," Stanley continued. "Not in terms of adherence to a single party, but faithful servants of democracy as a whole, which our great country is implementing globally with an energy that could be put to better use."

"Not bad, Stanley, not bad. If I'm in need of an expert in the composition of, say, press releases, I'll keep you in mind. After all, you'll be looking for a new job soon. If you're lucky enough to stay out of jail after you leave your current position, that is. Otherwise, I'll look you up in about twenty years."

"Twenty years? For what? What am I supposed to have done?" Stanley tipped his empty glass toward Frank, and the other man filled it again.

"As of now, you've broken twelve federal laws, McKnight. You can, of course, continue down the same road, but I'd advise you to take a moment to consider what you're doing. It's not too late to stop."

"I spend my days in an office, doing small transactions for our richest clients, and I'm breaking laws by the dozen? Without knowing anything about it?" Stanley pulled out another cigarette and lit it.

"We've been watching you for a long time, Stanley. Even in Moscow. And we know that you visited the Russian Ministry of Foreign Affairs, we know that Viktor Gagarin upped his deposit in your bank to $10 billion, and we know why you went to Berlin and what you brought back with you to Geneva."

Frank paused, seemingly lost in thought. He sipped from his glass.

"Are you okay, Comrade Dillon?" asked Stanley.

"Fine! We know about your lover, Viktor Gagarin's wife. Mila, right? Her father is a high-ranking official in the presidential administration.

Mila's mother is the daughter of a former USSR defense minister. Here's an interesting fact for you—your lover's maternal uncle was the last CIA double agent in the KGB to be shot under Communist rule."

"Have you considered a career as a screenwriter, Frank? I think you'd go far," said Stanley.

"Writing up storylines and filling in all the details is actually my official job. I'll leave you my card."

"Not your business card? Maybe you are CIA, after all? I'm just trying to understand, here."

Dillon only shook his head in reply.

"Your only way out of this is to cooperate with us."

"But I've never written screenplays, Frank! You heard what I can do— press releases, sure. But not scripts. I'm no good at composing dramatic storylines. Especially not for your audience."

"You put on a good show, McKnight, but it's time for intermission. The only way you can help yourself is by working with us and giving us the information we need."

"As the Russians say, 'Repent, and they'll shorten your sentence'!" Stanley said in Russian.

"I don't quite catch the meaning," Frank said, finishing his whiskey and pouring two fingers into the glass. "Is that something you heard from your new Russian friends?"

"From my great-grandfather. Or grandfather. You probably read in my dossier that I come from a Russian family."

"I just did, as a matter of fact. There it is, next to your couch. Want a look?"

"No, thanks."

"Up to you. At any rate, your roots aren't important in this matter. Listen, Stanley—"

"You know what, Frank, it's been a long day. Some particularly aggravating clients, a couple of meetings. I was getting ready to take a bath and get a good night's sleep, and you show up with your twenty years in prison. How about you get out of my room? Now!"

Frank calmly drank the rest of his whiskey and set the bottle down on the floor of the balcony.

"Of course, Mr. McKnight, of course! I won't bother you anymore. I'll leave you the bottle, please enjoy."

Dillon put on his jacket and dug around in an inner pocket.

"Here's my card. Call me any time."

He opened the door.

"And be careful with the wives of criminals, McKnight! Some jealous Russian might slit your throat over it."

The door closed. Stanley walked over to the table where the other man had left his card. There was no CIA or US government emblem. The card read: "Frank Dillon. Creative Director. Universal Studios."

McKnight flipped the card over and read the handwritten note: "Call any time. Look forward to speaking with you soon!"

Stanley paced the room, drinking his whiskey. "Son of a bitch! This is the last thing I need right now!" He tucked the card into his pocket and got out his phone.

Lagrange was initially pleasantly surprised to hear that McKnight had reconsidered joining them for dinner, but soon sensed that something was wrong.

"We'll be happy to have you, Stan," said Lagrange, "but I don't like the sound of your voice. Did something happen?"

"I just need to talk to you right away, Pierre. But everything's fine, just fine!"

"Ok, then…we'll be expecting you."

McKnight hung up and rang the front desk clerk for a clean shirt and a taxi. The shirt right away and the taxi in twenty minutes.

The imperturbable clerk just asked what size and color shirt he would prefer.

Someone brought the shirt while Stanley was still in the shower. He emerged to find it draped over the same couch that Frank Dillon had been lying on.

He gave the shirt a shake, as if trying to cleanse it of some infectious disease Frank was carrying.

Stanley told the driver the name of the restaurant, and after a couple of turns and a bridge crossing, they were pulling up in front of it.

"Do you need a receipt, sir?" the driver asked.

"No," Stanley replied, handing him a hundred francs.

"Shall I wait for you?" the astonished driver asked, but Stanley had already slammed the door shut behind him.

The maître d' gave an apologetic half bow as soon as Stanley walked in.

"I'm sorry, monsieur, but I'm afraid we don't have any tables available."

"I'm meeting a friend, table under the name of Monsieur Lagrange," said Stanley.

"Please follow me," said the maître d', turning swiftly and leading the way through the dining room.

Lagrange sat at the head of the table. Dino Bernasconi sat to his left, across from Andrea Kovalevich, her legs twined around each other as usual. The fourth chair was empty. Lagrange gave Stanley a friendly wave when he noticed him.

"Monsieur," said the maître d', bowing to Stanley, who slipped him a hundred-franc note.

"Nothing for me, thank you," Stanley told him and turned to his colleagues with a wide smile.

"We've been waiting for you, Stanley!" Lagrange gestured to the empty chair. "Have a seat, we've ordered a couple of seafood dishes and white wine."

Stanley shook Dino's hand, raised the back of Andrea's strong hand to his lips, and clapped Lagrange on the shoulder.

"I just need a word with you, Pierre!"

They stepped outside, a little away from the restaurant entrance.

Lagrange remained surprisingly calm during Stanley's recitation of Frank Dillon's visit to his hotel room. Stanley did leave some things out, however. That Dillon knew about his relationship with Mila for example. And that Dillon had left his card, and knew about their shipment of the cash, gold, and jewels.

Lagrange took Stanley by the arm, and led him around the corner into a side street. He took out a snuff box of cocaine.

"You need to calm down, my friend. Here, Stanley, do a bump, just a little, and don't worry about anything. Neither the Swiss police or the American agencies can do anything to you. They don't have any proof or any witnesses."

"No witnesses?" shouted Stanley. "He knows about our transactions with Gagarin. Where did he get that information? Either we have an informant, or Gagarin does. If they know something, they'll be able to find out everything."

"It won't matter if they do. They can know everything. They still won't be able to catch us. That's the way our business is set up. The way Swiss law is constructed. In our case, neither you nor I can be arrested. We have people who check the legality of incoming money, and all our transactions are conducted in accordance with the law. You want some coke?" Lagrange extended the snuff box toward Stanley.

Stanley took a long snort.

"They've tried to scare me too, you know," Lagrange said with a smile. "And nothing's ever come of it. Not once! Your guy didn't even tell you who he worked for. The ones who came to me showed me their official IDs, agent this and agent of that. And nothing! I told them to fuck off. And they went ahead and did just that."

"But you're not an American citizen, Pierre!" McKnight said, wiping his nose. "They wanted you as an informant. It was easier for you to get rid of them. But I've broken a dozen federal laws, according to this asshole, and they can arrest me for that wherever I am. I'm somewhat reluctant to spend twenty years in jail, crazy as that might sound."

"And you're not going to! I guarantee you that. Do you believe me?"

"I do, but—"

"No buts! You're not going to jail. Hang on. I'm going to call our chief of security, tell him what happened. Yes, I should be the one to make the call, and then we'll go do some serious drinking." Lagrange got out his telephone. "Just a minute, just a minute...hello! Yes, it's me..."

Lagrange stepped a few paces away. Stanley's head was buzzing. He felt that paralyzing fear beginning to dissipate. At the same time, no, he didn't believe Lagrange. He was too calm, too optimistic.

"What did you say his name was?" Lagrange was asking.

"Frank Dillon," Stanley replied, lighting a cigarette.

"Dillon, Frank Dillon," Lagrange repeated into the phone. "Yes, yes, of course."

Lagrange put his phone away and rested his hand on Stanley's shoulder.

"Everything's fine. They're going to figure out what's going on, who this joker is. Life will go back to normal, and the money's going to keep coming in."

"I don't need your money," Stanley whispered, starting off into the distance, exhausted.

"What did you say?"

"I said, I don't need your damned money," mumbled Stanley again.

Lagrange slapped him in the face, looked in his eyes, then slapped him again, shaking him by the shoulders.

"Wake up! Wake up, you American shithead! You fucking loser with your endless guilt. No, money doesn't make you happy. Okay, fine. But with money, you can buy any bitch you want. You know? The sweetest-looking bitch with the best legs in the entire world, and snort delicious fucking cocaine off her delicious smooth pussy! And I have never seen someone be unhappy snorting pure coke off some hot girl's smooth pussy. Maybe you have? Have you, motherfucker? Answer the fucking question, you dumbass American loser!"

McKnight shook his head silently, sighed deeply, then laughed, and snorted a little more coke.

"There you go! That's the Stanley I know and love." Lagrange let out a deafening laugh and slapped Stanley on the shoulder. "Let's go have a drink, it's going to be a good night."

They went back inside. Stanley ate a half-dozen oysters and ordered some tomato soup. He had several shots of Grey Goose vodka, and then moved on to bourbon.

"Nice shirt," Andrea whispered. When Stanley turned, her eyes were suddenly seemed very close and bottomless.

Stanley felt as if a veil was gradually dropping between him and everything else. He wasn't getting any drunker; he just couldn't stop talking. And he would lose his train of thought, jumping from topic to topic, either speaking too loudly, or softly enough that his companions had to ask him to repeat himself. The fear gradually left him. They ordered chocolate mousse for dessert, but Stanley couldn't eat his.

They all went back to the Beau-Rivage together; Lagrange had a room on the second floor there as well.

They had just sat down in Lagrange's room, where he was passing out cocaine again, when there was a knock at the door, and six girls came filing in. Stanley had been concentrating on the whiskey he was pouring, and looked up in surprise to find two girls sitting on either side of him.

"Part of your bonus!" Lagrange said with a wink.

Next thing he knew, Dino was dancing with a pretty blonde, comically bending his long legs. Three girls were tangled up together on the stairs, gradually tossing off articles of clothing. Stanley looked around for Andrea. He was thinking that ordering prostitutes with a female colleague present was a bit out of line when he realized that one of the women on the stairs was Andrea.

She was involved in a passionate kiss with an unusually lovely, light-complexioned black woman, unbuttoning the other girl's dress with her long fingers, which somehow reminded Stanley of Mila.

"Aren't you going to pour us a drink?" one of the girls asked Stanley.

"Of course, I am," said Stanley. When he tried to get up, though, he discovered that one of the girls had already unzipped his pants. Desire hit him like lightning. He tried to remember Dillon's face and couldn't. He got out a hundred-franc note, rolled it into a tube, and offered it to one of the girls. She leaned over the pile of cocaine on the table in front of them. The other girl slipped a cool hand into his underwear.

"This one's big," she said in Russian.

Stanley might have imagined that last part. He finished his drink in one swallow, listening to Andrea's moans as she passionately caressed her companions, and turned to the girl who had just inhaled a fat rail of cocaine.

"What's your name?" asked Stanley.

"What's your favorite name?" she replied, getting onto her knees in front of Stanley.

"I like all names."

"Well, that's my name." The girl smiled. "All names."

CHAPTER 30

S EVERAL DAYS AFTER THE FIRST shipment of Gagarin's cash and gold arrived in Zurich, on the eve of the trip to Berlin, Stanley and Lagrange were invited to Laville's home for dinner.

Lagrange assured Stanley that the invitation was a high honor. He, himself, had only been invited once, many years prior. As an expectant father, Laville had been living a fairly secluded life recently. He didn't visit his club, and barely spent any time in Geneva's restaurants. When the work day was over, he asked his staff not to disturb him at home, and dinners like the one to which McKnight and Lagrange were invited were practically a family affair. And Laville didn't simply invite his employees—he sent a helicopter to fetch them.

Stanley asked about the dress code, and initially regretted that decision.

"You look great, but the tux is a bit over-the-top," said Lagrange with a shake of the head, as Stanley exited the car. Lagrange was dressed elegantly, but less formally, in a tweed jacket, cravat, and pale-pink shirt. He kept up a running fashion commentary on the tuxedo all the way to the helicopter, until Stanley was heartily sick of it.

But as it happened, Lagrange was the one who looked out of place at their gathering. Laville was in formal evening wear, and his wife, Maria, a wide-eyed beauty with an indefinable air of sadness, concealed her pregnancy under the folds of an emerald Chanel gown.

The bankers were joined by an old friend of Laville's, the famous Polish film director Rajmund Lieblingsky.

Lieblingsky nodded silently to Stanley in greeting and shook his hand. He was a thin old man with disheveled gray hair. He reminded Stanley of Count Dracula from an old black-and-white movie.

"Jean-Michel has told me so much about you," Maria said, extending her slim hand in such a way that Stanley's only option was to bow over it.

"But I didn't tell you about Mr. McKnight's exquisite manners, my dear, since I didn't know, myself," said Laville, giving Stanley a friendly slap to the shoulder. He exchanged a firm handshake with Lagrange, and then offered everyone an aperitif. Stanley had vowed to go easy on the drinking, and only had two glasses of champagne.

Dinner was a feast, with several courses and many dishes, but Laville's wife excused herself after the soup, a pumpkin puree only served to her.

"Maria is having a difficult time with this pregnancy," Laville told them. "She thinks this child is taking away from her beauty. And the doctor is concerned with the results of her blood tests. But you know," Laville went on with a smug smile, "all my former wives had difficult pregnancies as well. And I came to the conclusion that I must be the reason why. Call me old-fashioned, but the man is always the root cause," Laville concluded adjusting the napkin on his lap.

"And what about that French saying: '*Cherchez la femme*'?" asked Lieblingsky.

"Ah, that's just for the sake of wit," said Lagrange. "The French love to drop a turn of phrase that makes everyone think. Not like the Russians. They don't have a single elegant saying. Everything is coarse, connected to hard labor or animalistic sex. Can you think of even a single Russian saying, McKnight?"

"Just the one you told me the other day," answered Stanley, covering his glass with his hand as Laville's butler was preparing to fill it with red wine.

"Oh?" Laville asked, looking to Stanley with a raised brow.

"'If you like to go sledding, learn to like pulling the sled back uphill,'" McKnight replied in Russian, then translated it to English.

"Well, judging from that proverb, Pierre is right," said Laville, taking a few sips of wine before setting his glass back down. "Now, of course, they're not carrying sleds, are they?" asked Laville with a half smile. "They've got bags of gold and suitcases full of cash instead. Remember, Lagrange, the last time someone transported cash and gold to us in those amounts?"

"How could I forget!" Lagrange swiped his mouth with a napkin, a sly look on his face. "It was the staff of Zaire's president, Marshal Mobutu Sese Seko Kuku Ngbendu wa za Banga."

Laville clapped his hands in delight. But Lagrange continued.

"Which can be translated from, if I'm remembering correctly, the Bantu language, as 'The great warrior Mobutu who goes from conquest to conquest, leaving a trail of fire in his path.'"

"And did he also send his deposits by diplomatic post?" asked McKnight, casting sidelong glances at Lieblingsky. Judging from Laville's reaction, however, they could speak freely in front of his Polish friend.

"No, they weren't quite so bold," Laville answered. "They didn't actually need any boldness, though. They simply stole from their people, and were never troubled by the slightest twinge of conscience. They believed that the unfortunate Bantu belonged to them, body and soul, and they didn't care what any international organizations or other countries had to say about it. They served a kleptocracy, unburdened by any compassion or moral restrictions or other such Western rubbish. Not too dissimilar from the current situation in Russia. Quite similar, actually."

"Come now, Jean-Michel," Lagrange objected with a smile. "They don't have the same level of poverty in Russia. Its citizens travel the world, run businesses, vacation in villas in Nice, and send their children to study in London, do they not?"

"Those differences are only quantitative," the Polish director broke in with a slight yawn. "How many Russians travel the world and don't live in poverty? Millions? No, maybe several hundred thousand. There were maybe fifteen hundred rich Zaireans. But qualitatively, there's no real difference. The same type of power. The same talk of greatness. Mobutu spoke about the glory of Zaire, the unique spirituality of the Zairean people, who starved so that he could live a life of unbelievable luxury. Same thing in Russia. The great, glorious history, the Russian soul. Lies, in both countries. Empty words!"

Stanley coughed.

"Did you find a bone, Mr. McKnight?" Laville shook his head. "My chef does sometimes make mistakes. But, in all seriousness, you wanted to ask, how is it that we can judge kleptocracies and still do business with them. Very easily, Mr. McKnight, very easily. We're cynics, and we have no principles. A principled banker is a nonsensical creature."

"Moreover, a principled banker is a dead banker!" added Lagrange.

Laville gave Lagrange a long look, swirling the wine in his glass.

"It's not a black-and-white world. More black-and-gray. After I graduated from Stanford, my father sent me to intern with my second cousin in Rome. He was a top manager at Banco Ambrosiano, and he was a very pious man who also served the church. After three years of Americanization, I was a little surprised by what I found at that bank," Laville said with a smile, "but my cousin soon set me on the right path."

"And what right path is that?" asked McKnight.

"You don't need to be afraid of your clients. Everything you dream of is located on the other side of your fear." Lieblingsky said, raising his wine and tapping Stanley's glass gently.

I've heard that somewhere before, thought Stanley.

"*Brillamment*! Let's drink to that!" exclaimed Lagrange.

"Is it really impossible to work for clients who earn their money honestly?" Stanley looked down into his glass as if the wine might answer.

"What is honestly earned money, Stanley?" Lagrange asked, spreading out his hands. "There's no such thing! Everyone steals. Who is honest? Even Zuckerberg stole his company. There is no honestly earned money. There is only money cleaned by time. Only time changes the nature of the money."

"You're putting together investment portfolios for Gagarin, looking for ways he can avoid paying taxes while building a mega-yacht, and Lagrange wanted to find for Mobutu..."

"I found an excellent personal hotel for him," Lagrange said proudly. "You've been to Paris, Stanley? Do you know Avenue Foch? A square millimeter there costs as much as your Porsche. Mobutu got a seven-story palace there through me, and only visited a couple of times, when he came to Paris to take his family shopping. He demanded he travel by Concorde. Air France refused at first, but Mobutu knew how to bargain. Through me, naturally. And the Concorde flew to Kinshasa. Have you been to Kinshasa, Stan? It's no San Francisco, far from it, and certainly no Zurich or Geneva, but good lord, the whores in Mobutu's palace were unbelievable! Such dark-skinned beauties, and what perfect asses!"

"Behave yourself, Lagrange!" said Laville and laughed.

"Sorry, boss!" Lagrange said. "My fault! And then we got that arrogant bastard a villa right near Monaco. In Roquebrune-Cap-Martin, on Avenue de l'Empress. Three swimming pools, a three-hectare garden, a personal helipad. The irony is, my dear Stan, that when they got rid of Mobutu..." Lagrange paused, and clapped his hand to his forehead. "Damn! It's been twenty years already! Do you miss him, boss?"

"Of course, I do. But now, thanks to the talented Mr. McKnight, we have Gagarin. Who has a new Mobutu at his back. So what was the irony, Lagrange?"

"The irony is, that when Mobutu and all his whores vacated that house on Empress Eugenie, a rich Russian bought it. And do you know how he came to buy it? I put together an investment proposal for him. I advised him to put his money in real estate. And he invested $200 million. Without giving it a second thought. Just stuck his hand in his pocket and pulled out a couple hundred million dollars."

"But that wasn't the end of it, Stan," Laville said, digging into his dessert. "That was just the beginning!"

"Exactly, boss! Because that Russian soon fell into debt, and another Russian, from the oil sector this time, acquired the villa. And do you know how that came to pass?"

"Let me guess: you put together an investment proposal?"

"Ah, you're no fun, Stan! You know everything!" Lagrange tossed his napkin onto the table. "But who's lounging around those pools now, Stanley? If you can tell me the answer, I'll owe you a bottle of 1965 Armagnac, from the cellar of my distant relative, Baron Lagrange. So?"

"Those same Russians? No? No...I've got it! Maybe the Russian president is vacationing there," said Stanley with a snap of his fingers.

"Nope! The Armagnac stays with me. Gagarin's lover is relaxing in that villa now, Madame Petrova. Do you know her?"

"Let him be, Lagrange," Laville put in. "You've tired Stanley out with your interrogation. Gagarin has a lover, a former diver..."

"Former tennis player, boss!" Lagrange corrected him.

"What's that? All right, a tennis player," agreed Laville. "By the way, I always wondered why Russian women put on so much weight. It looks like even the bones of their skulls expand, their faces get so wide. And forget about their..." Here Laville stood and patted his hips. "Russian men like that. They see that their investments aren't going to waste." Lagrange poured everyone more wine and drank, considering. "Or maybe they're trying to increase the amount of kissable area?"

"Possibly, very possible." Laville nodded. "But seriously, Stanley, it's not much of a stretch to compare Mobutu and the Russian president. Zaire had 'mobutism,' and Russia has 'assholism' or 'mudaizm' as they say in Russia; there are black people over there, and white people over here, but they're just the same inside—crooks. And us bankers, Mr. McKnight... well, you already know what we end up having to do! Cigars and coffee, please. By the way, Lagrange, I have a '37 Armagnac, we'll open it! Help yourselves, please!"

"I thought I noticed you having a bit of an internal struggle with the comparison between Zaire and modern-day Russia?" asked Lieblingsky, when they had all arranged themselves around the roaring fire with Cuban cigars and the delicious Armagnac. "Is that your Russian blood making itself known?"

"No, not at all," said Stanley. "It's not about who has actual 'Russian blood.' The vast majority of those you're talking about are just residents of Russia. If they're Russian, it's through culture alone. And you have a certain contempt for those people. You see them as a second-class kind of people, close to savages, part of a primitive, almost prehistoric culture."

"So you think Russian culture is sophisticated?" Lieblingsky asked with an ironic smile.

Lagrange laughed. "Now Stanley's going to start telling us about Tolstoy and Dostoyevsky. Isn't that right, McKnight?"

"And why shouldn't I?" Stanley felt a sudden burst of irritation at Lagrange, at Laville, and most of all against old Lieblingsky.

"Because, my dear Stanley, they're both long-dead. Like the nineteenth century in which they lived..."

"Tolstoy died in the twentieth century, though, didn't he?"

"Oh, who cares about the minor details, McKnight!" Laville thumped his glass down on the polished surface of the table. "What Russia had before, the people who were its pride and the pride of the entire human race, passed away long ago. Some of them got lucky and died in their beds, but most of them were killed by other Russians. During their civil war, and especially during the endless murders after that. The result? Everyone who had something to give to world culture rotted in their camps or was mowed down in their wars, and it's the killers and their descendants who survived. Russia has been host to a unique genetic experiment. An excellent illustration of what happens when the worst among us win. And the worst, the wardens, have no culture. Not a genuine, high culture. Russia and its culture are long-dead. Instead of Gagarin, the first cosmonaut, we have to deal with the crook who shares his name. Go ahead, name one Russian cultural figure, excluding the nineteenth century."

"Ok," nodded Stanley, "let me see—ah! Nabokov."

"Nabokov? All right. Anyone else?"

"That's not the best example, Stanley," said Lieblingsky. "He was an émigré, and did his best work in English. Anyway, is that all you've got?"

"I remember a Russian director winning an Oscar. And we suggested one of our clients invest in research on graphene, which Russians got a Nobel prize for."

"They haven't lived in Russia for a long time, and their discoveries were made in England and the Netherlands." Laville took a small sip. "Anyone else?"

"The automatic rifle. AK-47. A Russian invented it. The Kalashnikov," Stanley began to tire of the conversation and company of his bosses. He wished he could go home, kick off his shoes, loosen his collar, and drink a little whiskey before going to bed.

"Kalashnikov stole everything from Hugo Schmeisser," Laville said, slapping his knee. "They stole everything, all of them. They're all Mobutu. To one degree or another. The atom bomb, they stole that too. Have you seen their cars? They're a disgrace! Their modern writers—I was at an event with a Russian writer—he was a Mobutu too. He lived in Switzerland for a time, if you can believe it. I think he has a Swiss wife. Anyway, he put bits by other authors, little-known ones, from the nineteenth century in his novel, (which was published here in translation, of course). Not as a literary game. Just because he thought no one would notice. A Russian translator let me in on the secret at that event."

"I didn't realize you were so interested in literature, Jean-Michel," said Lagrange.

"I bought the publishing house," Laville said apologetically. "They published that Mobutu-Russian just before I acquired it. I wanted to get a look at that product of the kleptocracy. Well, Stanley? No more objections?"

"No, I don't have any good arguments. But I have the feeling that you're not right."

"I'm usually suspicious of feelings," said Laville. "But your recent successes owe a lot to your feelings, it seems to me. Or senses. So…"

"So let's drink!" Lagrange said loudly, raising his glass.

Laville's driver took them back to Zurich in a limo. Lagrange chattered incessantly, occasionally opening the bar, gradually emptying out the cube-like crystal liter decanter of whiskey until it was gone. Stanley responded with brief replies. Joked around. Then Lagrange fell asleep, and Stanley stared out into the darkness, trying to understand what was happening to him. He couldn't explain it, but felt like he was being gradually sucked into some kind of quagmire.

They dropped Lagrange off first. When they drew near Stanley's building, he asked the driver to stop.

"I'll walk the rest of the way, thanks!" he said.

The driver held the door open for him and wished him a good night.

He had to get up early the next day, and Stanley promised himself to take it easy for the next couple days. But tonight, he stopped into the first open bar he came across. His tuxedo made an impression—the bartender smirked at him when Stanley ordered a double bourbon and a beer. Then another bourbon.

"Where are you from, handsome?" asked the woman on the stool next to his. Her eyes were different colors, one light gray, the other brown, and she spoke with a slight lisp.

"California."

"Well, aren't you a long way from home!" She raised her glass. "Prost!"

CHAPTER 31

T HE ROBINSON HELICOPTER, LIKE A big-eyed white beetle, flew over the coastline. Below them, the unbroken blue expanse of the sea stretched out, and the pilot pointed ahead to their destination—the island of Hvar.

From above the island was red and brown with patches of greenery. Brown stone of the rocky island landscape, red brick rooftops, and the green tops of trees.

McKnight gazed out at the approaching island from the cabin of the helicopter. He was the only passenger on this flight, and the pilot had suggested he get comfortable in the seats in the back, but Stanley chose the copilot's seat instead.

The pilot had jokingly asked earlier whether Stanley was going to take over, and had he ever flown before. Stanley shook his head.

"I hate helicopters," he admitted, as they drove from the main building of the Split Airport to the hangar for private planes and helicopters. "I'm afraid to fly in them. In airplanes too, for that matter. I didn't used to be, but now I am…"

Stanley had actually been hoping to take a taxi to the marina and find a boat owner there willing to take him out to Gagarin's yacht.

When Stanley told the pilot that, the other man shook his head.

"It's impossible for security reasons," the pilot said. "Your boat could be booby-trapped with bombs, after all. And there are VIP guests on the yacht as well as the boss."

Stanley nodded. Safety first! God, he was sick of it. As if he couldn't strap explosives to a helicopter! He didn't say that to the pilot.

He had received an invitation from Gagarin the day before. Sent directly to him for the first time, not through Lagrange. Gagarin got in touch with Stanley personally on Telegram.

"Stanley, my savior!" said Gagarin when Stanley picked up. "What are you doing tomorrow?"

Gagarin sat on the deck, the sea and the sun at his back. Behind him, at the railing, Stanley saw a potbellied man with folds of fat at the neck, a hairy back, and a large bald spot, in long, sagging shorts, pawing at a thin girl with large, fake breasts. The girl tossed back her head and laughed loudly, exposing her thin neck. Laughter sounded from somewhere else on the boat. And music—Beethoven. "Ode to Joy."

"My work day starts pretty early—" Stanley began, but Gagarin cut him off.

"I'm your work. And I need you. Fly to Split. Biryuza will send you a ticket. And then come over here."

"But, Viktor—"

"I'll tell Lagrange."

"Pierre—"

"Pierre will stay in Zurich. He hasn't been able to hold his liquor lately. We like a man who can stay on top of his game. You know what I mean?"

"Someone who can drink a lot and stay sober?"

"Exactly! See you tomorrow."

Stanley headed to Lagrange's office. When he passed Barbara, he heard that she was talking to Lagrange's secretary. Barbara gestured for him to stop, and quickly finished her conversation.

"Monsieur Lagrange is in a rage," said Barbara. "I wanted to warn you ahead of time."

Lagrange really was in a state. He was offended that he hadn't been invited to Gagarin's new yacht. He was jealous of Stanley's relationship with Gagarin, jealous of Stanley's success. That was clear in every line of his posture, his sharp tone, in how he splashed whiskey out of Stanley's glass with his careless pour, leaving a puddle on the table's smooth surface.

"Stanley, Stanley, our golden boy," said Lagrange, pushing the glass of whiskey over to him. "You sure are lucky! A little midweek vacation on the yacht of a Russian billionaire. Do you know the 'Magnificent Five' are going to be there?"

"The magnificent what?"

"Five. The five people to whom our god, our benefactor, his Excellency Viktor Gagarin owes everything. They're the ones who made him a billionaire. To be precise…"

Lagrange fell silent, raising his glass and looking at the light through its contents.

"To be precise?"

"What?" Lagrange said, as if waking from sleep.

"You were talking. You started to say, 'To be precise,' and then you stopped." Stanley took a sip. "I've suspected for a while now that part, maybe even a significant part, of Gagarin's money doesn't belong to him."

"He suspected!" Lagrange finished his whiskey in one gulp. "Well, well. What a fast learner you are! Suspected! You have to know something with 100 percent certainty, not suspect it."

"And what exactly should I know, Pierre?" asked Stanley, in as relaxed a tone as he could manage: he was at sea, trying to figure out what, aside from not being invited to the yacht, had made Lagrange so irritated.

"That if you make a mistake, lose 20 percent, or even 30 percent, of Gagarin's money, Gagarin will survive. He'll steal even more, and the Magnificent Five, who you'll meet tomorrow, will help him do it. Of course, he'll be displeased, he'll be angry with you, but that will pass quickly. He'll pour you some vodka, you'll drink with him as usual, have your little kisses, and everything will be forgotten. But if he finds you on top of his wife, he's going to cut off your balls."

"Pierre! How many times do I have to tell you—"

"And you'll be lucky if Shamil does the cutting. He's a professional, at least. But if Gagarin does it personally, with a dull knife—"

"Pierre!"

"Don't say I didn't warn you!" Lagrange got up, and was ready to pour Stanley another drink. When he saw that Stanley's glass was still full, he just sighed and poured one for himself. "You think that this is just speculation on my part? That I was watching you, envious, *oh look at that pretty girl he gets to fuck*, that I imagined something? My dear Stanley! You can deny it all you want, but soon other people are going to find out what I already know."

* * *

The helicopter circled over Hvar Island. Yachts dotted the azure sea below in picturesque disorder. A cutter was pulling up to one of them, a white line of foam in its wake.

The helicopter began its descent. Stanley looked down and noticed girls sunbathing on one of the yachts. The sun played over the surface of the sea, which was calm in the bay, but further out the waves were topped with white.

Most of the yachts were motorized; sailing was becoming a thing of the past. Or already was. Sailing yachts were the exception now, rather than the rule. One of Stanley's London colleagues, an aristocrat who stood to inherit the title of earl, had invited a group of friends onto his yacht, and worked the sails himself, complaining about motor yachts.

"How can you call something a yacht if it's a big ship with a team of twenty people? Hah! I'll buy a decommissioned aircraft carrier, equip it for recreation, and according to their definition, it'll be a yacht! Everything intended for recreation is a yacht, they think. But a yacht is a craft like mine—made from mahogany, with a mast, sails, minimal electronics..."

The motor yachts were all big, but Gagarin's was so huge that it was anchored outside of the bay, in its own personal spot. No other yachts could come near it—there wasn't a single anchor buoy within a half-mile radius, probably at the request of the security services of Gagarin and his guests.

Stanley looked around the bay and imagined being on a small sailing yacht, in the company of good friends, then laughed at himself. He didn't have friends, and he hadn't been in good company since leaving college.

The helicopter hovered over Gagarin's yacht and began its descent to the helipad. Stanley saw the name of the yacht written in gold letters on the bow of the boat, and repeated along the length of the captain's bridge—*Alassio*.

The helicopter touched down gently, and its propeller made a few more rotations before coming to a halt.

Stanley thanked the pilot.

"At your service, sir!" he answered.

Michel Gauthier opened the door of the helicopter, a wide smile on his face, his eyes struggling and failing to focus on Stanley as he hopped down from the helicopter.

"Mr. McKnight! I have orders to meet you and I...I assure...Mr..."

"You're high as a kite, aren't you, Gauthier?"

Gauthier at last managed to focus, and shouted loud enough that Stanley stepped back in surprise: "Welcome aboard! Let me take your things!"

While Gauthier accompanied Stanley to his cabin in the lower deck, he managed to discourse on the glories of the yacht, including its two swimming pools and movie theater.

"I'd rather have two theaters and one pool," replied Stanley gloomily.

"Yeah? Why?" asked Gauthier in surprise, rubbing his nose.

"You can swim everywhere, but what if somebody wants to watch a comedy and somebody else wants a drama?"

"Well, here we all watch whatever the boss wants to watch," said Gauthier, and went on describing the details of this technological wonder; 510 feet in length, the yacht had a wine cellar (although not quite completed), a spa, a fully equipped medical station staffed with a doctor and two nurses, and even a library.

"And she has a cruising speed of twenty-one knots," finished Gauthier, nearly breathless with delight, and for some reason Stanley remembered an adult film with a busty dominatrix in a nurse's uniform that consisted of a very short skirt with a slit up the front and a red cross on each nipple.

"And where do you want to go at that speed?" asked Stanley.

"Oh, I don't know," said Gauthier, pushing the door of the cabin open with his shoulder. "Mila and I sailed here from Venice. We hung out there a couple of days. It was magical! Just magical. Lunch in half an hour." Gauthier put Stanley's things on the bunk. "They'll be expecting you on the upper deck."

Gauthier was walking out when Stanley called him back. The younger man turned with the look of someone expecting a tip.

"Michel, a word to the wise. On a yacht, or any other ship, there's only one person who can say, 'We sailed from,' or, 'I sailed.' That's the captain. Not the owner or the wife of the owner. Only the captain. Everyone else is just on board. I'm not sure if there is a captain on this yacht, though."

"Of course, there is! A real sea wolf, smokes a pipe!"

"Sounds like the real deal," agreed Stanley.

"So what am I supposed to say? We came from Venice?"

"Exactly! We came! We all come, and the captain sails, especially captains who smoke pipes..."

"Thanks, good to know," Gauthier said with a smile.

"No problem, Michel. If you want to know anything else, just let me know!"

McKnight wasn't hungry at all and wasn't looking forward to having to go up to the upper deck in half an hour. He looked at his watch—it wasn't close to lunchtime. But he would have to do as he was told. He opened his bag, got out a clean shirt, and was getting undressed to take a shower. Halfway through, he was hopping on one leg trying to get his sock off, when Mila walked into his cabin without knocking. Her eyes were slightly crossed from cocaine, her lips were moist, and her loose sarong was nearly transparent. He could see her dark-red nipples rising with her quick breaths through the sheer fabric.

"Ha, you've got the idea!" said Mila, closing the door behind her and turning the key. "You're already getting ready for me, excellent!"

She walked over to Stanley and kissed him on the lips. She smelled strongly of wine. Stanley tossed the sock in the corner.

"But why did they stick you in this hole? This is a cabin for the girls who work in the kitchen. I'll say something to Viktor. You should be on the upper deck. Hi, Stanley!"

"Hello, Mila."

"Aren't you happy to see me? Oh, Stanley, I was just miserable in fucking Venice. The canals stink, packs of tourists everywhere. Twelve euros for a cup of coffee. Twelve euros! Can you imagine? For a sip of coffee?"

"It's pretty unbelievable, but you can afford it."

"But then I found out you'd be coming, and even their nasty coffee started tasting nice. But why are you looking at me? The see-through fabric? No one cares about my tits here. Everyone's dressed like this."

Mila pressed herself against him.

"Do you care about them? My tits?"

"I was going to take a shower," said Stanley, trying to pull away.

"I'll come with you." Mila undid the knot of her sarong, stepping free of the thin cloth as it pooled around her feet. "If you don't take me now, I'll burst. Like a balloon."

She pushed Stanley toward the bathroom door.

"I'm all sweaty," muttered Stanley, sensing that he wouldn't be able to withstand Mila's pressure. "Hang on!"

Mila lowered her hands to his underwear.

"What is there to wait for?" She caressed him skillfully, making Stanley grind his teeth from the sudden rush of excitement. "Sweaty is good. I hate when men smell like deodorant, or even worse, male cosmetics. The smell of sweat and a big sweaty cock, like this one, that's what I want. Go on: turn on the water!"

They squeezed into the shower stall, and Stanley slid the door closed, turning on the water.

"Make it colder," said Mila, dropping to her knees. "I'll lick up your tasty sweat, honey. Oh, it's delicious."

After getting what she wanted from Stanley, Mila disappeared. Stanley glanced down at his watch to see that he was running late. And he realized that, over the course of only thirty minutes, this woman had made him come twice. The second time, she turned her back to him and demanded that Stanley be rougher, harder.

"Hit me! Harder! Hit me deep inside!" she cried out, with no concern that someone could hear her voice or her moans through the bulkhead between the cabins.

McKnight couldn't admit to Lagrange that he was, in fact, sleeping with Mila, but he acknowledged that Lagrange was right. His prediction about Gagarin and the dull knife was moving closer every day.

He arrived late to lunch; the host and all his guests were already seated.

Stanley found Gagarin's usual retinue on the upper deck, all familiar faces: Polina, her husband, Yulia, Biryuza, and Shamil, morose, all in black, and sitting off to the side, as he did. The core of the group gathered that day on the *Alassio* were new to him.

These were the Magnificent Five that Lagrange had mentioned, the high-ranking Moscow officials who had arrived a day before Stanley.

Biryuza was the first to greet Stanley. His handshake was as limp as always, but his whole attitude expressed goodwill toward the newcomer.

Apparently Anton thought of himself as something like a servant in this crowd, and saw McKnight as the same.

Gagarin was not at the head of the table as expected, but to the side of the table against the railing. He raised his glass of vodka, ice cubes rattling in greeting. Mila pretended happy surprise at Stanley's appearance.

"Mr. McKnight! Where did you come from?" she said. "What a surprise! How nice to see you."

"From there," McKnight said, pointing up to the sky. "I'm happy to see you as well, Mrs. Gagarin!"

Mila nodded and lit a cigarette, completely at ease. She was wearing a sleeveless white shirt with the message "I'd fuck me too" written on the front.

Gagarin gestured for Stanley to sit down across from him. McKnight found himself between Yulia and a girl with artificially swollen lips, her head resting on the thin and bony shoulder of a man Stanley didn't know.

"We've already had the aperitif, Stan, and we're about to begin with turtle soup. Do you like turtle soup, Valery Valeryevich?" Gagarin asked a broad-shouldered, thick-necked man in a colorful shirt sat at the head of the table. Valery Valeryevich had almost no chin and no expression in his large, dark eyes beneath thick brows and a high, balding forehead.

"I like pea soup," Valery Valeryevich replied in an unexpectedly high, squeaky voice.

"As you should, General!" put in another guest, dressed in a silk robe and sporting a bushy beard and greasy hair pulled back in a ponytail. Judging from his robe and the large cross hanging from his neck, he had to be a Russian Orthodox priest. He was also the only drunk member of the party, his cheeks flushed. Stanley was surprised to see that the muscular, handsome young man next to him was dressed only in pink swimming trunks.

"We should stick to our good old traditional food. Cabbage soup, pea soup, borscht—" the priest began, but General Valery Valeryevich cut him off sharply: "Next, you'll start talking about *pampushky*, Holy Father!" Stanley noticed the contemptuous emphasis with which the general pronounced 'Holy Father.' "We don't need your Ukrainian peasant slop!"

"What part of the Russian army does he command?" McKnight asked Yulia quietly.

"Army?" she snorted, and replied, barely moving her lips: "He's a general in the FSB. Zlatoust. Spent his whole career at a desk. Economic security; the head of the division. He has a gun made out of dollars."

"What about the bullets?" asked McKnight, stunned to be getting good intel from Yulia, of all people.

"Made of shit!" she said and turned away.

McKnight took a couple sips from the glass a silent waiter had filled with champagne. Another filled his bowl with turtle soup.

McKnight tasted it and then set his spoon back down.

"No good?" asked Yulia.

"It's good. I'm just not hungry."

"What's wrong—you're not feeling well?"

"I'm tired."

"I think I can diagnose your condition," Yulia said, waving a waiter over. "You have acute alcohol insufficiency. A double whiskey for the American."

"I'm just tired."

"And no wonder," she replied quietly. "Take care of yourself, Stanley. You'll come in handy yet."

CHAPTER 32

ON THE SURFACE, THE ATMOSPHERE over lunch seemed relaxed, but Stanley sensed a strange tension throughout the group. Everyone's jokes and remarks came out a little anxious, as if each speaker was trying to guess how they would be received by the Magnificent Five, and, most importantly of all, how the general at the head of the table would react. The general could barely turn his head, and it seemed as though he never blinked. The only member of the party who seemed to speak his mind without concern was the red-cheeked priest. He made the sign of the cross over the dishes on the table, dropped old-fashioned Ukrainian words into his conversation and, shunning the "foreign" drinks on offer, crossed his lips before each shot of vodka. He would also make a nasty face whenever he looked over at Stanley, always trying to turn the conversation to American wickedness and how to fight against it. He pointed his fat, crooked finger at Stanley and expounded on "foreigners" at length, and about how Russia was a kingdom of light, while the United States was a kingdom of darkness, debauchery, and godlessness. McKnight just nodded along, agreeing with everything the priest had to say, which came as quite a surprise to the good father.

He was eating for three, and the muscular young man at his side filled his plate again when it grew bare. The other glutton at the table was the bony man sitting next to the girl with the inflated lips.

When Gagarin finally got around to introducing Stanley to the Magnificent Five, he started with the bony man. Probably because he was the second most important member of that group. Mikhail Potyagaylo, according to Gagarin, was a federal minister, an indomitable fighter for the best and most advanced solutions, and a superior leader in whatever position the state appointed him. Potyagaylo had been a governor for a while and put up numerous monuments in his region, mostly to scientific and cultural figures as well as military leaders, who had had no connection to the region other than the fact that its governor, Potyagaylo, liked them.

Potyagaylo, like all of the Five, barely spoke, and when he did, it was lazily and disdainfully. Stanley noticed them displaying the same attitude to Gagarin. But it was obvious that there was nothing special about this Potyagaylo, or any of them. They were just people who had grown rich suddenly, and not through their talents or efforts, but due to luck of circumstance. Stanley was struck by their imperious tone.

After Gagarin praised him to the skies, for example, Potyagaylo began to argue that everyone attempted to distort Russian history and belittle Russian achievements. Great Russian rulers like Ivan the Terrible or Stalin, meanwhile, were wrongly portrayed as evil tyrants. Stanley was more than a little astonished to hear Potyagaylo allege that Ivan the Terrible hadn't killed his son. No, the son had died on the journey from Saratov to St. Petersburg, where the tsar had directed him to join the army.

Stanley wanted to object that neither St. Petersburg nor the city of Saratov existed when Ivan the Terrible was tsar, but when he opened his mouth to speak, Yulia and the girl with inflated lips hit his knees simultaneously under the table. So Stanley didn't say a word.

The other minister and member of the Five was Andron Alekseyevich Komarikhin, an enormous man with a triple chin. His eyes were set back in puffy lids, but his gaze was smart, vicious, and perceptive. Komarikhin looked over at Stanley with a sly smile, and gave him a wink, as if inviting him to step to the side if he wanted to hear some interesting information. His girlfriend or wife matched him well—she was stout and busty, with rosy cheeks and a braid that she twined around her fingers.

The other two members of the group, the deputy head of the Russian president's administration, Arseny Petrovich Zaikin, and a high-ranking member of the foreign intelligence service, Petr Sergeyevich Mamonov, bore a close resemblance to one another. They were short and stocky, with unmemorable faces and permanent fake smiles. They didn't contribute to the general conversation. Zaikin said something to his companion, whose long nose looked red, and her lips had the compressed and twisted look of someone who was on the verge of bursting into tears. Mamonov was alone, and looked around at the other guests as if wanting them to know that he knew more about them than they did. He directed several meaningless questions to Stanley, but when Stanley began to answer, he would lose interest, turning away or back to his plate.

Stanley noticed that when the Five spoke to each other, they used the respectful form of address in Russian, the first name and patronymic, and the formal form of the pronoun *you*. But they were all more casual with Gagarin, calling him simply 'Viktor' and using the informal *you*, and their tone was haughty, as if Gagarin was just a bit higher-ranking in their estimation than the waiters serving them dessert.

Stanley also realized that these people were well aware of who he was and what exactly he was doing for Gagarin.

"Ah yes, we've heard about you," said Komarikhin, unbuttoning one more button of his shirt and stroking his greasy, hairless chest with his short-fingered hand. "You're a man who knows how to do his job. Good work! Keep it up! Although I personally don't trust Americans."

"Oh, how right you are!" put in the priest. "You can't trust those American Judases. They'll turn on you! Sell you out!"

"Shut up, Father Vsevolod," Zaikin said. Gagarin had introduced him as a gifted political scientist, and an expert in psychology and the art of management. "You can trust everyone, but all the same, better not to trust the Americans. They're too set on laws, honesty, all that nonsense. Who needs honesty, eh? It's an anachronism!"

"I can vouch for Stanley," said Gagarin, looking Stanley in the eye. "Plus, Stanley's almost Russian."

Zlatoust interrupted Gagarin in a melancholy tone: "Be careful giving out your word, Viktor. You've only got one reputation. I'd watch out staking it on anyone else if I were you. I'd rather hear about how things are going with the diplomatic post. Everything good?"

Stanley was stunned. Even in these circles, talk of sending cash and valuables by diplomatic post would be decidedly inadvisable. But now it seemed as all of the Five not only knew about the operation, but were helping to provide cover for it. In fact, it seemed as if they were in charge of the transfer and Gagarin was just the front man, a figurehead acting on their behalf. If anything went wrong, these people could easily get rid of Gagarin and of Stanley. He could feel a chill creeping up his back between his shoulder blades. He devoured a huge piece of cake with ice cream; maybe it was the fear driving his appetite, and the realization that he was just a humble pawn, each move controlled by these unpleasant, arrogant people. The cake was greasy, and the ice cream was too.

When lunch was over, Stanley rose with relief, but then heard Mila, who had, as usual, overindulged on wine, demanding that Gagarin transfer Stanley to a more comfortable cabin, her voice quite shrill. *Now he's going to ask—how do you know what cabin he is in?* thought Stanley anxiously.

"How do you know what cabin he's in?" asked Gagarin.

"How?" Mila faltered. "I saw him arrive by helicopter, and Gauthier carrying his bags down. I visited him! What did you think?"

"I'm sorry, my love, sorry," said Gagarin in an unexpectedly affectionate tone. "I'll try to think of something. There is a cabin on the quarterdeck."

"Where?"

"The stern. A friend was supposed to fly in...ah, forget him! We love our Stanley, don't we? We'll figure it out, Milochka!"

"You do that, my sea wolf!" and Stanley heard a loud kiss.

Gagarin's guests dispersed; some, like Komarikhin, to sleep. Others went off to swim in one of the pools, while Mamonov called for a jet ski and took off into the sea, shrinking rapidly into a small dot against the horizon, where the sun was already beginning its descent.

McKnight walked back to his cabin. When he was safe inside, he locked the door and fell onto the bed. He'd already known that he'd gotten himself into a bad situation. Now he saw that he'd have to pay a very, very high price to extricate himself from this trap. He felt misery well up inside of him. He had never planned on becoming a millionaire, much less this way. But now he had no way out. He'd have to do the dirty work to get rich so he could stick his wealth in other people's faces. It was too late for him to just walk away.

Stanley pulled out his mobile and dialed Christine's number. When she answered, Stanley heard street noise and distant music in the background.

"Is something wrong, Stanley?"

"No, everything's fine. I just wanted to hear your voice."

"That's nice! It's been a long time since I've heard something like that from you."

"Then who have you heard it from?"

"From my boss, mostly. She's been working from home lately, and she..."

"I'm sorry, Christine, just feeling a bit jealous."

"That's nice to hear as well. But you sound quite sad."

"There's not much to laugh at right now."

"You have a lot of work?" he heard the London accent of the waiter on her end saying, "Here you are, ma'am!"

"You're in London?" Stanley asked.

"Yes, for three days. Our museum…well, long story short, I've finished my work here, but my boss bought me a nonrefundable ticket, so I'm killing time before my return flight."

"Excellent! I'll send you a ticket for tomorrow, a morning flight to Split—it's in Croatia, a beautiful place. Forget about your nonrefundable ticket. We'll find a scenic spot on the islands, and then…"

"Stanley, what's going on?"

"I'll see you tomorrow in Split!"

Stanley nodded off. His dream was vivid, disturbing; he tossed and turned, waking up and falling back to sleep several times, until he woke up for good bathed in sweat. He heard piercing screams coming from the upper deck. Stanley took a shower, got dressed, and walked up the gangway.

What he found shocked him. The upper deck was full of absolutely drunken people. Even Mamonov was drunk, but drunk like a professional spy—he moved with confidence and spoke clearly. But then he suddenly dropped to the deck as if his legs had just folded up under him. He lay there for a little while, then got up again, and walked with the stride of a sober man over to the bar, where he had another shot.

Komarikhin was dancing, his huge foot stomping heavily. Even Zlatoust, who had found a red Russian peasant shirt somewhere, was shouting at a deafening volume and trying to get down into a squat for a traditional dance.

It was the gypsies who were to blame for all of this; Stanley had no idea when or how they'd appeared on the yacht. Real gypsies with guitars—the women in long, colorful skirts and tambourines, the men with hoops in their ears, pleated pants, and accordions. They sang and danced, accompanied by an actual, live bear that stood on its hind legs and, to the delight of its audience, would seek out a person holding a full glass.

"Isn't this great?" Mila said, zooming over to Stanley.

"What is all this? Where did they come from?"

"Viktor sent his plane to Moscow for them. Don't they sing beautifully?" Mila was drunk again.

"They do," nodded Stanley, smiling at her. His main fear was that she would forget herself and throw her arms around him. But it was actually Father Vsevolod who did that, not Mila. He grabbed Stanley and embraced him so tightly that the priest's cross left a scratch on his face.

"They told me you were one of us!" Father Vsevolod shouted. "One of us! Our blood in your veins! And the sound of familiar Russian voices threading through yours! Let me kiss you! Come! You're a nobleman! *Barin*! A real noble, aren't you? Tell me!"

"I don't know what you mean. What do you mean by *barin*?"

"A nobleman!" Father Vsevolod tried to kiss him again, but Stanley turned away and the priest's wet lips met the warm Adriatic Sea air instead.

Everyone got sick of the gypsies pretty quickly after that. McKnight had noted before that his Russian clients often acted like small children—they'd fall in love with some toy, use it mercilessly, and then, a very short while later, they wouldn't even want to look at it. So it was this time. As if on cue, they all sobered up at the same time. Even Mamonov the spy, the folding man. They all started passing around headache pills and water with lemon juice, and then it was onto the next entertainment.

Gagarin, striking a picturesque pose against the setting sun, clapped his hands together and invited everyone to board the small boats tied to the yacht—dinner was waiting for them at a restaurant called Zori on the island of St. Clement, the largest of the Pakleni archipelago.

McKnight walked to the ladder. The guests passed by him, in a state of unnecessary nerves about descending from the steady deck of a giant yacht onto a boat in calm waters. The gypsies were not invited, and the drunken Father Vsevolod remained behind as well, blessing the rest of the group as they went.

"Don't sin, my children," he trumpeted. "Don't sin on land or on water..."

"Don't sin in the air!" said Stanley, picking up the refrain, and the priest shouted happily:

"You speak the truth, my son! The truth!" and made the sign of the cross over Stanley.

"Is it a long trip to this island?" Stanley asked the sailor who was helping the guests down into the boats.

"It's right over there, sir," the sailor replied, nodding toward the west, where the sun was already dipping below the horizon. "They're sometimes called Hell's Islands, but they're just the opposite; even though the word *pakao* in Croatian means 'hell,' the name actually comes from the word *paklina*, 'tar.' They used to tar ships there, and the sky over the islands would be covered in smoke."

"You sound more like a tour guide than just a simple sailor," said Stanley.

"They stuff some information into them before they set sail," said Mamonov, inserting himself into the conversation as he passed by. "So they'll have something to spout off in case someone asks. Isn't that right, Egor?"

"My name is Maxim, thank you," said the sailor.

"Well, well!" Mamonov raised his hands. "Maxim? You're Egor! Got it?"

"As you wish," said Maxim.

The small fast boats delivered them to the island in a matter of minutes. The disembarking was also accompanied by the squeals of the Magnificent Five's wives and girlfriends, all in high, spike heels and covered in jewels, who cursing fluently at both their own and others' clumsiness. The night that had fallen over the island was suddenly filled to the seams with pandemonium.

This continued in the restaurant as well. Some members of their party would study the menu meticulously, tormenting the waiters with detailed questions on each dish, and then their companions would get annoyed and start to hurry them along. Others just poked at the first thing on the menu. All this was going on under the general clanging and clatter of bottles—the table was suddenly laden with vodka and wine, and buckets of champagne appeared beside it.

Mila had consumed a fair bit of vodka since Stanley had seen her on the yacht, and was now drinking champagne. Stanley was afraid to even imagine how that would end up. Mamonov was being openly rude, this time to the waiter. Komarikhin was the first to order, and he was greedily sucking down oyster after oyster, an enormous napkin tucked into his collar. His companion drank herbal tea, her pinky finger pretentiously extended, and informed everyone loudly that she never ate after seven in the evening. She was, however, eventually tempted by the lobster and squirted everyone around her with the juice as she ate.

General Zlatoust and his pretty wife were tearing into a swordfish, Zaikin was digging into some shell with his fork and cursing through his teeth, and Potyagaylo, while stroking his girlfriend's leg, was busy explaining to a clearly uninterested Komarikhin why the future belonged to them, the Magnificent Five.

Gagarin was drinking vodka, as usual. He had a plate of mullet in front of him, and he glumly picked up one little fish after another, devouring them so thoroughly that only their brittle tails remained.

Stanley had somehow ended up next to Gagarin and across from Mila, Polina, and Yulia, to whom Gauthier occasionally offered cocaine, but Gagarin gave him scolding glances from across the table: What if the Croatian antinarcotics task force were to come bursting into the restaurant?

When Gagarin lost interest in observing Mila and her friends, he poured himself another shot, drank it down with a wheezing breath, and threw his arm over Stanley's shoulders.

"Not bad, huh?" asked Gagarin.

"It's wonderful, Viktor, just fabulous," answered Stanley. "Your friends seem really great."

"Ah, knock it off!"

"What's that?" Stanley asked, not understanding the Russian word Viktor had used.

"Ah, you don't know that one? It means, don't talk about what you don't understand. Don't make stuff up!"

Gagarin spoke quietly, almost directly into Stanley's ear. Stanley felt his hot breath and flecks of spit hit his neck and cheek, but suppressed his disgust and didn't move away.

"These friends of mine are ready at any moment—at any moment, you understand? To sell me out, turn me in, and trample me underfoot. They couldn't care less about me. They don't even care about my money. I'm rich, okay, but they're a hundred times, a million times richer than I am."

"Is that even possible, Viktor?" Stanley pretended to lean down for a spoonful of seafood mousse and covertly wiped Gagarin's spittle off his face.

"Oh it is, it is, when everything belongs to them. Well, almost everything. What do you know about them? A minister, another minister, a general… they've got all of Russia like this!" Gagarin raised his clenched fist in front of Stanley's nose. "And their money goes through me…"

And through me, thought Stanley. *And that could come to light. And then those years in prison that Dillon was threating me with will look like a weekend vacation.*

"But I don't care about anything anymore," Gagarin went on. "You helped me—no, don't argue—you helped me, and now we've got a whole system working, but I would give all of my money to see my mother just once more. I miss my mom so much."

Gagarin began to cry, but got control of it, blowing his nose into a cloth napkin and tossing it onto the floor. A waiter was there in a moment to offer him a fresh one.

"She died several years ago. I was very busy. Very. She didn't complain, but I could tell something was off. But I didn't insist that she go to the doctor. And when she did finally go, it was too late. She was gone in months. Terminal cancer."

Gagarin began to cry again.

"I'm sorry to hear that, Viktor," Stanley said sincerely. "I lost my mother recently too."

"Viktor!" Mila shouted across the table. "What are you sniveling about? Chin up!"

"I'll show you sniveling, you bitch!" Gagarin tried to leap out of his chair, but Stanley held him back, so Gagarin threw a half-empty shot glass at Mila, and hit Gauthier square in the forehead.

After dinner, they all got back in the boats. Stanley was secretly hoping that they would return to the yacht, but they passed by it, heading out into the bay. It seemed that the wives of the Magnificent Five wanted to dance in a club called Carpe Diem.

Stanley hadn't been in a club for a long time. He was struck by the roar of the music and conversation, but the other patrons at the club were in for a bigger shock when this pack of men and women dressed to the nines walked in. Most of the other visitors worked on yachts or sailed their own, and were all wearing comfortable clothes, shorts and T-shirts, the women dressed modestly. And suddenly, all these people appeared, women glinting with gold and the men's snow-white dress shirts flashing in the dim interior.

Stanley didn't plan on dancing. He snuck off to the bar unnoticed—or so he thought—to order a tequila. He could see the entire dance floor from his vantage point there, but the lighting was such that the people at the bar were nearly hidden from sight. He was on his second shot of tequila when the driving beat was replaced by the song "Slave to Love." Stanley had always been a fan of Bryan Ferry, his elegant style and genuine English charm. But just as Ferry sang, "How the strong get weak and the rich get poor," he felt a strong grip on his elbow. When he turned, Mila was there, in a short, sparkly dress, a rope of large pearls around her neck.

She literally dragged Stanley away from the bar, pressing up against him, and Stanley had no choice but to submit.

They were moving together on the nearly empty dance floor, in full view of everyone. Mila pressed up against him, closer and closer, and, when Stanley's back shielded her from the group of Gagarin's guests and the oligarch himself, reached up to kiss him quickly on the lips.

"Salty!" she said, jerking back before anyone saw them. "Have you been sweating again? I love the taste!"

"It's salt," said Stanley. "I was drinking tequila."

"Sweaty, but boring!" Mila stomped her foot petulantly. "You're a bore, but a good fuck. You're full of contradictions, but the fact that you're good in bed is the most important."

"You're drunk," said Stanley, praying for the song to end, but Ferry kept drawing it out: "*Slave to love, no I can't escape, I'm a slave to love...*"

The music finally came to end. Stanley took a half step back, and bowed formally. Mila curtsied in reply.

Stanley went downstairs to the bathroom, where he splashed cold water on his face. When he straightened up, he saw a hand extending a towel to him in the mirror.

"You're an idiot!" snapped Biryuza. "Have you lost your mind?"

"What do you mean, Anton? What happened?"

"Are you already fucking her? You can tell me the truth. I won't say anything."

"What truth? There's nothing to tell?" Stanley turned away and spit into the sink. "We were just dancing?"

"I'm gay, not blind, Stanley. You and her…anyway, fine, my business is business. You do what you want. But he'll cut off your head."

"My head? That's not so bad! He can have the head."

"You're an idiot! A fucking idiot!"

But neither Gagarin nor his guests were as observant as Biryuza.

Gagarin was sitting the whole time at the end of a leather sofa. He had gone so heavy on the vodka, in fact, that he had to be carried out of the club at dawn. The fresh sea breeze sobered him up a little.

On the boat, heading back to the yacht at last, he stood in the prow, threw his arms wide, and began reciting a poem:

Are you still living, oh mother of mine?
I'm here, I'm here, I greet you from afar!
Let the light of evening flow, sublime
In the fading sky above your home.

They write me that your aching worry
Drives you, restless, from the house at night
To pace in sorrow on your own,
In your old-fashioned threadbare dress.

Night after night in that blue darkness
You see a vision of me clear before you –
In the middle of a tavern brawl,
A stranger slips his knife between my ribs.

Gagarin's bald head was shining in the early-morning light. Shamil approached his boss several times, trying to pull him away from his dangerous position, but Gagarin just continued to shout westward into the receding darkness.

It's nothing, Mama, please don't fret.
Your mind is playing tricks, that's all.
I'm not such a hopeless drunkard,
To die before we meet again.

So set aside your restless worry,
And let your helpless sorrow go.
Don't walk out from your house at night
In that old-fashioned threadbare dress.

The sea was choppy, and when a wave rocked the boat, Gagarin flew overboard. Shamil was the first into the water, followed by Gauthier, who couldn't swim. Stanley also moved toward the railing, preparing to save the oligarch again, but Mila stopped him with a hand on his arm.

Stanley looked at her, stunned to see the absolute hatred in her eyes as she stared into the waves, and the depth of her disappointment when Shamil rose to the surface with Gagarin under his arm.

Stanley grabbed the exhausted Gauthier's hand and dragged him back on board.

"You saved me. You saved me too," whimpered Gauthier.

Several people helped Gagarin back on the boat, and Shamil climbed up after him, shouting hoarsely to the sailor to hurry it up—he didn't want their boss to catch cold, did he?

The gypsies and Father Vsevolod were waiting on deck to welcome Gagarin back. The gypsies chorused something like "he came back to us, our favorite," carrying a tray with a large shot of vodka and a poppy seed pastry. But as soon as Gagarin drank the shot and took a bite, the priest started on a lecture about how their benefactor was going to get sick. They needed to undress him, rub him down, get him warm. The priest's young companion, today in a revealing sailor's shirt, brought a blanket and wrapped Gagarin up. He demanded another vodka, and they brought that too.

"I thought you were going to save me again," Gagarin said to Stanley.

"But I'm not a savior, Viktor. I'm just a banker."

"Just, huh? Well, well…"

Back in his cabin, Stanley was just locking his door when he felt another person's weight pressing in from outside. He thought it was Shamil, coming to cut off his head, balls, or who knows what, and Stanley was almost ready to agree to any punishment, just as long as it was quick. But it was Mila.

"Were you scared?" asked Mila, locking the door behind her. "You were! They told you he was going to cut your head off?"

"Yes, and my balls."

"Your big, strong balls? Oh no, they're mine. All mine!"

It looked like Mila was getting ready to take the initiative again, walking toward him, but Stanley, without thinking what he was doing, reached out and slapped her across the face. Mila flew back into corner and fell, her dress riding up. Stanley stepped over to her and bent down, pinning her in place with his knee while he tore off her panties, throwing the torn scraps to the side.

Mila looked up at him like a little animal, with sweet fright in her eyes. There was a drop of blood at her lip. Stanley pulled his belt off and pushed down his pants. Then he pulled her up by her hair and turned her around, facing away from him. He raised the belt and brought it down sharply on her legs, and then her ass.

"Oh, yes! Like that, please! Again!" Mila breathed.

Stanley shoved her legs apart roughly with his knee, hitting her with the belt again.

"Yes! Please!" she said again.

Stanley entered here, feeling the soft, firm flesh, slippery wet. Then pulled out again.

"Where did you go? Come back!" moaned Mila.

"Shut up!" Stanley said, hitting her harder.

He entered her again, then, pulling out, pushed into her tight ass.

"Ah! Mama! You're going to tear me apart! Ah! It's so good! More! Hit me again!"

"Shut up!" Stanley shouted, driving into her as far as he could go. "Shut up!"

He was moving like a machine. Mila moaned and cried out for her mother. Stanley felt as if he was watching himself in a movie. Suddenly, light flooded into the cabin through the window, illuminating Stanley, crouched over a woman clinging to the wall, impaled on his throbbing member.

"I'm coming! Oh God, oh God!" Mila wailed, stamping her foot and breaking the heel of her shoe.

Stanley hit her again.

CHAPTER 33

V OICES CARRYING THROUGH THE BULKHEAD woke McKnight. Half awake, he couldn't make out what they were saying, but when he was finally fully conscious, he realized he could hear almost every word.

He lay on his bed, realizing with horror that his savage night with Mila had been audible to his neighbors down the entire corridor.

He sat up and got out of bed, stepping on something hard and sharp. He dropped back on to the bed and reached down to find the heel of Mila's shoe.

"Shit! Fuck! Shit!" he muttered, looking at the heel on his floor and listening to his neighbors' conversation.

"We need to say something," a young man's voice said in an affected drawl. "Otherwise, if he finds out from someone else, he'll ask why we didn't say anything. I heard everything they did, and then saw his wife come out of the room."

"First of all, my son, speak quietly—he speaks Russian, and if you didn't catch it already, you can hear everything on this ship!" said another man in a deep voice. "Secondly, I can tell you as a former major in the state security service, informing on someone is a sin. Unless the life of another person, or many people, depends on your words. Then I'd give my blessing."

Stanley realized that his neighbors must be Father Vsevolod and his muscular lover. But more importantly, the priest's lover knew about him and Mila. Stanley broke into a sweat.

"I was asked," the young voice began, but Father Vsevolod interrupted him.

"Say nothing to anyone! Let them deal with it themselves. We don't have to live with their sins. We have our own to overcome, don't we, Seryezhenka?"

"Oh, Father, what are you doing! That hurts!"

"It's no fun if it doesn't hurt," the priest's deep voice continued. "Remember: you're under my protection here. If you do something wrong, I'll curse you. And then when we get back to shore, or, God forbid, return to our long-suffering homeland, you'll be arrested. How many years in jail did I save you from, Seryezhenka? For your sins?"

"Eleven…"

"There you go! Eleven years. You just watch out! Keep quiet, or I'll say the word, and you're finished."

McKnight, the heel in his hand, got up, looking for other evidence that Mila had been in his room. He found the torn pieces of her panties in the corner. He picked the weightless, transparent fabric up off the floor, and brought them to his nose without thinking. The scent brought on such a rush of desire that Stanley was almost frightened. He almost thought of calling his wife and telling her that he was held up with work and couldn't meet after all, so that he could stay on the yacht.

He wrapped the heel up in the panties and hid them in his bag, then went to take a shower. The cold water helped ease his burning lust, but not his rapid heartrate. Lathering shower gel on himself, he resolved to get off this yacht as soon as he could.

He packed his things and zipped up the bag. His hand was already at the door when he thought that it might be wise to provide some plausible reason for his unexpected departure. McKnight pressed Lagrange's number on his smartphone.

"Hi, Stanley," his boss answered. "What's wrong? Hangover?"

"Yes, Pierre," he agreed, "a hangover."

He tried to speak as quietly as he could.

"Listen, I can't take it anymore. I'm tired of drinking so much, and I've got a lot of work waiting for me. Could you do something for me? Call Gagarin and tell him that Laville needs me, back in Geneva, maybe?"

"You could—"

"And I'll spend a day or two on the islands. Pull myself together. I've had enough of these Russians."

"You don't have to explain to me, McKnight. I completely understand—I went through the same thing, myself. Of course, I'll help you out. Just stay in touch, in case we really do need you."

"Absolutely, Pierre! See you soon! And thank you."

Shamil was quite surprised when McKnight came to tell him he wanted a flight off the yacht to the Split airport. The guard was sitting in a lounge chair on the middle deck, his feet up on the railing. He didn't move when Stanley addressed him, looking up through mirrored shades, so the only way that Stanley guessed his reaction was his voice on the phone when he placed a call.

"The banker wants to leave us," he said into the receiver. "Yes, immediately. Understood."

Shamil ended the call and raised his mirrored gaze to Stanley.

"Just a moment. The pilot is having breakfast. Maybe you would like to as well?"

"I'm not hungry."

"As you like," Shamil said, shrugging and turning away.

McKnight put his bag on the helipad and took a walk around the decks of the yacht. Everyone was still in their cabins. Only when he reached the upper deck did he encounter another guest—FSB General Zlatoust, in a robe that kept flapping open in the breeze to reveal his protruding stomach. Yulia stood next to him, the general pawing at her breast, his heavy brows raising and lowering, eyes half shut. Yulia saw Stanley, and gestured for him to stay away. Stanley nodded and went back down to find the pilot finishing up his sandwich.

"You're leaving us?" he asked.

"Yes, I have business to attend to."

"Too bad," the pilot replied, his voice expressing his complete indifference on the matter.

Stanley rented a car at the airport, using his personal credit card, issued back in San Francisco, for the transaction, instead of his corporate card. Then, as if remembering something, he asked: "Actually, could I pay in cash?"

"Of course, sir!"

Stanley counted out the money and went into the parking lot. After his recent cars, it felt strange to sit behind the wheel of a Mini Cooper, especially with its manual transmission. But he still enjoyed driving the—comparatively—imperfect car. It was only a short trip from the car-rental place to the parking lot, where he found an open spot with some difficulty.

There were many people waiting in the arrival hall of the airport. He had loads of time before the flight was due to arrive from London, and wandered over to a kiosk selling coffee. He was starving, but decided to wait until Christine arrived so they could have breakfast, or lunch, together.

He took his paper cup over to a table, stirring in packets of sugar with a plastic spoon. He thought how quickly he had become accustomed to luxury, how he was used to having his coffee prepared by specially trained baristas (except for the coffee he drank in the office, brewed by Barbara), putting special gourmet sugar in that coffee, and stirring it with a teaspoon, and certainly not one made out of plastic. He took a sip—it wasn't bad at all. Stanley looked around. The majority of people around him were dressed casually, in a style he was used to seeing at vacations and resorts. He stood out in his Brioni suit. He took another sip and then turned, sensing that someone was watching him. He tried to do it unnoticeably in his dark sunglasses, but he couldn't tell who it was. The coffee suddenly tasted bitter; the plastic spoon must have lent it an unpleasant aftertaste.

McKnight went outside, found a Smoking Area sign, and lit up a cigarette. Just because he couldn't see who was watching him didn't mean he was necessarily imagining things. McKnight trusted his gut. He remembered Dillon, that mysterious consultant, and his mood soured completely. But when he picked Christine out of the stream of passengers arriving from London, he was struck by her beauty, and felt a surge of new strength. Christine threw her arms around him and kissed him, then stepped back.

"Are you sad?" she asked.

"Not anymore," replied Stanley.

"Glad to hear it! What are your plans?"

"To spend at least a couple of days with you."

"Excellent!" Christine was not only beautiful, but efficient; "I found a lovely spot. I've rented a place for us there, for a couple days. Pag Island."

"I never heard of it," said Stanley, "Just the Pakleni Islands, where they burned some sinners."

"How awful? Did they really?"

"Yes, and they're still doing it today."

"Are you kidding, Stanley?"

"Yes, of course! Let's go," he said with a laugh.

Christine was a little surprised at Stanley's choice of car, but then said that the place where they were heading was probably not as chic as the resorts and hotels that he'd become accustomed to lately.

Stanley put their destination in his phone, and they left the parking lot.

"Why do you keep looking in the rearview mirror?" asked Christine. "Is someone following us?"

"Oh, ha ha, of course not!" said Stanley. "I'm just not used to this car yet."

"You could have rented a different one!"

"No, no this one's fine!"

Stanley drove from the airport at high speed along the Franjo Tudjman coastal highway, avoiding any traffic jams, and turned onto Prince Trpimir Street, once again shifting into the left lane.

"What's the rush?" Christine checked her seatbelt. "You act like you're trying to outrun someone."

"There you go again! First someone's following us, now I'm trying to outrun someone. I just want to get there as soon as I can. So, we just need to go straight along the E65, until the turn onto 160th, and then straight again. Are you hungry?"

"I only had a coffee at the airport."

"Same here."

As they drove, they kept an eye out for café or restaurant signs but kept missing the exits. They finally stopped at the Fortuna pizzeria after the toll at Posedarje.

"The Swiss banker is going to have pizza as well?" Christine teased him.

"Swiss bankers not only eat pizza; they also go to the toilet like ordinary people."

"I don't believe it! Then I'll go there as well."

They had a lunch of pizza and Coke. It was noisy in the pizzeria, but they were in the very back of the room, against the wall. Stanley was intensely thirsty, and the Coke didn't help, only making him thirstier.

"You've changed. A lot," said Christine.

"I've always liked Coke. Just didn't admit it," he said, trying to joke.

"You know what I'm talking about."

"What, exactly?"

"You've grown even quieter. You look around you from time to time like you're anxious about something. You're more wrapped up in your own thoughts. I can tell that you're happy to see me, but something is weighing on you. Are you sick, Stanley?"

"I'm as healthy as a horse," he said with a laugh.

He had a sudden, desperate urge to tell Christine absolutely everything, here in this provincial pizzeria. Everything except Mila, that is, but he was even prepared to tell her about his brief relationships with his neighbor and with Elise.

Stanley looked into Christine's eyes and realized that he didn't have the courage to tell her about his job or that the CIA was trying to contact him. Christine would understand about the other women, but if he told her about work and everything related to it, she would panic.

"I'm as healthy as a horse," he repeated. "It's just that this is the first time in a long while that I haven't had to rush off anywhere else, and it's making me nervous. I keep expecting a call from my office or a client. To be honest, I'm terribly, awfully tired."

Christine took his hand.

"Drink up your coke and let's go," she said.

Twenty minutes later, they were crossing the Paski bridge onto Pag Island. They were driving directly above the sea, the sun playing on the waves to their left. They crossed nearly the entire island, taking the 107 through the town of Novalja until they finally stopped at the Boskinac, a hotel and winery.

They arrived to find that their room wasn't ready yet, and the apologetic manager led them out onto the veranda, which had a marvelous view of the Novalja valley. He offered them a bottle of local wine on the house and suggested a local cheese with olive oil to go with it. Stanley asked for something more substantial in addition to the cheese, and the manager promised to send the waiter with freshly made lamb and baby vegetables.

Stanley filled their glasses and took a sip from his before tossing it all back in one gulp. The wine was fabulous. He poured himself another glass and asked the waiter who had just arrived with their cheese to bring another bottle.

"You're so tired you've decided to get drunk?" Christine asked.

"I'm not getting drunk. Remember that line? I'm just drinking a little wine," said Stanley, but then admitted: "Yes, actually, I wouldn't mind getting drunk. Not at all."

"So—it's not just exhaustion that's bothering you?"

Stanley raised his glass to watch the clouds through his wine, and sighed deeply.

"Not just that," he said and nodded as he pulled out his cigarettes.

"Ha," said Christine, "Now you're having a cigarette, after the second bottle you're going to be offering me marijuana, and then, before ordering your fourth, you're going to pull out the cocaine."

"I hate to disappoint you," said Stanley with a grim chuckle. "But if I did have marijuana or cocaine, I'd offer them to you."

He drank down half his glass. Christine followed his example.

"I don't want you to have to go it alone," she explained and drank the rest of her wine.

"It really is delicious, isn't it?"

"Okay, so what's going on, Stanley?"

"What? Oh, sorry…the thing is…"

McKnight fell silent. The waiter was approaching their table at the edge of the veranda with two large plates. McKnight thanked him and tried the meat.

"Excellent!" he said, and set his fork back down when the man had left.

"The problem is, Christine, that my work is tied to dirty money. Russian money. I'm covering up criminal transactions and laundering illegally obtained income. That's the short version. I can give you the long version, but there's no point."

"What! But your bank is one of the most respected financial institutions in the world! You said…"

"Well, that doesn't stop the bank from doing business with Russian oligarchs. Just yesterday I was on one of their yachts. A guy by the name of Gagarin. On that same yacht, he had Russian ministers, an FSB general, and staff from the Russian president's administration. They're all in the same group. And this Gagarin represents them. He's their front man. *Frontovik*. Billions of dollars flow through him, and his bank accounts, which I provide. Billions!"

"That's their personal money?" Christine was so stunned that she had forgotten all about the food. She just drank her glass of wine and held it out to Stanley for more. He complied, and topped up his own glass, before waving the waiter over and ordering another bottle.

"You could call it that. Their personal money. They appropriate huge sums from the national budget, interest from various deals, money raised from the tribute they all extort from Russian businessmen. But the important thing is that this personal money is all illegally acquired. And then they send it out of Russia using diplomatic mail; art, gold, jewels, and enormous sums of cash."

"But you don't have to deal with that, right?"

"I have to deal with that as well. I ensure that these packages are delivered. I accompany them. Oversee their placement in bank storage. In a word, Christine, I'm up to my ears in shit." McKnight drank his wine and lit up a cigarette.

"You could leave. Couldn't you just drop everything and go?"

"Not anymore. I can't go. I can't hide. I'm dirty now too, and the CIA came to see me."

"The CIA? What do they have to do with it?"

"The CIA is interested in illegal financial transactions, Christine. Especially if American citizens are involved."

"And you're sure that it was actually the CIA?"

"I can't be sure, no. It could have been the CIA, or maybe the Department of Justice. Who the hell knows? But that man who..." McKnight faltered. "Anyway, forget the minor details about how we met."

"Yes, stick to the main point!"

"He introduced himself as a consultant. A consultant working with the United States government. He got right down to it, told me he knew all about what I was doing, my contacts, and my ties to the Russians."

"So he says!"

"Christine, men like him don't bluff. If he knows about it, he can probably prove it in court."

"In court."

"Yes. Twenty years."

"Twenty years?" Christine, in shock, poked at her plate and raised the fork to her mouth, and when the piece of eggplant fell off, she just licked the tines, and her mouth automatically made several chewing motions as if the food had reached it. Despite the context, McKnight had to smile.

"Twenty years in prison, Christine. They promised me that. But they also promised that if I cooperated, they wouldn't press charges. It's up to me."

He drank his wine and lit yet another cigarette. Christine said nothing.

"You know what, I've lost my appetite," Stanley said.

"Me too."

"Want to take a walk?"

"Let's."

Outside, they chose a shady trail heading up the mountain. The sea was behind them, and the trunks of the pines on either side had been twisted by years of maritime winds. The pine needles scattering the ground made a soft, springy carpet beneath their feet. Stanley walked ahead, breathing deeply in the fresh air, and Christine held his hand.

"Where are we going?" she asked.

"I have no idea," McKnight replied. "Does it matter?"

Christine laughed and stopped.

"What's wrong?" he asked. "Tired already?"

"I'll always support you, Stanley," Christine began, her smile disappearing, now focused and intent. "Whatever happens. And not just when you ask for it. I'll offer you my support when I feel like you need it. And right now, I think there are several things you need to do."

"Christine..."

"Let me talk, please!"

"Ok, sorry, go ahead."

"First of all, you have to agree to cooperate with the government. They'll keep their word."

"How many times have they gone back on their word?"

"I wasn't finished!"

"Sorry, sorry."

"Secondly, you have to come back."

"To you?"

Christine laughed drily.

"Let's not worry about that for the moment. I mean come home, to America. Nothing good is going to come out of you staying in Europe. Especially working with Russians. They, especially, don't keep their word."

"How do you know that? From books?" Stanley brushed her face with his hand. "Movies?"

"It doesn't matter! I know! This isn't your game, and you're going to lose. You'll be lucky if prison is the worst of it. These people have no mercy. They'll find a way to get to you anyway, unless you make a deal with the government. Then you'll have a chance. Right?"

Stanley looked over Christine's shoulder. A yacht, tiny in the distance, crawled lazily over the waves of the bay. A bird was singing somewhere in the branches nearby.

"Right," nodded Stanley. "You're right, of course. But you don't know the details—there are reasons I can't act right away. I'll need time to get everything arranged."

"How much?"

"How much what?"

"How much time do you need?"

"A month. Yeah, I think I can do it in a month."

"Okay, then, in a month, you'll buy a ticket to San Francisco. And you'll contact the government. Agreed?"

"Agreed."

"Promise me."

"I promise."

Stanley pulled his arms around her, felt her skin against his, now warm from the sun, inhaled the scent of her hair. He stepped to the side of the path, pulling Christine behind him, and they were hidden from view behind a high, thick bush.

"We have the whole night ahead of us, Stan," she said, her voice hushed, as she unbuckled his belt.

Stanley thought about how he had used this same belt less than twenty-four hours ago to strike Mila's behind as she writhed and moaned beneath him. He closed his eyes, trying to chase the memory away, and raised the hem of Christine's skirt, gently slipping his fingers under her panties. Now she was unzipping his pants and taking him in her hand with such tenderness that his vision darkened with pleasure. Then she pushed his chest, down onto the covering of pine needles. Stanley lay down, and she lowered herself on top of him. The sun was behind her back, her face in shadow, but Stanley sensed her happy smile. He could feel her light weight, her inner wetness matching his pulsing length within her. He felt that he loved this woman. Her alone.

They had breakfast on the hotel veranda the next morning. It had been a long night—they made love, fell asleep, and woke up to make love again, over and over. They hardly spoke. In the dim hotel room their bodies clung together, one mouth finding the other. It was dawn when they finally went to sleep for good, and they woke up fresh and energized.

"Why can't you do it right away?" asked Christine, sipping her coffee.

"Do what?" Stanley took a piece of bacon from his plate.

"You said you needed a month to set everything up. Maybe you shouldn't delay? The sooner you talk to the government, the better."

"No, no, I need to prepare. I need to find out what they know."

"But that man you talked to said they knew everything, right?"

"The Russians call it *vzyat na pont*—I guess the closest translation would be to bluff, to act like you're in charge of a situation. That consultant, or adviser—that man, at any rate—could just be trying to intimidate me. He threatened me with prosecution, but does he have enough evidence to actually bring the case to trial? I could find myself in a really idiotic position."

McKnight split open his boiled egg in a cup, and dipped a piece of cheese into the yolk. Even if he did manage to put together the dossier of materials he needed, it still might not be enough to get himself out of the situation he was in. Moreover, he was starting to distrust that promise that he would escape prosecution. His experience interacting and doing business with the Russians had fundamentally changed his views on human nature. He saw people as dishonest and self-interested at their core. Before, not twelve months ago, he would have thought differently.

"An idiotic position is better than a jail term." Christine said emphatically.

"Trust me," said Stanley. "I'm doing this the right way."

They were planning to spend at least two days at the hotel, but when Stanley turned his phone on after breakfast (he had turned it off yesterday before they set off on their walk) he saw that Lagrange had been trying to contact him.

"Stanley! Where the hell have you been? Why didn't you answer your phone? Where are you?"

"Like I said, on the islands. In Croatia. Has someone been looking for me?"

"My dear McKnight, have you been on the internet? Watched television? The European news? No?"

"I've just been sleeping and eating." Stanley turned to Christine and took her hand.

"Lucky! But I'd watch the news if I were you."

"I will. But what's going on? And you didn't tell me whether someone was trying to get in touch with me."

"In order: Biryuza called, and I said what we had agreed, that you were in Geneva, in an important meeting. As for the news, it's about Gagarin. They announced a journalistic investigation of his affairs. Some fucking anticorruption foundation! They called him the front man of a group of corrupt Russian politicians."

Stanley felt his fingers holding the phone go numb.

"Are you listening to me?"

"Yes, Pierre. Go on."

"And in that damn press release, they name our bank. As the place where he launders his money!"

"Shit!"

"That's right, Stanley! It's all bad. And it's going to get worse. Okay, I'm going to call you back shortly. Don't turn off your phone anymore."

"What happened?" asked Christine, when Stanley set his phone down on the table.

Stanley briefly summarized his conversation with Lagrange.

"What are you going to do?" asked Christine.

"Go swimming with you."

"You're not going to watch the news?"

"What do I need the news for? Everything's clear as it is!"

Stanley and Christine walked down to the beach and took a swim. The water was pristine, transparent.

Stanley dove deep after a small stone and pretended for a moment there, underwater, that when he surfaced again, he would have gone back in time, before any investigations. He swam back to shore and saw that Lagrange had called him twice already.

"Yes, Pierre, did something else happen?"

"I've been talking to some of our contacts. It's not looking good for Gagarin. He just called Laville. Gagarin's in a panic—he could be accused of laundering money."

"That was to be expected," said McKnight, and immediately regretted it.

"Yes," agreed Lagrange. "It was. But he's going to take us all down with him. Actually, he's going to hide away in his Russia, and we're going to go down. Is that what you want?"

"No, Pierre, it is not."

"You're suspiciously calm."

"What do you want from me? Should I go drown myself? I haven't paid my hotel bill yet. Or returned my rental car. Let alone all my other responsibilities. If I run around shouting—we're lost! We're lost!—will that help?"

"Fine, fine, but you should know that we've already gotten calls from FINMA and the Swiss prosecutor's office."

"They're just doing their jobs, Pierre. I would…"

"Enough, McKnight! Gagarin is worried his assets will be frozen. That they'll seize his deposits with us. He wants to move his gold, diamonds, and paintings somewhere. So pay for your damn room and your damn car and get your ass to Singapore. Got it?"

"Got it."

"And Gagarin says hi. And hello from his wife. Did you get caught hip deep over there? His voice was displeased when he mentioned his wife."

"No, I didn't. There was nothing to catch."

"Ok, someone will meet you in Singapore. Take care, McKnight!"

"And you, Pierre, all the best!"

McKnight put the phone on the beach chair, and it slipped through a crack and fell onto a small pebble with a dull sound.

"Is it bad?" asked Christine.

"It's all bad," agreed McKnight. "But it's going to get worse!"

"You're turning into such an optimist, honey. Don't worry!" Christine put her arms around his neck and kissed his cheek. "If you don't hurt yourself, no one can hurt you."

CHAPTER 34

THEY WERE SITTING IN THE interior courtyard of the Raffles Hotel. The Singapore afternoon was hot, humid, and smelled of rotting fruit mixed with Indian fragrances.

The southwestern monsoon was in its second month, but had yet to bring any relief from the heat.

McKnight inwardly cursed the tropical climate, suffering as he was from unexpected allergy attacks, but he forced himself to smile and nod along with Mila's hysterical stupidity. Then agree with Biryuza's pompous pronouncements, listening with the air of an expert seriously considering the other man's comments.

The endless warm rain pounded on the glass roof sheltering the courtyard. The huge fan blades on the ceiling had some success at dispelling the oppressive heat and humidity, but did nothing to improve Stanley's terrible mood. Everything irritated him—Mila and Biryuza, the attentiveness of the hotel staff, the starched white tablecloth, and the intoxicating aroma of the strange flowers blooming from the bushes growing in the courtyard.

Biryuza insisted that he and Stanley order a mint julep with a double shot of bourbon.

Mila was, as usual, going heavy on the champagne. As her drunkenness progressed, she gradually took full possession of the ice bucket holding the bottle, waving the hovering waiter away. Eventually, she called for another bottle to replace the empty one, cursing through clenched teeth to shut Biryuza up as he tried to talk her out of it.

"I'm sorry, Mila, but that's the third bottle. Your third, Mila." Biryuza spoke softly but insistently.

"If I finish a third, I'll order a fourth," said Mila, seemingly unaffected by the champagne. "What's it to you?"

"It's unhealthy to drink so much champagne," he replied. "Have you heard of the Zelda syndrome? Named after the wife of F. Scott Fitzgerald. She drank champagne by the bucket and developed—"

"I'm going to develop something if you don't shut up," Mila said, hatred in her gaze. "You know what's going to develop, Stanley?"

Mila barely looked at Stanley. She gave every appearance of disliking him intensely. This seemed to surprise Biryuza, but Stanley understood her game—she would do everything she could to get him alone, and who would think anything of it, if he was so obviously unpleasant to her?

"Yes," replied Stanley, "I do."

"So?"

"You're going to tear this place apart."

"Aren't you the clever one!"

When the waiter came by, Biryuza had a long conversation with him about what kinds of bourbon could be used to make this cocktail. Then he asked Stanley about his favorite bourbons. Fighting back the desire to tell Biryuza to fuck off with his questions, Stanley rejected Jim Beam and Pappy Van Winkle, but approved Old Forester.

"An excellent choice," said the waiter.

"You have to remind him that the syrup should be from cane sugar," added Biryuza, but Stanley noted that in this hotel, they were likely already aware of that, without any advice from their guests.

The mint juleps were served in the traditional fashion of the American South, in chilled silver cups. Biryuza began a lecture on how to properly hold them so as not to disturb the lovely frost on the cup's exterior, and reduce the transfer of heat from one's hand. Stanley had no choice but to hear him out.

The cocktail, when McKnight finally tried it, was stellar. This mollified him somewhat, but then Biryuza started in on the architecture and history of the hotel. He asked Mila: "Do you know that this is where Vertinsky first sang his famous song, 'In Banana-Lemon Singapore'?"

"Who cares!" Mila said, finishing her glass and lighting a cigarette.

"And you?" Biryuza asked Stanley.

"I did not." McKnight took the pack of cigarettes from Mila and lit one of his own. "I don't know who Vertinsky is, as a matter of fact. Another of your rock stars from the USSR?"

"You ignorant American!" Biryuza gestured to the waiter for another round. "Do you at least know that it was named in honor of Sir Thomas Raffles, the founder of Singapore, or that it was built by Armenians, the Sarkies brothers?"

"Oh shut up, Biryuza!" Mila said. She lifted the bottle out of her bucket, knocking it over onto the marble floor with a crash. "Everyone's had enough of you!"

One waiter rushed over to clean up the ice, and another dashed off for a new bucket.

"Yes, yes, I'm the one they have had enough of." Biryuza thanked a third waiter, arriving with their cocktails. "You don't know anything, you're not interested in anything, and I'm trying to enlighten you! Show you the world. Like those gold plaques over there, do you know what they're for? McKnight?"

Stanley watched grimly as the frost on his cocktail glass grew thicker. There was no escape from the humidity here.

"McKnight?" Biryuza repeated.

"I didn't see any gold plaques," responded Stanley. "I have no interest in the features of hotel architecture."

"If you read them, you'll learn that Somerset Maugham, Joseph Conrad, and Rudyard Kipling have all stayed here. I suppose you don't know anything about them, either?"

"Listen, Biryuza," Mila began, "if you don't change the topic and your tone, I'm going to break this bottle over your head."

"Maugham called this hotel a symbol of Singapore, and you—"

Enraged, Mila grabbed the neck of the Kristal bottle sticking out of the bucket.

"All right, all right!" Biryuza raised his hands in surrender and sighed. "What am I going to do with you incurious wretches?" He took a sip of his drink.

After a pause he began again, "What would you say to moving here to work? It's a lovely place."

"And live in this hotel for $3,000 a night?"

"I'm sure you can afford it, McKnight."

"No, thanks!"

"Well, you could rent an apartment as well. Or buy one, really."

"The climate's not for me, thanks. It's a damned sauna."

"But everything's better here in terms of personal capital than in your precious Switzerland. The banks are more reliable, they have better credit ratings, and they are less politically biased."

"Sure, that's a great idea," Stanley agreed indifferently.

"I imagine there's going to be an outflow of Russian money from Switzerland to here soon. Are you even listening to me, McKnight?"

"Huh? Yes, I'm listening. You're right: this cocktail has the right balance of flavors, not too sweet."

"Ah, forget it! All right, let's order another."

Stanley felt himself beginning to get drunk, but at least the allergies tormenting him had eased up. The julep was light and refreshing, but Stanley was a bit worried about what would happen if he tried to walk away from the table. Then he decided it didn't matter. Maybe he wouldn't live to try.

He had arrived in Singapore early that morning, changing time zones in the more difficult direction, from west to east. He felt like a boxer who'd taken too many punches to the head. When he reached the hotel, all he wanted was to fall into bed and sleep just a little, but then Mila showed up at his door.

Stanley knew who it was before he looked through the peephole from the sound of her nails scratching against the wood.

She always scratched doors with a certain rhythm, as if playing a song. Stanley opened the door, and she slipped past him into the room.

McKnight was sick to death of meeting her like this, over and over— he'd arrive somewhere, and Mila would appear at his door, slip inside and tell him they had to make love quickly, since they were expected at lunch, breakfast, or dinner, or they had to drive somewhere to meet someone.

Everything was different this time. Mila looked tired. Her full lips were dry and cracked, there were dark circles under her eyes, and it looked as though she hadn't washed her hair quite some time.

Stanley said hello, but Mila didn't respond. She sat down in an armchair, crossed her legs, and lit a cigarette.

"Did you rush over here to save my dear husband?"

"What are you talking about, Mila?"

"I'm surrounded by assholes. Cowards. Garbage." It was as if she hadn't heard him at all. "Not a single real man. Oh, some of their dicks are good enough. But a real man is more than just his dick. That's something else. Do you know what, McKnight?"

Stanley opened the minibar and offered Mila a drink. She pointed at the bottle of vodka.

"With orange juice," she said, then repeated, "So, do you know what it is or not?"

"Mila," sighed McKnight, "I'm very tired." He mixed her drink and opened a bottle of Coke for himself, downing half of it in greedy gulps.

"Exactly!" Mila poked him with one long finger. "All the men around me only talk about themselves. I! I! I'm tired. I'm this, I'm that, I shit myself...or I want! I want this! I want that! Honey, wipe my nose! Honey, I want a hand job!"

"What do you want, Mila?" He was seized with the sudden desire to hit her across the head with the bottle in his hand. "Why did you come here?"

Again, she seemed not to hear him.

"You can tell a real man, Stanley, by his actions. And not just any actions, but the right action, the right action at the right moment, that's important too."

"Mila, I'm not a child. I don't need you to teach me how to live."

"Shut up! If you were a man, you would take some action. You'd get money, and we'd run away together."

"And now you shut up," Stanley said harshly. "You thought I was one of your things, just another toy like everyone else around you. But I'm not a toy. And we need to end this. And I'm certainly not going to take money from anyone."

"End this? End what?"

"Our relationship."

"You'll do what I decide. And we'll end our relationship when I want. Did you forget that you still owe me one wish?"

"Enough, Mila!"

"Do you want me to tell Viktor everything? Who's he going to believe if I tell him that you forced me, if I tell him that you tried to get the numbers to his personal accounts from me?"

"I know them already," Stanley said, sinking into a chair, exhausted. "What the hell do I need his accounts for?"

"You don't really know him yet, you stupid man. You should be more careful with me. And I don't want to hear anything—*anything*—more about breaking up!" She tossed the remainder of her vodka cocktail at Stanley. "You need to change."

Mila looked even worse now, in the courtyard at lunch, despite her heavy makeup and thick layer of lipstick. Her hands shook occasionally. He pitied her, but he was sure he had made the right decision—he had to end their relationship at all costs. He also thought that if Mila tried to tell Gagarin something in this condition, her husband would be more likely to believe Stanley than his own wife.

Mila sensed Stanley's covert observation and, with a defiant air, took a packet of cocaine out of her pocket and pulled the tablecloth back to pour out a little onto the marble surface of the table. She pulled out her credit card to make a line.

Stanley understood the reason for her behavior—she was high all the time—several hours ago when she'd shown up at his door, and now, drunk on champagne. And she was using something stronger than cocaine.

"Mila!" cried Biryuza. "What are you doing? That's illegal!"

"Fuck off!"

"We're in Singapore, Mila," Stanley said, trying to come to Biryuza's aid.

"And you can go right to hell too!"

McKnight realized that if the police arrived (and the staff here would definitely call the police) he might be detained, which he did not want at all. He started looking around, as if seeking out an escape route. Then his salvation appeared through the doorway of the courtyard—a twitchy, nervous Gagarin trailed by Durand.

Gagarin quickly took in the situation. He strode over and brushed the coke onto the floor and flipped the tablecloth back into place.

"You idiot!" Gagarin roared at Mila. "No more of this! And get out of here! Scram! Now!"

"Viktor, honey! I'm happy to see you too!" Mila leaned back in her chair. "How was your morning? Have you had breakfast?"

"Idiot woman!"

"Calm down, Viktor," Durand hissed into his hear. "Don't shout!"

But Gagarin did not, or could not, calm down. He swung at Mila, who meekly turned to take the blow. Gagarin didn't hit her, though, and rammed his fist into the table instead. He howled in pain and began cradling his injured hand, rocking it back and forth.

"You came close to making a serious mistake, Mila," Durand said. "If you get caught with drugs in Singapore, it's a death sentence, and not even your husband's money could save you. Twenty-five years in prison would be the best-case scenario."

"You can fuck right off too," Mila replied with a sweet smile and then knocked the bucket with champagne onto the floor with one quick blow and burst into tears.

"Nobody here loves me!" Tears were streaming down her face, and she sniffled as she talked. "Everyone turns on me. Nobody thinks about me. So what if I go to jail or…" She looked at Durand with sudden interest.

"How do they execute people in Singapore?"

"Goddamn it, Mila!" Gagarin growled. "I told you to get out of here. Go to your room! You can snort as much coke as you want there. But it would be a better idea to go to sleep!"

"Sleep? How will I make it to my room?" Mila made an attempt to stand and nearly fell over. McKnight caught her elbow.

"Stanley will help you," said Gagarin.

"This damn Yankee? This ruthless, despicable banker? Nothing is sacred to him!" Mila's speech was growing less and less intelligible. "He's just as heartless as all of you. But he…" Mila stuttered to a stop.

McKnight thought that now would be a good time for the local police to show up. If they took Mila in and charged her with a drug crime, that would solve a lot of his problems. He also thought that Mila was on the verge of saying something that would betray their secret to Gagarin.

Gagarin ignored Mila entirely. "Stanley, I'm sorry to ask, buddy, but can you help me out here?"

"No problem, Viktor. I'll take your wife to her room."

"Thank you, my friend! And then come right back down to the lobby—we need to go to Freeport."

CHAPTER 35

MILA WAS SILENT AND COMPLIANT as McKnight guided her through the inner courtyard to the elevators, his hand at her elbow.

She could barely walk. The hotel employee who called the elevator for them kept his face blank, but McKnight noticed a worried look in his eyes as he took in Mila's pale face. She was breathing heavily and licking her lips; she'd eaten all the lipstick away already.

"Can I help you, sir?" he asked very quietly.

"I'll manage," said McKnight, and they went into the elevators.

They made it to Mila's room without any adventures, aside from a few stumbles on the way. She spent a long time looking for her key card at the door. Stanley finally took her purse, squatted down, and dumped all its contents onto the hallway floor. The card wasn't there.

"Maybe Viktor has it?" Stanley asked, looking up at Mila.

Mila shrugged and sighed heavily.

"Does someone have an extra key? Maybe Shamil?"

"I don't know. I don't know!" Mila said, leaning against the wall and sliding slowly down it onto the floor. "I. Don't. Care." She stretched out her legs. "I…"

Her head dropped onto her chest.

His phone rang. It was Gagarin calling, wondering how much longer they'd have to wait.

"I'm sorry, Viktor, but we can't find the key card to the room. Mila is about to pass out, she's sitting on the floor, and it's not in her purse."

"You'll have to pick her up, McKnight. The card's in her back pocket. I wouldn't trust anybody else to do it, but you're like a brother to me—I know you're not going to grope my wife. Go on. I'll wait."

"Okay, hang on!"

McKnight picked Mila up, so that she was hanging over his shoulder, and felt around in her pockets. The card was there.

"Finally," muttered Mila. "That's so nice. Stick your hand deeper. Come on, Stanley. Don't be shy. Stick your finger in my ass."

"Did you find it?" asked Gagarin. "What's she saying? I can't hear her."

"I can't make it out," said Stanley. "She's mumbling. Yes! I found it!"

"Excellent! Get her in and put her in bed. But face down, remember—face down!"

"Yes, I've got it."

McKnight opened the door, dragged Mila in, pulled her all the way to the bedroom, and put her in bed, following Gagarin's instructions. Then he went back into the hallway and gathered everything from the floor back into her purse. When he returned, Mila wasn't in her bed.

"Shit! Motherfucker!" he cursed, turned around, and took a blow to the face from something large and heavy. The object Mila had hit him with shattered into pieces at the impact.

"Asshole! You think you can do me like that, huh? I'll kill you, you son of a bitch!"

Stanley realized that Mila had hit him with one of the vases from the table in her bedroom. She picked up another, which looked to be made out of metal. Stanley grabbed her wrist, and she dropped the vase.

"You're hurting me, you animal!" She tried to knee him, but McKnight pushed her away.

He pushed her harder than he had intended, and she flew into the table, knocking the other vases onto the floor. One or two broke. Mila fell down, then tried and failed to get up. She grabbed onto Stanley's leg instead.

"I'm sorry, baby," she said quickly. "Please forgive me. I'm so sorry! Stay with me! Please, I'm sorry. I can't live without you! I'll kill myself! I'll cut my wrists, stay! I'm begging you, please, don't leave me!"

McKnight bent down and pried her fingers off his leg. He felt the blood trickling from his head wound, and got out a handkerchief, pressing it to the cut.

Mila got on her fours, then her knees. Her smeared mascara made her eyes look huge. Tears streamed down her cheeks.

"Don't leave me! Or, no, let's run away together, today, right now. No one will catch us, I know how to hide from him. It's not hard. He's such an idiot. I hate him. Baby!"

She started crawling toward Stanley.

"Forget it, Mila! It's not going to happen. This was a mistake, Mila. This is over. Everything is finished between us. Do you understand?"

Stanley's words pushed her back into a state of rage. She came up swinging, and McKnight threw up his arm to block her. She landed a painful blow on his forearm.

"So that's how you want it?" she said. "Fine!" She tried to kick him, but he dodged and ran to the door.

"Running away?" he heard her call hoarsely. "Run, you bastard! I wish you were dead!"

Same to you, thought Stanley. When he made it to the hallway he turned back. Mila was standing in the doorway.

"Damn you to hell."

McKnight went downstairs, still holding the handkerchief to his wound.

He was close to giving up and leaving. Just leaving. He'd resign by email to Lagrange—no, directly to Laville. Leave everything in his apartment in Zurich and his Porsche in the parking lot. He could hire someone to deal with them later. He'd transfer all his money to some small bank in the Midwest, then the Cayman Islands, to his own offshore account. He could close that and take the cash. Buy a plane ticket, get Christine, and move to Napa. They could buy a vineyard, make their own wine. They'd call it Chateau McKnight...no, Lagrange knew he loved Napa, and he might have mentioned it to Gagarin as well. Okay, so they'd go somewhere else, then, maybe Los Angeles—he had a friend there who had some ties to the less savory side of the city, and who he had heard could provide people with new documents and identities. They would need that—he couldn't simply quit this job, even if he tried to disappear. He knew too much; they would look for him, and they would find him. Of this, McKnight was certain.

Stanley went into the restroom next to the hotel's front desk. When he lifted the handkerchief from his head, it reopened the wound and started the bleeding again. He wet the handkerchief and put it back in place. Then he went out and asked the clerk there for a Band-Aid, and the man grew alarmed, started asking a string of questions: what happened? Where was he wounded? Did he need a doctor? But Stanley told him that he had banged his head on a corner leaving his room, and that he didn't need a doctor, all he needed was a Band-Aid. He refused any further help and went to put it on himself.

He washed the cut in the bathroom, wiping around it with a soft, scented hotel towel, and stuck the Band-Aid over it. He felt something scratching his neck. When he reached back, he discovered a shard of the vase Mila had broken over his head, caught between the collar of his jacket and the collar of his shirt.

Stanley picked it out and, considering, decided not to throw it out. He stuck it in his pocket. When he exited the hotel, he saw an enormous black limousine at the curb, with Gagarin pacing nervously alongside it. Gagarin's figure and balding head were reflected in the mirror shine of the vehicle's black paint.

McKnight laughed to himself, despite his condition. This limousine would be inconvenient and unwieldy on the streets of Singapore, but matched Gagarin's appearance perfectly. It was either parody or a hint of something serious, some kind of threat.

McKnight looked around. Ah, the threat was close at hand—a Jeep with security guards was parked nearby, with Shamil leaning out of the driver's side.

"What took you so long, Stan!" Gagarin rushed over. "We've been waiting and waiting, and you…hey, what's this? What happened?"

"It's nothing." Stanley tried to back up, but Gagarin got a firm grip on his elbow and walked him out from under the hotel awning and into the light so he could examine the wound.

"Who did this? It was her, wasn't it?" Gagarin's eyes grew hard. "You can tell me the truth."

"I did it myself, running into the corner of the door. When she couldn't open the door and I found it by looking through her pockets, she thought…"

"That you were groping her, and took a swing at you?"

"No, Viktor, she just stumbled backward, and I was trying to keep her from falling, and hit myself. It's not her fault, it was just an accident, really."

Gagarin lit a cigarette, looking him over. "Hmm, somehow I don't quite believe you, McKnight! All right, get in and let's go. They're expecting us."

Gagarin pushed aside the driver in a cap with gold braid and opened the back door himself. The door swung open backward, and Gagarin ushered Stanley in first and then followed him. Durand and Biryuza were already inside.

"Uh-oh!" said Biryuza at the sight of Stanley's face.

"Come on. Let's go!" ordered Gagarin.

The limousine pulled smoothly away from the curb, followed by the Jeep with security guards. All four passengers sat in the back, Gagarin and Durand facing forward, and Biryuza and Stanley with their backs to the driver.

"I love the roads here," said Biryuza. "Or, how they organize the flow of traffic, to be more precise—their interchanges are excellent!"

"It's not the intersections that do it," said Durand. "Or not alone, anyway. The founder of modern Singapore, Lee Kuan Yew, instituted a rule that you needed to buy a certificate to own a private car. Those certificates might cost two or three times what your car is worth. They're sold at auctions, and that money is used to fund public transport. 'Dracula' cars are popular here."

"What are you talking about, Robert?" Gagarin said gloomily, as if rousing from sleep.

"Draculas—cars that you can only drive from sunset to sunrise and on the weekends. Certificates for them are cheaper, and they're sold outside of auctions."

"That wouldn't be possible in Russia," Biryuza said, shaking his head.

"Nothing's impossible in Russia," replied Gagarin. "All you can do in Russia is make money, and not everyone can...sorry, I interrupted you, Robert."

"No, no, that's fine, Viktor. It wasn't important."

The limousine stopped suddenly. The driver rolled down the window separating their compartments.

"Sir," he said to Gagarin, "there's an accident ahead, and the road is closed. Okay to choose a different route?"

"Talk to Shamil. If he says yes, we'll go around. And don't bother us again!" Gagarin closed the window.

"And these are the roads and traffic system you were praising!" said Gagarin. "Everything works, but if it starts raining, everything falls apart."

"But this happens all over the world," replied Durand.

"There are always accidents in Russia. It's the exception when the roads are functioning normally," snorted Biryuza. "Why do you think they've managed to figure it out in Singapore and not in Russia, Robert?"

"I'm not sure I understand the question."

"Okay, look—Singapore has an authoritarian regime; Russia has an authoritarian regime. Singapore's leaders remain in power; Russia's leaders remain in power. Outsiders call what is happening in both places 'authoritarian modernization,' while inside Russia they only talk about modernization, but nothing changes, even though we've got more authoritarianism than you can shake a stick at. How should we understand that?"

"Probably because the population here is Chinese, Malaysian, and Indian, and Russia has Russians. Different kinds of brains."

"What does that have to do with anything?" Biryuza looked at Durand, surprised. "You don't like Russians? Think they're incompetent? Unskilled? You think everything depends on race and nationality?"

"Not completely, but it does have an impact. The Chinese are good at things that the French, say, can't do. Everyone knows that, right? Singapore moved from the third world into the first mostly because of their particular mentality."

"And what do you think?" Biryuza asked Stanley.

Judging by the fact that they weren't taking a detour, Shamil must not have approved any shortcuts. The limousine did start moving slowly forward, though. A traffic policeman was waving the driver around the jam.

"I think that cultural mentality may have an impact, but it's not the main factor," said Stanley.

"Well, well! So what's the main factor, then?"

"The most important thing is motive. The leader here fought for his country and the welfare of its citizens. But in Russia, the nation isn't their main focus, let alone its inhabitants…"

"This is interesting," Gagarin broke in, looking up from his text-message correspondence. "So what's most important to the leaders in Russia?"

"Power. Only power. It's a means to an end in the rest of the world, but in Russia, it is the end. I just realized that recently, and I've seen a lot of evidence to support my theory since then," said Stanley. He immediately regretted his words when he saw Gagarin's expression grow harsh and angry.

But then his frown disappeared, and he slapped Stanley's knee.

"You're right, my friend. You're so right!"

Everyone laughed, relieved. McKnight laughed the loudest, and Gagarin picked up his phone to make a call after getting another text.

"Yes, Stewart, keep going up. Up, I said."

He ended the call, but kept his eyes on his phone; he seemed to be on a video call. He nodded approvingly from time to time.

"I'm buying something at Sotheby's in Hong Kong," said Gagarin, sensing his companions' curiosity. "Chinese porcelain, a bowl, over a thousand years old, from the Song dynasty. Do you like porcelain, McKnight?"

"I'm a practical man," replied Stanley. "If I can't use something in my everyday life, I'm not that interested in it."

"That's a soulless American for you!" laughed Gagarin. "You don't understand the sublime. But I love things for their beauty. I like to think about the long history of an object. Recently—"

A phone call interrupted his rumination.

"I said go up! It doesn't matter, Stewart. I want that bowl, and it's going to be mine! Yes, fine!"

Gagarin turned off his phone and flopped back onto the seat, looking pleased.

"I recently bought a vase by the same craftsman for ten million. Ten million dollars, Stanley. Exquisite! It's in my room. Quite a heavy vase."

McKnight watched Gagarin carefully. He didn't believe this talk about his love of beauty; he knew that money was all Gagarin cared about, and how to better invest it. And money was the only interest he had in Chinese porcelain, regardless of its age or the dynasty in which the bowl or vase or anything else was made. Only money, always money. Moreover, Stanley suddenly realized that this vase was what Mila had hit him with, and that she had intentionally grabbed that valuable vase. With one blow, she struck out at the lover who was trying to leave her and the husband she despised.

McKnight slipped his hand in his pocket, touching the shard of the vase. He struggled against the temptation to hold it up and ask, "Is this your million-dollar vase, then?"

"Yes!" Gagarin pumped his fist in the air. "It's mine! My agent knows what he's doing, held on till the end. The vase is mine! Biryuza, get in touch with him, and have him send it here, to that—what do you call it? Where we're headed."

"To Freeport," Biryuza prompted his boss.

CHAPTER 36

At the Freeport storage facility, situated next to the Changi Airport, they were met by two senior employees of the company. When Stanley heard them speaking French, he realized Gagarin had brought Durand as his interpreter. Although Biryuza boasted of his excellent French skills, he, too, soon grew tired of deciphering their rapid speech and asked Durand for assistance as well.

What Stanley couldn't understand was the purpose behind his own presence there. But he chose not to fight it. Gagarin was clearly trying to draw him in closer, strengthen the ties binding him, and one of those ropes was this visit to the storage facility.

The two employees played their parts like actors on the stage—the first, tall and bony, would begin, and the second, short and plump, would finish for him. And if the first man walked ahead, the second would bring up the rear, letting the guests walk in front of him. Then they would switch positions, as if rehearsed ahead of time.

"Le Freeport Singapore provides the safe storage of precious metals, antiques, works of art, vintage automobiles, rare wines and cigars, diamonds, and jewelry," began the first.

The second waited for Durand to translate, then continued, "Wealthy clients of Freeport also have the opportunity to buy and sell valuables without paying duties or taxes."

They passed through several guard posts and took the elevator down to the vault.

"Le Freeport offers direct access to the airport terminal, twenty-four-hour security, temperature and humidity control, restoration services, and has fully equipped offices and showrooms for select guests wishing to hold private auctions, as well as providing full logistical support," said the second.

"Our clients include well-known companies like Christie's Fine Art Storage Services, Fine Art Logistics, Malca-Amit Singapore, and Stamford Cellars, who use our services for the transport, storage, and sale of valuable objects," the first man went on.

"The activity at Le Freeport is monitored by the Monetary Authority of Singapore, the Ministry of Home Affairs, and the Ministry of Finance, in order to prevent money laundering and financial terrorism," said the plump employee, looking meaningfully at Gagarin.

"What's that all about?" Gagarin asked suspiciously.

"Everything has already been settled!" Durand said. "Don't worry, Viktor. We won't have any problems."

"I'm not worried. It's your job to worry."

"We have the strictest possible security policies, including the electronic monitoring of our staff, clients, and stored items, and armed guards patrol the grounds. The temperature and humidity of our storage area is carefully controlled to protect the items kept there. Any damage or spoilage of valuables as a result of improper temperature and humidity or other errors is grounds for the termination of a contract, and for compensation from the operator, logistics company, or other organization working at Le Freeport," the thin man said, his explanation accompanied by theatrical gestures.

Another employee was waiting for them at the door to Gagarin's personal vault. He entered a code into a remote and then tactfully stepped to the side as Gagarin entered his own passcode. The door opened, and the guests went inside.

"And what if you need to get in when I'm not here?" asked Gagarin.

"A good question, monsieur!" the employees exclaimed in unison. "In that case, we have the option of entering a particular combination of our own passcodes, together with several other employees, including the head of the security service on duty. That combination alone will open the door of your vault in your absence."

"This is necessary, because the customs service has the right to visit all sections of the Freeport to carry out inspections and investigations at any time," the shorter man said.

"You see, license holders operating at Le Freeport must comply with the laws of Singapore regarding money laundering and financial terrorism as well as legislation to combat corruption, narcotics, and other serious crimes. And those laws give them the right to conduct any manner of inspection," concluded the tall man.

"Can I ask a question?" Stanley interjected, raising his hand like a student at a lecture.

"Of course, sir!"

"What about confidentiality?"

"We maintain the strictest confidentiality regarding client information, and do not disclose details on client agreements to third parties," the tall man answered with a smile.

"Hey, McKnight," Gagarin called, "Look over here!"

Gagarin's paintings hung on the walls of his vault. A video camera was pointed at each one.

"I have monitors in frames hanging on the walls of my house in Moscow," Gagarin proclaimed, "that show the video feed of the originals from the Freeport. That way I can enjoy the paintings all the time at home. High-quality video! You can see every brush stroke. Three-fucking-D! Not bad, eh?"

"Not bad, Viktor," said Stanley, and nodded, rubbing his finger along the fragment of the ten-million-dollar vase in his pocket. "Not bad at all!"

Gagarin sang praises to the Freeport all the way back to the hotel. He said that he was sick of Europe, and he was going to transfer all of his assets to Singapore, including his valuables from Laville's storage, as soon as possible. He cast sneaking glances at Stanley throughout his rant, but the latter only shrugged and nodded.

There's not a single bank in Singapore that would take a client like Gagarin, Stanley thought. *You've got too bad a reputation for that, buddy; compliance would turn you away at the door.*

Gagarin obviously wanted Stanley to object, to defend the benefits of Swiss banks, but Stanley chose not to. Instead, he said that times were changing, that players shifted on the field, but that Swiss banks in general, and Laville in particular, would survive, even if serious clients like Gagarin left them.

Gagarin was clearly unhappy to hear this. Something nasty flashed in his expression, but he just grimaced and huffed contemptuously. He didn't say anything the rest of the ride.

When they arrived, McKnight immediately set off for his room, declining Biryuza's offer of another mint julep or two. He hung the Do Not Disturb sign on his door, locked it, and secured the chain for good measure, before taking a shower.

For a long time afterward, he sat naked in an armchair, staring off into space. Then he stood abruptly, took out his wallet, and found Frank Dillon's business card in a secret compartment.

He felt like the card was burning his fingers. He stroked the edges, aware that he would be taking an irreversible step by making that call. He keyed in the numbers on his cell phone.

A young woman replied, her tone flat and professional. She asked whom he was calling.

"I'm looking for Mr. Dillon," said Stanley. "I thought this was his personal number."

"It is. Mostly," the woman said, seemingly fatigued by the performance of her duties. "Mr. Dillon will return your call shortly."

In two minutes, the hotel phone rang.

"Good afternoon, Stanley McKnight. I'm happy that you called," said Dillon. "It's better that we avoid cell phone calls, since your Russian friends can listen to all your conversations."

"Is that so?" said Stanley. "What about this number?"

"We have equipment that can be hooked up to fixed-line phones. It will make our conversation unintelligible for anyone listening in. All they'll hear is some gurgling noises."

"Then they'll realize right away that we're trying to hide something."

"Maybe they will, and maybe they won't. There's always a risk. You want a 100 percent guarantee? That doesn't exist. But I take it you didn't call just to chat, am I right?"

"Right. I'm ready to talk about working together."

"Excellent, McKnight, excellent! You're in Singapore, I hear. You're just back from Freeport Singapore, having a rest…ok, come on back to the US. You're from California? I'll be there, as it happens, maybe even by tomorrow. Go see your wife, and I'll be in touch. You don't need to worry about getting in touch with me. And remember: you're being watched."

"Your people?"

"That would be great, but unfortunately, not just mine. Don't do anything stupid, and try not to attract Shamil's attention—that's the name of Gagarin's head of security, right? And please, act natural. Calm. If they invite you to have a drink, next time, don't say no."

"How do you know about that?"

"I don't know anything, McKnight. I just guess." Dillon chuckled into the receiver and added in Russian, "Do svidaniya!"

McKnight had planned to have room service deliver his dinner and spend the rest of the evening in his room. But after the conversation with Dillon, he realized that would arouse unnecessary suspicion.

McKnight cleaned himself up a little and went down to the lobby, where he ran into Biryuza. The other man was delighted to see him, and invited him to come along to the Geylang district. When Stanley asked what there was to do in Geylang, Biryuza just laughed and told him he'd find out.

Twenty minutes later, they were walking along narrow streets toward the Parkway Parade shopping center. Soon, they were practically surrounded by girls offering to spend some time with them, but Biryuza, clearly not a first-time visitor to the neighborhood, pulled Stanley through the crowd behind him.

Finally, they reached a small karaoke restaurant. They sat down, and were soon joined by an extraordinarily beautiful girl with bronze skin, sky-blue eyes tilted upward at the corners, and fabulous breasts. After a couple minutes, Stanley came to the conclusion that she had started out life as a man.

"This is Sili," Biryuza said, "Where are your girlfriends, Sili?"

"Busy, always busy," Sili replied in English with a heavy Chinese accent. "But I can still find them.

"But make sure they're girls!" put in McKnight, just in case.

Sili gave Stanley a disdainful look and turned away. The girl who she gestured over was just as beautiful, but her eyes were green.

"Where are you beautiful girls from?" asked Stanley.

"The Philippines," giggled the girls.

When Stanley came down for breakfast the next morning, he found the whole group sitting at the same table. Biryuza greeted him warmly, Mila had a twisted smile on her face, and Durand and Shamil nodded; Gagarin alone showed no reaction to his appearance.

McKnight sat down next to Biryuza, across from Mila and Gagarin.

"Where did you disappear yesterday?" asked Biryuza in a whisper.

"I left. You should have warned me! I didn't expect her to have a dick!" Stanley replied in the same stage whisper. "I specifically checked—no Adam's apple, so I figured…"

"There's a special surgery to remove the Adam's apple, and anyway, women have them too, they're just less pronounced. But forget that: tell me how it went!"

McKnight laughed. Sili's friend had been affectionate and sweet, but he still decided not to stay. He left her payment anyway, for the services that she hadn't had a chance to perform.

"Everything went great," he said. "Thanks for a pleasant evening."

"What are you two lovebirds whispering about?" Gagarin asked loudly. "What's the secret?"

"They're homos," Mila said, her voice hoarse. "They've recently become lovers. You didn't know, Viktor? The Singapore vice squad caught them last night."

"I'd shut up if I were you, the girl who was about to do a line of cocaine in public," Gagarin said.

"So?" he glared at Biryuza. "I'm waiting?"

"We visited some prostitutes in Geylang last night," Biryuza replied calmly. "Had some Filipino food for dinner…"

"They fucked some Filipina whores," Mila interrupted. "Or got fucked, more likely. How are you, Stanley? Your ass isn't too sore?"

"That's enough, Mila," Gagarin said.

"I'm just curious!"

"It's time for you to shut up. Now." Gagarin put enough threat into those words that even Mila got scared.

Gagarin broke into happy laughter.

"Who else got scared?" he asked. "McKnight?"

"I'm always scared," answered Stanley, putting some avocado salad on his plate.

"Don't be scared, my friend. In a week, we'll be having the time of our life, and there'll be more than enough to be afraid of then. Have you ever been to the running of the bulls?"

"No, I never have."

"Uncultured swine! We go to Pamplona every year. Always! Mila," Gagarin began, putting his arm around his wife's shoulders, but she brushed it off with a snort, "always demands that she be allowed to join in, but it's man's game. Men only."

"Especially if you put about five grams of coke up your nose beforehand," Biryuza added quietly.

"Those are the times we're living in, Stanley—people can't just enjoy something. They have to add coke or alcohol. But if I have to choose, I'll take vodka. We'll expect you in Pamplona in five days. I won't take no for an answer."

"How could he say no, Viktor?" Mila looked over at Stanley with hatred in her eyes. "He's one of your minions."

"Didn't I tell you to shut your mouth? Are you looking for trouble?"

Mila hunched her shoulders and lit a cigarette. Gagarin waited a moment and then went on as if nothing out of the ordinary had occurred.

"I really like it here. Not the hotel, although it's not bad. Could be better, but not bad. I'm talking about Singapore itself. I might buy a house here. My darling drunk wife smashed up a vase worth millions of dollars yesterday. I forgave her, of course, but I decided to give her a task to complete—to find us a house. A good house. In one night. And what do you know—she found one! A villa on Sentosa Island, for about $25 million, with a private beach; it even has a helipad. I want to go there and have a look. We'll go with Mila, have lunch somewhere. McKnight!"

"Yes, Viktor?" Stanley, his omelet finished, wiped his mouth and looked up at Gagarin.

"You'll join us, of course?"

"I'm afraid I'll have to decline, Viktor. When the documents for the purchase are ready, send them to me, but otherwise, you don't need my services for this. I need to fly to California as soon as possible."

"California? What do you need to go to the States for?"

Stanley caught a note of wariness in Gagarin's voice; it wasn't the first time, either. He was watching McKnight as if he suspected him of something. Stanley wondered what was worse—that he was having an affair with the wife of a Russian oligarch or that he planned to sell that oligarch out, hand him over, along with all his politician and bureaucrat friends, to the American government? He decided there wasn't much difference in the level of betrayal and that the end result of both would be the same. And smiled.

"Something funny, Stanley?" Gagarin asked.

"Nothing's funny, Viktor," answered McKnight. "I just might happen to have my own personal life, that's all. And if you recall, I do have a wife living in the States. Who I need to see. A family matter, if you will."

"The same woman who came to Moscow?" Mila asked with a sneer. "Oh yes, I saw her picture. Shamil showed me. Surprised, Viktor? I asked him to. After all, it has to do with your security, doesn't it?"

"Thank you, my sweet. I just don't know what I would do without your tender care."

"As for you, Stan, I have to say that I'm not very impressed with your taste."

"It is what it is," said McKnight, realizing that there was no conflict between Gagarin and Mila—he had forgiven her for the vase and her hysterics. He remembered a Russian proverb: a husband and wife are the same devil, and he felt again that he had made the right choice, breaking things off with Mila.

"Go to hell, McKnight!" Mila exclaimed, as if reading his thoughts, and Gagarin laughed.

"And a good day to you," Stanley replied calmly.

CHAPTER 37

S TANLEY LEFT ON THE NEXT flight to Los Angeles out of the Changi Airport. He could have waited for a direct flight to San Francisco, but that would have meant another seven hours in Singapore, and he wanted to get out of town as soon as possible.

He went through registration and security, and when he was waiting at the gate, Barbara called him. She wanted to know where he was, and Stanley told her that he was very tired, and needed to see his wife, and would she please ask Lagrange to call him. But as soon as she hung up, he switched off his phone.

Stanley got settled in business class, ordered a double bourbon, drank it, and asked the stewardess not to disturb him. He was asleep before the plane had reached cruising altitude. When he awoke, it was night outside the plane, and he was powerfully thirsty. He ordered a water and another bourbon. The stewardess told him that he had missed an excellent dinner, but she could bring him some black caviar and champagne. Stanley turned down the champagne, but enjoyed the caviar with another bourbon before falling asleep again.

Stanley half expected Dillon to be waiting for him in the Los Angeles airport. After all, his people were undoubtedly tracking Stanley's movements, so Frank surely knew what flight he was on. Then he scolded himself for acting like some teenage shut-in who believed in an all-powerful CIA, and cloak-and-dagger spy games. No one was there to meet him, of course.

Stanley turned his phone back on as he made his way toward the car-rental companies. Barbara called him immediately. It seemed that the Swiss prosecutor's office had conducted a search in the bank's Zurich office and the headquarters in Geneva, although it wasn't quite a search. The prosecutor's office gave them a warrant with a list of documents they wanted to see. Barbara sent the list to Stanley over email. She asked him when he'd be coming back, and Stanley told her he'd be back just as soon as he saw his wife, so the day after next.

He rented a Toyota, had a burger and a Sprite, and headed out on World Way at a leisurely pace, turning onto Center Way and then making a smooth turn onto Vicksburg Avenue, enjoying the clarity of the road signs in comparison with Europe; he hardly even needed his GPS.

Lagrange called when Stanley was turning onto Interstate 5.

"McKnight! Finally!" Lagrange was panting like he'd just been on a run. "Barbara told me that you're in the States. You decided to go back to your wife? You Americans are too focused on your family ties."

"I have some problems to resolve, Pierre."

"Then go ahead and solve them, McKnight, but...wait, wait a minute!"

Stanley heard a gurgling sound. Lagrange must have been pouring himself some of his beloved whiskey.

"Okay." Lagrange took a sip and gave a sigh of satisfaction. "Okay, my friend, we have some problems of our own. The Department of Justice from your home country has launched an investigation. I don't know why you Americans have to stick your nose everywhere, but your compatriots are suddenly so intensely interested in our bank that the Swiss prosecutor's office is standing at attention and ready to take orders."

Lagrange took another sip.

"In a word, they're on the hunt. They're just taking practice shots now, but the real shooting is going to start soon. Laville is running around, trying to figure out who and what they're so interested in, but...where are you now, anyway?"

"I'm on Interstate 5, Pierre, heading toward San Francisco. I'll be there in about five hours."

"Interstate 5? That doesn't tell me anything. I need you here. Do you understand?"

"I'm supposed to be in Pamplona soon."

"What the fuck are you talking about, McKnight? Pamplona? The running of the bulls? Are you a bull, or are they going to be chasing you?"

"Gagarin is our biggest bull. He only let me leave Singapore when I promised to come with them to Pamplona. Considering that he's planning to move his valuables out of our vault to Singapore..."

"Okay, your trip to Pamplona could salvage our working relationship with this jerk-off. So let's do this—you do your thing in shitty San Francisco, fly here, we'll meet with Laville, and then you fly over to our bull. Right?"

"Right, Pierre."

"And stay calm, Stan!"

"Why wouldn't I?"

"I don't know! I was nervous when the people from the prosecutor's office were here. By the way, we need to put together the documents they asked for. Will you give Barbara your instructions? Excellent. Go on, then, Stan. Say hello to your wife! She'll be in your arms in five hours, you lucky man."

"I will, Pierre, thanks!"

"Of course."

A little over three hours later, Stanley turned on Highway 152 toward San Jose, then took Gilroy to 101 toward Market Street. After that, he was on automatic pilot, choosing his route and taking a shortcut home without conscious thought. Only when he was parking in his driveway did he realize that he hadn't told Christine he was flying home. He knocked and rang the bell, but no one answered. In the end, he called Christine's cell number. She was at work, but delighted to hear from him; she said she would leave the office and meet him at home as soon as she could.

McKnight took a walk around the neighborhood, stopping to buy wine and cheese in a shop where the owner remembered him and greeted him by name, as well as a bouquet of flowers at the shop next door.

Christine arrived, and they walked in together. Stanley was immediately enveloped by a feeling of calm and security. Christine suggested ordering a pizza, and they opened the bottle of wine. But partway into their first glass, the phone on the kitchen wall rang. Accustomed as they both were to the sound of their cell phones, it was a while before they realized where the ringing noise was coming from. When Stanley finally picked up the receiver of the phone on the wall, he heard Frank Dillon on the line.

"Where the hell have you been, Frank? I've been waiting for your call," said McKnight.

"Do you know how the devil torments people for their sins, McKnight?" said Frank with a laugh. "He makes them wait."

"Are you the devil, then?"

"No, no, I'm much worse."

"I only know one thing—people aren't punished for their sins. People are punished with their sins."

"Maybe so, McKnight, maybe so. Do you know the Ethiopian restaurant the Goose & Gridiron?"

"No, I've never been."

"It's in South Berkeley on Telegraph Ave. Can you come now?"

"Yes, of course."

"All right, I'll be waiting!"

Christine shot Stanley a sad look, but said nothing. Stanley took her car, and was walking into the restaurant within half an hour. The room was nearly empty, and he spotted Frank sitting with a short man of about forty with a Mediterranean cast to his features, who Frank introduced as Marco Monti.

"My partner," said Frank.

"Do you like Ethiopian food, Mr. McKnight?" asked Marco.

"Call me Stanley. You know, I've never tried it, somehow." Stanley sat down across from Frank and Marco.

"Well, we went ahead and ordered for the table—*doro wot*, slow-cooked lamb stew, *kitfo*, and a lot of vegetables."

"Hm, that doesn't tell me much."

"You'll like it. Just keep in mind that the sauce is very spicy. And there's a flatbread called *injera* you can wrap the food in, very tasty! I'm a vegan myself, and it's a good vegetarian option."

"Ah, an animal lover?"

"The Ethiopian church—orthodox, like the Russian, by the way—has more holidays requiring abstinence from meat and poultry than the Catholic one. That's why there are so many vegetarian options in Ethiopian cuisine."

"Marco, our Swiss banker here will figure the food out on his own," Frank interrupted his partner, waving over their portly waiter, who began setting out steaming dishes of bread and vegetables.

"What are you drinking?" Frank asked in a sympathetic tone of voice. "We're having Coke."

"I'm drinking vodka," said Stanley. "Do they have vodka? An Ethiopian version?"

"They'll find some! For you…" Frank tore off a piece of bread and dipped it in the sauce. "Stanley, I understood from your call that you're ready to work with us—am I right?"

"You're right. And tonic, please, with ice. Lots of ice! Separately."

"Well, then, I can tell you that Marco and I represent the American government. We have sufficient authority to make a preliminary agreement with you on the terms of our deal."

"Deal?"

"That's right. You'll need a good deal to save your ass, McKnight. You won't try and deny that you're a criminal and belong in jail, will you?"

"Really?" Stanley winced from the heat of the spicy sauce. "You still need to prove that."

"Don't test us, McKnight! I could arrest you right here," Marco hissed, his mask of Italian goodwill dropping for a moment.

Dillon held up a hand to his partner.

"Maybe you weren't aware, Comrade Stanley, but laundering money through banks, such as the one where you have been working so productively, is a threat to the national security of the United States. Especially dirty money from Russian oligarchs. People like your client Viktor Gagarin."

Frank fell silent; the waiter was approaching with a tall, narrow glass of vodka, and set it down in front of Stanley.

"What kind of vodka is this?" he asked.

"Polish vodka."

Stanley drank the vodka, winced again, and took a bite of flatbread and spicy lamb, which set fire to his mouth.

"Wash that down with some tonic, McKnight," Frank suggested, and went on: "So you're a threat to national security. We can't guarantee your safety, but if you give us the information we need, and testify in court, we can protect you."

"Let me stop you there, Frank," Stanley said, placing his empty glass on the table. "I have zero confidence in our judicial system, our police, or our security agencies, CIA or NSA. By the way, do you work for the State Department or the Treasury Department? OFAC? Who are you guys?" Stanley pushed his plate away and took out a cigarette.

His companions paused for a moment, studying his cigarette silently.

"You can't smoke here, McKnight. You're not in Moscow," said Frank.

"Or are you CIA after all?" McKnight squinted and blew a stream of smoke into Dillon's face. "Excellent! What's next, I fall to my knees and kiss your hands? I need...damn it...I need another vodka."

Stanley raised his hand and snapped his fingers. The waiter appeared.

"Another Polish vodka!" Stanley told him. "It seems to me"—Stanley looked first Marco, then Frank in the eye—"that you're quite interested in me. You won't get anything without my help. Not from the Swiss, who would tear out your throat to protect banking secrecy, or from the Russians, who'll just mow down anyone in the way with a Kalashnikov without stopping to check who's from the CIA and who's from OFAC. We're talking about billions of dollars here. Not about tax evasion by some little shop owner, or some modest offshore accounts. Tens of billions of dollars. Maybe even a trillion or two of dirty money. Corruption at the highest levels. About that fucked-up Russia, where you can buy anything for five cents, and the corruption creeping out of there, eating away at all those mechanisms that you clean-living, clever people believe to invulnerable. And I can pull back the curtain for you. And here you sit, telling me 'we can't guarantee,' as if I've come crawling on my knees to you!"

The waiter brought the second glass of vodka. Stanley downed it in one gulp, took a drag, and rolled some raw, thinly sliced beef up in the *injera* without taking the cigarette out of his mouth. "Mmmm, delicious. What do you call this one?"

"*Kitfo*."

"Although a bit spicy for me, I must say."

"They'll have a blander version for you in prison," Marco said in another hiss.

Stanley pretended not to have heard him.

"I have a product, gentleman, an exclusive product. Why don't you try and make me a reasonable offer for it? And not just me—my wife as well. Are we clear?"

Dillon and Marco exchanged glances. They looked a bit stunned. Dillon nodded.

"We'll do everything in our power," said Marco.

"Listen, Monti, I don't need anything that rests on your personal power. You're a cog in the system, and while you may be very smart and very professional, I need a 100 percent guarantee. A guarantee that won't depend on, say, a jury verdict. After all, it's possible that some, or even all, of my bank clients will be acquitted. Or avoid a trial entirely. And I'll stand up proudly in court and wait for my head to be blown off when I step outside? No, thanks. Which is why I'm sorry to say that you two aren't ready to meet with me. For some reason, you thought I'd already shit my pants and I'd be grateful to you for wiping my ass. Well, let me assure you that I know how to wipe my own ass. Do you get me?"

"We understand you perfectly," Dillon said. "And you'll get the protection you need, for yourself and your wife."

"Now that's a different story." Stanley rose, and ground out his cigarette on his plate. "You know where to find me. And I don't like Ethiopian food. Next time, let's meet at Starbucks."

PART FIVE:
BULL MARKET

CHAPTER 38

S TANLEY ENTERED HIS HOTEL ROOM, slipped the porter a hundred euros, and fell onto the bed closest to the balcony door.

"Shall I open the balcony door for you, sir?" asked the porter, shutting the closet where he had placed Stanley's small suitcase.

"What for?"

"So you can hear the city preparing for the running of the bulls."

"Go ahead." Stanley squinted and saw white pants, a white shirt, and a red necktie on the bed next to him. There was a pair of white canvas shoes with rubber soles on the floor.

"Those are authentic shoes from the era when Señor Ernest stayed in this room," the porter said, as if he had personally encountered the famous guest.

He opened up the balcony door, letting in a muffled hum of city noise: the voices of passersby on Estafeta Street and the sounds of distant cars moving around the Plaza del Castillo.

"We've kept the room exactly the same as it was when—"

"Yes, thank you, I'm aware," Stanley interrupted the porter. "What about the shoes? Are they my size?"

"Of course, sir. And if anything doesn't fit right—"

"Yes, yes, thank you! Everything is great, just please make sure that I'm not disturbed."

"Of course, sir!"

The porter left the room, and McKnight got up and shut the balcony door. It made little sense in this heat (it was nearly 100 degrees Fahrenheit outside) to sit in a room with a working air conditioner and leave a door open.

Stanley kicked off his shoes, opened the minibar, and mixed himself a vodka and tonic, tossing some ice cubes into the glass. He took a big swallow, then put the drink on his nightstand and lay back down.

Tall glass shelves with works by Hemingway stood in the corners of the room; he saw *A Movable Feast*, that endless feast, in different languages, as well as a bronze bust of the author. Another bust faced him from on top of the closet.

The first thing Biryuza had told Stanley when he picked him up at the airport was that he'd be staying in the famous Gran Hotel la Perla, and not in just any old room, but in the actual room named after Ernest Hemingway.

"This used to be Room 217. Now it's 201, but everyone calls it 'Papa's Room.' Do you have any idea how much this cost Viktor? This room is booked during the San Fermin festival years in advance. But he told me to get this room, whatever it took. I had to find the Australian millionaire who was planning to stay there with his girlfriend, negotiate with them, find them a different hotel, pay their cancellation fee, and give them a generous gift."

"And this was all for me?" asked Stanley.

"Don't get too proud, Stan. Viktor instructed me to make sure this room was available, and he also rented a villa, where he will stay and receive his guests. Some people will stay in the city. You're one of 'some people.'"

Then Biryuza paused, waiting for Stanley to react to "some people."

"We drew straws," Biryuza finally went on. "You got Hemingway's room. So it was just luck. But you should make the most of it!"

McKnight finished his vodka and made himself another, then searched around on the bedside table for the remote. He switched on the enormous flat-screen TV on the wall. "Just think," Stanley told himself sarcastically, "Hemingway watched this very TV!" He flipped through the channels until he landed on *Abbott and Costello Meet Frankenstein*—he and Christine had met at a screening many years before.

The old black-and-white movie went well with the décor of the room.

Stanley took a few more sips, watching as Dracula, played by Bela Lugosi, hypnotized Wilbur, the bumbling and cowardly clerk played by Lou Costello, so that he'd remain motionless while Dracula freed Frankenstein from his box.

McKnight made himself a third cocktail and got out a cigarette. He looked around before lighting it, trying to find a smoke detector. Smoking was probably forbidden here, but he didn't put out his cigarette—it would be disrespectful to the memory of the great writer not to enjoy a cigarette in his room. Or not to have a drink there, for that matter.

He remembered his meeting with the agents. He'd surprised even himself with his boldness and determination. He recalled Dillon's stunned expression and laughed. It had probably been a while since the confident and self-assured Dillon had encountered someone like him.

Meanwhile, onscreen, Dracula and Frankenstein had arrived at the island of Dr. Sandra Mornay, the unfortunate Wilbur's ex-girlfriend. The actress playing Sandra reminded Stanley a little of Mila—her character was just as unprincipled and cynical.

Stanley had felt much better after his meeting with Dillon and Monti in the Ethiopian restaurant. It had been as if he'd had the chance to view himself from the outside, and he'd felt strong, ready for anything. So when he'd come home to find his wife in a state of anxiety, he'd had no trouble reassuring her. He'd spoken quietly, in a measured tone of voice, trying not to let on that the main danger they faced—Stanley was sure of it now—wasn't the consequences of defying the US federal government, but Gagarin, and his henchmen and friends. More precisely, those Magnificent Five.

Even if they did decide to prosecute Stanley, the trial process could go on for years. There would be appeals, jury selections and rejections, and other judicial twists and turns.

But Stanley thought that the federal government would rather reach an agreement with him than let it become known how they had instigated the violation of laws, or at least delayed the investigation.

But Gagarin and his Five weren't bound by any judicial conditions or moral codes. For them, Stanley had no doubt there were no boundaries they wouldn't cross, no restrictions on their actions. They wouldn't hesitate to send hired killers, would collude with any group—from Mexican cartels and the Italian mafia in Brooklyn, to Northern Irish militants or veterans of the Balkan wars. The long arm of the law couldn't reach them because they could always hide in Russia if necessary and quickly recoup any loss of laundered funds or valuables.

Christine had kept saying that she understood, but that Stanley was in danger now. He was between a rock and a hard place, and she couldn't see how he would make his way out.

His confidence had gradually won her over. She'd clung to him and told him that if he was so sure of everything, he should let her come to Zurich. She could talk to her boss about a leave of absence, or she could quit, even, and maybe they would let her have her job back when it was all over. It had taken Stanley some effort to talk her out of it. They'd talked nearly till dawn, then made love, and slept till noon.

Lagrange had called while Stanley and Christine had been eating breakfast. He was still in the office, he'd said, dealing with the devastation. He'd sounded frustrated and had complained of being utterly abandoned, responsible for everything, and cleaning up after everyone—he'd said he wouldn't mind taking a break either. Stanley had tried to say that he'd be back to work soon, and would be happy to do his part clearing out the rubble, but Lagrange had just laughed.

"Stan, you're hardly a bank staffer any more. Your main job is to be our authorized representative at the court of his majesty Gagarin. Believe me, my friend: that's the most important thing right now. You might think that you're not fulfilling your duties, but what matters to us most is that you are with Gagarin, even when he's visiting Singaporean prostitutes. We can barely keep up with his deliveries. It seems like he's trying to stuff our vaults with every single treasure in goddamned Russia. And he'll keep doing that, as long as you're with him. You're our guarantee to him. People like Viktor only trust personal relationships. So you maintain yours on behalf of our bank. Where are you now?"

"San Francisco. And tomorrow I'm flying to Pamplona."

"Ah, Pamplona, of course! San Fermin, right? Your life is just one big party, eh? I'm starting to get jealous, Stan, pretty jealous."

"Don't envy me, Pierre. Believe it or not, I wish more than anything that I was in Zurich, heading into the office in the morning."

"More than lying side by side with your pretty wife? All right, go run with the bulls, get a horn in your ass, then come back to work. We'll get you a standing desk till you recover. Tell Gagarin and his wife I said hello. Is she there? Do you remember what I told you? Watch out. Viktor will finish what the bulls start if you're not careful."

The conversation with Lagrange had left Stanley feeling concerned. His colleague wasn't simply annoyed—he'd been simmering with rage, because this wasn't the first time that Gagarin had failed to invite Pierre to join them. Lagrange was jealous that Stanley was having the fun that he used to have.

Smoking and watching Dracula fight a werewolf, Stanley began to consider the fact that Lagrange never forgave insults. If he couldn't get Gagarin back somehow, he would take it out on Stanley. "If you're enjoying a place in the sun, you're blocking someone else's light."

He had to take two connecting flights to reach Pamplona and the trip took almost twenty-four hours. Christine offered to drive Stanley to the airport, but he got a message from Marco Monti that evening, asking him to meet at the airport to discuss matters before Stanley left, and he decided to take a taxi there. He didn't want Monti to see him with his wife.

McKnight was walking through the airport when Monti appeared beside him out of nowhere. The agent nodded and gestured for McKnight to follow him. They passed through security and a police checkpoint and walked down a long corridor to a door with a keypad lock. Inside was a small, windowless room, dimly lit. The only furnishings were a table, two chairs, and an empty bookshelf.

"Have a seat, McKnight," Monti said. "And don't worry—the plane won't take off without you."

"I hope not," Stanley said. "I paid about fifteen K for that ticket, all told."

"Just don't tell me you paid with your blood money," Monti said, sitting across from Stanley and putting a plastic object on the table.

"Dillon's already in Europe," Monti went on. "He asked me to give you instructions."

"So you are fully guaranteeing immunity for myself and my wife? Complete protection? You guarantee that I'll get to keep my bank accounts and real estate holdings? You've accepted all my conditions? If not, you'll just be wasting your breath."

"We fully accept your conditions, Mr. McKnight," Monti said. "We give you our full guarantee. The situation has changed, and—you were right— we've come to an agreement with our directors. We can't conduct this operation without you. You might have wanted a written guarantee, but—"

"That's not necessary. At least, not yet. I'll prepare a detailed list of my terms and give them to Dillon when we meet. I'll be seeing him in Europe?"

"Yes. He'll be in Pamplona."

"Excellent. And what do you have here?"

"This is a special kind of flash drive," Monti said with a smile. "When you return to Zurich from Pamplona, you'll go into the office, stick this flash drive in any bank computer on a Friday night, and take it out on Monday morning."

"You do realize that if I get caught with this, I'm going to have some serious trouble? Employees are forbidden from hooking up any personal tech items to the bank's internal systems."

"Even if you do get caught, all the bank's security service will find on the drive is pictures of you, Mr. McKnight, and your wife."

"Where did you get them?"

"Well, there are certain skills we haven't entirely lost. The flash drive is really only a transmitter. Over the weekend, our team will use it to hack into the bank system and copy everything we need, remotely. Nothing will remain on the drive itself. So you put it in, copy at least one photo onto your desktop. You missed your wife, you see, and wanted to print a photo of her, something like that. Clear?"

"Clear." Stanley nodded, tucking the drive into his pocket.

"That's not all." Monti held out a hand when Stanley made as if to stand. "Our main interest isn't really the data we'll get with this flash drive. Don't get me wrong, it's important, and your assistance will be critical in getting it. But the 'Magnificent Five,' as you call them, are going to be in Pamplona for the festival, and they're the ones we want. They're not coming to run with the bulls or see a bullfight. Although they probably will go at least once. But they're worried about recent events, about the Swiss prosecutor's investigation into Gagarin. That's their money, after all, their channels, their reserve aerodromes. They're also concerned about the possibility of international sanctions against them and their close friends."

"Oh come on, Marco!" Stanley huffed. "No one's going to touch them. They're thick as thieves with the elites in the West. They have businesses in common—"

"This isn't a business matter. It's about big-league politics. Really big-league. John Fort, the president's national security adviser, is flying from Washington to Pamplona—and I don't think he's there to watch the bullfight. He's probably interested in holding talks with the Magnificent Five."

Stanley was stunned.

"Are you trying to tell me that John Fort is involved in these deals with the Russians? And you want to use me against him or something?"

"No comment on that. But your job is to get the Magnificent Five to trust you, and, if possible, get any information on their talks with Fort. We don't even know what they'll be discussing."

"Well, that's not too difficult to guess. They'll negotiate on concessions for Russians involved in sanctions in exchange for contracts going to American oil companies."

Marco shrugged.

"Maybe yes, maybe no. They could be discussing anything, from oil, as you say, to Iranian nuclear capabilities. So…"

Marco got out a pack of cigarettes and pulled something out of it about an inch in length, resembling a wire or a thick strand of human hair.

"This is the world's most advanced listening device. There are none like it. You'll need to attach it to Gagarin's clothes. It'll 'live' for about twenty-four hours, and then it'll just fall off, so there's no danger to you. The Russians don't have this technology yet. Secretary Fort will have all the rooms swept for bugs, but his instruments won't find this one."

"So I'll have to stick a bug on Gagarin every day?"

"Yeah. Try. And on as many of the Five as you can. There are ten bugs in this pack, and Dillon'll give you another ten in Spain. Keep in mind that each one costs over $15,000."

"Wow, Marco, you've got quite the budget—bugs, flights, hotels. I'll try to wrap this up as quickly as possible for you."

But Monti gazed at him directly and said that although they had accepted all of Stanley's conditions, he shouldn't expect that their cooperation would end any time soon.

"The only thing I can do quickly is put you in jail," Monti said. His polite and sympathetic mask was slipping again. Stanley saw the real man before him, a cynical and cold agent.

"Until we have an accurate picture of Gagarin and Company's money-laundering schemes, and bank transactions showing compromising material on the Magnificent Five," concluded Monti, "you've got no hope of retiring."

It was a typical move from an officer in the security services. Promise, agree, then take a step back, then another, until your opponent had no moves left, and no way back.

Stanley thought about the trouble he was in the entire eight-hour flight to New York. He had only an hour to make his connecting flight to Madrid, but he managed to stretch his legs and have a cup of coffee. He found himself thinking cowardly thoughts—of just stepping out of JFK, clearing all the money out of his accounts, buying a big American car, and driving back west.

"Sir, we're waiting for you!" a flight attendant at the gate told him.

McKnight threw his half-finished cup of coffee into the trash can and trotted down the sloped corridor to the plane.

The flight from New York to Spain was over thirteen hours. Stanley was prepared for the worst, but everything went quite smoothly. It was an evening flight, so he fell asleep almost immediately, and awoke to a sunny morning—no surprise there—in Madrid. He did have seven hours to kill at until his next flight, so he took a taxi to the Puerta del Sol. The driver asked if it was his first time in Madrid, and Stanley told him that he just wanted to have a walk around a bit and have a nice lunch. He ate bean soup and ham at

314

Casa Botin and drank nearly a liter and a half of wine; in the end, he didn't have time for a walk. He returned to the airport, and was back in the air on an Iberia flight at six that evening, arriving in Pamplona just an hour later.

CHAPTER 39

T HE HOTEL PHONE RANG. McKNIGHT, half asleep, was watching Dracula turn into a bat and couldn't figure out which phone was ringing at first.

"I asked not to be disturbed!" he said when he finally picked up the receiver.

"Yes, sir, but your colleague insisted that we put him through," the clerk said apologetically.

Stanley thought that it must be Lagrange, and prepared himself for the taunts and jokes to come.

"Go ahead!" he said, but to his surprise, it was Bernard on the line.

"Stanley!" Bernard sounded like he'd won the lottery or hit the bull's-eye in a shooting competition. "I'm right next to you!"

Stanley looked around in confusion. "What do you mean, next to me?" he asked.

"I'm in the same hotel as you, Stanley," Bernard said, still delighted. "One floor below you, I think. What a nice place, huh? Lagrange sent me. He didn't want to go, busy with work and all. But he sent me. He said you could use some support."

"Support with what?" Stanley finished his vodka, but the ice had melted long ago, and it tasted terrible.

"With investment matters for Gagarin, of course! Pierre said that you should introduce me to Gagarin's circle, and asked me to prepare some new proposals for him. So here I am…"

Stanley was not at all pleased that Lagrange had sent Bernard to Pamplona without any advance discussion. It was an unpleasant surprise: in his opinion, Bernard was simply a stupid, boring, Swiss gnome with no initiative. Bernard had previously only been involved in structuring investments for Gagarin's portfolio, so Lagrange's instructions meant that he had to, in a manner of speaking, move several levels up at once. Lagrange wanting him closer to Gagarin simply meant that the older banker suspected something, maybe even that Stanley was thinking about leaving the game. Could he be preparing Bernard as a replacement?

"Great," McKnight said, trying to sound friendly. "That's great, Bernard. Glad to hear it. Let's meet in the bar—how about in half an hour?"

"Of course, of course, that's fine. I've prepared some really interesting offers! First of all—"

Bernard was still talking, but Stanley hung up. This eager young banker, purely by accident, might just screw everything up for him. He would try to get in between him and Gagarin, get close to the Magnificent Five, curry favor with their wives and girlfriends with conversation and compliments. This was a terrible turn of events.

McKnight got undressed and stepped into the shower. Lathering himself with orange-scented Hermès soap, he wondered how he should behave with Mila. She would definitely use the festival atmosphere to try to slip into Stanley's room. He couldn't turn her away. In fact, he would have to do whatever necessary to keep her happy to avoid any scenes and hysterics. And now, in addition to the usual spies, Stanley had the eager Bernard under foot.

He stood under the warm stream of water and sighed. He couldn't figure out where the CIA had gotten pictures of him and Christine. He should look on that drive and see what pictures they had. But then he decided just to wait until he got to his office computer, no need to rush.

Bernard was reclining in a chair, his legs crossed, when Stanley came down. This wasn't the uptight, obsequious bank clerk he knew from the office. Nor even the Bernard he remembered from their trip to Moscow.

He was dressed in a light suit, soft shoes, and his hair was slightly, artfully disheveled. Everything about him said he was cool and only getting cooler.

"Hi, McKnight!" he said, jumping up. "How are you liking Pamplona?"

"I couldn't say yet," Stanley said, shaking the other man's proffered hand. "I just got off the plane."

"Then how about a cocktail?" Bernard suggested. "Do you know that Ernest Hemingway stayed in this hotel? We should have a daquiri in his honor. Let's order at the bar."

"First of all, I'm staying in Hemingway's room," said McKnight, interrupting Bernard's cheerful flow of conversation. "Second of all, you drink daquiris in Cuba. We're going to drink what Hemingway drank here, in Pamplona—some Rioja Alta wine. But not in the hotel bar, but on Estafeta, in the Buddha Café. Follow me, Bernard!"

"Was that here in Hemingway's time?" asked Bernard.

"Of course!" said Stanley, who had no idea whether Papa Hemingway had, in fact, ever been there. "It was his favorite café. He wrote some of the key scenes of his most famous works there."

He'd grown accustomed to strong drinks lately, and easily downed two glasses of wine. Bernard looked at him in surprise as he savored small sips from his own glass.

"Thirsty," explained Stanley. "I've been thirsty the whole trip from San Francisco."

Bernard tried to speak to the waiter in Spanish, but he just gave them a sour and smile and responded in German, then switched to French, and finally English. Bernard ordered another bottle, although he'd barely finished one glass.

"Is it far from here to the café Stedzip?" asked Stanley.

"That depends on what you consider far, señor. I can call a taxi."

"No, we'll walk," said Stanley, ignoring Bernard's nodding in favor of a taxi.

"That's an excellent choice, señor. You'll have a lovely stroll. Turn left from here onto Cortes de Navarra, then right on Paulino Caballero, cross Baja Navarra Avenue, and right again on Leyre. It will be a lovely walk. Shall I bring some more wine?"

"Of course! It will be a difficult walk without more wine."

Bernard chattered on without pause the whole walk to the restaurant. He talked about everything—the stressful work with Gagarin's investment portfolio, about his fiancée, a journalist who wrote about cosmetics who had her own blog, about how much he got out of working with Stanley, how he envied him—with the best of intentions, of course—and how he'd love to have a peek at the Ernest Hemingway room if Stanley wouldn't mind, although (and here Bernard paused, lowering his head sadly) he had to admit that he had never, in his entire life, read a single line by Hemingway, although he had googled the author on the flight here and looked through a couple of articles about him.

There were so many people around that they lost each other several times. Once Bernard accidently directed a long discourse about the complexities of working as an investment consultant at an elderly Spaniard with a violin in a white suit and red necktie.

Stanley tried to grab Bernard's arm, but lost him again. They only reunited when Bernard called him, and they arranged to meet at a Kutxabank.

Bernard went in the wrong direction nevertheless, and Stanley had to direct him on speakerphone while reading the map on his smartphone.

Hundreds of tourists and locals streamed past them, all excited in anticipation of tomorrow's events. The air smelled of alcohol, danger, and sweat, and Stanley thought he could hear, in the distance, the anxious lowing of the bulls being readied for the slaughter. Stanley finally picked out Bernard in the crowd, and followed behind, directing him over the phone, still, until they reached Stedzip.

"You know the city so well," exclaimed Bernard. "Have you been many times?"

"I'm going to tell you something important, Bernard. If you want to have any kind of career in banking, you have to know how to do a couple of pretty basic things. You can learn them, but they're usually innate skills. Three, in all. First, you have to be able to do math quickly in your head. For example, how much is 14.5 percent of 2,343?"

"Ummm, hang on…"

"Not ummm, but 339.735. The second skill, which might not seem so essential in this age of gadgets, but is actually just as necessary, is to be able to navigate by looking at a map and remembering it, quickly following directions someone has given you."

"What use is that to a banker?"

"At the very least, to be able to run away if you're arrested in Moscow like Michael Calvey."

"Are you serious, McKnight?"

"Absolutely."

"Well, I was a scout with my youth organization in school."

"Oh, I could tell that right away! Last, you have to be good at languages. I have to admit that's not my strongest suit, but I can tell someone off in ten different languages…and we're here!"

Gagarin had reserved an entire room in the restaurant, and the entrance was manned by some broad-shouldered young men with sharp eyes whom Stanley didn't recognize. They stood, shoulder to shoulder, blocking Stanley and Bernard's way in, but Shamil appeared and whispered something, and they stepped aside.

Gagarin's entire group was seated at one long table, but Gagarin wasn't at its head. Arseny Zaikin was, the deputy head of the presidential administration, whom Stanley had seen on the yacht *Alassio*, with Gagarin at his left. In fact, all of the Magnificent Five were in attendance, with the same wives or lovers in tow.

It was difficult to distinguish between the Russian oligarchs' women, however—they were almost all blond, with high cheekbones and inflated lips, fluttering fake eyelashes and clenching their teeth so as not to accidentally let anything stupid slip out.

Even the fat, red-cheeked priest who had called Stanley a 'nobleman,' Father Vsevolod, was here, wearing a light silk robe and wolfing down a Galician stew.

The FSB general, Zlatoust, was here, surveying the scene with his steady, piercing gaze, in the company of two blondes, close enough in appearance to be twins. There were so many unfamiliar faces that Stanley even experienced some warm feelings when he saw Polina and her husband Krapiva, Gauthier, and Biryuza, and even Yulia, wearing her habitual expression of general contempt. He might even have felt some concern when he noticed Mila's absence.

Biryuza was the first to notice Stanley and Bernard. He clapped loudly and stood.

"McKnight! Well, finally! Now we'll get things going!" Biryuza strode over to meet them. "Now we'll show those bulls! We're going to give 'em hell, right, Stan?"

He hugged Stanley tightly and kissed him three times in greeting. McKnight stoically endured these sloppy kisses, repressing the urge to get out his handkerchief and wipe his face. A smiling Gagarin was the next to approach.

"Here he is! Our hero! My savior! My adviser and friend, finally! I'm delighted to see you!"

So Stanley had to kiss three times with Gagarin. But while Biryuza was high as a kite on something, Gagarin was simply drunk.

Gauthier took the opportunity of Stanley's appearance to tap his knife against the side of his glass and suggest that they all fill their glasses and drink to friendship and true friends. Stanley got a glass with vodka.

"Who's that with you?" Gagarin asked in a whisper.

"Bernard, he's an employee at our bank—your personal investment consultant, by the way, and my subordinate. Lagrange sent him in his place."

"So Pierre decided not to come?" Gagarin pursed his thin lips in a familiar gesture, and his face took on a nasty expression, despite his intoxication. "Well, well..." He turned to Bernard and said, "Have a seat anywhere, monsieur!"

He turned back to the rest of his guests.

"What are we drinking to?" asked Gagarin.

"You forgot already, Viktor?" a high, thin voice cut through the general hubbub. It was the minister, Komarikhin, looking even fatter than before. Next to him sat a stout young woman with enormous breasts, but not the same one from the yacht; this one had short hair and wary, dark eyes.

"To friendship and friends!" Komarikhin pronounced, raising his wineglass.

"To friendship and friends!" Stanley repeated after him in Russian, deftly sticking the listening device onto Gagarin's jacket.

"Don't smoke here," said Gagarin, noticing the pack in Stanley's hands, and said in his ear: "Only those five are allowed to, and they don't smoke, the bastards. Bad for their health. So, to friends!"

CHAPTER 40

A FTER THE VODKA AND TONIC in his hotel room, and the wine on the way to the restaurant, as soon as Stanley finished his glass, the room began to swim before his eyes.

He dropped into the chair next to Biryuza, and Bernard sat down across from him and a little to the left. He ordered baked lamb.

"What are you ordering, Stanley?" Bernard asked loudly across the table. "Is it good?"

"He's driving me crazy with the questions," Stanley said quietly to Biryuza.

"What does he ask about?"

"Everything! What's the meaning behind the bullfights, the running of the bulls? He wants meaning!"

"I ordered lamb, Bernard," Stanley answered. "You should try it." And he added, to Biryuza, "You answer him too. Give him one of your lectures."

Biryuza took Stanley's suggestion seriously, and began a long, overly detailed account of the tradition of bullfighting, and the history of the running of the bulls, which, he said, began in the sixteenth century. It used to be mostly Spaniards and Basque men running from the bulls, but now the majority of the participants are from America, New Zealand, and Australia, and they're all on drugs or tipsy on sangria, and it's the drunk and high ones who fall victim to the bulls.

Gauthier brought around a silver tray of cocaine; Stanley and Biryuza venerated several times under the astonished gaze of Bernard.

Biryuza paused, and Bernard, well into his wine by this point, giggled and, looking around slyly, asked why Russians in general, and Gagarin in particular, loved the running of the bulls so much.

"After all, a Russian running from a bull—it's pretty funny!" said Bernard, and laughed at his own words.

There were few seconds of silence, and Stanley thought the tactless Swiss banker's neighbors, already three sheets to the wind, were going to bash his head in.

Biryuza was the first to recover. He continued his lecture—Hemingway was very popular during Gagarin's youth in the USSR, and everyone read *A Movable Feast* and *The Sun Also Rises*, hence the adult Gagarin's interest in bullfighting. Bernard continued to wonder, however, and Stanley's irritation grew. Father Vsevolod saved the situation. He rose and began to sing, in a deep, heavy bass, the song that all the runners were supposed to sing before the bulls were released.

When Father Vsevolod finished singing, everyone applauded and forgot about Bernard.

"What a voice!" cried Gagarin.

"A beautiful voice, indeed!" said Biryuza. "Too bad Mila couldn't hear it."

"By the way, Anton, where is she?" asked Stanley.

"Gagarin sent her to Promises," Biryuza replied quietly.

"Where?"

"An addiction treatment clinic. In California."

"No way!" Stanley said, successfully concealing his joy beneath an expression of surprise.

After that, it was chaos. Gauthier came around several more times with the cocaine tray. Gagarin demanded several times that Stanley drink vodka with him and his Magnificent Five friends, whom Stanley generously decorated with listening devices.

Stumbling, his vision hazy, Stanley went outside to smoke and use the toilet. Passing through the restaurant, he saw a surprising number of guests who looked like Dillon.

One Dillon clone was enjoying a plate of seafood and spilling white wine on himself. Stanley thought it would be hilarious to go up to the man, slap him on the shoulder, and explain to his companion, a large-boned woman with a horsey face that he was a friend from college, some small college in Nebraska or Indiana.

McKnight didn't even remember how he got back to his room early that morning, or for that matter getting dressed in the white clothes and red necktie, grabbing his newspaper rolled up into a tube, and coming back down to Estafeta Street.

He took a few sips of strong coffee in a café there and looked at his watch. It was just after 7:00 AM. The street was full of people dressed in white like Stanley, all with rolled newspapers.

The smell of alcohol still hung in the air. Bernard appeared from somewhere, pale and rumpled. He kept coughing, a nervous tic, maybe. He seemed worried about the upcoming run.

"I woke up in my room," said Bernard. "But how did I get there? I don't remember."

"The same thing happened to me," nodded Stanley. "Shamil must have taken us."

"That big one?"

"Yes. There he is, by the way."

Shamil approached. He was also in all white, making his athletic figure look all the more impressive.

"Ready?" he asked hoarsely.

"My head hurts," complained Bernard, but Shamil didn't even glance his way.

"Ready," answered Stanley.

"Remember: never, under any circumstances, run all the way to the arena. Try for about five hundred to seven hundred meters from where you're standing, and after that, either jump over the barriers or climb up. Don't run into anyone, and if someone falls down, don't stay to help them up. Understand?"

McKnight nodded and looked up to see Dillon standing on one of the balconies overlooking the street. The horse-faced woman stood next to him. Dillon waved to someone, and Stanley looked away.

Shamil looked at his watch.

"Where are they?" he muttered irritably.

"Who are we waiting for?" asked Bernard.

"Gagarin and Biryuza—who else? Ah, here they are!"

Gagarin and Biryuza arrived, pushing through the crowd.

"Stanley, you American son of a bitch!" shouted Gagarin. "How are you?"

"Excellent, Viktor!"

"Do you remember how you danced yesterday?"

"Danced? Me?"

"Yeah, with Komarikhin's girlfriend. You practically trashed the entire restaurant."

Stanley didn't have a

"I don't believe it!" The incident was erased from his memory entirely. "What happened to the restaurant?"

"The restaurant manager tried to reason with you. He thought you were Russian, and when he spoke to you in Russian, you started to curse with such virtuosity that even Zlatoust was impressed. Where did you pick that up?"

Stanley didn't have a chance to answer. At seven fifty-five, everyone broke into the song that Father Vsevolod had performed for them the night before:

The street was flooded with people, and the noise of their singing was deafening. A group of guys next to them sang in Basque:

"Entzun, arren, San Fermin zu zaitugu patroi,
zuzendu gure oinak entzierro hontan otoi.
¡Viva San Fermín! ¡Viva!, Gora San Fermín! Gora!"

The song was repeated twice more, and as soon as the singing ended, a deafening clap sounded as a firecracker burst over the city, and the crowd started to move.

The gates of San Domingo, the bulls' corral, opened, and twelve enraged bulls began the race along the narrow cobblestone streets of old Pamplona, to the cheers of thousands and thousands of spectators. They soon turned onto Estafeta, and the crowd raced past.

McKnight wanted to join the crowd, but Shamil held him back, only letting go when he saw the horns of the bulls approaching. He shouted "Go!" and took off himself, protecting Gagarin.

McKnight ran quickly, trying to keep Bernard in sight. Suddenly, he felt someone's breath on his right hand, almost hot enough to burn, and then something wet and just as hot poked him in the back. He looked over his shoulder, directly into the eyes of a huge, dark-brown bull.

The bull snorted, as if telling him to make way, and McKnight moved to the left, hit the bull with the rolled newspaper on its strong rump, and looked back again to see Shamil helping Gagarin over the barrier. Bernard had disappeared somewhere. Biryuza caught up to Stanley and wriggled over the barrier after Gagarin to safety. That's when Stanley caught sight of Bernard. The other man was swinging his elbows to fight his way through the crowd, near where three bulls were tossing people aside with swings of their heads.

The street turned, and several people slipped on the slick cobblestones. One bull stumbled over a fallen runner and nearly fell himself before continuing to run.

At the next turn, McKnight saw Bernard fall. Stanley tried to grab him by the arm, but a big man running from behind got in the way. In fact, he knocked Stanley down as well. Stanley fell right by the barrier and saw Bernard lying in the path of the oncoming bulls, trying to rise.

"Don't get up!" shouted Stanley. "Stay down! Don't get up!"

But Bernard didn't listen. He rose and turned to face the approaching bulls. He managed to dodge one of them, but another tossed its head and gored Bernard with its horn. For a moment, Bernard hung from the horn until the bull shook its head and dropped Bernard onto the cobblestones. His body hit the ground loudly, and another bull jumped over him. Bernard curled into a ball and screamed. A puddle of blood pooled out from beneath him. The crowd, and yet another bull, rushed past the man on the ground.

Stanley ran over. Bernard was trying to stop the blood pulsing from the wound.

"Call an ambulance! We need a stretcher and an ambulance!" Stanley shouted into the crowd, his voice breaking. "It hit an artery!"

McKnight returned to the hotel covered in sweat, dirt, and blood.

The receptionist asked anxiously how Bernard was feeling. Stanley told him the doctors had managed to stop the bleeding, but he was weak. The doctors had reassured him that they'd seen much worse after the running of the bulls.

Back in his room, McKnight drew himself a bath, and had just sunk down into the fragrant water when he heard a knock at the door.

"What the hell do you want?" shouted Stanley.

"You ordered cigarettes," said a vaguely familiar voice.

McKnight pulled on a robe and padded on bare feet to the door. He looked through the peephole and saw Dillon standing outside in a white shirt and bow tie.

"Here are your cigarettes, sir," he said when Stanley opened the door. "You went through a lot yesterday. We're already receiving information."

"I'm happy for you," barked Stanley.

"I hope your friend is well."

"Thank you! I'm sure he'll be fine."

He returned to the bathroom, where he opened the pack, and saw a little packet with the bugs tucked inside. Stanley lit a cigarette and sank back into the bath.

326

He didn't have the time to soak as long as he wanted. First, Christine called, offended that Stanley hadn't, and anxious that something had happened to him. Stanley apologized and told her that the festival and all the surrounding chaos had simply made him forget all his promises—he should have called yesterday after arriving in Pamplona. They held to their agreement not to discuss anything relating to Stanley's work with the Feds over the phone, but Stanley did tell her about Bernard's injury, which shocked her. She asked him several times if he was sure he was okay as well. Then, as they had agreed for security purposes, she went into detail about her own affairs. Finally, Christine sent her regards to Bernard and hung up.

McKnight got out of the tub, opened a bottle of beer, and called Lagrange.

Their manager was also stunned to hear what had happened to Bernard, and asked for the telephone number of the hospital, promising to get in touch with one of the bank's staff doctors. He said that one of them could travel to Pamplona to assist the Spanish doctors if necessary.

"You didn't take care of him, Stan!" said Lagrange. "You should have been watching out for him, and instead…"

"I told him, more than once, not to stand, but he didn't listen. You really think this is my fault? Why the hell did you send him here anyway?"

"Yes, I do. You were probably covering Gagarin's ass and didn't give a shit about Bernard."

"I really hope you're joking, Pierre."

"Well, I'm not!"

"Then you can kiss my ass!" Stanley said, but Lagrange had already hung up the phone.

Stanley was in a foul mood after that. He thought he could at least get some sleep, but Gauthier called and said Gagarin was waiting for Stanley at the villa.

Stanley called a taxi and called the hospital one more time before leaving. The doctor said that the patient's condition was stable but serious and that he would do everything he could for him.

The car was waiting for him in the square. Stanley gave the driver a piece of paper with the address.

"A lovely place," said the driver. "Is that your castle, or are you just visiting?"

"Do I look like I own a castle?"

"Well, the porter told me that you're staying in Papa's room."

"That was just happenstance, my friend."

327

"Chance makes the world go round," the driver began philosophically, maneuvering through the raucous crowd in the square. "Today, for example, the Swedish man, why did he get up? They tell everyone not to, ahead of time."

"Swiss, not Swedish. He's a friend of mine."

"Damn!" cried the driver. "That's terrible—bad luck."

"Yes...chance," agreed Stanley.

There was a festive atmosphere at the enormous villa Gagarin was renting, situated on a picturesque plot of land. No one remembered about poor Bernard, of course.

McKnight immediately received his portion of coke from Gauthier and a glass of vodka from Gagarin, which he poured out onto the ground when no one was looking. Komarikhin's girlfriend gave him a friendly wave with her big hand. Stanley walked over and kissed that hand, which smelled strongly of tanning lotion.

He noticed a limousine in the parking lot, guarded by a man who resembled a Secret Service agent.

McKnight poured himself a tall glass of sangria and bumped into the US president's national security adviser in the inner courtyard.

John Fort was obviously in a hurry to meet with Gagarin and the members of the Magnificent Five.

"Good afternoon, sir," said McKnight in Russian.

"Hello," nodded Fort, a tall, thin, gray-haired man. "Have we met?"

"I don't think so, sir," Stanley said, switching to English. "My name is Stanley McKnight. We're compatriots, I'm happy to say."

Fort stopped and looked at Stanley with interest.

"Indeed, McKnight, that is a good thing," he said with a smile. "What do you do?"

"I turn crap into chocolate, sir. I'm a banker."

"Not bad, McKnight, well said. I'll have to remember that one. I do pretty much the same. Another time!"

They shook hands; Stanley managed to press the bug he had ready onto Fort's jacket.

Fort walked briskly into the house, and Stanley would have given a lot to know what such a high-ranking staffer from the US president's cabinet was discussing with Russian oligarchs.

McKnight found an unoccupied sun lounger by the pool. The girlfriends of the Russian tycoons splashed and squealed in the pool. Stanley took several sips of his sangria. Then Biryuza sat down in the chair next to his.

"How is our man doing?" he asked.

"Bernard? Let me find out."

Stanley called the hospital. The doctor hemmed and hawed but finally pulled himself together and informed Stanley that Bernard had passed away from blood loss eight minutes previously.

CHAPTER 41

M CKNIGHT PLANNED TO LEAVE PAMPLONA in the morning. He wanted to go even earlier, but couldn't force himself to get out of bed. He was comforted by the thought that he wouldn't have made the earliest flights from Madrid to Zurich anyway. Then he decided to have a decent breakfast, realized he wouldn't make the three PM flight, and finally booked a business-class seat on a Helvetic flight for seven that evening. It was a small plane, a Fokker, with good service. Stanley loved to fly in that type of aircraft.

He could have flown out of Pamplona, from the closest airport. His status as a guest of Gagarin gave him access to a full range of services and benefits. But after Bernard's death, Stanley had a physical aversion to being in the Russian oligarch's presence. The cynicism with which these money-stuffed players reacted to the death of someone they had recently dined with hit him hard.

Biryuza was surprised to hear that Stanley was renting a car and driving to Madrid.

"We could fly you to Zurich on a private plane. We don't have any in Pamplona, they all reserved for Viktor's guests, but you could fly out of San Sebastian, from the Donostia Airport," said Biryuza. "Why do you want to drive, anyway? We could have a chauffeur take you."

"Thanks, Anton, really, but I want to drive." Stanley put out his cigarette in the urn by the hospital doors.

The tobacco tasted sour. Stanley had just come from the pathology department, where he had signed a stack of papers in the presence of Spanish government officials and bank security service personnel who had come to bring Bernard's body back.

"I need to be alone," said Stanley. "No offense."

"It was his own fault, you know," Biryuza said, his lip curling upward. "He was told how to act. It's natural selection. He should have stayed down. He was just an idiot. He'd been warned."

"He was scared, Anton," Stanley said, squinting in the sunlight. "He just got scared."

"Serves him right, then! No reason to panic." Biryuza fell silent, then asked, "What kind of car are you going to find here, anyway? Some junker?"

"Not a problem, I can make it in a junker."

The porter helped him load his things into the trunk, and expressed his condolences again for Bernard's death. Stanley thanked him, and they shook hands.

He got in and entered his destination into the GPS—Madrid, Barajas Airport, terminal 2, then pulled away, and saw the porter waving in his rearview mirror. He waved back through the open window.

Christine called as he was approaching Madrid on the N-113. She was in London for a couple of days, with several meetings planned for the evening, followed by dinner with some British collectors, and a visit to an antiques auction the next day.

McKnight turned on video calling. Christine was lying on a wide bed in a semitransparent nightgown, and Stanley couldn't tear his eyes away from her enticing body.

"Video calls have been the cause of many deaths," he said.

"Why is that?" Christine lit a long cigarette.

"You're distracting me," admitted Stanley. "I almost hit the bumper of the car ahead of me just now. I'm going to have turn off the picture and just leave the sound."

"Oh no, don't! I like to watch you drive. You just peek at the screen from time to time, don't stare at it."

"That's the problem, I can't. I want to be next to you, not driving to damned Madrid."

"Madrid? So you can fly to Zurich? Why didn't you fly from Pamplona?"

"Christine, do you think you could find the time to come to Zurich for a couple days? I'm not asking for more than that."

"Of course, I can come tomorrow evening after the auction. I'll come on flight—"

"It doesn't matter which one! I'll meet you anyway."

"But you didn't answer me—why are you driving to Madrid?"

"Because I just wanted to get away from Gagarin and his people, at least for a little while. I can't look at those faces anymore. I'd rather spend an extra four hours driving than fly on one of his planes, use his cars, or eat on his tab."

"But you have to admit you said they had some curious features that interested you," Christine put in.

"Yeah, curious is the right word! You can watch them like animals in the zoo. Dangerous animals. Don't get too close and don't feed them. They don't care about anything but their own welfare and their own money. They heard about Bernard's death, and a minute later they were already back to the party, drinking and feasting."

"Well, that's how most people react. Somebody died, but we're still alive," said Christine. "Alive, healthy, and rich. And besides, you said that Bernard—"

"Yes, strictly speaking, he was to blame. I admit it. He was told not to stand up. But he got scared. I think I'd be scared too, if a bull was standing over me, snorting."

"You're not to be blamed for his death, Stanley."

"I know."

"But you sound like you're feeling guilty. Stanley, honey, it's not your fault. You did everything you could. Do you hear me?"

"I know...oh, sorry, I'm getting a call from Zurich. It's Lagrange. Can you hang on?"

"Of course, honey!"

He could hear the deep exhaustion in Lagrange's voice. He spoke slowly, as if carefully choosing each word.

"McKnight, my dear torero!"

"Hi, Pierre, how are you?"

"Great! Where are you? Are you done running with the bulls?"

"Yes, Pierre, you know..."

"Oh yes, I know about your outstanding achievements in Pamplona. Bernard's body arrived in Zurich today. Back to his parents. He was their only son, didn't you know?"

"No, Pierre."

"But you won't be able to attend the funeral and comfort them with an account of the last minutes of their son's life, I'm afraid. You need to fly to St. Petersburg. Do you know where that is? Not the one in Florida, the one in Russia."

"Yes, Pierre, I know."

"Don't interrupt! They're holding the International Economic Forum there. You have a hotel reservation. You're accredited, all set."

"Damn it, Pierre, I'm driving to Madrid to fly back to Zurich."

"So you'll fly to St. Petersburg instead!"

"But that's your forum! You go there every year."

"And this year I can't!" Lagrange's voice hardened. "While you're vacationing and hanging out, traveling around the world from Singapore to Pamplona, I'm cleaning up our problems. And believe me: they're growing by the day. Our Russian clients are one problem, and you're going to take that one on, get me? You've dealt with them in the past, but now you'll be handling them on your own. I have a different focus now."

"Does Laville know?"

"Come on, Stanley, You sound like a child. Of course he knows. It's his orders. Now you're the head of Russia and the CIS markets, and your new title is managing director—how do you like that?"

"I'd prefer to head up a different market, Pierre. How about Latin America?"

"Very funny, McKnight! But there would be other Gagarins waiting for you there, anyway. We've got some hard times coming up. Inspections. And now, Bernard. His photograph is all over the papers. All the forums are talking about the young banker who died running with the bulls. They even put his picture in front of our building, and people are bringing flowers. Idiocy!"

Stanley almost ran off the road, but the navigator beeped a warning, and Stanley got back in his lane. He had to get back to the bank as soon as possible to put the flash drive in his computer, and now this was postponed. And he was tired; truly, deeply tired. Fly to St. Petersburg! There was no direct flight from Madrid that he knew of, so he'd have to take connecting flights. A six-hour trip, minimum. He cursed under his breath.

"Okay, Pierre, I understand. I understand everything," he said. "Flowers, photographs. Okay…when do I need to be there?"

"Where? Oh, St. Petersburg. You have time. Tomorrow. Tomorrow at nine AM local time registration starts. Our dear friends, Gagarin et al., will all be there. You're already missing them, I imagine?"

"Pierre, I'm not in the mood to joke. And I don't feel like listening to your jokes at all."

"Why's that, old pal?"

333

"I got a letter today. From FINMA. An official letter. They've asked me to come in for a talk. They want to clarify some details. They said that this invite was cleared by bank management."

"And you're worried about that? Forget it! It's no big deal. Yes, I know about it. But the few days you spend in St. Petersburg won't change anything. You can write and tell them you're on a business trip and will come see them when you get back. The local authorities never come after their own. You're a Swiss resident; you count. They'll talk to you and let you go. Then you can relax. Get some sleep, at least. Was Mila at the festival?"

"No."

"So you didn't get any while you were there? Remember, McKnight: abstinence is bad for you! So where was our pretty girl? Has she been fired? Gagarin decided to get a divorce?"

"She's in treatment. For alcohol and drug addiction."

"Her addiction is between her legs."

Stanley understood that Lagrange was intentionally trying to provoke him, was waiting for him to blow up. He might even be recording this conversation. For what reason? Stanley didn't know, but this conversation convinced him that something was going on. He was filled with a vague sense of foreboding.

"And that's her whole problem," Lagrange went on. "Gagarin can't satisfy this bitch, and then you turn up—don't even try to tell me there's nothing going on between you, I won't believe you—but you don't fuck her very often, and she's started to drink more and more. When you get back from St. Petersburg, I'll give you a couple days off, and you can go get Mila out of that clinic, fuck her right, and everything will be okay. You still there, Stanley?"

The Swiss authorities would be happy to make a scapegoat out of him, Stanley thought. An American, an outsider who colluded with Russians. We Swiss are upright and honest. It's those people who only care about money and don't give a damn about reputation. *So be it*, thought Stanley.

"Can you hear me, McKnight.?"

"Yes."

"Great. I'll get someone to find a ticket for you from Madrid to St. Petersburg. And you think about that trip to Mila. Maybe it's fate, eh?"

"Could be," said Stanley. "Goodbye, Lagrange!"

"Bye, Stanley!"

Stanley switched back to the other call. Christine appeared onscreen, now wearing nothing at all. She lay in the pose from Goya's "Nude Maja."

"Beautiful, damn it, so beautiful!" said Stanley.

"I knew you'd like it." Christine covered her naked breasts. "This is even more seductive, no?"

"Yes, much more! But I have very unpleasant news, love."

"What's happened?"

"Nothing much yet, but I'm flying to St. Petersburg instead of Zurich. If your visa's still valid…"

"It is!"

"Then I'll show you the white nights."

"The what? Did you watch an adult movie and come up with a new name for it?"

"Ha ha. No, there really are white nights in the summer there, daytime at night. I've never seen it myself, but I've heard about it."

"I can't wait to spend those nights with you!"

"Me neither! I'll see you soon, love you!"

"Me too! Bye!"

It only took him ten minutes to exchange his ticket to Zurich for one to St. Petersburg. Moreover, the girl working at the Helvetic counter was kind enough to take him over to her friend at Iberia, where it turned out that Stanley's new flight was leaving Barajas a half hour earlier than the flight that he was supposed to take to Zurich. He would be arriving in St. Petersburg's Pulkovo airport at 12:30 AM.

"Have a good flight," said the girl at the counter after checking Stanley in, shooting him a wide smile.

The border guard at passport control smiled just as much, but he pressed a button under his table, anyway, and man in civilian clothes appeared, asking Stanley to follow him.

They went through a door that the man opened with a combination and walked down a narrow corridor to another door. He pushed it open and ushered Stanley in. Dillon and Monti were sitting at the table.

Dillon was looking at some papers, and he gave some to Monti, who put them in a folder.

"Thank you, Garcia," said Dillon, rising, and held out a hand to Stanley.

"Please accept my condolences on the loss of your colleague."

"Thank you, but the best thing you could do for me would be to hurry— my plane is about to start boarding."

"You'll make it," said Marco, waving his hand. "We're in touch with Helvetic. We can hold the flight."

"What the hell does Helvetic have to do with anything!" Stanley sat on the hard chair. "I'm flying on Iberia."

"On Iberia?" Marco whistled. "They changed your flight?"

"And destination. On the way from Pamplona. I'm flying to Russia, St. Petersburg."

"What?" Dillon sat down. "We had an agreement! You have to get that flash drive in ASAP!"

"My dear Frank," Stanley said, pulling out a pack of cigarettes. He glanced at the sign banning smoking in this room, then lit one. "When my boss, Pierre Lagrange, called and said that I had to take his place at the St. Petersburg Economic Forum, what was I supposed to do? Tell him I couldn't go because I have instructions from the CIA to steal all of Laville & Cie's information? He wouldn't get it."

Marco opened his laptop.

"Flight 383?" he asked.

McKnight nodded.

"Okay, you don't have much time. We can't hold Iberia."

"So," began Dillon.

"My plans changed on Lagrange's orders," McKnight interrupted. "And I don't like it at all. Not because of your flash drive, but because he was speaking to me very strangely. As if he suspected something, or something happened that he doesn't want to tell me about. And I got the feeling that he doesn't want me in Zurich right now."

"Details, please," said Dillon. "What was strange about it? And what do you think he might suspect? What might have happened?"

"Anything could have happened, Frank! He could have left his girlfriend and be sleeping on the couch in his office, which is why he's tired and out of sorts, or he could have learned about my contact with you. Maybe there's trouble related to sanctions against our Russian clients. I don't know, Frank! To be honest, I'm exhausted. The bulls, Bernard's death, all this travel. And the insane amount of alcohol." Stanley ground out his cigarette with his heel. "I'm sorry for making a mess, but there's no ashtray, and I have to catch my plane."

"This is all very strange," said Dillon. "As far as we know, Lagrange was supposed to speak at the forum. He has meetings planned. Did he tell you?"

"No."

"And he didn't promise to send you the text of his speeches? Ask you to give the talks in his place? Very strange. So what are you going to do there?"

"Drink. And try to fight off the girls they'll be throwing at me."

"Do you know that Gagarin's wife Mila checked out of the clinic early, and is on her way to Russia?" asked Marco.

"No, I didn't. So I'll be fighting her off as well. My wife will be coming tomorrow or the day after, though."

Dillon and Monti exchanged glances.

"A visit from your wife there is suboptimal," said Dillon. "Any chance you could cancel?"

Stanley shook his head.

"Okay, just be careful. Lagrange's behavior lately has us worried. He's been having some suspicious phone calls to a number in Cuba, using a protected line. Encoded. As soon as our specialists figure out the code, he or the person he's talking to change the code."

"What was he talking about?" asked Stanley.

"Very suspicious stuff—spicy sauce for chicken, based on red pepper, ginger, and certain herbs."

"Certain herbs?"

"Our specialists worked it out. They use those herbs in Caribbean cooking. Why did they need a code?"

Stanley felt a chill go down his spine. He thought he was close to the answer, why Lagrange was using protected lines and talking about herbs, but then he waved the thought, or the start of a thought, away. It was too unbelievable.

"Maybe he's planning to open a Caribbean restaurant in Zurich? There aren't any yet."

"Really? Well, you know better. Okay..." Dillon slapped his hand on the table. "You have to go. You'll be back in Zurich in a couple of days, get some sleep, and put that flash drive in a computer. Meanwhile, I'm going to ask you to stick as close to Lagrange as you can. Call him all the time, ask his advice on the most minor questions. Most of the Russia's top leadership will probably be at the forum. So—here you go."

Dillon handed Stanley a package with several packs of cigarettes.

"Please don't tell me those are more bugs," said Stanley. "I feel like an idiot with these bugs."

"They are, Stanley, but what's the big deal? Just do what you can. You see an important oligarch or official at the forum, shake his hand, give him a pat, and you're good to go. Take them, Stanley, go on. This is part of our agreement."

"Go to hell, Frank!" Stanley said. But took the package anyway and left the room.

CHAPTER 42

E VERY SEAT WAS OCCUPIED IN business class. Two tall blondes were raising their voices at a stewardess, who nodded along deferentially to their narrative.

The blondes were demanding that their friend, who had by some accident ended up in economy, be moved up to business class. The stewardess replied that she would have to ask a current business-class passenger to give up his or her seat to make that happen, and she couldn't do that. One of the blondes, scanning the cabin, met Stanley's eyes before he could turn away.

"Hey, mister," she drawled. "Would you be a gentleman and switch places for us? We would be so grateful. We were on a shopping trip—do you know how hard it is for an honest girl to get a Kelly purse? We're completely exhausted; our friend just won't survive this entire flight in economy."

McKnight, listening carefully to her accent as she spoke, was certain she was Russian.

"My sympathies, of course, I'm a regular at Hermès, myself," replied Stanley in Russian. "But I'm afraid you'll have to make peace with the current situation. I, for one, won't be switching seats for you. Make peace with it, my child. Accept the strong hand of God." And he made the sign of the cross over the blonde just as Father Vsevolod had to him.

The astonished girl whispered something to her companion, and they both glanced warily back at McKnight before giving up their tirade and going back to their seats.

The stewardess brought a flute of champagne over to Stanley.

"Thank you, sir!" she said.

"Not a problem! If you have any other Russian problems, don't hesitate to call on me—that's what I do for living."

"I certainly will, sir! Another glass?"

"Absolutely."

After three glasses of champagne, Stanley fell into such a deep, sweet sleep that he had trouble waking up for lunch. He asked for a shot of vodka and then had five double bourbons after lunch. He was staggering a bit by the time he got off the plane.

He got through customs and exited the green corridor to find a familiar face—Gala was waiting for him, dressed in slacks, a light jacket, and a white shirt.

"Hello, Mr. McKnight! I was sent by—"

"I'll stop you there, Gala, I know who sent you."

"Excellent, then let's go! They're waiting for us."

McKnight waited until Gala was maneuvering out of the parking lot and onto the highway before asking,

"They're waiting in the office?"

"Of course!"

"Right now?"

"Yes."

"Gala, my dear. I'm completely worn out. I can barely keep my eyes open. There's no way I can do any business right now. Can you help me?"

Gala examined Stanley's face carefully in the rearview mirror.

"Yeah, you look like crap. Okay, I'll try…Shamil!" She pressed a button on the dashboard to call her boss, and a blue light went on in the headphone over her elegant ear. "Yes, I picked him up, but he's not doing so good. Hm? No, he seems sober, but he said his blood pressure is high, and he looks pale and sweaty. The doctor? I suggested it, but he just wants to go to bed. To sleep, what do you think? Of course…you'll tell the boss? Okay, I'll wait!"

Gala put the conversation on hold.

"He's gone to tell Gagarin. It's a good idea, really—Viktor's been drinking since the flight back from Spain. You had a terrible time there, didn't you? They said that young guy gored by the bulls was the one who came with you to Moscow?"

"That's right, Gala. He passed away." ˒

"Oh, that's terrible! That's how it always is with bulls, the weak…"

But Stanley never got the chance to hear how it always was; they lost the thread of that conversation when Shamil came back to tell them that Viktor had agreed to move their meeting to the next morning. Gala promised to pick him up beforehand.

The car flew down Mitrofanevskoye Highway, and Gala turned at the Baltic Gardens to cross the Obvodny Canal, then down Izmailovskoye Avenue to cross the Fontanka. She described the sights of the city to Stanley as they went along, and Stanley fought his drowsiness to watch St. Petersburg at night pass by his window. The city looked enormous, gloomy, full of mystery and danger.

They drove down Voznesensky Avenue and through the square where St. Isaac's Cathedral stood before pulling up to the hotel.

"This is one of the best hotels in the city," Gala told him. "Get a good night's sleep, and then you have to try Cococo for breakfast. The owner is a country girl named Elena, who goes by Brunhilde now. She's the girlfriend of a local rock star, and she's big on the scene here."

"Thank you, Gala," said McKnight as he got out. "I'll definitely stop in."

One porter was already carrying his bag over to the glass doors, and another closed the door of the Mercedes behind him.

Stanley took a deep breath. The air was humid and full of the scents of the old city, car exhaust, and the smell of either algae or rotting trash on the breeze from the gulf.

"Mr. McKnight? Thank you for choosing our hotel! Here's your card. Is there anything I can do for you? Anything at all?"

"I'd like to have a whole night of dreamless sleep," said McKnight, picking up his key card from the counter and sticking his passport in his pocket.

"We can guarantee you that, sir!"

But despite the clerk's assurances, McKnight slept restlessly.

He dreamed that the two blondes from the plane were chasing him through St. Petersburg's narrow streets, dressed in little black dresses and Louboutin shoes. Even in high heels, they were faster than Stanley, who was moving as though underwater. Sometimes he managed to pull a little ahead, but then the clack of their heels on the pavement would grow louder, and the furious girls would be right behind him again, reaching out to snatch him and tear him to pieces.

People were throwing dishwater and trash out of the windows above him, and Stanley just managed to dodge. Then he ended up in a small square with a fountain and gulped down the rusty, hydrogen sulfide-scented water, and got into an old, bright-red Volvo. But he hadn't lost the blondes—now they were behind him on a mountain road in a white car, revving its engine constantly, not overtaking him, but maintaining the same distance behind him.

Swerving wildly, he flew into the wall bordering the road. The hood of his car crumpled, and white steam poured out of it as he was thrown forward through the windscreen. He opened his eyes; it was morning.

He ate breakfast: a cup of chicken broth, which the waiter assured him would be an excellent hangover cure, an omelet, and coffee.

McKnight had just returned to his room and was thinking about lying down again for a nap when Gala called. He sighed and pulled his jacket back on. "I'll be right down!"

Gagarin, his face pale and haggard, was seated at an enormous desk populated only with a closed laptop, pack of cigarettes, telephone, lighter, and an overflowing ashtray, despite the early hour.

His eyes were half closed, and he was slowly massaging his temples when Stanley entered. Biryuza sat in a chair by the wall, searching for something on his phone.

"Ah, McKnight! It's been a long time!" Gagarin said, without looking up. "We were expecting Lagrange, actually. He's on the list of presenters. He's even supposed to take part in some talks with our bankers from VTB and Sberbank. Did you rearrange everything over there in Zurich? Are you going to present, then?"

"No, Viktor, I'm not planning on presenting," said McKnight, nodding to Biryuza and sitting down across from Gagarin. "I'm not the best public speaker, to tell the truth. Maybe if Pierre had sent me with some notes for his presentations, but as it is…"

"Yeah, screw this economic forum, anyway." Gagarin emptied the ashtray into the trash bin and lit a fresh cigarette. "We wanted to discuss something with your boss, but I think you'll be able to answer our questions better." Gagarin took a deep drag on his cigarette, paused, then let out a stream of smoke toward Stanley. "Are you after his job, by the way?"

"Not just now, no. Lagrange isn't planning on retiring anytime soon."

"Sorry to be so blunt. How are you settled in? Hotel okay?"

"Yes, I slept well, thanks."

"Well, that's the most important thing. So you're not gunning for your boss's job? You should be! You should always be striving to move up. There's nothing sweeter than maneuvering your boss out of a job. I've done it a couple times in my life, and it's a pure delight. And satisfaction. So here's the thing…"

"The Americans, that is, you," put in Biryuza, "are going to put Viktor on the sanctions list."

"You see what's going on here, McKnight? Well, not here, but there. Sanctions! Fuck them! Fuck their sanctions! Did you hear about this shit?"

Stanley nodded.

"Of course, you have! And those fucking Swiss bastards have opened a money-laundering investigation against me."

"And we got a summons from the UK," Biryuza interrupted. "They're asking Viktor to come in for questioning about our latest real estate acquisitions in London. And not just there. Viktor thinks…"

"Shut your mouth, Biryuza!" barked Gagarin. "I'll say what I think, what I want, and what I'm worried about!"

"Sorry, boss, I just wanted to update the banker," said Biryuza, so startled by his boss's outburst that he almost dropped his phone.

"I know what you wanted," Gagarin said, switching instantaneously from rage to magnanimity. "But let me speak for myself…ok, forget about the details. The main thing is that they've started to roll the barrel on me!"

"They've started to do what, now?" asked Stanley.

"It's a Russian expression…roll the barrel, digging into my affairs, going after me…that's always the way, a bunch of committees and audits, all at once, on several different fronts." Gagarin ground out his cigarette and lit another. "Have you heard anything? Like about the sanctions lists?"

McKnight thought of telling Gagarin about his call to FINMA and MROS, got out his own pack of cigarettes, and lit one up. It seemed premature to talk about potential problems with the Swiss government.

"I know a bit," nodded Stanley. "They haven't approved the lists yet, but a special commission is putting them together. There are two lists, a full one, with even family members included, and another, which…"

"That, I know already," interrupted Gagarin. "I read the papers and watch television as well. Tell me this—what can your Swiss bank do to provide me with evidence that my deposits with you are clean, and to ensure that my assets won't get frozen if I end up on those lists? Can you get any kind of guarantee from your management?" Gagarin paused. "I know the Swiss are the most cowardly and dishonest when it comes to taking risks of their own."

"Those Judases will give us up," Biryuza added.

"I think so, yes. A guarantee is possible." McKnight decided to promise whatever necessary to buy more time. "But where are you getting the intel that you might end up on the sanctions lists?"

"We have reliable sources," Biryuza muttered.

McKnight nodded. He assumed that their reliable source was none other than the adviser to the American president, John Fort, who he had encountered in Spain.

"So you need to go after the lobbyists working with the Treasury Department and the Justice Department, the lobbyists in Congress," Stanley suggested. "I can recommend some good lobbyists, the lawyers from Zakin Bump, for example…"

"That's all slow and expensive," sighed Gagarin. "What do I have in your bank? After the latest deposits?"

"I can't give you a precise figure offhand, of course," McKnight replied. "But I'd say the equivalent of $10 billion in cash and securities. The rest has been transferred out to storage in Luxembourg and Singapore as well as Chinese and Korean banks. We've already diversified your investment portfolio, transitioning completely from the US dollar to other currencies and gold. As you requested."

"We have another request for you." Biryuza rose and went over to the chair next to the desk, facing Stanley. "We need to open an account in Mila's name, in your bank. And transfer about five billion to it. Then split it into accounts in the same Chinese and Korean banks, leaving about five billion in your bank."

"That's easy enough to do, but why, if I may ask?"

"Why split the accounts?"

"That part I understand. Why open an account in Mila's name?"

"Viktor has just filed for divorce ahead of his potential difficulties," Biryuza explained with a sigh. "This amount will be officially registered as a divorce settlement."

Stanley barely held back a smirk. He had really screwed up by not accepting her offer of marriage! A rich bride like that, she'd have no end of potential suitors.

"And another billion should go to your bank's Dubai branch, and everything else—to private bank UBO in Argentina and Chile."

"UBO? I've never heard of this bank."

"So listen harder, McKnight! Get to work—find that bank and set up the transaction." Biryuza hadn't used that tone of voice with Stanley in some time. "That's your job, isn't it?"

"Indeed, it is," said McKnight with a nod. "I'll get to work and take care of things."

"Don't take offense, Stanley," Gagarin said, smoking again and checking his watch. "We're just on edge. And I promised myself I wouldn't drink before noon, and it's still seven minutes away, goddamn it. I'm dying over here, Stanley!"

"I'm not offended, Viktor, I understand perfectly. But as far as I know, you have new legislation on capital amnesty. Russians can now bring their money back into the country without fines or other problems. Why not consider that option?"

Gagarin and Biryuza broke into nearly hysterical laughter, Biryuza squealing, Gagarin letting out loud guffaws that turned into hacking coughs.

"Stanley, my friend," Gagarin began, wiping away his tears, "why would I bring money back to my homeland? I have plenty of money in Russia as it is. So much, that I don't know what to do with it. It's of no great value here in Russia."

"All the benefits of money lie in the possibility of using it," said Biryuza, raising his finger pedantically.

"That's right, Biryuza. Your time at MGIMO University wasn't wasted!" said Gagarin as he laughed. "What would I spend it on? Gorge on black caviar? The doctor says it's bad for me. Buy another house in Crimea? And get on another sanctions list? Money's only valuable to us when it's completely clean and deposited in reputable European banks. That's it. Anyone who believes in the government amnesty is either an idiot or trying to use it to move up in the government. I'm not an idiot, and the path to power is too heavily populated for me."

"Ah, I see now," Stanley said, arranging his face into an amused expression.

"But now your American government is going to ruin everything," sighed Gagarin. "You hear me, McKnight? You are going to ruin everything. America...goddamned America! The whole country is one big mistake."

There was a knock at the door. Gagarin looked at his watch, which showed twelve o'clock on the dot, and nodded with satisfaction. He shouted an invitation, and a pretty brunette in a very short skirt walked in, her long, tanned legs gleaming, carrying a tray with bottles and glasses. She smiled as she set the tray down on the table, and walked out with a fluid grace, as if floating out of the room. Gagarin followed her with his eyes and then poured them all vodkas with a shaking hand.

"To the success of your transactions, McKnight!" Gagarin toasted.

"I'll need a couple of days to put together all the necessary authorizations and do the transfers for such large sums leaving the bank," Stanley said, raising his glass.

"So get to work, my dear Yankee!"

He didn't have any trouble with accreditation at the economic forum. The administration had already been informed that Stanley McKnight would be representing Laville & Cie in place of Pierre Lagrange, and Stanley got his red badge right away. They asked whether he would be giving his own presentation during Lagrange's slot in the agenda, or would he just be participating in the roundtable conversation?

Stanley assured them that he would only take part in the general discussion, and proceeded into the main hall with Biryuza. Gagarin was already there, standing to welcome the next presenter along with all the business bigwigs, politicians, and bankers.

"Why is he getting so much applause?" Stanley asked Biryuza.

"Are you for real, McKnight?" said Biryuza with a laugh. "That's the Russian president! Follow me. I see two free seats."

They sat in the third row, with Biryuza on the end. On Stanley's other side sat a short man with fine features and curly hair.

The president was already speaking, but the curly-haired man continued to carry on a whispered video call. McKnight glanced sideways at his screen and saw a girl in a bathrobe sitting in a kitchen.

The president was giving the audience some heartening news: "Automobile sales are up as well as mortgages issued. Economists see those indicators as key signs of economic recovery and rising consumer demand."

"Did you hear that?" Stanley's neighbor asked the girl on his screen. "Now there's some news!"

"Investment rose 2.3 percent in the first quarter. I want to emphasize that we have a situation today where investment is increasing faster than the GDP. That's yet another indicator of what I've said already. The economy is entering another growth phase and laying the foundations for future development."

Optimism continued to flow from the stage: "I'm calling on all the leaders of the Russian regions—it's necessary to continually increase our efforts, provide business with new opportunities for successful, unimpeded action."

The curly-haired man yawned, covering his mouth with his hand. The president continued: "It is of utmost, essential importance for entrepreneurs, and for all citizens, that we have effective protection of their rights, business, and property. Private capital should be a source of additional investment, but the high levels of risk is holding investors back. Thus, we must establish clear, stable regulations protecting the interests of investors..."

"Will you be investing money in the Russian economy?" Stanley's neighbor asked him in a whisper, glancing down at his badge. "You're a respectable bank, I think; you financed a yacht for me a couple of years ago."

"We prefer to receive the investments of others," McKnight whispered back. "But I won't be advising my clients to invest in Russia."

"And right you are...how do you speak such good Russian? Did you study it in college? Or are you a CIA agent?"

"My family is Russian. Just maintaining the tradition."

"Tradition—that's what we're lacking, and that's the root of all our troubles."

Several people in the row ahead of them turned around and shushed them. The president, meanwhile, had finished his speech, and was answering questions. To a question about income inequality in Russia, he replied: "We can't just go around throwing money out of a helicopter to everyone who wants some. The point is, our economy needs to generate more growth; people will then see their own incomes rise. The only way to make that happen is by investing in new technologies, including digital technologies."

"And now are you going to advise your clients to invest in Russia?" Stanley's neighbor whispered again.

Stanley laughed. "Especially not now."

"I'd like to talk with you some more," the other man said and handed Stanley his card.

Stanley saw that it read *Obik Investments*, and his new friend was named Leonid. He passed along his own card.

"Till next time, Mr. McKnight," said Leonid, and started to rise.

Biryuza also stood up, offering the curly-haired man an obsequious greeting.

"There won't be anything else before the break, Stanley," he said. "Let's go have a drink and a bump! I got some high-quality coke from Argentina."

"No, I can't," Stanley replied. "I need to go back to the hotel—my wife is supposed to be arriving this morning, and I want to meet her there."

"Your wife's coming? Excellent, I've been wanting to meet her. Oh, and we've moved you to the Four Seasons, just around the corner from where you were last night. It's just a bit more suited to your and Viktor's status. Viktor can't have his banker staying at some second-rate hotel, you understand."

"Naturally."

They left the hall.

"There's a reception at the Hermitage this evening," Biryuza went on. "Gala's going to come pick you up. She's at your service during your stay—call her if you need a ride, and she'll pick you up now. Excuse me, I have to go find Gagarin."

"No problem, Anton. By the way, who was that sitting next to me?"

"A major businessman. Independent player. He doesn't bend to the whims of the government, and thumbs his nose at their bans and prohibitions."

"I see."

"Until tonight, McKnight! Bring your wife. Robbie Williams and Elton John are going to be at the party."

"Really?"

"Really. Not to mention the purest cocaine on the whole goddamned planet."

"Okay, see you then!"

CHAPTER 43

THE FOUR SEASONS WAS ALMOST directly across from the hotel Stanley had spent the previous night.

Almost as soon as he walked into his new room, the phone by the bed rang.

"Yes?" he answered.

"Everything okay, Stan?" a male voice asked.

"Who is this?"

"It's Frank. Everything okay?"

"How did you…? Okay, never mind. Yes, everything's fine. Why do you ask? Where are you?"

"I'm going to be close to you from now on, McKnight. Maybe not geographically, but we are nearby. My colleague and I. We've invested too much in you, and have too much riding on you. So we're going to watch out for you. And here's a tip—not everything is ok right now. Do you know why you were moved to a different hotel?"

"It was a matter of prestige for Gagarin. Although the other hotel was fine."

"Bullshit. Gagarin and his head of security simply hadn't managed to bug your room in the other hotel. But they have everything set up at the Four Seasons. Every time you sneeze, every word you say—they're listening. So be on your toes. Keep your mouth shut about anything important! And warn your wife, although—not to be sexist—women are responsible for most of our failures. You get me?"

"About women?"

"Don't joke around, Stanley! This is serious. They'll stop at nothing. You need to keep quiet. It sounds silly, but if you need to tell your wife something important, either whisper in her ear or write notes. Come up with a way to communicate—turn the music up loud, for example."

"But why have they decided to start bugging me? Do they suspect something?"

"Nothing concrete for now, but after this business with sanctions, the real estate problem in London, and accounts investigation in Switzerland, the people behind Gagarin are getting anxious. They think someone is leaking information. Someone of theirs, or working for the people who work for them. You fall under suspicion automatically."

"I see. Where are you, anyway? Outside? In a car?"

"In the car of that lesbian Gala? You know she can hit a half-dollar coin with a Glock from fifty meters? Keep that in mind, just in case. And her car is packed with listening devices, of course. Ones that can catch a conversation outside from 150 meters away. You won't even notice the person eavesdropping on you. Russians have made good progress in the surveillance field."

"I see. Listen, Frank, I have to go. My wife should be here any minute; I just got a message that she's on her way."

"Okay, okay, just remember what I said."

"Another thing, Frank. Will you come if I need you?"

"How do you picture that, Stanley? Even if we were close, right nearby, what would we do? Beat up the bad guys and shoot a bunch of Russians on their own territory? Come on, McKnight! You'll have to depend on yourself. Or, mostly…"

McKnight heard a sound from the bathroom, and realized Christine was already in the room—she'd been in the shower.

"Is that you, Stan?" she shouted over the sound of the water when McKnight walked into the enormous bathroom.

"Were you expecting someone else?" Stanley said, starting to undress.

He got into the shower with Christine and put his arms around her.

"Watch it, you!" She laughed, pressing against him. "Let me at least rinse out the shampoo first!"

"I like you better this way!" he said, pulling her closer.

Christine slid her hand down his body.

"Oh, what do we have here?" she said, gripping the root of his member and stroking upward. "What could this be?"

"That is my good friend, who missed you very much."

"Let's take care of him, then."

"Wait, I have to whisper something in your ear first!"

McKnight recounted the main points of his conversation with Frank, told her what precautionary measures they had to take, and to be careful not to discuss any matters of importance out loud.

Christine listened, nodding, her hand continuing its rhythmic motion, but when Stanley advised her not to come with him to the Hermitage reception, she squeezed him tightly in her fist, and Stanley moaned, out of pain and pleasure at the same time.

Stanley didn't want Christine at the reception—not out of concern for her safety, but because he knew that Mila would be there. There was no telling how a meeting between the two of them would end.

"Oh no," Christine replied. "What do you expect me to do, wait for you in the hotel room? I've never been to this city or the Hermitage, and even if I do come some other time, I'll never have the chance to go to another party like this. You better take me with you, or else."

"Or else?"

"Or else I'll leave you in this condition, and you'll have to finish what I started. Is that what you want, baby?"

"No, no, anything but that."

Two hours later, Stanley and Christine approached the doors of the Hermitage, flanked by two enormous atlantes holding up the portico.

"It's beautiful!" whispered Christine.

Stanley laughed. "You can use your regular voice here. We're not in the room or the car."

"How beautiful!" Christine repeated louder. "By the way, about the car, who was that in the car, a guy or a girl? And why did they give you a thumbs-up?"

"That was Gala, a driver and guard who works for Gagarin. She was letting me know she approved of you."

"Well, well, well! She approves, does she?" Christine said irritably, and the doors swung open to admit them.

The footmen were wearing eighteenth-century livery and powdered wigs, and accompanied each guest down the stairs, where the host of the ball hit the marble floor with his staff and loudly announced their names.

"Mr. and Mrs. McKnight," the host proclaimed. Stanley and Christine picked up flutes of champagne from the tray of a passing waiter and proceeded further into the room.

The high-ceilinged rooms were crowded with guests. Music played, and the conductor, who had the look of a man who had just smoked a good joint, his bald head shining and face covered with a five o'clock shadow, made a half bow to the assembled crowd. He nodded to Stanley.

"Do you know him?" Christine asked.

"I don't think so," he said, and then felt someone embrace him from behind, and the moist press of a kiss to his cheek. He stepped back, and saw Mila, in a beige silk dress, pale, and looking taller than usual.

"Stanley!" cried Mila. "I've missed you so much!"

Stanley freed himself from her embrace.

"Mila, this is my wife, Christine. Christine, this is Mila, Viktor Gagarin's wife."

"Ha!" Mila exclaimed. "Finally! I've been dying to meet you." She extended her hand to Christine, who shook it with a tight smile on her face.

"Where is your husband?" asked Stanley.

"My former husband, you mean," corrected Mila. "Where do you think? Pushing his deals with some officials or some other assholes. Boring! You know," Mila said, turning to Christine, "your husband and I are great friends."

Stanley shot a quick glance at his wife. Her mouth no longer held a smile, and she looked from Mila back to Stanley in surprise.

"He brightened up my lonely days with this pack of idiots. Your husband is the only one who can understand me lately. He knows how to entertain like no one else. Maybe you like to have fun as well?"

"I try to keep it within limits," said Christine, at a loss.

"That's a big mistake!" Mila replied. "I've learned one thing in my short life…"

"What's that?" asked Stanley nervously.

"Not to limit myself in anything!"

"Hm, maybe you should be a bit…reasonable in your pursuits?" Stanley hedged.

"No, you idiot," Mila said, giving Stanley a pinch on the cheek. "Any experience is better than lack of experience. That's the meaning of life. Oh, damn!"

Shamil, dressed all in black, was headed their way.

"Hi, McKnight," barked Shamil. "Mila, Viktor wants to see you. Right now!"

"We'll talk more later, Stanley," Mila said, giving Christine a brief nod and following after Shamil. Stanley sighed and took a drink of champagne.

"Who was that?" asked Christine.

"I told you, Gagarin's wife."

"No, the scary guy who came for her."

"He's Gagarin's head of security."

"Does he also shoot well?"

"Why are you asking?"

"Forget it!" Christine's mood had turned; she looked around her with clear displeasure, walking unwillingly along with Stanley. She finished her champagne and took another.

"What's wrong, honey?" asked Stanley, taking Christine's hand.

"Nothing!"

"But I can tell that something…"

"Shut up, Stanley! Look, your Mila's coming back."

"She's not my Mila at all," began Stanley, but didn't finish his sentence. Gagarin was approaching, Mila's arm in his. The pair looked a bit comical, Stanley thought—a short, unkempt man, unshaven and with tufts of hair sticking out around his bald spot, and the tall, slender Mila with her perfectly coiffed hair. The only thing they had in common was their pale skin and dark circles under their eyes. Gagarin eyes were full of appreciation as he took in Christine.

"Well, introduce us, Stanley!" Gagarin said. "Actually, let me do the honors. I'm Viktor, and you must be Christine. He's hidden you away from us for too long." Viktor wagged a finger at Stanley. "How could he, the scoundrel. Mila just told me—look at this beauty, that's our Stanley's wife! So how do you like St. Petersburg?"

"It's okay," Christine said with a shrug of her shoulders.

"Okay! I can't believe it, the first time I ever heard that! Okay! Come with me. Let me show you something and introduce you to a few people. Leave your boring banker behind!" Gagarin ceremoniously offered Christine his arm, and she looked back at Stanley with a grimace before taking his arm and disappearing into the crowd with him.

"Stanley," Mila whined, "I'm so unhappy, Stanley…"

"Not now, Mila! Later!"

"Later? Why did you drag your American wife here?"

"Because I'm an American! Because I love her. Because…"

"You love her, huh?" Mila interrupted. "Well, well, you be careful and make sure you don't get yourself castrated."

"Not now, Mila!" Stanley said, pasting a wide, fake smile on his face as a billionaire oil baron passed by and nodded at them. "We'll talk later." He put his empty glass on a tray carried by a passing footman. "I'll be back."

Stanley moved into the crowd, circling the room several times, but couldn't find Christine or Gagarin anywhere. He was surprised to see Father Vsevolod, then the members of the Famous Five, not all together, but each at the head of small groups of guests. Finally, tired of searching for his wife, he stood by the food table and took two tartlets with black caviar.

Scanning the crowd from this position, he finally spotted Christine. She was alone, looking lost. Her face was unhappy. Stanley walked over and took her arm.

"Christine!"

"I've been looking for you," she said. "To say that you're a fucking asshole, Stan. Your lover, that stupid, arrogant girl…"

"What lover, Christine, what are you talking about?"

"Not what, but who. Mila! Have you slept with her? Well?"

"Christy!"

"Have you?"

"Okay, if you insist…what do you think? We were separated, close to a divorce. I haven't asked you, and I'm not going to, whether you were with someone then. That's the past. Our present is what matters."

"I'd slap the hell out of you, if this crowd wasn't so important for your job. Look, they're already staring. You can go to hell, Stanley McKnight!"

She shook off Stanley's hand, turned, and left the hall in tears.

Stanley was about to rush after her, but Biryuza stopped him.

"Russians have a saying—lovers' quarrels are soon mended. You get me?" Biryuza was quite drunk, but holding himself together.

"Not really."

"Never mind! Don't you worry, Stanley! Let's go to Shatush! You know it? Come on!"

There was a big crowd in front of the restaurant on the Moika embankment when they arrived. Some were gathered in small tents by the entrance. To get in, you had to meet the approval of the host, a man well over six feet with a face displaying no emotion.

This dispassionate oligarch—one of the richest men in Russia, according to Biryuza, was dressed in a black Adidas sweatshirt and personally greeted each new arrival.

He would occasionally spot a pretty girl in line and literally push her into the restaurant. Parked cars packed the narrow street in two rows, with taxis and cars with special accreditation for the economic forum barely squeezing through the remaining space to drop off new guests also fleeing the official ball.

Biryuza greeted the oligarch like an old friend and led Stanley into the restaurant. Inside, music played loudly, and there were so many people that Stanley was pressed against the wall, and Biryuza disappeared somewhere. Looking for some way to entertain himself, Stanley took out his pack of cigarettes and began sticking the tiny bugs onto every Russian who passed by, enjoying the thought of Frank and Marco losing their minds trying to decipher the recordings.

The show began after another surge of guests entered. A band started to play a deafening song, and there was endless vodka and champagne.

The drunker everyone got, the more it started to resemble a wild college party. The group started to play a song that Stanley recognized from the yacht, "Earth Through the Porthole," and the entire crowd sang along with the vocalist.

The upper torso of the oligarch rose over the dancing crowd. Stanley squeezed in between the girls and the host, palmed one of the bugs, and cautiously placed his hand on the oligarch's shoulder.

The tall man turned toward Stanley at the touch and shot him an unexpectedly welcoming grin and shouted something in his ear about basketball. *I wonder who he took me for?* thought Stanley. He gave the giant a friendly slap on the shoulder in reply, checking to make sure the bug was in place, and headed off to the bar, all without having said a word.

He was distracted from his pursuits by the ringing of his phone. He looked down at the screen to see that it was Barbara calling.

"Hi, hello!" answered Stanley, but couldn't hear a thing over the din of the music. He hung up, squeezing through the crowd and dispersing bugs as he went, to the bar, where he took a double bourbon.

Barbara called again, and Stanley had to go outside.

"Hi, what's up!"

"Where are you, Stanley?"

"As usual, drinking and having a bit to eat. Damn it, Barbara, what does it matter? Why are you calling this late?"

"The transfers from Gagarin's accounts aren't going through," she said. "And I can't understand why."

"Have you asked Lagrange?"

"I've tried. I can't reach him."

"Well, I guess he decided to rest. It is late in the evening after all. Call again tomorrow."

"But you told me to get the transfers done today."

"Nothing terrible will happen if the transfers aren't completed until tomorrow. Especially since I'm planning to fly to Zurich. There's nothing for me to do here, and I've already spoken with Gagarin. The day after tomorrow at the very latest. Don't worry. We'll talk in the morning, okay?"

While Stanley was talking to Barbara, an unusually beautiful girl appeared beside him. As soon as he hung up, she began asking him in broken English to take her back into the restaurant with him.

"No problem, pretty girl," replied Stanley in Russian.

"Are you Russian?" the girl asked, seeming disappointed.

"Not for a long time, no," answered Stanley.

He walked back to the hotel on foot that night, even though Gala called him several times offering to pick him up.

Christine was sitting on the balcony when he walked in, a half-empty bottle of wine beside her chair.

Stanley dropped his tuxedo jacket onto the couch and stopped at the door onto the balcony.

"Hi," he said. "You know, I feel like a real asshole. I shouldn't have done it. However you look at it, I betrayed you. And…"

"Oh, just be quiet, Stanley. Listen to the sounds of this city. Entirely different from the ones we're used to. And the air! The air is marvelous here."

"Forgive me, Christine, please."

Christine rose from her chair.

"There's no better sight than a repentant Stanley McKnight. Go on. Repent some more! Just get undressed while you do it!"

Christine's fingers flew as she undid the bowtie at Stanley's collar.

"Faster, Stanley!" she walked to the bedroom, slipping out of her dress on the way. When Stanley followed her in, she was lying on the bed. She opened her arms, and Stanley stepped out of the rest of his clothes.

"You're taking too long, Stan!"

He lay down beside her and kissed her chest.

"You're never going to cheat on me again, Stanley. It's my fault. You were alone too long. I shouldn't have left you alone in Zurich."

"I promise you, Christine. I'm going to leave everything behind soon and come back to you. For good."

Stanley lay beside Christine, and he felt that he would love her forever. He wanted to tell her that, but thought that any words right now would come out wrong.

"Now you don't have to hurry, baby," whispered Christine.

A phone call from Barbara woke Stanley at six the next morning. Stanley looked at his watch, surprised that Barbara was at work so early.

Barbara said that Stanley must have misunderstood her the day before, as he had been too calm about it and then hung up for some reason. Because they really had serious problems with transfers. When Stanley asked why Barbara couldn't go to Lagrange for help, she replied that she still couldn't get through to him.

"So what's going on?" Stanley shuffled over to bar on bare feet, and poured himself a full glass of orange juice.

Barbara coughed and said that Gagarin's account had insufficient funds.

"What do you mean, insufficient? What the hell?"

"I thought you would know, Stanley."

"How much less does he have than needed?"

Barbara paused.

"Two billion. Two billion dollars."

"What the hell!" Stanley was suddenly having trouble catching his breath. "That's not possible."

He fell silent and heard Barbara sobbing on the other end of the line.

"I'll be there as soon as I can," said Stanley. He hung up and finished his juice.

"What happened, honey?" asked Christine when Stanley came back to the bedroom.

"Nothing. I just want you!"

He put a finger to his lips, sat down on the bed, and whispered into her ear that he had very, very serious problems, and he was going to fly to Zurich, but that Christine could spend the morning in the hotel, go to a museum, and he would send her a ticket when he got to Zurich. She would have to leave the hotel in a taxi without anyone seeing her, no later than this evening, and fly back to America.

"And I can't spend some more time here?" whispered Christine.

"For your own safety—no."

"I wanted to spend a couple of days walking around the museum."

"No!" whispered Stanley forcefully. "Don't you understand that it could be deadly? You have to leave today. Do you hear me, my love? Today! Promise me."

"Okay, honey."

"Promise me!"

"I promise. I promise."

PART SIX: PAYBACK

CHAPTER 44

T HE FOREFATHERS OF JEAN-MICHEL LAVILLE looked down on Stanley from the walls of the bank's main meeting room.

  The portrait of the bank's founder hung over the fireplace, and his descendants were situated on either side.

As for Jean-Michel, his was a small portrait, right by the door.

His smile was reserved, the sky shone blue above him, and the tips of waves rose from the sea behind. A respectable client of the bank left that room feeling as if he was accompanied by the optimism of the bank's owner, imbued with his confidence in their long-term and mutually beneficial cooperation.

Now Jean-Michel was wearing a different smile. Stanley could feel his gaze burning on his cheek.

Jean-Michel and all his ancestors, now looking daggers at him as well, seemed to suspect Stanley McKnight, now sitting in a soft chair with his back to the window, of planning to deprive Laville & Cie of a significant sum of money as well as the most valuable thing in the business of banking—its centuries-old reputation.

McKnight arrived from St. Petersburg completely worn down. The long flights, transferring from one airplane to another, the cocaine, the alcohol, the lack of opportunity to get a good night's rest—they'd all done their part.

He didn't even feel like someone who worked at a bank anymore. He forgot the last time he had opened his clients' investment portfolios, or checked the stock market and banking news.

He had turned into either a professional partygoer or a traveling salesman. The only thing Stanley wanted to do during his flight was open his laptop and check his business email. He read a letter addressed to all the senior bankers that, in accordance with a new bank policy, charges to the corporate credit card for strippers and prostitutes would no longer be reimbursed. Then he was stunned to see his access to the bank's information system suddenly cut off. He tried to get in touch with Barbara, but she didn't answer the phone.

Stanley thought it must be some IT glitch, a temporary breakdown, a poor connection thirty thousand feet in the air, maybe, or automatic blocks set up by the bank.

When he'd landed and made it through passport control, Stanley called Barbara. First, she didn't answer. Then she did, and asked Stanley to come to the office immediately, her voice cold.

Stanley told her he'd have to stop off home first, at least to take a shower. Barbara was passing on Stanley's words to someone else and listening to their instructions, told him they'd expect him at the bank in an hour and a half.

An hour later, Stanley approached the bank entrance, but his key card didn't work on the second set of doors. He tried again. Same thing. The guard sitting at the desk located between the two sets of doors looked familiar to Stanley.

"Hi, Karl!" Stanley said.

The guard lifted his colorless eyes to Stanley. The desk hid the lower half of his face and the rest of his body. Sparse strands of blond hair framed his narrow skull.

"Karl, my card's not working. Probably got demagnetized after so many flights! I should have left it at home."

"That's against the rules," the guard replied, his voice sounding worn and gray.

"I know that the card should remain with the owner at all times," Stanley answered, happy at least that the guard was talking, "but could you open the door for me? They're expecting me, and I've just flown in urgently from Russia. By the way, hello from St. Petersburg." Stanley pulled out a postcard with views of the city that he'd taken from his room, and placed it on the desk. "A souvenir for you!"

The guard gave a barely perceptible nod, but didn't buzz Stanley through. Instead, a small door opened behind the desk, and a senior security officer emerged.

"Mr. McKnight!" he said with a polite smile. "Nice to see you again. They've asked me to walk you over."

"There's no need, I know the way to my own office, if Karl would just open the door," Stanley said, beginning to lose patience. "What the hell is going on?"

"His name is Kurt, Mr. McKnight. And management has asked me to accompany you. So, let us go."

Another guard, looking like Kurt's identical twin, joined the senior guard. "How could I forget his name?" wondered Stanley. "I always have a perfect memory for names! Even for mannequins like these guys."

Kurt, previously known as Karl, opened the door. Stanley, flanked by guards, proceeded down a corridor, but not the one that led to the employee elevator—to the one for visitors.

"Where are you taking me?" asked Stanley. "What's the meaning of all this?"

They didn't answer him. Stanley repeated the question.

"Mr. McKnight, I was told to bring you to the meeting room, the main one on the second floor. That's all I know. Please come along now."

The elevator doors opened up.

"Please hand over your briefcase," the senior guard said when the elevator began to ascend.

"Have you lost your mind?" Stanley exclaimed.

"At the instruction of Mr. Laville. Please don't make any problems."

Stanley exhaled. The situation was growing ridiculous.

"Do what you like!" said Stanley, and handed over the briefcase.

After several minutes waiting in the meeting room, Stanley began to feel like the founder of Laville & Cie, a man with a high forehead, bushy eyebrows, and a thin neck, really was watching him from the painting. *Damn it*, thought Stanley, *I'm the one who's losing his mind. What is going on here!*

The doors opened, and the head of compliance, Michel Poiccard, walked in, followed by Barbara, her expression tenser than usual, and a shabby-looking man who Stanley had seen once in Lagrange's office and who Lagrange had introduced as the head of security.

The shabby man, without saying a word, unbuttoned his jacket, sat down across from Stanley, and fastidiously brushed some invisible dust from his sleeve.

Stanley noticed a gun in the man's shoulder holster as he did so.

"Hello, sir," Barbara said, with effort.

"Hi, hi," said McKnight with a nod, and looked at Poiccard—he was placing a red folder on the lacquered, perfectly smooth surface of the table.

362

"What's going on?" Stanley asked him. "I'm getting pretty tired of asking the same question over and over again."

"We have big problems, thanks to you, McKnight." Poiccard drew a high-backed chair away from the table and sat, crossing his legs. Stanley saw that he was wearing red-and-yellow-striped socks and smiled.

"Something funny?" the head of security asked. His voice was as colorless as his appearance.

"What problems, Poiccard?" asked Stanley, ignoring the other man.

"A large sum of money has disappeared from the account of your client." Poiccard opened the red folder. "Mr. ...yes, Mr. Gagarin. And we believe that you are responsible for that disappearance."

"Are you joking?"

"No."

"What amount are we talking about? Barbara said something about two billion, but I thought it was a joke. A bad joke."

"It's no joke, McKnight!"

"Ah, so I'm such an idiot that I stole money from a Russian oligarch who would tear off your head over 500 euros, and now, like a little boy who's gotten into the jam jar, have come strolling back here thinking that the loss of a little jam—i.e., billions of dollars—will go unnoticed? I'm not offended that you suspect me, that means you think I've got balls, but since I'm here and not on the run, that means you think I have no brains. I'd punch you in the face, Poiccard, but your friend here has a gun."

"Don't get worked up, McKnight!"

"Don't get worked up? Are you a complete and absolute idiot, Poiccard? Of course, I'm worked up! I'm so worked up I'm about to start tearing this place apart. We are missing—if you're not playing some kind of game—funds belonging to my client, one of the richest people in the world, I'm a suspect, and you expect me to be calm? Who withdrew those funds? How? Where did they go? Come on, Poiccard! Give us the report!"

Poiccard looked down at his folder.

"Eighty transfers were made over the last week amounting to approximately $2 billion."

"That's impossible."

"Is that so, McKnight?" Poiccard snorted and flipped through some papers.

"No more than $30 million have ever been transferred out of Gagarin's accounts," Stanley said, rubbing his temples. "Money came to our bank but never left! There were small payments, mostly on fuel for the yacht, a

363

couple times he bought little things at Graff for his wife, and he recently purchased a house in Sentosa. Altogether, that's maximum thirty million. Maximum! He used other banks to pay for his other expenses, and we were his most reliable piggy bank, where he only added money."

"And he did," exclaimed Poiccard, "until you decided to add your client's money to your own wallet!"

"Con man," Barbara said, shaking her head.

"Have you all lost your minds?" Stanley said, jumping out of his seat.

"Sit down, McKnight. Sit down," said the head of security, moving his jacket to the side.

"I'll say it again—idiots." Stanley sat back down. "I don't know about any transfers. Even if there have been transfers, I didn't have anything to do with them."

Poiccard pulled several papers out of the folder.

"Is that so, Mr. McKnight? And how do you explain your personal authorization on all these transfers?"

"Let me see." McKnight practically snatched the papers out of Poiccard's hands. All the papers had his signature and Lagrange's personal stamp. For internal purposes, this was all the authorization needed for any transfer under $100 million.

"I've never seen these forms before in my life. And they're copies of documents, at that. A signature is easy enough to copy from old transfer forms—where are the originals?"

"It is your signature, McKnight."

"A child could copy a signature with a Xerox machine." Stanley picked up a pen from the table and spun it around a couple times before setting it back down. Only one person could explain what was going on. Even though Stanley already sensed, already knew deep down what had happened, his mind was refusing to accept it.

"Where's Lagrange?" Stanley asked quietly.

"You'd know better where your accomplice is, McKnight. We're looking for him, and we're going to find him."

"I repeat," said Stanley, "everything you've said here is complete and total nonsense. The only thing I'm convinced of is that you're looking for a scapegoat. And I'm an ideal candidate. Okay, carry on, but in the meantime, I'd like to go for a walk."

"I'm afraid you'll have to stay here," replied the head of security.

"I have to take a leak," snorted Stanley. "Excuse me, Barbara. Or are you going to bring me a pot? At least an empty water bottle. And then, my dear friends and colleagues, no one in this room can order me to do anything. I don't report to any of you. Nor am I under arrest. Isn't that right?"

"No, however, you'll have to—" began the security adviser, but Stanley stood. He looked around and saw the Japanese vases standing next to the tall mirror, Laville's prized pieces. He claimed that each of them was worth the same as a private plane.

Stanley thought that the police would be arriving any minute. These idiots would have called them as soon as he showed up at the bank. Without the police and official charges against him, neither Poiccard or security had any right to hold him.

They'd have to hand him off to the authorities. Now he could hear the distant sound of police sirens approaching through the armored windows of the bank. *That's probably not for me. They'll come for me without any sirens, quietly and discretely, but I don't have much time at all!* thought Stanley.

"Barbara, would you be so kind as to turn around for a moment?" he asked, going over to the vases, and demonstratively reaching for the zipper of his pants.

"Stop this nonsense, McKnight!" cried Barbara. "Do something, Poiccard!"

"Indeed, McKnight, there's no need for this vulgar display," began Poiccard, but the security adviser broke in.

"I don't see a problem with allowing our dear colleague to visit the restroom."

He spoke formally, looking at Stanley without blinking, and was clearly very happy that the party responsible for the loss of funds, this devious American thief who had wormed his way into their reputable bank, had been caught, and was about to be handed over to the police.

"The police will be here soon," he went on, "and my man will assist you, Poiccard. That is, if Mr. McKnight tries anything foolish. Like making a run for it, say."

"Excellent!" said Stanley, and headed for the door. Poiccard followed him. Another security guard stood on the other side of the door, either Kurt or Karl, tense and ready for anything. Kurt or Karl led the way, followed by Stanley, and then Poiccard bringing up the rear.

The guard remained in the hallway, and Poiccard went in first. The man had obviously watched more than his fair share of action movies and decided to act like a policeman—he checked both stalls (they were empty), and, just to be safe, banged on the hand dryer a couple times and examined the high window with tinted glass panes.

"I doubt I'd be able to jump that high," said Stanley, observing Poiccard's actions with interest. "Can I take a piss now?"

"Ok, ok, McKnight, don't get an attitude. I'll leave you alone, but don't take too long."

Poiccard went out. Stanley immediately locked the door to the restroom, went into a stall, and stood on the toilet. From that height, he managed to reach the lock on the window frame, turned it, and yanked the frame roughly toward himself.

From that sharp tug, the frame banged on the wall, and the glass flew out, barely missing Stanley and shattering on the tile floor. But as it turned out, even if Stanley had been able to pull himself up and climb out the window, it wouldn't have done him any good—bars covered it from the outside.

Poiccard hammered on the door from the hallway.

"What's going on in there, McKnight! Open up! Open this door!" Then, to the guard, "Break it down!"

Stanley didn't wait for them to break it down. He swung the door open, and putting all his strength and frustration into the swing, punched Poiccard in the jaw.

"I hate compliance!" said Stanley.

Because of the narrow entrance, Poiccard didn't fall down, and his body protected Stanley from the reach of the security guard.

Stanley moved toward the guard, staying behind the unconscious Poiccard. He waited for the right moment, then shoved the motionless body to the side—Poiccard's head banged loudly against the edge of the toilet as he fell—and came at the guard, whose hand was already raised to strike.

Stanley's kick caught the guard right in the groin, and the other man screamed, doubling over. Stanley grabbed his collar and slammed his head repeatedly against the toilet as well.

Blood sprayed from his fractured cheekbone. Ignoring the man's moans, Stanley stuffed him and Poiccard into a stall, slammed the door behind him, and leaped out of the room.

McKnight ran down the hallway leading to the stairway, but met Barbara around the corner.

Like a soccer goalie gearing up to face off against an oncoming striker, she stretched her hands out wide and crouched down slightly, taking a couple steps toward him.

"You won't get away, you American bastard!" she hissed. "You dirty thief!"

Stanley didn't hesitate for a second. He ran into her full force, and her body crumpled inward and dropped to the floor. But as he stepped over her prone form, he felt her latch onto his left ankle. *Principled little witch,* he thought. He stopped and turned, trying to free his leg. But he moved a little too forcefully, and his boot slammed into Barbara's forehead. Her grip relaxed, and her eyes rolled up as she slumped back down.

Stanley bent over and patted Barbara on the cheek. "Nothing personal, honey, nothing personal!" He tore the magnetic key card from her neck and ran on.

But when he opened the door to the stairway, he heard voices from below. When he peered over the banister, Stanley saw the senior security officer, two men in civilian clothing, and a policeman in uniform. The only path left to him was up.

He tried to not to run and attract attention, but still moved quickly as he made his way up to the top, fourth floor. He opened the door with his key and entered a hallway that led to another stairway. This narrow spiral staircase went up to the roof, where the bank maintained a small garden and smoking area.

When he was almost at the door to the roof staircase, Stanley remembered the flash drive in his pocket. He looked around him, and saw that the door to a small office was partially open. These offices belonged to the bank's most junior IT employees, and one of them, it seemed, had gone up to smoke on the roof and forgotten to close his door tightly behind him—which was strictly prohibited.

McKnight cracked the door open. The room was windowless and dim, with two desks facing each other. The two occupants of this office would have to stare at each other's faces all day long. The chairs were empty; apparently they were both smoking on the roof.

Stanley slipped into the office. It was equipped with old desktop computers, powerful enough and reliable, but nothing like the latest high-speed models in the offices of the bank's senior management and leadership. Stanley took the flash drive out and crouched down, ducking under the desk and feeling around on the back of the system unit of one of the computers for a USB slot. He plugged the drive in. Now, even if the bank's security detected the drive's intrusion into their system, they would have a difficult time finding it. Stanley was too busy savoring his minor revenge to be careful and banged his head soundly on the underside of the desk as he got back up.

Rubbing the bruised spot, Stanley went back out into the hallway and trotted toward the spiral staircase.

Several bank employees were up on the roof when he got out, and they all stared in surprise at the panting man.

Just his presence here was surprise enough—employees at his level of seniority could smoke in their offices, equipped with powerful vents. Moreover, Stanley hadn't been in the office much lately, involved as he was with work for his Russian clients.

"Good afternoon, ladies and gentlemen!" Stanley greeted the smokers, although he didn't see any women among them.

"Hello, Mr. McKnight!" answered a tall, thin man whom Stanley had seen in the hallway several times. "What's going on down there? We saw a police car."

"Who knows?" Stanley replied, and walked over to the edge of the roof. If he took a running jump, he could make it to the roof of the next building.

He looked again. *Or I could fall short and end up in the custody of these cretins with two broken legs.*

"But they had all their lights and sirens going!" the thin man continued. "As if someone had broken into the vault or something."

"Well, in a manner of speaking, someone has," muttered Stanley. He looked around one more time and decided to jump. It would be a tricky business: before leaping from the edge of the building, he would have to jump up onto the short wall around the roof without slowing down. Stanley turned his back toward the edge of the roof and began to count off his steps.

"Is everything okay?" asked one of the smokers.

"Everything is excellent!" answered Stanley, and finished his count: *...twelve, thirteen, fourteen...that's enough, I think!*

"Maybe you'd like a cigarette?" asked another.

"Later." Stanley took a deep breath, slapped his legs to get the blood moving, and took off at a run.

He jumped with the complete certainty that he wouldn't make it to the roof of the neighboring building. It wasn't a suicide attempt, but it was his only option; he simply couldn't allow himself to be led out of that building in handcuffs, suspected of stealing Gagarin's money. But all the cards were stacked against him! The signature, the transactions done with his codes, with his personal passwords, from his computer. He knew that it would be practically impossible to prove his innocence, to show that he was the victim of someone's cunning plot, the pawn in a carefully planned and skillfully executed operation. They would pin it all on him. That is, if he survived until the trial, a highly unlikely outcome. So—he jumped.

He saw the stunned faces of his smoking audience. This was the very last thing they'd expected to see when they went upstairs for a break. Stanley's dormant athletics skills had risen to the fore somehow, even though it had been fifteen years since he'd run track in college.

He leaped easily from the edge of the roof, pushing off with great force, and flew over the gap between the buildings. His speed and jump were actually too strong—he crashed onto neighboring roof, lessening the blow with his hands, rolled quickly to his feet, straightened, ran, and leaped onto the next roof. He picked up speed, crossed it, crouched, and jumped yet again.

I could win a parkour contest like this, he thought. *Maybe when I get out of prison.*

That thought finally brought him up short. He stopped, panting. He looked himself over—his suit showed no visible damage, his shoes weren't scratched, he didn't have any bruises or scrapes, and nothing had fallen out of his pockets.

He walked to the far end of this roof to the top of a fire escape.

Gagarin was probably already coming after him, after his blood. He wouldn't stop to figure out who was innocent and who was guilty. People like him just struck out with their knives left and right, so their own throats didn't get cut.

He saw that the fire escape descended into an interior courtyard, and he started to climb down.

Strangely enough, his heart, which had been so calm earlier, was now trying to beat its way out of his chest. He hadn't been anxious jumping off the roof, but was sick with the fear that one of his hands would slip on a rung and he would go tumbling down.

Stanley thought that dying in a fall like that would be the best option. He imagined lying in a hospital bed under guard, paralyzed, pissing in a bed pan, with police and prosecutors visiting, and Gagarin's thugs trying to get at him. The image amused him for some reason, and he clambered easily down the last rungs of the staircase and jumped onto the ground.

CHAPTER 45

H E ENDED UP DIRECTLY ACROSS from the service entrance to the kitchen of a small restaurant. The gates leading out into the alley from the courtyard were locked. Just then, the kitchen door opened, and a Chinese worker came out carrying a large back trash bag.

"Can I help you, Herr?" he asked in surprise.

"I was in the bathroom," Stanley replied, "and I got turned around on the way out."

"It happens!" the man said with a smile.

He held the door open, pointing Stanley in the right direction. Stanley walked through the kitchen, then the dining room, and onto the street.

He turned right and soon came out onto Banhofstrasse next to the Chanel store.

Respectable white-collar workers streamed past him. A police car sped by, its siren on.

Stanley tightened his tie and walked along the right side of the street toward the train station. He had managed to escape from security and the police at the bank, but what now? Where could he go?

He had very little cash in his pocket, and he couldn't use any of his cards or go back to his apartment. It would be best not to use his phone, either.

Cursing the triumph of gadgets over the human memory, Stanley sat at the table of an outdoor café and copied down some numbers from his telephone. He remembered Christine's number, and he only needed a few others—Dillon, Monte, Lagrange, and, just in case, Durand, Biryuza, and Gagarin's personal cell.

The waiter came over, but Stanley told him he would just have an espresso at the bar. The strong coffee gave him a boost. Stanley went to their restroom, washed his hands, and carefully examined his reflection in the mirror. With the black bags under his eyes and his haggard look, he was the spitting image of a long-term drug addict.

He winked at himself in the mirror, then took the SIM card out of his phone, dropped it into the toilet, and threw the telephone into the trash.

Stanley left the café and walked to the nearest side street. Small, cheap shops unable to afford the high-street rents lurked here, and he was looking for the shabbiest option. Luck was on his side; he found a hole-in-the-wall shop selling everything from cheap pens to discount laptops, which were arranged in stacks in the shop's window.

Several minutes later, he came out with long-out-of-date cell phone. The owner had somehow sensed Stanley's desperate need for the phone, and had jacked up the price. Stanley had haggled a little, but hadn't managed to bring him down much. He'd had to part with most of his cash for the dark-red Motorola flip phone and a new SIM card.

As Stanley had turned to go, the owner, wishing to send him off on a pleasant note, had said, "That phone does have an excellent antenna, and the SIM card isn't traceable. Have a good weekend, Herr!"

Stanley turned on Bahnofstrasse and continued toward the train station, even though his remaining money wouldn't get him far, far away, which is where he wanted to be.

The first person he called was Christine, but she didn't pick up. Operating his new phone with some difficulty, Stanley left her a message asking her to call him back. Then he called Frank.

"You learn quick, McKnight," Frank said in place of a greeting. "You got rid of your old phone? Threw away the SIM card? Good work! And you absolutely must not use your bank cards. We know your accounts, and we'll get you access to them a little later."

"Okay," said Stanley, "that's good news. Now give me the bad news."

"As you wish! We know what's going on. That you were accused of stealing from the bank. We found out just after you were detained in the bank's meeting room."

"How, Frank? Do you have an informant? Surveillance?"

"Let us keep some of our secrets, Stanley. Just a few. So, they've loosed the hounds, and they're tracking you. Two breeds—Swiss racers and Russian fighters. You can guess which is the more dangerous, but what you need to know is that I can't help you on Swiss territory."

"So you're just abandoning me here?"

"Take it easy, McKnight! What I mean to say is, I can't send an agent to rescue you. I don't have one to spare, and I can't stop the Swiss police. They're happy to pin it all on you. You're a perfect gift—a bit of revenge for the humiliations Swiss banks have endured from the American authorities in the past."

"Could you cut to the chase, sir?" Stanley said, striving to put the maximum amount of sarcasm in his voice. "I'm not sure this is exactly the right time for a history lecture."

"You're right, you're right, you know all about William Tell. I need to get you out of the country by any means necessary."

"The point, Frank!"

"The Hyatt hotel, underground parking, a black Audi A-6, license plate 140388. The car will be unlocked, key under the driver's seat, a mobile phone and envelope with a couple hundred euros in the glove compartment, and a parking pass on the passenger seat."

"Two hundred! Is that all I'm worth to you?"

"Get moving! Don't take a taxi, and remember: the Swiss police are the least of your problems—it's Gagarin's people you should be worried about. They're already on your tail, McKnight, and as I said, I don't have an agent to send you."

Stanley walked down the block, crossed the street, and turned onto Pelikanstrasse.

He walked at a relaxed, measured pace. He remembered the sunglasses in his inside jacket pocket and slipped them on. Then he lit a cigarette.

He crossed a bridge over the river Limmat and walked along the embankment. There weren't many other pedestrians; lunch hour was over and all the clerks and office workers had returned to their desks. Ahead, he saw two policemen walking toward him, a tall, heavy woman and a shorter man. They cast him indifferent glances as they passed on.

Stanley carefully put out his cigarette and tossed it into a trashcan, then stopped into La Stanza for another espresso before walking up the embankment to Dreikönigstrasse and turning on Beethovenstrasse. He saw the Hyatt up ahead.

He quickly found the car. As he approached, he heard the telephone ringing inside.

He sat in the driver's seat and picked up.

"You weren't exactly hurrying, were you?" said Frank.

"I stopped for a coffee."

"McKnight, you're too used to living the good life, and it's going to get you killed. I've sent a dependable specialist to help you out. From Bern. He's a problem-solver. Named Alexander. Drive to Wädenswil and wait for him in your car at the train station parking lot."

"How will I recognize him?"

"He'll find you. Be there in twenty-five minutes. Don't be late! Get going!"

Stanley pulled out of the underground parking garage and turned right, then right again onto General-Guisan-Quai. His GPS suggested that he take Alfred Escher-Strasse onto the A3W, but he turned onto Mythenquai instead and drove along the shore of the lake. This route was a bit shorter, but often congested with traffic, and there were numerous speed limit signs.

Traffic wasn't great, but things loosened up after Mythenquai merged into Seestrasse. The weather had taken a turn for the worse. Dark clouds covered the sun and it began to rain.

The Lindt chocolate factory flashed by on his left, and Stanley caught a sweet scent in the air. He checked the time and grew concerned that he was going to be late. He overtook one car, then other, honking to get the Mercedes in front of him out of the way, and stepped on the gas.

"I wonder where the speeding ticket for this will go?" thought Stanley, clenching his teeth as he got ready to pass another car. A half mile later, he passed two cars at once, flew into the oncoming lane, and swerved back just in time to avoid crashing into a bus. Only a couple of minutes until he was supposed to be there. He *had* to make it.

Stanley pulled into the Wädenswil train station parking lot twenty-seven minutes after leaving Zurich. The light rain had turned into a full-fledged summer downpour, slow and steady.

Stanley chose a spot a fair distance from the station, enough to see its doors and the tracks beyond. He shut off the engine, then rolled down his window and lit a cigarette. He tried to get in touch with Christine again. This time her phone was switched off, and he decided that she must be in the air already.

He smoked another cigarette, lighting it from the cherry of his first. His mouth was dry. He looked in the glove compartment, in the driver's side door, under the passenger's seat—and there he felt a plastic bottle. It was mineral water, and as he was drinking it gratefully, he saw over the top of the bottle a figure in a black trench coat emerge from the station and head directly toward him.

"And here's Alexander," whispered Stanley. He took another couple of sips, screwed the cap back on, and started the engine. He checked the instrument panel automatically and noted that the gas tank was nearly full. Several moments later, he noticed another two men wearing similar black coats as the first.

They were moving toward his car from the left and right, and when they got closer Stanley saw that they had short buzz cuts and Slavic faces, just like the guards he'd seen in Gagarin's office and at his parties.

"That's not Alexander," whispered Stanley. "Shit, shit, shit! What am I going to do?"

The man who had come out of the train station reached the car first. The other two stood back. The first put his hand under his coat and took out a handgun with a silencer and tapped on Stanley's window, gesturing for him to open the door.

Realizing it was too late to make a run for it, Stanley rolled down his window and glanced over at the others again—their guns were out as well, and they stood silently, one hand folded over the other, the rain falling on the black metal of the guns.

"Please step out of the car, Mr. McKnight," the first man said in a Russian accent, smiling. "We're not going to hurt you. We just got sent to pick you up. Some people want to talk to you."

Stanley remembered his cigarette and brought it to his mouth. The long ash fell on his suit as he did.

"Ay-yi-yi, you're going to ruin your suit. And smoking is bad for you. Come out, please!"

Stanley took a drag.

"Get out of the fucking car!" The man drew his hand back to hit the door with his gun, but Stanley heard a muffled click somewhere nearby, and a piece of the Russian's forehead hit his suit right next to the ash.

"What the hell?" said Stanley, but the first click was followed by two more in quick succession and the man on the right fell, his face slamming into the fender on his way down.

Acting on instinct, Stanley crouched down in his seat, trying to slide to the floor, but his seatbelt prevented it. He heard a light clapping sound—Gagarin's third man was shooting—but there was another dry click, and the last of the Russians fell onto the parking lot asphalt.

McKnight tossed his cigarette out the window, turned on the engine, and heard a knock coming from the passenger's side window. Once again, someone was tapping the glass with a gun.

A girl was standing next to the car, in jeans and a dark-gray jacket, the hood pulled over her face. All Stanley could see were her narrow, dark eyes, high cheekbones, and full lips. He lowered the window.

"McKnight, right?"

"Yes, I'm McKnight, but who are you?"

"Open the door! I'm Alexander. Come on, open up!"

Stanley unlocked the door, and Alexander hopped in.

"Let's go, McKnight!"

More Russians came running out of the building toward the car, and Stanley heard the sound of bullets slamming into the car with the rhythm of the rain.

"Are you awake?" Alexander swung back her hand as far as the narrow confines of the car would allow and slapped him across the face. "Drive! Drive, you fucker! They're going to shoot us like a couple of rabbits!"

Stanley hit the gas then, coming to his senses. He shifted into drive and pressed the pedal down again, and the car jerked forward.

"I was expecting someone else…"

"A man? Rambo? And all you got was little old me," said Alexander.

She reached out with her gloved hand for a handshake, but she was still holding the gun.

"Sorry," she said, tucking the gun under her arm. "I don't like silencers. They affect my aim. It's not a problem to shoot from a meter away, of course, but still…"

"Where to now?" asked Stanley at the parking lot exit, amazed by how calm he was.

"Go left. We need to backtrack a little. And I apologize for running late—Swiss trains aren't as punctual as they used to be."

"No problem," muttered Stanley.

"What was that?"

"I said, where are we going?"

"Kilchberg. Just ten minutes away. We should have met there, really, but never mind. It has one spot I've always loved there. We'll do something there."

"Really? Just like that?"

"Mister, I've had quick romances. But right away, after three corpses, with a complete stranger?"

"Well, it is the best way to get to know someone."

"Indeed. But we've got something else on the agenda. So relax. We won't be testing out your manhood."

"That's good, because I'm not at my best today, I have to tell you."

Stanley glanced down and saw the piece of forehead from the man Alexander had killed on his jacket. He slammed sharply on the brakes, and the car behind nearly crashed into them but managed to swerve to the left.

"What happened?" shouted Alexander.

"That! It flew in the window. That's a piece of his head! I'm going to be sick."

"Like I said, you're too easily rattled." Alexander took the clump of skin, bone, and hair, and threw it out her window. "That was a nice suit! What are you waiting for? You want those assholes to catch up? They could. Drive!"

"What's with your name?" Stanley asked five minutes later.

"My parents were hippies. I was conceived at the top of the Eiffel Tower, you see, and they named me in honor of the engineer who built the damned thing, Alexander Eiffel. That's the name on my birth certificate—Alexander."

"You're lucky they didn't decide to conceive you in the Trump Tower. Can I call you Alex? Alexander's a bit too masculine."

"I insist! That's what everyone calls me. Ok, turn here, right here, a little bit further. Stop on that dirt road, right up. There's an excellent view of the lake here. Keep going, keep going, right to the edge of the ravine, and... stop! Get out of the car."

"Why?"

"Out!"

The view truly was superb. The light from the setting sun played across the water, turning the white sails of a yacht flying across the lake's surface red.

Stanley let out a deep sigh and looked around warily. What was Alex up to? *I'm about to get a bullet to the head*, thought Stanley. *They don't need me anymore, either. I'm just a burden. The flash drive is operational, information is coming, and they'd need to put a lot of effort into me. Well, go ahead and shoot, pretty girl.* He squeezed his eyes shut.

"Do your eyes hurt?" Alex asked.

"No, I'm fine," Stanley said, opening his eyes. "The view really is amazing, isn't it?"

"I'm not a fan of all this fresh water. I like to swim in the sea, to come out of the water with salt on my skin. It's good to lick off..."

"Yourself?"

"Sometimes, but I prefer a handsome man with a good body. Like you, for example. All right, get undressed."

"Why? There's no ocean nearby. I won't be salty."

"Listen, Stanley. Frank told me you're a cocky guy, but for fuck's sake, please just do what I tell you. I saved your life fifteen minutes ago. If you want to go on living, get undressed! And this is not a seduction!"

"Then why?"

"Do you only get undressed when you're about to fuck? A real macho man. Get undressed! We have to get rid of your clothes."

"Why?"

"To make sure we don't have any bugs. They could have stuck them on you anywhere. You put them on other people in St. Petersburg. From a cigarette pack that Frank gave you? How many did you hand out? Ten? Two? Three? You think somebody else couldn't do the same to you? They could, easily. Come on, we don't have much time."

Stanley took off his jacket, shoes, and pants.

"Goddamn it! Shirt! Underwear! Socks! Put your wallet here, I'll check it. You have your passport? Put it here as well. Telephone. Okay, that's the one you just bought? You can keep it."

Stanley took everything off. He was completely naked and instinctively put both hands in front of his groin.

"Don't worry. I'm not looking. Although you're doing all right in that department," Alex said. "Your watch!"

"Oh no! That's a collector's Rolex. It cost 50,000 francs, and I never take it off."

"Don't lie!"

"Ok, I have taken it off, but..."

Alex took a small device out of the glove compartment. It looked like a portable electric razor, and she ran it over Stanley's left wrist, through his hair, forcing him to hold up his arms.

"I'm not looking. I'm not looking," she repeated, then opened the trunk and pressed a button. The floor of the trunk slid to one side, revealing a hollow space beneath.

"Get in!"

"This is really necessary?"

"We need to get out of Swiss territory as quickly as possible. The best way for you to do that is in the trunk of a car."

"And if the border guards catch us?"

"This is a magical trunk. Once you get in, the panel slides shut. And anyway, calm down! I'm going to go throw your clothes in the lake. Then will you be you ready to go?"

"You couldn't check my clothes with your little thingie?"

"The clothes stained with the blood of a Russian gangster? You want to auction them off later? Two thousand dollars? Wait, I see two thousand five hundred! Don't be foolish, Mr. McKnight!"

"Why so formal all of a sudden?"

"I always treat naked men with respect. Especially if I'm dressed. Ok, it's time! Hop in."

Stanley sighed and put his foot into the trunk.

"Don't hit your head on the roof of the trunk, sir!" Alex said with a laugh, her hand on his head.

"What exactly is funny about this?"

"It looks like danger gets you hard. That's a sign of your virility. You, sir, must be a warrior. You just didn't know it and became a banker by mistake. We'll fix that. Give it time."

Stanley readied himself for a long trip. He didn't have room to stretch, so he lay there clutching his knees to his chest. The car threw him around a little at first, but when they made it back onto the asphalt road, the ride smoothed out. His eyes gradually grew accustomed to the dark, and he saw that this space intended for the secret transport of humans was equipped with certain comforts.

A slightly illuminated tube stuck out from the wall, and Stanley managed to drink something out of it. The trunk's upholstery was comfortable, and the car's heating system was right beneath it. Little by little, Stanley calmed down. He believed that Alex would protect him. He liked her, although he was a bit concerned by how calmly she'd dispatched the three Russian thugs.

CHAPTER 46

T HE RIDE CALMED STANLEY DOWN. He dozed off and woke only when the car stopped. He heard the door slam, and the beep of the electronic lock.

Alex soon returned and the engine started again. By the sound of it, they were now driving through a city. Alex made several turns and then stopped. She got out of the car and locked it again. When she stopped for a third time, Stanley thought they were probably in a multilevel parking garage based on the tight turns they had made on a steady incline.

The trunk opened.

"Get out quick," Alex ordered. "Into the back seat. It took me a while to find a place without a camera. You're freezing! Here, get dressed. There's bags with clothing on the back seat."

"I didn't tell you my size, but these look right..." They were indeed at the far end of a multilevel garage, Stanley noted. "Where are we, by the way?"

"Konstanz. A charming, quiet town on Lake Constance. As for the size, you have the same build as my ex. If something doesn't fit, don't worry. We'll exchange it."

Alex clearly knew her way around men's fashion. And she wasn't short on funds. The soft English suede shoes fitted just right, as did the jeans, T-shirt, and an excellent shirt to go over the T-shirt. He topped off the outfit with a nice suede jacket.

"I bought that at the market," Alex said, watching as Stanley dressed. "Gently used. Don't take offense. New clothes would be a little too pricey for the taxpayers. And, damn, I forgot socks."

"I noticed."

"The underwear isn't too tight?"

"You must have really known your ex's body. Why did you break up? Sorry for asking, but I think we've gotten pretty close, don't you?"

"I'll admit this isn't the first time I've had to undress a man to check for listening devices. You're lucky I didn't tell you to bend over so I could check your behind."

"I sure am! So why did you?"

"He got tired of my business trips. He thought I worked in fashion, setting up shows, traveling to look for models. Idiotic work—I could never do it."

"Instead you're an excellent shooter."

"You sound like you're judging me for it! Sit up front. We need to drive to the Steigenberger Hotel. We're supposed to get instructions from Frank there."

"Why there, specifically?"

"I'm not used to questioning these things. I was told to wait in the café of the Steigenberger Hotel. So, we'll wait there. Let's go!"

Alex sped down the spiral ramp and turned right. They passed Mayura, and Stanley smelled Indian spices wafting from the restaurant. Alex turned again, onto a street running alongside the lake. Stanley just managed to read the sign—Konzilstrasse—and they turned right into the hotel's parking lot.

"My Russian friends love hotels like this," said Stanley.

"I'm not surprised. It's got five stars. I usually choose more modest places. Or rather, they get chosen for me."

"That sounds like a complaint."

"On the contrary! I don't really like fancy establishments. You're the one who's used to them."

They got out of the car, walked through the lobby into the hotel's café, and sat by a large window. It was growing dark.

"What will you have?" asked Stanley.

"Are you buying? A double espresso, no sugar."

"I'll have one as well," said Stanley to the waiter who had instantaneously appeared at their table. "It's strange. All I've had the entire day is cups of coffee, but I don't feel hungry at all," he said.

"It's nerves. Later you're going to want to eat and eat until you're stuffed. By the way, you're on TV. They're showing you on the television by the bar. And while I was running around buying clothes, your face was everywhere. You're quite popular—everyone's looking for you. Keep calm!"

Alex put her hand over Stanley's.

"Don't worry! No one would even think of looking for you here. In the picture they're showing, you're in a suit and tie. A rich banker. Ha ha! Come on, smile! Act like you're happy to be on a date with a girl like me."

Stanley smiled, but it came out a little sour.

"Also, I got a message on the way. Our people are already getting a lot of the information they need from your flash drive. Soon we're going to have all the dirt on your bank and on your criminal clients. All you'll have to do is testify, but you can do that back in the US."

"I'll do it if I manage to survive till then. I'm the subject of a manhunt here, remember?"

"Ha." Alex slapped him on the shoulder. "Now they're showing the bodies in the parking lot. The ticker says, 'A criminal war between mafia families has made its way to Switzerland.' Damn! I never get the recognition for my accomplishments. But don't you worry, Stanley. You'll be taken care of. We'll get you back to America in good condition."

Frank called as they were finishing their coffee. His instructions were something of a surprise—Stanley was to take a train to Marseille, where he would board a boat back home.

"That'll take at least a week!" he exclaimed.

"It's a week on a nice cruise ship. You'll probably be on some cargo ship, and they take twice that long. You'll get the chance to catch up on your sleep, at least. And you'll have dependable protection." Alex tossed a bill onto the table. "Come on. They're already waiting for us."

At the station, Alex handed Stanley off to a colleague named Thomas, a thin, middle-aged man who spoke English with a strong German accent. She gave Stanley an encouraging smile, noticing his disappointment that they were parting ways.

"See you later, Stanley!" said Alex.

"I sincerely hope so."

"You don't have to worry about a thing with Thomas here. Bye!"

Stanley watched her leave until she joined the crowd by the exit to the station and disappeared. Thomas handed Stanley his ticket and a small bag.

"What's this?" he asked. The bag was quite heavy.

"Dog food. Some rags," Thomas answered in a raspy voice. "It's just a bit of cover. A man traveling across half of Europe without any luggage arouses suspicion."

The train was already at the platform, but Thomas asked Stanley to wait by an ice cream kiosk while he went to the bathroom in the train station. When Thomas was out of sight, Stanley called Christine.

Her phone rang for a long time, but she finally picked up. The connection was terrible. He asked where and how she was, and she replied that everything was fine, and that she was in Milan. She finally asked where Stanley was, and he told her he was on his way from Konstanz to Marseille.

Something in her voice made Stanley uneasy. She stammered a little, repeating the same word several times.

"Is everything okay, honey?" asked Stanley. "You sound drunk."

"Everything's fine, baby. I'm drinking Campari Spritz in Milan, and I'm flying to San Francisco in two hours."

"How are you?"

"Everything's really good!" answered Christine. "Where are you going from Marseille?" she asked.

"I'm flying to New York tomorrow." Stanley had suddenly realized it might be a mistake to tell Christine his travel plans. What if they were listening to his calls? And he decided to fix things with a little lie. "Yes, flying out tomorrow!" He saw Thomas approaching. "Love you. Bye!"

"Who were you talking to?" Thomas asked, displeased. "You're not allowed to talk on the phone."

"Since when? Calm down. I was just talking to my wife. Are you married?"

"It's not allowed," the German repeated. "Give me the phone."

Stanley handed it over.

"You're a strict guy. I'm lucky you weren't one of the ones looking for me in Switzerland."

Stanley made some more attempts to start a conversation with Thomas, asking if he knew where Frank was, but Thomas turned out to be the grim, silent type.

He seemed to know absolutely nothing about Frank, seemed not to have known Stanley was married, and his only concern seemed to be getting Stanley off his hands as quickly as possible. Thomas explained at great length that Stanley must stay as close to him as possible and not leave his side for any reason. If a situation arose in which they were separated, Stanley should find a man named Kirk Baltz in the old port of Marseille, where he owned a fish restaurant. Baltz would help him.

Thomas's droning voice put Stanley to sleep before he heard the rest of the details.

He dreamed that he was strolling down a long pier in Berkeley, with Mila on his left and Christine on his right. They each held his hand and were both acting nicely, with no arguments or jealousy, a happy little family.

They walked along, discussing the life they all shared, which they were all quite pleased with. When they approached the end of the pier, Mila and Christine suddenly started to pull him forward. He thought it was a joke, but they were stronger, and they pulled him off the edge into the San Francisco Bay. They fell together beneath the surface, and he began to sink, choking and struggling, until he woke up in horror.

"Where are we?" asked Stanley.

"We're in France already," Thomas said, looking up from his mobile phone. "You slept for a long time. We'll be in Marseille soon."

"Okay. I'm going to take a piss." Stanley got up and immediately fell back against the seat as the train jerked to a stop. "What the fuck was that?"

"The train stopped!"

"I'm sober, but I can't stand up straight," Stanley said, rubbing his temples.

"Something's wrong, McKnight. Somebody pulled the emergency break."

"Now we're going to be late to Marseille. I think I'll go back to sleep."

"Get up, McKnight," ordered Thomas. "I don't like this! We need to get out of here."

Thomas yanked Stanley, still drowsy, to his feet and pulled him forward. "Let's go!"

They walked from their carriage into the next and saw two men in black suits walking toward them. When the men saw them, they picked up their pace, and Stanley had no doubt who they were.

"Shit, Thomas. We have to go back."

"Russians."

"I can see that they're not Buddhist monks!"

"We have a problem. They're everywhere. They've got us surrounded."

Stanley turned and saw another group of men entering the carriage, led by Shamil.

"Now we've got more than a problem, Thomas. This is the end."

Shamil saw Stanley and grinned, and a gun appeared in his hand. The passengers started screaming in panic. Some jumped out of their seats, others fell to the floor. Stanley watched it all like a movie on screen. Shots rang out.

"This way! Wake up!" Thomas pushed Stanley toward the doors, pulling out his own gun and pulling the emergency lever to open the doors.

"Jump!" ordered Thomas, and started to shoot. "Jump!"

Stanley jumped into the darkness, but Thomas didn't follow. He sank slowly to the floor of the train, a small hole in his forehead. Blood smeared the wall behind him.

Stanley saw all this and took off, running toward the forest. *Too much death*, he thought, and the phrase repeated over and over in his head. *Too much death for one day.* He ran as hard as he could, turning back occasionally to see if anyone was chasing him. But all he could see in the darkness was the lights of the train.

Past the tree line, he felt safe enough to slow down and began to make his way through the trees and brush. He couldn't hear any sounds of pursuit. He wandered for several hours through the woods, and it was morning before he came across a small village. The fog lay thickly over everything, and his hands were numb with cold.

He hesitated, unsure of what to do, but soon realized he only had one option. He walked over to the nearest house and rang the bell. It took a long time for the elderly man who opened the door to understand what Stanley wanted, but eventually Stanley was able to make it clear that he needed the phone.

"Police?" asked the farmer in French. "I should call the police?"

"No, no police. I just need your phone! Telephone!" Stanley was practically shouting.

The farmer nodded and gestured for Stanley to come in, leading him to the living room and pointing out an ancient stationary phone with a rotary dial.

Stanley dialed Frank's number.

"Frank!" Stanley cried when the other man picked up. "They're here! Thomas is dead. Gagarin's people are after me."

"Are you okay, McKnight?"

"No, I'm not okay, goddamn it! I'm very fucking far from okay."

"Where are you calling from?"

"I have no idea. A village."

"A village?"

"Yes. A fucking village somewhere in France."

"Stay calm, Stanley. Don't panic. Stay where you are. I'll send my people to pick you up. What's the name of the village?"

"Hang on. I'll ask."

McKnight set the receiver down next to the phone and went into the kitchen. The farmer wasn't there, and Stanley walked down the hallway to see if he was on the porch. He opened the front door and came face-to-face with his host, his eyes open wide in fright. Then something struck Stanley on the back of the head. He lost consciousness.

When he came to, he was in the trunk of a car. He heard the sound of a conversation in Russian and the radio playing "Never Let Me Down."

Stanley smiled grimly, thinking that this was the end of the line—the Russians would never let him go. That thought brought with it a strange sense of calm. Stanley felt himself slipping back into that dream from the train, Christine and Mila dragging him under the water. He tried to break free, but it was no use. He sighed, closed his eyes, and everything faded to black.

CHAPTER 47

STANLEY MANAGED TO OPEN HIS eyes with some difficulty. He was surrounded by total darkness. His head ached, and he was lying on a painfully hard surface. His hands and feet were bound to metal pipes running next to where he lay. There was a gag in his mouth, and he was having trouble getting enough air.

He tried to get free, or at least move his arms and legs, but he couldn't do it. The next thing he noticed was the cold; it was terribly cold. It took him a surprisingly long time to realize that he was bound, helpless, motionless, completely naked.

He struggled to get free again, even though he knew it was pointless. He tensed all his muscles and tried to move left, then right. He felt something else binding him across the chest to the hard surface beneath him, maybe duct tape.

His efforts weren't completely in vain, however. The surface he was on moved slightly. He tried rocking from side to side again, then to lift himself upward and down as much as he could. He thought he felt movement beneath him again, and guessed that he was tied to a stretcher, on something like a hospital gurney.

Stanley took a break, breathing the damp, musty air, preparing to try the same maneuvers again. But then he heard the sound of a key in a lock, and a heavy door opening. The light switched on.

He squinted, trying to turn away from the light coming from a lamp hanging directly overhead. Several people approached his gurney. The first to reach him smelled like stale booze and cigarette smoke, and he bent over Stanley, shading his face. But Stanley couldn't make out who it was in the sudden brightness.

"Look, Shamil. He managed to move!" Gagarin said. "I told you we needed to put a brake on these fucking wheels. Didn't I tell you? And what did you say?"

"Viktor," Shamil answered in his distinctive hoarse, slow voice. "Where is he going to go? He can't make out of this hangar."

"Okay, probably not, but still. Jesus Christ, that's the same thing I thought when I heard about the missing money. Where could it go? Ah? A bank with a 150-year-old sterling reputation! But it did go missing, didn't it? They stole it! This motherfucker stole it!"

Gagarin kicked the cart and swore at the pain of the impact, hopping on one foot. Stanley's gurney rolled across the rough floor of the hangar. The wheels hit something, and then it rocked back and forth. Stanley had one moment of anxious anticipation before it tipped over on its side.

"Get him up!" shouted Gagarin. "We can't have him getting banged up! Get him up. Gala, Biryuza, what are you doing just standing there? Help Shamil!"

Stanley felt the gurney lifting up, heard Biryuza's labored breathing and Shamil's sniff.

"You see how well we're taking care of you, McKnight?" Gagarin said, leaning over Stanley again. "Your comfort and health are what matter most to us. You look like you have some doubts about that. *Tsk tsk*. What's that you say?"

Gagarin leaned closer.

"What? Shamil, I can't understand what he's saying."

"He's got a gag in his mouth, Viktor," said Biryuza.

"A gag? No! What sadist would do such a thing? Bring him here!" Gagarin shouted as if someone had just slammed his own fingers in the door. "I'll teach that son of a bitch to treat our dear, precious Stanley McKnight that way."

"You put the gag there, boss," said Gala with a giggle.

"Me? It's not possible! I've never put a gag in anyone's mouth. My dick, sure, but a gag—that's too rough." Gagarin bent over Stanley again. "Isn't that right, Stanley? I've always been courteous and respectful, even with a fucking scumbag like you. Right? Well? Answer me!"

At that, Gagarin punched Stanley full force in the chest, then again in the face, then began pummeling everywhere like he was a punching bag in the gym. Stanley screamed from the pain, nearly choking on the spit in his mouth, and the blood from his split lips soaked the gag.

"He's not answering!" complained Gagarin to Shamil, lifting his hands up. "He doesn't want to talk to me. Fucker. All right, pull out the gag."

Shamil tore the gag out of his mouth. Stanley turned his head to the side and spat out a mouthful of blood and saliva. He inhaled, and blood, saliva, and mucus went down his windpipe. He started to choke.

He moaned, rasping and coughing.

"He'll die like that," Biryuza said thoughtfully, observing Stanley's suffering.

"I don't think so," said Gagarin, shaking his head. He cleaned his hands with a paper napkin. "He's good at surviving. And fucking. Look at the size of that thing. He's packing quite the equipment, isn't he?"

He reached out to the side, grabbed a rubber baton, and hit Stanley in the crotch. Stanley screeched in pain and began to lose consciousness from the lack of air.

"Viktor, you'll kill him," Biryuza said, his voice strained.

"So help him! Sit him up and slap him on the back. Do CPR. Mouth-to-mouth. You like that sort of thing. Go on!"

Biryuza and Shamil cut off the tape binding Stanley to the stretcher, untied his hands, and set him upright. Shamil gave him two hard slaps on the back, and Biryuza held up a napkin for him to blow his nose on, and wiped his face.

Stanley coughed, hacking up the fluid in his windpipe.

"Give him something to drink," Gagarin said. "I want to ask him something before we fuck him up."

Biryuza held up a plastic bottle for Stanley to drink from and poured a little over his head.

"Just drink! You're so caring, Anton." Gagarin lit a cigarette. "I'm thirsty too, by the way."

Biryuza held the water out to him.

Gagarin snatched it out of Biryuza's hand and threw it on the floor.

"How about a clean bottle, you idiot?"

"Sorry. Sorry, Viktor."

"Ok! Bring me a chair! And tie him back up. No reason for him to sit here watching us."

The short time he'd been freed from the tape and ropes on his hands had given Stanley the chance to look around. He was in an empty hangar, possibly built to house small boats. There were metal shelves on the walls. In one corner were tables with bottles of water, some folders and packets, and a multitude of instruments. The bright light was still blinding him.

"Quickly, quickly," said Gagarin from his seat. "I have an important meeting soon. And it stinks here. What is that smell? Can you smell that, Stanley?"

"Viktor," rasped Stanley. "What is going on? Why are you doing this?"

Gagarin laughed out loud.

"What is going on?" he repeated. "He's got a nerve! This bastard yank steals my money, then sits here asking, nice as you please, what's going on? So, guys, what's going on?"

Shamil tied Stanley's wrists to the stretcher and stretched the tape back over his chest.

"Are you comfortable, Stanley?" asked Gagarin. "Your comfort is key, because once we start our serious conversation, man-to-man, it'll be too late to change anything. So, comfortable?"

"I didn't do it, Viktor!"

"You didn't do it? Really? Then why did you run? Why did you get involved with some Americans? Who was the guy we shot in the head? FBI? CIA? Or the State Department? Who?"

"That was just...just my friend. I just ran into him."

"And the guy who shot up my people in the parking lot? Another friend who you just happened to run into? Come on, Stanley. I am, of course, as my ex-wife Mila believes, a total fucking idiot, but not to that extent. You simply don't respect me if that's what you think of me. Okay, I think we need to wrap this up. Shamil!"

"Yes, boss!"

"It's time!" Gagarin got up and stood over Stanley.

"You know what it smells like in here, buddy? I said it smelled, right? So, what?"

"You said it stinks," corrected Stanley.

"Ah, so you haven't lost your nerve. You're a tough guy. Yes, indeed, I said it stinks in here. Do you know what it smells like?"

"Paint? Mildew?" asked Biryuza.

"A man?" Gala squeamishly poked her finger into Stanley's stomach, then drew her nail down from belly button to groin, leaving a red stripe on his skin.

"All true," said Gagarin. "But most of all it stinks of betrayal. What does betrayal smell like? Eh? Who reeks of it? Who, McKnight?"

"I don't know."

"You don't know. I'll tell you. The stink is coming from you, Stanley. Shamil!"

"I'm ready, boss!"

"So go ahead already. What the fuck are you waiting for?"

Shamil slowly pulled on a pair of latex gloves with great ceremony. He turned to Gala, who unbuttoned his leather jacket and took it off. Shamil was wearing an expensive silk shirt under his jacket.

"Apron!" ordered Shamil, and Gala helped him put on a blue medical apron, then protective sleeves of the same color.

Gagarin got a flask out of his back pocket, unscrewed the cap, and took several swigs, then lit a cigarette.

"Okay, Stanley, here's how things are going to go. Shamil is going to work on you a little bit. Then I'm going to ask you some questions. Depending on your answers, Shamil is then going to either beat the shit out of you or just knock you around a little, purely as a formality. If you disappoint us, we'll introduce other procedures. Specifically? Well, I'll let that remain a secret for now."

"I didn't do it, Viktor!" shouted Stanley desperately. "I didn't take the money! I was as surprised as you were."

"Gag him!" ordered Gagarin.

Biryuza held Stanley's head in place, and Gala stuck the gag in his mouth.

"This might also surprise you, Stanley, but we're not going to start with the money. First...but no, I'm getting ahead of myself. Shamil!"

"Wait a minute," said Biryuza, "Can I have this asshole's watch? It's a museum piece."

"Come the fuck on, Biryuza. You don't have enough money to buy your own?"

"This is a special collector's piece," Biryuza explained apologetically, hurriedly unstrapping it from Stanley's wrist. "You can't just go out and buy it."

Gala giggled and slapped Biryuza on the shoulder.

"You're distracting us, Biryuza! Let us give this American a Russian punishment!"

Shamil began to strike Stanley, over and over again, like Gagarin had, as if he were a punching bag. But unlike his boss, Shamil's blows were hard and painful but professionally delivered, so as not to cause lasting injury.

At first Stanley tried to concentrate, to prepare for each blow, to lessen the pain by even a little, but soon realized that he couldn't keep up with Shamil's fists. All he could do was moan in pain. He closed his eyes. Eventually, Shamil stopped.

Stanley exhaled and opened his eyes. Shamil was holding the rubber baton.

"Judging by your wide eyes, you're expecting something bad, Stanley," said Gagarin. "You're right. This is going to be bad. But it's going to get much worse, so don't pay attention to Shamil; listen to what I'm going to say to you…Shamil!"

Shamil raised the bat and brought it down sharply onto Stanley's shin. The pain was so intense, it felt like an electric shock running through his entire body.

Gagarin lit a fresh cigarette from the end of his first. "Try and pay attention to me, Stanley. I know it's difficult at the moment, but you have to. Are you listening, Stanley?"

Shamil brought the baton down on Stanley's legs at a measured, methodical pace, gradually going higher and higher.

"Just don't smash his balls off. Not yet, anyway," Gagarin said, taking another swig from his flask. "So, we have a lot to talk about. Hey, Biryuza! Where are you? Are you feeling sorry for him? All right, all right. Go ahead, but come back soon. And bring me some vodka. This French cognac is giving me heartburn. And something to eat. Some hamburgers…American style."

Biryuza nodded and went out.

Shamil, breathing heavily, took a break. Stanley's legs were covered in streaks of blood. The soles of his feet were particularly bad—Shamil had focused a lot of attention on them.

"What is this? You on vacation? Get to work, Shamil!"

Shamil wiped the sweat from his forehead and picked up the baton.

"Okay, Stanley. I'm interested in two things. They're more important, more significant than the question of where you put my money. First is the question of betrayal. Because you did betray me, didn't you, Stanley? What are you whimpering about? You're mumbling. You betrayed me!"

Gagarin upended the flask, finishing the cognac. Lit another cigarette.

"I should get compensation for damages," he said, "Not only do I have to look at you, I have to deal with the stress, all this stress, smoking, alcohol… Where did Biryuza get off to?"

Stanley started to lose consciousness from the pain. Gagarin's words traveled to him through a thick fog, clumping into hard blocks that hit him with almost physical force.

"You, Stanley, are a traitor, and belong in the ninth circle of hell. Have you read Dante? Hmm? Okay, hush, hush. I seem to remember reading that

391

your shitty American schools teach Dante at some point. He puts traitors in the ninth circle of hell where Lucifer sits in the center, the prince of darkness—another traitor, by the way. Lucifer continuously devours three traitors with his three mouths—Judas, Brutus, and Cassius. You've heard of them, I think? You're not on their level, Stanley. You're a piece of shit on one of their shoes. But you'll still end up in the circle with them. We'll take care of that, won't we, Shamil? Okay, take a break."

Shamil sat down on a folding stool, and, following his boss's example, lit up a cigarette.

"Do you know what the ninth circle looks like?" Gagarin went on. "I'll remind you. There's a huge, frozen lake, Cocytus. Traitors with cold hearts, like you, Stanley, don't burn in hell—they freeze. But that's not the worst part. Traitors can end up in that lake while they're still alive. I remember the lines from years ago, 'I found one such of you, that, for his deeds, in soul he bathes already in Cocytus, and seems in body still alive above.' Do you understand? Those traitors experience the torments of hell while they're still above ground. Like you, for example. Although your earthly life is nearing its end."

The hangar door opened, and Biryuza appeared, carrying a large McDonald's bag. He unpacked its contents onto the table next to Gagarin—a frozen bottle of Russian vodka, cups, four hamburgers on a plastic plate, fries, and pickles, then set down a couple of cans of beer next to the vodka.

"Now, that's more like it!" Gagarin said approvingly. "Nice work, Biryuza."

Gagarin poured himself a half glass of vodka, drank it, huffed, and followed it up with pickles. Then he bit into one of the hamburgers. Ketchup dripped onto his chin.

"After I treated you like a son," Gagarin said, his mouth full. "I really liked you. Smart, handsome, not arrogant. Did everything I asked for. Someone I could depend on. How am I supposed to trust people now, Anton?"

"You can't, boss!"

"That's what I say. Shamil!"

Shamil got up and approached the stretcher. He put out his cigarette on Stanley's bare chest.

"That's the way, Shamil! I like the initiative!" Gagarin gestured for Biryuza to pour more vodka into his glass, drank it, ate a pickle, and then finished his hamburger.

Shamil got down to beating Stanley's body with the baton while Gagarin was eating. Gagarin wiped his mouth with a napkin.

"Now I want to ask you something." Gagarin opened a can of beer and took several deep swallows. "I'm thirsty, Stanley. I'm dying of thirst."

He got up to stand next the gurney, opposite Shamil, who continued to methodically batter Stanley. Small sprays of blood flew up from the stretcher, and some spattered Gagarin's starched white shirt.

"You know what I'm dying to do?" Gagarin leaned down to whisper in his ear. "To fucking destroy you!" he screamed, right into Stanley's ear. "To beat you into a million tiny pieces. But first, you're going to tell me everything."

Gagarin motioned to Shamil, and he pulled out the gag.

"Tell me, who was with you in the parking lot? Who killed my people?" Gagarin took several fries out of the bag and shoved them hungrily into his mouth.

"No?" He took out a couple more and shoved them up Stanley's nostrils. "Here's what I want to know—is the man we shot the same person who killed my guys?"

Stanley nodded.

"Okay, we're making some progress. Unless, of course, you're lying to me. So, that was your friend? Where'd he get the gun? Where did he learn to shoot?"

"He—" Stanley began, then sneezed, and a fry flew out of one nostril. "He served in Iraq, and was recuperating in Switzerland after being wounded. He works for a security firm. He's either a former Navy SEAL or a paratrooper. He had a permit for his gun. I told him people were following me, that I didn't know who they were or what they wanted. I told him that people in my bank suspected me of stealing money, but that I was innocent and the police were looking for me. My friend doesn't like the police. At all. He told me that he'd help me, help me get to Marseille, that he knew people there that could get me on a boat home. Your people started first, Viktor! They took out their guns, and my friend reacted. I would have gone with your people. I have nothing to hide, but he—"

Gagarin put his hand over Stanley's mouth.

"Okay, that will be our working version for now. Time for act two, Shamil. Look at me, Stanley. Shamil has just stepped away for a moment. Do you miss him already? He's going to give it to you good now. So, where did you put my money, and where is Lagrange? You can do it, Stanley. I need answers. Go ahead and lie if you have to, but make it believable. Go on!"

"I...I didn't take your money. And I don't know where Lagrange went."

"Those are bad answers! Shamil!"

Shamil rolled a small table on wheels over to the gurney. On it was a small device with a dial, and a handle on the side.

"Do you know what that is, handsome?" asked Shamil, "It's called a megohmmeter."

"Strange word, isn't it, McKnight?" Gala put in.

"See these two wires leading from it? They have clamps at the end that we're going to clip to your ears, like this, and then we'll turn the dial, like this."

An electrical current shocked Stanley. He felt like his head was going to explode. The first shock was followed by another.

"Where's my money?" Stanley heard Gagarin's voice, as if from far away.

"I don't know! I didn't take it!"

"Where's Lagrange?"

"I don't know!"

"Shamil!"

Shamil turned the dial back up. The electrical current hit him with such force that he fainted.

He came to when they poured cold water over him. Gagarin was no longer in the hangar.

"He turned out to be weak," Stanley heard Shamil saying. "He seemed strong, but all Americans are weak."

"I can't watch this!" said Biryuza.

"Oh, give it a rest," laughed Shamil. "Or are you into him? You want him to fuck you? If I shock him good, he'll have a hard-on you can use."

"You're a pig, Shamil!" said Biryuza.

"Sorry, sweetheart!" Shamil went on, laughing. "Hey, where are you going? We need to move him!"

"I'll send someone," Biryuza replied, and walked toward the exit.

Shamil lit a cigarette. He saw that Stanley was awake.

"Welcome back," he said. He took a deep drag, then put out the cigarette on Stanley's chest again.

Two men entered the hangar. They were nearly identical, both tall and broad-shouldered, with buzz cuts, heavy faces, and low foreheads.

"Okay, wheel him out and load him up," instructed Shamil, pointing toward the gurney where Stanley was bound. "Did you bring the car around? Good."

The two low-browed men pushed the gurney out of the hangar, rolled it to the open doors of a minibus, and took the stretcher off the gurney. But they moved too forcefully and dropped it. Shamil stood watching impassively.

"Sorry, boss," one of them said, clearly expecting a blow to the head.

"Excellent!" said Shamil. "Do it again, but then toss the stretcher in the back. And don't be gentle about it. Just don't kill him."

Stanley understood that the beatings and shocks weren't going to stop. He also knew that Shamil would keep coming up with new ways to hurt him. But he didn't have the slightest chance to escape the torture. If he did know something, where Gagarin's money or Lagrange was, he would have told them immediately, after one or two punches, way before they brought out the electrical currents. He would have admitted to everything. He was afraid of the pain, but mostly he didn't see any point in refusing to confess. He didn't believe there was anyone who could withstand torture. And he didn't see any point in trying to.

The only thing he was guilty of, if the word *guilty* applied here, was agreeing to work with Frank Dillon, and of taking the flash drive and connecting it to the bank's network. But Gagarin didn't even suspect him of that and wasn't going to ask about it. Moreover, Gagarin had seemed satisfied with the explanation that Alex (who his people had taken for a man, apparently not believing that a woman could shoot that well and/or that quickly) was Stanley's old friend, Iraq war vet and employee of a private security company.

That would have been good if Gagarin's main concern was the identity of the person who had killed his men. But Gagarin didn't care about anyone; money was all that mattered to him. Stanley lost consciousness again.

CHAPTER 48

THE MINIBUS DOORS SLAMMED SHUT.

"One of you up front with me," said Shamil.

He sat in the driver's seat and started it up.

"How are you doing back there, Stanley?" he asked loudly, and then, to the man sitting next to him, "Make sure he's tied up tightly back there. And check the gag! The last thing we need is him shouting *help* if we have to brake somewhere along the Promenade des Anglais."

The guard got into the back seat of the minibus. His thick fingers felt along the knots on Stanley's hands and feet and tugged on the gag.

"Everything's good!"

"Okay, stay back there with him. And keep an eye on him!"

The minibus started moving.

Promenade des Anglais. The phrase echoed in Stanley's head. *That sounds familiar. Hmm, Nice, I think. Gagarin has a villa in Nice. We must be heading there.*

Shamil was a sloppy driver, braking and accelerating sharply. The stretcher slid back and forth across the floor until the guard with Stanley pressed his foot down on a corner. The temporary peace let Stanley return to his train of thought.

Sure, Gagarin could talk about betrayal, could quote Dante, and maybe it did actually hurt him that—from his point of view—everyone betrayed him and Stanley had too, but money was what mattered to him. Only his money. Most of which didn't even belong to him, but to those Russian officials, general, and other members of the government mafia who entrusted Gagarin to oversee their funds. Losing it was a death sentence for him. It was just too bad that Stanley wouldn't live to see it. Shamil would make sure of that.

Stanley let out a stifled laugh.

"Boss!" the guard next to him said. "His lips are moving!"

"Yeah? Check his pulse. Make sure he's breathing. We'll be in for a world of shit if he dies."

"Seems to be breathing, and his pulse is normal."

"Normal? I'm not doing my damn job! I beat the shit out of him and shocked him so hard that smoke was practically coming out of his ears, and his pulse is normal? All right, you fucking Yankee, I'm going to really give it to you next time."

Money, money, money. That was what all Gagarin wanted, in the end. And Stanley couldn't do a thing for him there. He didn't know anything. He refused to believe that Lagrange had pulled off a scam for Gagarin's money. He had to know it was death sentence.

Or maybe Lagrange had accomplices, and he'd planned a long time for this. Maybe he was getting an operation to change his appearance, moving to a different country, different continent. Maybe he was running one of the world's most grandiose banking schemes and Stanley would end up paying for it. Or perhaps Lagrange was operating with the consent of one of the oligarchs who'd been on Gagarin's yacht. He couldn't rule that out. Anything was possible. But for now, everything looked bad for Stanley. They were going to torture him until they maimed him, and then pour cement over his feet and drop him in the sea. They wouldn't be able to just return what was left of him to the bank, after all.

"Boss," shouted the guard. "He wants something!"

"How do you know?"

"I can see it in his eyes!"

"Take out the gag, ask, then put it back in place."

The guard pulled out the gag.

"Let me have a smoke," said Stanley, surprised at how firm his voice sounded.

"He wants a smoke!" the guard shouted to Shamil.

"I heard him," replied Shamil. "I don't like his voice. Too cheerful. As if I haven't just fucked him up. Okay, I'll do my best to rectify that. Well, we're not animals. Let him have a smoke. Hey, Stanley! Can you hear me?"

"Yeah."

"I've got good news for you. Viktor asked me to tell you—you're going to see your wife soon. Did you miss her?"

Stanley's heart seized up. *Please, not Christine. God, no. Did they catch her before she made it out of Russia?*

Shamil decided to head to Nice via Toulon, made a U-turn onto the A50, and hit the gas.

He did everything he could to demonstrate his kindness to Stanley on the way. He instructed the guard to put out his cigarettes on Stanley's chest—clearly a favorite pastime of his—where the burns were forming a large open wound. He seemed to delight in Stanley's cries of pain and curses, only ordering the guard to put in the gag again when it was time to beat him with the baton. But the guard was less skilled as Shamil and, wanting to impress his boss, overdid it a little—Stanley passed out from the pain, and woke up to Shamil swearing at the guard.

"Asshole! You'll kill him like that! Torture, but don't kill. Maim, but so he can still walk. Hit him in the balls, but don't tear the balls off," he lectured. The guard listened with the guilty expression of a schoolboy with bad grades. "I have to teach you everything. You don't know how to do anything! Where did they find you idiots?"

The minibus turned off the highway, drove along the coast, and then through open gates and onto the territory of an enormous villa.

Shamil drove down the drive to a pier that extended out into the sea. Two motorboats and a small yacht made of mahogany were anchored nearby. He parked by a squat, two-story building that looked like a house for staff.

Two men came hurrying out of the house to help the guard pull Stanley's stretcher out of the bus and carry it inside.

They untied his hands and feet, took out his gag, and doused him with water. Then they put him in a room that Shamil considered the best torture chamber in the world, although he acknowledged that not everyone could use it well—torture was a science, he told his people, and gave them instructions to stand guard over Stanley and watch him closely. Then he went off to have lunch.

Stanley came to his senses soon enough, roused by the unbearable, glaring light. But it wasn't the same light that had blinded him in the hangar. He couldn't figure out where it was coming from. There was no way to turn away from it. His whole body hurt, his bruises ached, but Stanley sat up, with great effort, and looked around.

He was in a small room with a white floor, walls, and ceiling. The panels over the powerful lights on the ceiling and walls were also white. There was no furniture in the room. A white toilet sat in the corner, and a bucket with water next to it, also painted white. Next to Stanley on the floor was a white plastic plate with a mound of white rice topped with a drop of soy sauce.

Stanley remembered reading an article about torture. Conditions like these were used when you wanted to break someone's spirit, oppress them emotionally, deprive them of the will to resist. He thought that maybe they wouldn't beat him anymore, but had to tell himself not to be naive—Shamil's greatest joy in life was causing pain. He wasn't going to stop torturing Stanley.

He tried to stand up, but could barely manage it. His body was covered in bruises, and black spots marked the places where Shamil had attached the electrodes from his little machine.

Stanley was surprised by the reserves of strength he found within. But even though he'd only been in the white room for a short while, he knew he couldn't survive in these conditions for long. Again, he regretted his absolute lack of knowledge. He would have been happy to tell everything he knew about Lagrange and his theft—and Stanley was now certain that Lagrange was the one who'd stolen the money, who'd set Stanley up. He would have been so delighted to sic Shamil the maniac and his thick-headed henchmen on that traitorous bastard.

He tried to walk across the room. This proved very difficult. The white light and white color worked together to create the illusion of distance; it seemed to Stanley that the closest wall was a meter or two away, but, in actuality, the wall was barely centimeters away, and he banged his head badly against it, and fell with a groan. Neither the floor or the walls were padded. Stanley covered his face with his hands. The bright light got through anyway. It started to drill into his brain, causing physical pain.

Then he heard a light humming noise, starting soft and gradually growing louder. It started on a low note, and climbed higher and higher, eventually turning into a high-pitched squeal, almost ultrasonic. Stanley crawled over to the plastic plate, gathered up some of the sodden rice, and stuffed it in his ears. That helped a little.

Stanley couldn't tell how long the torture with sound, light, and color lasted. It might have been several hours, or several days. When he passed out, someone came into his cell, checked him over, nodded approvingly, and left the room again silently. Stanley woke up, crawled over to the toilet, and threw up. He curled up into a ball next to it on the floor. And sank back into oblivion once more.

Stanley woke up to someone standing over him and kicking his foot. He couldn't see who it was, just got an impression of dark glasses.

"You don't recognize me?" Gagarin asked. "Look at you, lying around. This isn't a resort! How do you like our little room? It's equipped with the latest in technology—we got help from someone who used to work at MI5. Nice, huh? I like it too. Sorry we had to take a break. I had some more urgent things to attend to, and I didn't want to put Shamil completely in charge of you. He likes you so much that I had to tell him three times not to touch you while I was gone."

Gagarin squatted down next to Stanley.

"He would have killed you already, I think."

"Where's my wife?" Stanley asked, although he had some trouble operating his tongue.

"Wife? What wife?"

"Shamil said she was with you."

"Ah yes, your wife! She's here. You can see her now. Have a chat. You'll have time while Shamil works you over. Under my supervision, of course. Don't worry, he's not going to kill you, maybe just maim you a little. Foot, hand, knee. Get up, fucker!" Gagarin stood and kicked Stanley with the toe of his shoe. "Stand up! We haven't finished our discussion. You can't? I'll get some help. Hey!"

Two men appeared at Gagarin's shout. They picked Stanley up and dragged him out of the white room, along a hallway, and down a staircase to the basement. The basement had a low ceiling and was cluttered with shelves. Part of it was fenced off by an opaque plastic curtain, and a large metal tub occupied another part. The men raised Stanley up and tied him to a table that looked like a carpenter's workbench. Gagarin sat in a chair, and one of the men who'd dragged Stanley in lit a cigarette for him. Then Gagarin sent them off with a wave of his hand.

"Shamil got held up," Gagarin nodded toward the curtain. "He's busy with something over there. Can you hear that rustling? He'll be free in a minute. You're not in a rush, are you?"

"No."

"Louder! Speak up, goddamn it."

"No!"

"Well, I am. Ah, here's Shamil…What were you doing over there?"

Shamil went over to Gagarin and whispered something in his ear.

"Really?" Gagarin jerked back in surprise. "Well, that's unexpected! Anyway, we have to get started."

Shamil came over to the workbench and wrapped Stanley's head in two layers of fabric, then clamped his head into a wooden vice.

"Ok, my dear Swiss banker, let's start from where we stopped last time. Shamil!"

Shamil began to pour water on Stanley's cloth-covered face. He poured water from a hose until the outline of an open mouth appeared in the cloth and Stanley's body began to arch upward. He took a break, and then started again.

"Where's Lagrange?" asked Gagarin during the break, but called for Shamil again before Stanley had the chance to answer.

The water torture continued. Water got into Stanley's lungs, and he tried to spit it out, arched his back, and cough, but the pain was too great. His body convulsed.

"Where's Lagrange, Stanley? Tell me, and we'll give you an easy death." Gagarin, as usual, took out his flask, took several sips, and lit a cigarette. "Otherwise you'll die in agony. Shamil, take that rag off his face. Talk! Otherwise you'll die like her!"

Shamil unwrapped Stanley's head and pulled back the plastic curtain. Someone was hanging by their hands from a hook on the ceiling, their arms twisted up and back behind them.

"Wipe his eyes, Shamil," Gagarin said. "Recognize her?" He nodded toward the hanging body.

Stanley tried to focus, but his vision was still blurry.

"Recognize her?" Gagarin asked again.

It was Christine, his Christine, her head bent back, her legs tied, covered with bruises. Her hair covered her face, and there was a bloody cut across her neck.

"I see that you have." Gagarin nodded and laughed. "What did you expect? The ones who love us must share our fates. And she did love you, Stanley. But you didn't love her! You loved fucking my wife every way you could get it, and we couldn't fuck yours? That's not fair! We believe in fairness, don't we, McKnight? American justice. What are you getting all worked up about? Look, Shamil. He's twitching around, making all kinds of noises. McKnight, you poor thing. Are you crying?"

Gagarin walked over to Christine's hanging body and pushed her leg. The body began to sway lightly on the hook.

"It's just Old Testament principles—an eye for an eye, a tooth for a tooth. You fuck someone else's wife, someone fucks yours. Biryuza described your meetings for me in detail. Gathered info. So it turns out you betrayed me twice. And that's just too much. Shamil got a little out of hand, put a little too much elbow grease into it. Your wife was too delicate, not like my slut. Mine is happy taking it any way you want to give it, but yours couldn't handle it. Go on, Shamil!"

Shamil wrapped Stanley's head back up and started pouring water again. When Stanley started to choke, Shamil brought the table with the megohmmeter over, hooked up the electrodes, and gave Stanley a shock.

Gagarin smoked calmly, observing the torture, sipping from his flask and asking the same question over and over: "Where's Lagrange, Stanley? Where's Lagrange?"

But the torture was set up so that even when Stanley wanted to say something, either his mouth was covered with cloth and had water pouring over it, or he was being shocked, and foam came out of his mouth instead of words.

Gagarin finally stood up.

"I need to make a few calls. Your wife can hang there so you'll have something to look at during the break. You won't have much time for that, but still. Shamil, take a break, and then back to it!"

But Shamil didn't want a smoke. He carried on, alternating methodically between water torture and electric shock. When he got tired, he dropped Stanley into the iron tub, which was filled with muddy, filthy water. To keep from drowning, Stanley had to hang on to the rough sides with his teeth. It was those moments when Shamil took the time for a cigarette and frank conversation. He told Stanley that even though he didn't like women, he had liked Christine.

"She was a stuck-up bitch, Stanley. But only till I started fucking her in the ass. What are you mumbling about, Stanley? I can't hear you. Anyway, your wife was the first American woman I ever had, and I have to say, it wasn't bad at all."

Shamil grabbed Stanley's nose and started swinging his head back and forth.

"And you know what, Stanley? I was choking her while I fucked her, and she came. Can you imagine? She came right before she died. I felt it. What a slut, huh? That was your wife, man! What a whore! And you're a piece of work, yourself," Shamil said, patting Stanley on the cheek before clamping his hand down over Stanley's throat.

"Open your eyes, Stanley! Don't worry, I'm going to fuck you too, handsome, when the time is right. And you know what that's going to mean for you? Open your eyes, Stanley! Do you hear me? That'll be it for you. Death. When you feel my cock in your ass, that's going to be the end. On the one hand, you'll probably be upset to be taking it up the ass. On the other hand, you'll know that your suffering is almost over. So are you already looking forward to me fucking you? What do you think, McKnight?"

Stanley was close to passing out, again. But he tried to fight through the pain. He didn't look at Christine's body. He didn't think about anything but the fact that he had to live through the torture, no matter how terrible it was. He had to survive so he could get revenge. On his own, without help from anyone.

There was no hope of salvation. It was simply an illusion. Stanley prepared for death, but the desire for revenge helped him endure the pain. It was as if he'd moved into a different reality. Lost track of time. He didn't know how long it went on. Maybe several days, maybe several hours.

Shamil dragged Stanley out of the tub and hit him several times with the electric shock, then he passed out. Christine's body continued to hang in front of his eyes like a reminder: *you must endure everything, survive to get revenge.*

The next time he came to his senses, Gagarin stood next to Shamil. Gagarin looked at Stanley as if he wasn't a person, but an earthworm crushed beneath someone's boot.

"Well, friend," said Gagarin, "how are things? I'll say it again—you have a choice. More torture, or you tell the truth. Where's Lagrange hiding? You're in on it with him, right? If so, you'll die easy. It's up to you."

Stanley squinted and saw that Shamil and Gala were unpacking a case of surgical instruments.

"Yeah, they're going to cut you up into little pieces next." Gagarin smiled, seeing the direction of Stanley's gaze.

Shamil began by slowly pulling the nails off Stanley's thumb and forefinger with a pair of pliers. Blood poured down his mangled hand.

"Wait, wait!" rasped Stanley.

"What happened?"

"Lagrange…I know where Lagrange is."

"So why did you wait so long to tell us, McKnight?"

"Maybe he's a masochist," said Gala. "And kept quiet on purpose to prolong his enjoyment. I've met a few like that."

"So where is he?"

"He's in Cuba. I remember him saying once that he's got a secret place in Cuba. A refuge, all set up. Where he could hide away."

"You believe that, Shamil?" Gagarin asked.

"He's lying, boss!" Shamil said, letting out a laugh.

"How about you, Gala?"

"I'm telling you, Stanley's a masochist. He likes being tortured. Can I cut off his balls?"

"I love my people's enthusiasm." Gagarin chuckled. "I agree. I think Stanley is lying to protect his partner." Gagarin bent down and picked up a case with a drill from under the table.

"Look what we've got here, Stanley. Nice drill, German quality. Bosch. The best company in the world. American drills are shit, right, Shamil? Black and Decker is garbage. But Bosch, now, that's quality. Too bad the drill bit is only ten millimeters. In the nineties, I used twenty-five-millimeter bits. But this is all Shamil could buy in the local French supermarket. The frogs let me down completely."

Gagarin put the bit into the drill and passed the cord to Shamil, who plugged it into the socket.

"I'll make the first hole, then I have another conference call—Credit Suisse wants to sell me a capital protected note. Shamil will take over while I'm gone. I haven't lost my touch, have I, Shamil?"

"You're a master, boss!"

"Well, well! Nothing sweeter than drilling a hole in a traitor!" Gagarin pressed a button, and the drill began to spin wildly. Then, as if remembering something, he switched the drill off and thoughtfully pressed its still-rotating bit against Stanley's chest.

"When I was a kid, there was nothing worse than a traitor. I learned that with my mother's milk. You know the Soviet tale about a little boy called *Malchish-Kibalchish*? Why am I asking? Of course you don't know that old story. I'll tell you.

"Once upon a time, the bourgeoisie attacked a Soviet country beyond the Black Mountains. All the grown-ups went off to war, and only very young boys remained behind in the village. And when Red Army soldiers came for help, but found no one, Malchish-Kibalchish called on his young friends and led them off to fight. A fight to the death!

"But one bad boy, named *Baddun*, decided to betray his comrades and his great Soviet country for a barrel of jam and a basket of cookies. Fucking bastard! The bourgeoisie captured Malchish-Kibalchish and put him through terrible torture to find out military secrets. But the boy laughed in their faces. The Red Army soon came and defeated the bourgeoisie, but it was too late. Malchish-Kibalchish had been killed. They buried him on a green hill by a blue river and placed a red flag over his grave."

Gagarin lifted the hand holding the drill and felt around for the start button with his finger.

"And the tale about Malchish-Kibalchish ends like this, Stanley: 'The ships pass by his grave and call out—hello, Malchish!'"

The drill switched on again, and the bit sank deep into Stanley's knee.

"Pilots fly by his grave—hello, Malchish!"

Stanley howled in pain. Gagarin pulled the drill out, picked a spot just above, and drilled down into the knee again.

"Trains run by his grave—hello, Malchish!"

Gagarin switched to the other leg and stuck the drill all the way in his other knee.

"And scouts walk by—we salute you, Malchish!"

Stanley screamed and passed out from the unbearable pain.

"Look how easily he comes in and out! Shamil, take the drill. Your turn! Right there in the center of the knee. Perfect."

CHAPTER 49

ONSCIOUSNESS RETURNED SLOWLY. STANLEY FELT like he was being carried, then as if he was floating in a small, fragile boat on a stormy sea.

He manned the oars, trying to face the boat into the high waves, but he kept getting turned sideways. Christine sat in the stern of the boat. She wasn't scared at all; she laughed infectiously.

She was alive and beautiful, and she told Stanley not to worry, assured him that everything would be okay. All their misfortunes and difficulties would soon be behind them, with only joy and love ahead. Then the sea suddenly grew hard, as if covered with iron, and he was thrown from the boat. He hit his head, but didn't lose consciousness.

He found himself on a street full of people wearing light, casual clothes. He heard the ocean nearby, and the cars that passed him were out-of-date models from decades ago. The wall nearby was covered with a poster of a bearded man. *That was Fidel Castro*, thought Stanley, and remembered what he'd told Gagarin about Lagrange.

Vengeance. He imagined placing the electrodes against Shamil's ears, turning the dial of that evil, black machine. Drilling into Gagarin's chest, smashing Lagrange's skull with a hammer, and shooting Gagarin's guards, the low-browed thugs.

These were sweet illusions, but they helped him forget his suffering, his inhuman pain. For a little while he was lost to the world, but then Shamil came into the white room and doused him with freezing water from the bucket.

Stanley's whole body shook. He saw to his surprise that he wasn't tied up at all.

"How are the knees?" Shamil asked with a smile. "They hurt? You passed out so fast. Weak! That's all right. Everything's going to stop hurting soon. An end to your suffering. Rejoice! Viktor lost his patience, and he's gone for good. You're no use, and it's time for you to die. But we're going to have some fun first, just like I promised."

Shamil lowered the zipper on his jeans and pushed them down. He bent over Stanley.

"Now I'm going to fuck you, banker, and then choke you to death. Well, to be precise—you like precision, don't you, banker?—I'm going to choke you and fuck you at the same time. After I kill you, I'll hang you up next to your wife."

"Are you joking?" whispered Stanley.

"You think this is funny, American? Let's have a laugh together, then."

Stanley sighed. "Bend down."

"What?" Shamil couldn't make out Stanley's words.

"Bend down," Stanley said again, his words barely audible. "I'll give you a kiss."

"You'll do what?"

"Give you a kiss…before the end."

"You'll kiss me?" Shamil laughed and began to take off his jacket. "Go ahead, then! Where do you want to kiss me?" Shamil bent over Stanley. "Here you go, give me a kiss…"

Shamil got on his knees, his jeans pushed down, his hands behind his back pulling off his jacket. He bent down lower and turned his cheek to Stanley.

"Here you are, a bloody kiss. That's such a turn on!"

Stanley pressed his lips to Shamil's cheek, then extended his tongue and ran it slowly down his executioner's rough skin. Gathering all his strength, forgetting about his punctured knees, Stanley wrapped his arms around Shamil's head, burying his face deep in the other man's neck, and bit down hard, tearing at the pulsing vein beneath his mouth, not giving Shamil time to fight back.

Stanley felt hot, salty blood pour over him, then he bit down into Shamil's Adam's apple, ripped it out with his teeth and spit it out, then bit down again on the spot where blood was gushing out, chewing on it deeper, almost choking, trying to breathe in fits and starts, snorting as the blood poured down his throat like molten lead. His hands still gripped Shamil by the neck.

Shamil arched upward, gasped. His feet drummed on the ground. He tried to free his arms from the jacket trapping them. But Stanley tore at his throat again and again. Finally, Shamil's struggles lessened. He arched up once more, twice, then lay still. The flow of blood trailed off.

Stanley pushed the body off him and noticed the pain in the fingers missing their nails. He tried to get up and dropped immediately from the agonizing pain in his knees. He lay on his stomach and vomited up Shamil's blood, slipping into unconsciousness for several minutes.

When he became aware again, Stanley looked around. Bright-red blood ruined the purity of the white room.

He tried to figure out where they had installed the camera the guards could observe him with. But he couldn't see one.

Stanley lay down next to Shamil's body, resting a little and using his good hand to search the dead man. He pulled a gun out of Shamil's holster, a heavy Stechkin. Wincing in pain, he checked to see if there were rounds in the clip and racked the slide, trying to figure out what to do next. The attack had taken a lot out of him. Stanley blacked out for a little while.

When he woke, he decided it was time to get out, even with the risk of encountering guards, even if he had to crawl. He had to get out or die trying. He realized then, though, that he was still completely naked. *Strange*, thought Stanley, *just a little while ago, when I was being tortured, I wasn't worried about that at all.*

Suddenly, he heard the sound of steps approaching. He sat up, leaned against the wall, and raised the gun with shaking hands. He removed the safety and pointed the gun at the door of the white room.

A moment later Biryuza appeared on the threshold. He was in a light-gray suit and a shirt in his favorite color, pink. He saw Stanley and froze. Gala came in after him and reached toward the holster under her jacket. Biryuza put out a hand to stop her.

"Jesus." Biryuza looked around the room in horror, at Shamil lying dead and Stanley naked, covered in blood.

Stanley waved his guests in with the gun.

"Step in and close the door," he ordered.

Biryuza obeyed, slowly. "Where the hell did you come from?" he asked, pronouncing each syllable distinctly.

"From Disneyland." Stanley tried to aim, but his hands shook so badly that the gun nearly fell to the ground.

Once Biryuza saw his condition, he laughed in relief.

"You know what they say about slugs? They always leave a trail of slime on their path. You planning on going far, Stanley?"

"Home."

"Home?" Biryuza laughed. "You're a fucking comedian. You're staying here. Just look at his hands shaking, Gala. He's so scared he's about to shit himself."

"Death is close enough for me not to fear for my life," whispered Stanley, trying to aim at Biryuza's head.

"A philosopher! Put a bullet in your head, Stan. You'll feel better."

Stanley was silent, trying to settle his shaking hands, but the gun still wavered back and forth, inciting Biryuza's mockery. He didn't have much strength left. He could hold on for another minute, maybe two, and then he was going to drop the gun.

"What are we going to do?" asked Gala quietly.

"Kill him," Biryuza said, and made a grab for the gun.

Stanley shot first. The bullet hit Biryuza right between the eyes, and blood splashed onto the white wall behind him. He waved his hands in an absurd pantomime for a moment, then fell down dead.

Gala pulled out her gun and leaped forward, shooting at Stanley nearly point-blank. He felt bullets burn into his arm and neck. He closed his eyes tight and shot in front of him.

Silence fell over the room, and Stanley, deafened by the shots, finally opened his eyes. Gala lay wheezing on the floor, a bullet in her throat. She watched Stanley, unblinking, bloody bubbles coming out of her mouth.

The noise of the guns had been ear-splitting, but no one had come to check on them. There were probably no other guards nearby. He put the gun on the ground with a shaky hand and crawled over to Shamil. He searched his pockets and found a pack of cigarettes. He took out a cigarette, which grew wet instantly with the blood from his hands. Stanley wiped his hands on Shamil's clothes, then took out another cigarette and lit it.

His head spun after the first drag. Stanley checked himself over. It looked as though the bullets had just winged him. Blood flowed from the bullet holes, but no faster than from his other wounds. He took a deep drag on the cigarette, down to the filter, and put it out in the pool of blood on the floor. Gala's wheezing grew louder, then cut off. She gasped silently like a fish out of water, then grew still.

"Okay, stay calm," he told himself. "You need to get out. You have to. If you can't walk, crawl."

So he crawled. He crawled over Biryuza's body and flopped down next to him. He reached around for Biryuza's right wrist and took his watch off. Then he sighed and crawled on.

Every inch cost him greatly. He couldn't use his legs because of his drilled knees, but he couldn't use his hands fully, either, because of the torn fingers on his left hand.

Stanley pushed off the floor with his right hand, scooting his stomach along the floor, resting after each push forward, then starting again. He put the gun in front of him, then dragged himself toward it. Put the gun in front. Dragged forward again. When he crawled over the threshold of the white room, he banged his knee against the frame and grimaced in pain.

Out in the hallway, he saw a staircase going down. He reached the top and looked down.

He could roll down, but there was a risk he'd break his already maimed legs. He lay on the top step, his head hanging over it, and tossed the gun down. The gun bounced down the stairs and hit the door, which seemed to lead to the staff quarters. Then Stanley began to slowly descend the stairs, supporting his body weight with his one good hand.

The wounds that had just begun to close over opened up again. Stanley was leaving a trail of blood behind him. Each movement caused him horrific pain. Sometimes he banged his head into the wall, and came close to passing out from the pain.

He finally made it to the door. He tried to push it open with his forehead, but finally had to twist himself into an awkward curve to reach the handle. He climbed out of the house and onto the porch.

Stanley saw several cars near the house, but they were all parked on a gravel lot. "Oh God, not that," moaned Stanley. But he put the gun out in front of him and kept pushing forward, scratching his chest, shoulders, and hips on the small stones.

With great effort, he made it to the first car, a black Bentley cabrio. With the last of his strength, Stanley did a fast push-up off the floor, reached the door handle, hung on it, and fell back down.

He tried again. Fell down again. Tried again, and this time the car door opened. Stanley used his good arm to pull his body in. Howling in pain, he shut the door behind him. The key was on the dashboard.

He put his hands and head on the wheel and took a breath, then started the engine and pushed down on the gas pedal. He almost blacked out from the sharp pain in his knee. The car jerked forward and stopped. He tried pressing down on the gas with his left knee, but that was even worse.

Stanley wept in despair; there was no way out.

After a few minutes, he calmed down. Looked around. The pier was directly in front of him, half hidden by the branches of pine trees. A small motorboat was tied up there. He bit his lip, opened the door, and fell out of the car. Then he began to crawl toward the pier.

Now pine needles and gravel were working their way into his wounds. His knees were swollen and bleeding. After moving forward a foot or two, he had to rest, losing consciousness several times, then waking up to crawl forward.

After hours of crawling, he made it to the wooden pier. If someone saw his wormlike movements, he thought, they probably wouldn't even think there was a human intruder on the pier. He started to laugh, harder and harder, until his laughter turned into tears. Then he howled like a homeless dog. He forced himself to calm down, but the last few feet were the hardest—the planks of the pier were old, and a long splinter lodged in his skin as he crawled along.

When he was even with the boat, he thought that a funny end to all this would be missing the boat and ending up drowning in the shallow water. Praying that the boat didn't need a key to start, he threw himself off the pier and fell onto the boat, hitting his head on a metal bench and losing consciousness yet again.

The light of the setting sun on his face woke him. He sat up and reached for the instruments. The boat didn't need a key. All you had to do was turn the power switch and hit the starter button. He hit the switch and pressed the button. The motor coughed and started up.

Not sparing his wounded hands any more, Stanley lifted the loop of rope off the bollard. Keeping his healthy hand on the wheel, Stanley pushed the speed lever up with his nose. The boat hit the pier, then moved slowly off toward the open sea.

"Ah-ha!" exclaimed Stanley, nosing the lever up all the way. "How do you like that, motherfuckers?" he said in Russian.

The wind rushed over Stanley's face. He took a deep breath in and turned to see the foaming water in his wake.

CHAPTER 50

D AY AND NIGHT BLURRED TOGETHER, and the nightmares followed him everywhere he went. The daytime nightmares were the worst.

Stanley spent the days alone, in a damp, cramped, airless cabin in the bowels of a rusted old ship. Condensation ran down the walls of the cabin. The ceiling leaked. It stank of engine oil.

The moment he closed his eyes, however, he dreamed he was walking through the streets of various cities, running into people he was supposed to know, but who he was actually seeing for the first time.

The sun was always scorching hot in these nightmares. Then it would turn black, the smells of the city would intensify, and the air would grow so thick he had to push it apart with his hands as he walked. Now and then he thought he heard someone calling out to him; that someone who was actually silent was asking him a question.

At night, he lay in the darkness, knowing that there was no one lying beside him. But still, faces and voices emerged, one after the other. They called him by name, trying to convince him of something, accusing him, reproaching him for his mistakes, saying that he was to blame for everything, that he had been weak.

"You wanted money? Well now, you've got it all!" a high-pitched, grating voice said.

"No, he just wanted to be better than other people."

Another voice laughed. "He wanted people to envy him. He certainly is better than everyone else now."

His first nightmare was of Christine. Her face and body were covered in bruises. She moved slowly around him, as if in orbit. Even though her cracked lips were pressed tightly together, Stanley heard her voice clearly.

She repeated the same phrase, over and over: "We must share the fates of those we love." Clear, translucent tears fell from her eyes.

He thrashed around, tried to sit up, but the man sitting at the head of his bed wouldn't let him. Stanley lay on his stomach, his head and legs covered in needles. He looked like a giant hedgehog.

Stanley came back to reality and remembered that the man in his cabin wasn't part of the nightmare, but an actual person. That was Mao, an ageless man with a small face, wrinkled as an old apple. Mao took care of Stanley. They had been introduced by another Chinese man, young, tall, and broad-shouldered, named *Huojin*.

Stanley had met Huojin in a small dive bar by the docks of the Marseille port. He'd sat down next to Stanley, ordered them a round, and introduced himself, noting that his name meant "man of iron."

"And what does your name mean?" Huojin had asked.

Stanley had shrugged.

"I never thought about it."

"Your name is your fate," Huojin had said. "And yours is a difficult one. You need help. I can tell. I'll help you. What will you give me in return?"

"Money?" said Stanley.

"Hmm. It doesn't seem like you're doing too well on money." Huojin had laughed. "Or are you planning to get some? Someone owes you money? You're trying to find the debtor?"

Stanley had thought he might be dreaming. He'd even pinched his arm. No, Huojin hadn't disappeared. The beer in front of him had been just as cold and intoxicating.

Huojin had seen the pinch and laughed again.

"I noticed you right away," he'd said. "I knew immediately what you need. I do business without papers, no documents. I know everybody in this port and every other. You need to get out of here, am I right?"

"That's right." Stanley had taken the cigarette Huojin was offering.

"Where to?"

"Cuba," Stanley had said after some consideration. "And I'll need documents. Any documents. Doesn't matter what name."

"Easy. This is Marseille, after all. But you'll be at sea a long time. You'll leave the day after tomorrow. You can pay when you get that money back."

"I've got money. How much?"

"However much you see fit."

413

"Why are you doing this?" asked Stanley.

"You might be useful to me," Huojin had said with a smile. "Later. I help you. You help me. But the documents will be expensive. I'll get you a South African passport. That's simple. I've got lots of friends there. You'll get it when you're about to arrive to Cuba. Just so you don't do anything foolish before."

Huojin had taken Stanley to the ship and handed him over to Mao, giving the latter instructions in Chinese. Mao had followed those instructions (Stanley assumed) without a murmur. He'd put Stanley in the cabin and begun to treat him with acupuncture, had fed him rice and vegetables, had brought him jugs with harsh Chinese vodka, and had left several joints of hashish.

On his way out, Huojin had told Stanley that, when he found his enemy, it would be better to leave them alive.

"Why?" Stanley had asked.

"We live as long as our enemies do," Huojin had said over his shoulder. "Without them, we become like this old man. Kind and useless. Obediently fulfilling the orders of men like us, who have enemies everywhere, enemies who we protect and keep."

Stanley couldn't figure out how to steer the small boat he'd used to escape from Gagarin's villa. By that point, he didn't much care. The thirst for vengeance had made him grit his teeth and suffer through unbearable pain, but deep inside, he felt a rising indifference. Christine's death, her terrible, cruel death had brought him low. A death that he was to blame for.

He locked the handle for the gas in place, and the boat's motor made a strained humming noise. Stanley slid from the side of the boat down into the cockpit. He knocked open the door of the small cabinet holding the steering wheel in place, and discovered a mini-fridge inside. Stanley pulled out two cans of beer. He popped the top off the first and downed it almost instantly, foam spilling all over him, and opened the second. Then he threw up and passed out.

The boat hit the shore at full speed, a rocky, fenced-off section of beach accessed by granite stairs leading down from a villa above.

The impact threw Stanley forward; he ended up with a cut on his forehead, a swollen wrist, and more damage to his already suffering knees. The pain brought him back to consciousness for a little while, but then he slipped back into the fog.

Early the next morning, the villa's owner came down to the beach for a swim. Jacques was shorter than average, and suffered from multiple untreatable illnesses, the main one being his unrestrained, severe alcoholism.

After struggling all night with a bottle of cognac, Jacques decided to refresh himself at dawn. He threw a robe onto his lean but muscular body, and slid his blue-veined feet into rubber shoes. He lit his traditional morning Galois and took the stairs down to the water.

His wife stood at the very top, taking small sips of coffee from a large drinking bowl, into which she dipped a croissant, nibbling it down, piece by piece.

Jacques threw off his robe and stepped into the water nude, stroking slowly through the cold water as it cleared away his hangover. It was only on turning back toward shore that he noticed the boat that had crashed into his private beach. He swam toward it, jumped to his feet, and peered into the cockpit. Stanley lay there, unconscious.

"Lucy!" he called, but his wife continued to sip calmly at her coffee.

Jacques may have been short, but he wasn't lacking in strength. He had been a well-known professional boxer in his youth, and had literally acquired his beach through his fists. It was nothing for him to jump into the boat, grab Stanley under the arms, and pull him to shore.

Lucy had come down to meet him by that point, and she set her coffee down on the stone of their short pier, brushing crumbs off her full chin.

"What are you doing down there, my fighter?" she asked, squinting at her husband. "And what the devil is that?"

"It's a naked guy! Wearing an expensive watch!" Jacques proclaimed happily. "And not a bad boat! Probably got drunk at a party and decided to go for a ride."

Lucy came closer. She looked Stanley over as he began to slowly come to. At the sight of his body, she wrapped her robe tighter, gripping the edges.

"I think he had a bit of a fight before he decided to go for a joyride. Say, twelve rounds."

"Clearly, now you mention it," agreed Jacques, looking closer. "With a heavyweight. Who was also a kickboxer and worked his knees over pretty good."

Stanley moaned, and his arms twitched.

"I think we should call the police," Lucy said. "And don't you hurt yourself. Leave this Marcel Cerdan where he was! I think he was tortured."

"Maybe he needs help," said Jacques, but nonetheless set his burden down.

Stanley's head hit the side of the boat with a loud thunk, and he fainted again.

"Another couple moves like that, Monsieur Jacques, and there'll be no helping him!" Lucy helped her husband out of the boat. "Go, call. I'll watch him!"

The police and the ambulance arrived at the same time. The EMTs pulled Stanley from the boat and put him on a stretcher, covered him with a sheet, and got him into the vehicle. Jacques, meanwhile, told his story to the police, with Lucy's corrections and additions. When the police had what they needed, they took off after the ambulance.

Stanley was taken to the hospital and placed in a ward with six other beds, but with a curtain for privacy. A detective came to visit him, but found the patient in a twilight state, only mumbling meaningless sounds in response to questions, his gaze clouded and senseless. The detective took his fingerprints and left.

The doctor appeared after a considerable delay and gave Stanley a brief once-over. He told the nurses to wash the patient thoroughly, then send him to surgery. There, Stanley was examined again, his blood was drawn, and his wounds were treated and sutured.

Stanley suddenly came to life then, started shouting something, and tried to escape from the restraining hands of the nurses. They had to call a larger male nurse to assist; the hefty Algerian man held Stanley down and strapped him to the stretcher, then administered a sedative.

The doctor examined Stanley again. He wrapped up his knees and put on special braces. He also prescribed antibiotics.

The detective came back, having forgotten to photograph Stanley on his first visit. He took several shots with his cell phone and went back to the station. In the end, he never uploaded the photos of the mysterious stranger. Later that evening he was called to an incident after a soccer match between Marseille and Rennes, where a quick-fingered Marseilles fan lifted the cell from his back pocket. So Stanley had several days of peace in quiet in his hospital bed with no one asking who he was, where he had gotten the boat, or where he had come from.

He regained consciousness and ate with appetite. The nurses enjoyed taking care of their handsome patient, who spoke almost no French but made cute jokes in English. When the doctor looked in on him a few days later, he was quite satisfied with the patient's progress, but surprised that, in all this time, no one had even tried to discover his name. He asked the nurses. They answered that "Monsieur Anglais" was enough for them, although they thought that the patient wasn't English at all, but American.

The doctor pulled back the curtain. Stanley was sleeping peacefully. The doctor patted him on the shoulder, and Stanley woke.

"Hello. I'm your doctor."

"Yes, I know. I remember you."

"What is your name?"

"That, I don't remember," said Stanley.

"Hmm," the doctor replied, and called a psychiatrist in to examine Stanley, calling the police at the same time to find out what they were planning to do. This was of greater concern to the administration of the hospital than the doctor—who was going to pay for the significant expense of his treatment and care?

The psychiatrist conversed with Stanley in good English and diagnosed him with dissociative amnesia with dissociative fugue. He subsequently explained the condition to the detective and his partner, a small woman with an enormous gun, during their next visit.

"He doesn't remember the facts of his personal life, or his name, but he has retained general knowledge. He remembers, for example, how to use a fork and knife, he recognized the song on another patient's ringtone. But he has periods where he is not present, mentally. We need to do a tomography, then decide on a treatment plan. Maybe transfer him to the psychiatric department; that would be for the best."

"Can I ask him some questions?"

"You may, but don't tire him out."

"Monsieur," the detective addressed Stanley. "Can you tell us where you came from?"

"No."

"Do you know why the boat doesn't have a registration number? Can you remember?"

"No."

"There was a gun in the locker under a seat in the boat. Is it yours?"

"No."

The police left, discussing on the way that it was usually drug couriers who used boats without registration numbers, to ferry drugs from big ships to the shore. The fact that the gun (which did not have Stanley's prints on it) was Russian-made indicated the Russian mafia. Piece by piece, the file on the mystery man who arrived from parts unknown began to grow in size, but still contained no photograph of its central figure. The police commissioner noted this lack, and sent the detectives back to take another picture.

Stanley, who could more or less decipher the conversations between the doctors and nurses as well as between the detectives, came to the conclusion that, even with their general disorganization and seeming indifference, the police would figure out who he was in two days, three at most. It was simple enough. They'd upload his photo into the ID database and get a hit.

The next step would be the arrival of the Swiss police and deportation to a Swiss hospital. Probably with an attack by Gagarin's people on the way. Viktor had to be beside himself with rage after Stanley's escape and the deaths of Shamil and Biryuza. It would take a most unlikely streak of luck to survive until he was able to reach Frank Dillon and the charming Alex.

He had been feeling reasonably fit for several days. Even his sleeping was back on track, though his nightmares tormented him. The nurses took good care of him.

One nurse, a pretty, mixed-race woman who spoke decent English, was particularly kind to him. She had overheard the detectives talking in the hospital cafeteria, and told Stanley that they suspected him being a member of a Colombian drug cartel, and just pretending to be an American who had lost his memory. Especially since there had recently been a terrible shootout at a villa on the outskirts of Marseille, and witnesses driving by the villa and on the shore had seen several people escape by boat.

"You know I'm not a drug dealer, darling. I don't know who the monsters are that took a drill to my knees." Stanley shurugged.

"Oh! Mon pauvre cheri! Of course not, you handsome thing," said the woman, stroking his hair.

The next day, she hurried up to Stanley's bed with a wheelchair, and quickly detached the heart monitor sensors from his chest and the blood pressure bracelet from his wrist.

"It's time for your procedures, Monsieur Forgetful!"

Stanley realized immediately that they weren't going to any procedures, and his suspicions were confirmed when the nurse parked him in a secluded corner and came back with pair of crutches and a bag. The bag held a change of clothes.

"You'll get fired!" Stanley said.

"Eh, to hell with him!"

"With who?"

"The detective is my ex. I'd do anything to screw with that asshole. Anyway—here."

She showed Stanley a piece of paper. He shrugged, not understanding.

"It says here that you're being transferred to the Edouard Toulouse Hospital."

"What's that?"

"A psychiatric clinic. My current boyfriend works there. He'll sort the paper trail somehow. He knows his way around! And one last thing."

She handed Stanley his watch.

"Get dressed and get out of here!"

Stanley sold the watch at the port for 12,000 euros. The buyer, who owned a small store on Estienne d'Orves square, saw at once that he could make a low offer, even though the watch was worth many times that. Stanley didn't try to bargain.

As he lay in the hospital, he had planned on contacting Frank. But then he realized it had nothing to do with them now. There was no benefit to their federal government. Their special services had no oversight in this matter. It was his personal business now. Actually, it wasn't business anymore. Just personal. And so everything was up to him, and him alone.

The ship moved slowly from one Mediterranean Sea port to another. Sometimes it seemed to Stanley that he was traveling in a circle, that the squeaky old ship would never make it out to the ocean. He asked Mao when they would finally set a course for Cuba.

"Never," answered Mao.

"What do you mean? Is this a joke?"

"You'll go to Cuba in a tanker. Big tanker. It's waiting for us at a shipyard in the Canary Islands. Waiting for us and others. It's carrying oil, oil stolen from bad people. They're taking it to the Cubans. We need to collect other goods and deliver them to the tanker. The tanker won't go anywhere until we deliver our goods and other people deliver theirs."

"And what am I supposed to do?"

"Get better. I'll treat you. You'll be walking good by the time you board the tanker. Your knees won't even hurt! And I'm going to feed you rice. Rice and vegetables. Good for your health. You'll drink tea and baijiu. You like baijiu?"

"Is it this nasty stuff?" Stanley sniffed at the contents of the drinking bowl he was holding.

"Yes, that's it. Good drink?"

"It's swill! You don't have anything better?"

"You want Maotai?"

"Maotai? What's that?"

"The best vodka. Chairman Mao thought highly of it. Maotai is also baijiu, but an expensive kind, and not as strong as what you're drinking. No, sir, you don't have the money for Maotai. Drink what I pour you. More?"

"Go on!"

Stanley couldn't get drunk, even after several bowls of the Chinese vodka. He never had understood why Russians put such value on the ability to drink without getting drunk. He liked feeling intoxicated, but thought that drinking as a sport, where the one who can drink more is the toughest, was total idiocy. Like much of what his former Russian friends valued.

Mao usually locked the cabin when he went out so that the other crew wouldn't see him, particularly the captain, a gloomy Romanian, and his first mate, an enormous Ukrainian man. They didn't know that they had the most wanted Swiss banker in the world in their very own hold.

The faithful Mao let Stanley out at night, only under cover of darkness. One night, Stanley climbed quietly from the hold to the deck and found a secluded spot to smoke. The clouds hung low overhead, and the ship rolled from wave to wave. Sometimes there were lights in the distance, either another ship, or lights from the shore.

Stanley tried to figure out what part of the Mediterranean they were in. Maybe that was Malta, or maybe Alexandria. The ship slowed down, then started to drift. A larger ship loomed out of the fog, and thin black men began to climb to its deck via rope ladders.

One by one, they disappeared into the open deck hatches. Two men with automatic weapons over their shoulders were in charge. One of them, sensing he was being watched, looked up and saw Stanley. His hand started for his weapon, but then he just smiled, and brought his finger to his lips.

When Stanley got back to the cabin, an anxious Mao was waiting for him.

"You shouldn't have gone out tonight!" he said. "You might have been spotted. That would have been very bad!"

"Who were they loading onto the ship?" asked Stanley.

"Slaves. From Africa. Europe wouldn't take them, now they can't go back home. They'll work for pennies somewhere. Like all of us."

Another time, lost in the bowels of the ship, he encountered a small, elegant woman, frightening them both. The woman shrank back against the peeling paint of the wall, and Stanley squeezed by her, catching a faint scent of perfume as he went by. It was a familiar smell. The same expensive perfume he'd given to Christine.

He looked up. She was beautiful, but for the dark rings around her eyes, and her swollen, peeling lips.

"Sorry."

The woman just watched him as if she didn't understand.

"Do you speak English?"

"I do, but I'm trying to hide it." She laughed suddenly.

"Why?" asked Stanley.

"I'm hanging out in the hold with a bunch of Sudanese, Berber, and Eastern European girls. I told them I'm Greek, since I speak Greek, and have lived there. Are you American?"

"Yes. And you?"

"And who do you pretend to be?" she asked, without answering his question.

"Chinese."

She laughed melodically. "Somehow, you don't look very Chinese. But, hmm, maybe if I look a little closer." She laughed again.

"Your perfume," said Stanley. "Is it Mzinov?"

"How about that?" the woman replied in surprise. "On a half-rusted-out Chinese ship filled with stench and shit, a man who recognizes Ralph Lauren perfume! Who are you?"

"I'm looking for a way up on deck. But one that I can use without any of the crew seeing me. And what are you looking for?"

"In general? Or here?"

"Here." Stanley smiled.

"A shower. There's none in the hold. The Sudanese women wash using buckets. It's about to drive me crazy."

"I've got a shower in my cabin," said Stanley. "And some good hashish. And Chinese vodka. I'm happy to share."

"Are you suggesting we shower together?"

"You can take the shower by yourself, but we'll share the joint and the vodka."

"If I come back to the Sudanese women clean, they'll suspect me of being a plant and strangle me. Thanks. I'll stay dirty for now. And anyway, I'll lose the hint of my old perfume if I shower. Thanks anyway, stranger!"

"You're welcome! Good luck!"

"To you as well!"

Stanley and the woman went their separate ways.

A couple of days later, Mao said that the ship had finally turned toward Gibraltar. When they were out in the ocean, he told Stanley that there had been a knife fight between some of the women in the hold that left two Sudanese women and one white woman dead.

"A short, Greek woman? Pretty?" asked Stanley.

"You went to the women? Ay ay ay, that's no good! They'll catch you! Mao will get it bad! And you, mister, it will be bad for you. Very bad!"

"Which woman?"

"Yes, the Greek. They cut her. Dumped her overboard."

Stanley lay down and turned his face to the wall.

"Hey, Yankee, what's wrong? Be happy! We'll reach Cuba soon!"

Stanley didn't answer.

He thought that if this woman pretending to be Greek, who was probably running some kind of con, an aristocratic thief, or a high-class prostitute, if she had come to his cabin, she might still be alive. Or maybe the Sudanese women would have strangled her right then. He tried to understand the nature of his feelings. He understood that he didn't actually know this woman, that he wasn't hurt by her death, not really, but it nonetheless somehow intensified his sorrow and his bitterness.

He lay for hours looking at the wall. He decided that if he couldn't find Lagrange in Cuba, he wouldn't work with Frank anymore, either. He just wouldn't have any strength left to continue the fight. Only the belief that Lagrange was hiding from the world in Cuba gave him strength to go on. Each day, as the ship swayed through the Mediterranean, passing Gibraltar, toward the Canary Islands, Stanley turned over and over in his head how he would kill Lagrange, and what he would say before he did it.

In his mind, he hacked Lagrange up with a blunt knife, sawed off his arms and legs, shot or drilled through his knees, clubbed him with a baseball bat. He watched himself in these internal movies, spattered with Lagrange's blood, heard himself talking, but everything he said sounded artificial, stupid, pointless.

He was transported to the tanker at night, in the same rowboat as a silent Sudanese woman wrapped in striped cloth.

The tanker was enormous, like an entire city towering over the surface of the sea. Almost all its lights were dark that night. Mao warned Stanley not to talk to anyone, and to follow the crew's instructions to the letter. One of the sailors led Stanley to a narrow, cramped cabin.

The cabin had a porthole. Stanley opened it and breathed in the slightly bitter scent of the Old World, blowing in from the east. The gigantic hull of the tanker shuddered as it prepared to move, its bulkheads creaking. Stanley lay down on the bunk. His knees, thanks to Mao's treatments, hardly hurt. Only a slight limp remained of the torture he had endured. But he didn't have to walk very far anyway—food was brought to him on a tray, and he was forbidden to go on deck.

It was also nighttime, about a month later, when Stanley was transported to the Cuban shore. Alone.

CHAPTER 51

A FTER PAYING FOR HIS PASSPORT, Stanley had about $3,000 left. This, he reckoned, should be enough for a couple months of searching. According to his new green passport book, Stanley was now called Clyde Griffiths. He liked the name. He looked sharp in the photograph, taken in the basement of a Marseille dive; it fitted his state of mind.

"My name is Clyde. I'm from Pretoria, but I haven't been there in almost twenty years. I worked in Switzerland. I'm a cigar aficionado," Stanley repeated, making his way along the shore toward some lights in the distance. "I will find Lagrange. I will find fucking Lagrange. I'll find him."

Stanley had no stamp in his passport showing he had crossed the Cuban border, but that didn't seem to bother anyone. Everything he'd heard about the easygoing attitude of Cubans proved to be entirely true. He found a room in a small hotel on the outskirts of Havana and paid in dollars, raising him even higher in the estimation of the hotel clerk. The other man liked that his new guest was unpretentious, that he traveled only with a small bag over his shoulder (which Stanley had stuffed with various rags to look full). And he'd never seen a South African passport before.

"How are things in Africa, Mr. Griffiths?" the clerk asked, handing Stanley his room key.

"We've got lots…"

"Lots of what?"

"Lots of wild monkeys!"

The next morning, Stanley went for a stroll and met an elderly Cuban woman in a bar who rented out rooms to solo tourists like the man he was pretending to be.

Stanley's new landlady also found him a car, or rather, she took him to the owner of a small garage who had several cars to rent. At first, he took a liking to an old Soviet model with the strange name of Zhiguli. He gave it a test drive, but when he got in, his head almost hit the ceiling and the gears shifted with such a screech that he slapped his hands over his ears.

The owner of the garage suggested a different car, and he pulled the tarp off it to reveal a Ford Fairlane 1957. It wasn't in the best condition, with paint peeling in some spots and rust showing in others, but the seat was fine, and when the owner installed a battery and started the engine, Stanley was pleasantly surprised by the rich sound.

They didn't bargain long over the price, and Stanley left a deposit while the owner promised to do a maintenance check on the car.

He spent another couple of days hanging out in bars, where he started up conversations about cigars, asking where the best plantations for cigar tobacco were to be found. He believed that Lagrange, as a true cigar lover, would set up his secret refuge near such a plantation.

He soon learned that the best region for cigars was Vuelta Abajo, on the western edge of the island. They grew the best tobacco there, and there were three large cigar factories where they rolled the tobacco from the nearby plantations into the cigars sold by the world's most prestigious brands.

Once the Ford received a clean bill of health, Stanley set off to visit the area. His first trip, on which the car drove like a dream, was to San Luis. The land around the city was known to produce the best wrapper leaves. Over lunch at a small café, Stanley learned that the farm of the legendary Cuban grower Alejandro Robaina wasn't far away.

"It would be nice to meet him!" said Stanley, but the waiter informed him that it would be impossible now to meet with Señor Robaina, as the man had been in the nearby cemetery for the last ten years. He was surprised that the guest from South Africa hadn't already been aware of this.

"It was such a tragedy! Condolences from all over the world! From Schwarzenegger, from Depardieu! His grandson, Hiroshi, is in charge there now. I think you would find him an interesting conversationalist, Señor Griffiths."

Stanley got directions and set off for the Robaina farm. Hiroshi didn't resemble his idea of the typical tobacco grower or the typical Latin American—no rubber boots, no hat, only sneakers, jeans, and a T-shirt.

Stanley apologized for taking up the time of one of the world's best cigar producers and told Hiroshi that he represented a small tobacco company interested in starting cigar production in the Natal Province.

Here, Stanley's experience as a banker and investor came in handy. He spoke at length about the financial prospects and the benefit to Hiroshi should he choose to get involved.

Stanley said that his partners would be proud to collaborate with Vegas Robaina, one of the top cigar makers in the world. Toward the end of their conversation, he asked if Señor Hiroshi knew any foreigners who had bought tobacco plantations in Cuba in the last few years, even small ones?

Hiroshi thought for a moment.

"Yes, Señor Griffiths, I do. Not personally. But I heard of it. The plantation is called Acrecabot, in Vuelta Arriba. They don't grow cigar tobacco there, mostly wrapper leaves. The taste is not so important for those, you know, the taste that comes from the composition of the soil. The beautiful appearance matters more, which you can get easily—it's enough to simply take care of the plant. Of course, between us, our wrapper leaves are better. But there is a cigar plantation there, yes. It was bought by—"

"A Frenchman?"

"Yes, yes, a Frenchman! You know, he bought it long ago, when my grandfather and El Comandante were still around. The plantation was considered to be rented, then. I don't know how he managed it. I can't say for sure, but he probably thanked someone for it quite generously. He has quite a bit of money, I think, and renovated a villa not far from the town. He used to come a couple times a year, but now the locals see him all the time."

Stanley returned to Havana. He was on Lagrange's trail now. He could feel it. Close to having Lagrange in his snare.

He needed to prepare so that, if the French owner of the plantation did indeed turn out to be Lagrange, he wouldn't have to act hastily.

Stanley found a small hardware store and was shocked at the scarcity of goods, but was able to buy a large knife, pliers, rope, wide duct tape, and a flashlight. He asked if they had binoculars, and the sales clerk produced an ancient, worn pair from beneath the counter. They were of Soviet origin, he said, sold long ago by a Soviet soldier for a bottle of rum.

Stanley was checking out a drill as well, but it was too expensive. The clerk, seeing Stanley's hesitation, advised him to buy a secondhand drill, or better yet, rent one.

"What size drills do you have?"

"What is the señor planning to drill?" the clerk asked.

"Nothing harder than concrete. I'm looking for a twenty-five-millimeter drill."

"What for?"

"I need to help a friend with some repairs," answered Stanley.

"A man must help his friends, señor. Holy Mary bless you! Everyone rents tools from us, except for people working in cooperatives."

So Stanley did, but he bought new drill bits, the newest, cleanest, and largest the store had to offer. As he paid, he was already imagining the pliers tearing off Lagrange's nails, the drill going into his knees, the long bits entering the bone.

Stanley had a hearty dinner and went to bed. He got up early in the morning, had coffee, and set off on his way.

The road ran along the ocean shore. He drove at a leisurely place, trying to ease his agitation. He rolled down a window and smoked the cigar he'd bought from Hiroshi, checking the paper map the garage owner had given him.

He stopped in Santa Clara, where he had another coffee, and then went on toward San Antonio de las Vueltas, where he had a lunch of rice, black beans, and fried beef, and asked around about the plantation.

"Yes, that's not far," the café's pretty owner told him. "The owner came by recently, had a beer. What? Yes, he's French. You want to visit him? Business? Of course. We used to fight for communism, and now it's business everywhere. Would you like coffee?"

Stanley drank his coffee and smoked another cigar. He asked about a room and got one right over the café. As she gave him his key, the owner asked if the señor would be interested in a young girl.

"Thank you, no," said Stanley.

"She's only fourteen, tall and pretty, nearly a virgin. Yes?"

"No, thank you."

"Perhaps a woman? An experienced one such as myself?"

"An experienced woman would suffer with an inexperienced man like me," said Stanley, "and I try to reduce the amount of suffering in this world."

"You're a wise man, Señor Griffiths." The owner laughed.

Stanley sat on a wicker chair on the balcony of his room. He drank a bottle of rum, smoked a few cigars, and watched local life play out in the street below until evening. Then he napped for half an hour. When it was dark, he took an ice-cold shower, drank a bottle of beer, and headed off in the direction of the plantation.

He parked outside the town and went on foot from there, keeping close to the forest. He reached the plantation owner's house after half an hour.

He crouched beneath a wide-branched tree, a knife at his side just in case. The lights of the mansion were quite close.

A pediment on columns at the front, a well-manicured garden—it was clear that the colonial-style house was in caring hands. Stanley saw through his binoculars that the walls were freshly painted, the roof redone, the window frames were new, and the glass within was clean.

There were two vintage cars in perfect condition parked in front, a 1930s BMW and a 1960s Ford pickup, both carefully washed, wheel rims shining.

The light curtains at the open living room window were blowing in the breeze, and slow music drifted out toward him. From the fullness of the sound, the clarity of the high notes, and the depth of the low notes, Stanley could tell that the owner appreciated expensive sound equipment, and that he was playing a collector's vinyl record on a high-quality player.

It was completely dark now, and Stanley changed position to get a better view through the open window.

He raised the binoculars to his eyes and saw a beautiful, and completely naked, Cuban girl pouring rum into glasses. She added ice and juice and danced in place, laughing, as she sipped one of the drinks she'd prepared. Another beauty soon entered the room, her skin nearly black, in bright-pink underwear.

Stanley hid the binoculars and, slowly, trying not to make a sound, crawled through the high grass to the house. He reached the garden and stood next to a tall eucalyptus plant, considering the best way to make it to the window unnoticed.

Suddenly, the door to the patio banged open, and someone came out. Stanley hit the ground and rolled toward the tree. Over the music, he heard a voice. A painfully familiar voice. Trying not to make a sound, Stanley lifted himself up on his elbows and peered out of his hiding place.

Lagrange, thinner, tan, wearing only white shorts and a straw hat, swayed on his bare feet and looked up at the night sky.

The girls came out behind him, carrying the bottle of rum, glasses, and ice bucket. They all settled into wicker chairs in the garden.

Lagrange poured half a glass of rum down his throat and began the slow process of lighting a long cigar. The naked girl perched on his knees and kissed him passionately on the mouth.

Lagrange irritably raised the cigar over his head, grabbed a fistful of the girl's hair, and pulled her back from his face, arching her head back so that her chin pointed up to the sky. He held her in place like that for a few moments, then jerked harder on her hair, and she tumbled onto the grass.

Lagrange laughed, gulped down the rest of the rum and ice, and pushed the girl further away with his foot. Then he gave an order in Spanish, and both girls got on their hands and knees, and crawled toward him, like dogs.

Laughing, the girls reached Lagrange's feet and pulled his shorts down to his ankles. He continued telling the girls something funny, the cigar sticking out of the corner of his mouth. Then he put it out and wrapped each girl's hair around one fist, then pulled their heads between his legs.

A few minutes later, Lagrange shuddered, finished, then slapped his hat on the head of one of the girls who'd just given him a blowjob, and pulled up his shorts.

"Oh, c'etait très bien!" he shouted, his voice loud over the music.

"You motherfucking bastard," whispered Stanley. He was ready to attack now, knife in hand, ready to cut his throat or gouge out his eyes. But that would be too easy, and besides, he didn't want unnecessary witnesses.

Stanley waited a few minutes, then crept cautiously back through the bushes the way he had come.

He had intended to sleep for the rest of the night, but it wasn't to be. First, the owner of the café turned out to be a night owl, and was sitting alone when Stanley returned, a half-empty bottle of rum and a full ashtray on the table in front of her.

She offered Stanley a drink, and he didn't have the strength to refuse. They slowly drank that bottle, then made their way just as slowly through a second.

Next, he found out that the owner lived in the room across from his, and when they both went upstairs, they went to the wrong rooms by mistake. Then they both ended up in Stanley's room, then her room, then in Stanley's bed, which was too narrow to fit them both, then in her bed, which was less stable than expected—when the owner tried to kick Stanley out of her bed, one of the posts broke and the next thing he knew she was on top of him and could not seem to get off.

Finally, she told Stanley not to be an idiot, and unbuttoned his pants while she pulled off her underwear, but Stanley was already asleep.

In the morning, she brought him coffee and asked how much longer he was planning to stay. As he sipped the hot, rich drink Stanley inquired why she wanted to know—was he bothering anyone? He was prepared to pay. He slid fifty dollars over to her.

"The police might be interested in you," she said, slipping the money into a pocket of her dress. "The commissioner came around already. If you're still here tomorrow, I'll have to bring your passport to the station."

"I'll be gone by tomorrow."

"Too bad, honey!" she said and slipped her hand under the sheet covering him.

Stanley slept most of the day. It was evening by the time he went downstairs. He had lobster for dinner and a couple of bottles of beer. Then he paid, got in his car, and drove to Lagrange's house. He parked a couple of miles away from the house and walked the rest of the way along the already familiar path.

There were no cars parked in front, so Stanley guessed that neither the girls nor Lagrange was at home. He walked around the house, chose a window facing the forest, broke it with a rock, then climbed inside.

Lagrange's sanctuary was luxuriously and tastefully furnished. The first floor housed the kitchen, several guest rooms, and an enormous living room, over four hundred square feet, with high ceilings, floor-to-ceiling-windows, and brand-new mahogany furniture. A large bar occupied one corner, stocked with what looked like a hundred bottles of rum, vodka, and whiskey.

Stanley strolled around the kitchen, which was spotless and perfectly organized. The master bedroom was probably on the second floor, but Stanley decided not to go up.

He returned to the living room, and was surprised to find Zvenigorod whiskey at the bar. *That fucking crook even managed to get Russian whiskey shipped to Cuba.* Stanley shook his head and filled a wide crystal tumbler half full of ice, then poured whiskey up to the top. Glass in hand, he went out to the garden to wait.

As he sat there, shooting pains pierced his left knee, which had taken the most damage during his torture; his agitation was having an effect, it seemed. Stanley winced and put his leg up on another chair, taking a big gulp of whiskey. The pain gradually subsided, and Stanley relaxed. He took out a cigar, but then thought better of it—Lagrange might smell the smoke when he got out of his car. He put the cigar back in his pocket.

He mulled over the best place to meet Lagrange. Should he wait by the front door or just inside? He finally decided to wait in the utility room in the short hallway between kitchen and living room. If Lagrange returned with guests, he'd have to wait till they left.

Lagrange pulled up in his BMW at twilight, when the bottle of whiskey was almost empty. At the sound of the engine, Stanley's heart began to pound. He quickly poured the rest of the whiskey onto the grass and hurried silently into the house, empty bottle in hand.

From his hiding place, he heard a rustling at the lock, and Lagrange came in, humming quietly to himself. Through a crack in the door, Stanley saw the light go on in the living room. Judging by the sounds, Lagrange was alone.

Stanley waited a few more minutes, his heart nearly beating out of his chest. He tried to calm his breathing, but then his knee began to ache with pain again.

Gripping the empty bottle firmly in his right hand, Stanley headed out to the living room. As he opened the door and went into the hallway, he looked around slowly, trying to accustom his eyes to the light. Lagrange stood, facing the other direction, about thirty feet away. He was mixing a drink at the bar, and singing in French to himself.

"Salut, Pierre!"

Lagrange turned, shock on his face, and Stanley rushed toward him and swung the bottle into his left temple. Lagrange shuddered, reaching forward as he tipped backward, knocking a tower of bottles off the bar. Stanley hit him again, and this time the glass broke over his head. Lagrange slid down the side of the bar and lost consciousness.

Stanley bound Lagrange's hands and feet with duct tape. When he was done, he stood and looked down at the motionless body.

His heartbeat had slowed, and Stanley exhaled, looked around for an unbroken glass on the bar, and poured himself a rum on the rocks.

"How're things, Lagrange?"

Stanley kicked Lagrange's torso lightly.

"Wake up!"

The prone man showed no signs of life.

"Stop pretending! Can you hear me, Pierre? Wakey, wakey."

Stanley gave him several light slaps across the face.

"Open your eyes! Okay, you're a tricky one, aren't you?" Stanley stood and examined the room. "Maybe a little music to get you going? How about some music, *mon ami*?"

Stanley flipped through the vinyl albums by the record player.

"Oh ho! What a collection! You've got everything—Rolling Stones, Rod Steward, ELO—one of my favorites, by the way—T. Rex, Eric Clapton. What's this shit, now? Mylène Farmer, seriously? Don't tell me you listen to that French garbage. What about the classics, Pierre? Ah? Nothing to say? Maybe we'll listen to a little Dylan, I've always liked Dylan. You don't mind, do you, Pierre?"

Stanley flipped the record around and put the needle down. The sounds of "Knockin on Heaven's Door" filled the house.

"A little too on the nose, I agree. But since it's your last day on earth, it'll get you in the right frame of mind. My gift to you."

Stanley lit a cigarette, danced a bit to the song, sipping on his rom, slowly moving toward Lagrange.

"Come the fuck on, Pierre. Just look at yourself."

Stanley crouched down beside the body and shook his head, looking over his former boss's body. Blood was streaming from the wound on Lagrange's forehead.

"Knock, knock!" Stanley said, tapping his glass on Lagrange's forehead in time with the rhythm. The other man didn't move.

"Jesus Christ, you're all bloody. That wound needs to be disinfected. Don't worry. I'll help you out."

Stanley poured the remainder of his rum on Lagrange's forehead, and Lagrange groaned quietly, then opened his eyes and focused on Stanley.

"It's you!" Lagrange said with a weak smile. "I expected you sooner."

"Oh, really!" Stanley laughed. "Is that so? I think you never expected to see me again. You thought either the police or Gagarin would take care of me, you bastard. But I've given you a bit of a surprise, haven't I?" Stanley tapped his cigarette ash onto Lagrange's face and stood. He went out into the hallway and came back with his bag full of tools.

"You hit me pretty hard. I think the cut is going to need stitches. I'm going to need the hospital," said Lagrange.

"You're a funny guy," said Stanley. "About to die and still making jokes."

"What's funny? What are you doing?"

Stanley began to lay his tools out neatly on the floor without a word.

"What is this, Stan? Stanley! What the fuck are you doing?"

Stanley pressed his finger onto one of the knives to test its sharpness, then set it back down.

"What do you know about pain? Absolute, all-encompassing pain? Were you aware, for example, that the desire for vengeance and pain activate the same region in the human brain? Interesting, right?"

Lagrange watched Stanley in silent horror.

"But I discovered an interesting paradox. When the pain grows too intense, when it fills you completely, you start to adapt to it, accept it as the new baseline of normal. Can you imagine? When they were torturing me, there were moments when I reached a truly calm, meditative state."

"Jesus, Stanley…"

"Desire is the foundation of all suffering. When I stopped desiring anything—salvation, death, whatever, my pain went away, and the torture seemed like child's play." Stanley fell silent. "Then they killed Christine."

"Who?"

"Christine. My wife. And I rediscovered desire. My new desire was to find you and kill you. And so my pain returned."

"I'm sorry. I didn't know, Stanley."

"And now I'm here to send your straight to hell."

"Wait, Stan, wait! I'm not to blame for that. What do I have to do with that? Put the knife away. I'm begging you. Get the knife out of my face, Jesus Christ, McKnight! I had to run because I lost…I got careless investing those fucking Russians' money. You understand?"

"No."

"At first, they didn't care where their 30 percent annual profits were coming from, but when the markets took a nosedive, I had to start taking risks, doing little tricks. Move money from one account to another, so the account statements wouldn't arouse any suspicion. I was distributing the losses, evening it out. I even placed bets in the casino, but I lost. They would have killed me if Gagarin found out about the missing money!"

"And so they killed my wife instead of you." Stanley ground out his cigarette and blew the smoke into Lagrange's face.

"They're fucking animals. There are rules! Wives and children are untouchable. Those Russian bastards don't follow any rules!"

"You're behind the times, Pierre! The rules were broken long ago. Starting with you. You broke the rule not to steal from men like Gagarin. Nobody robs the Russians."

"I thought you would figure it out, Stanley, while you were still in St. Petersburg. I didn't think you'd go back to Zurich. You're so smart, Stanley! You could have guessed, goddamned it!"

"No, I didn't figure it out. You left a real surprise for me."

"Stanley, forgive me," Lagrange said, trying to smile. "But life is one big surprise, is it not?"

"Is that so…" Stanley's hand trembled as he cut shallowly into the skin of Lagrange's neck. "Then maybe death will be just another big surprise for you, motherfucker."

"Wait, Stanley! Don't go crazy: I'm begging you! What are you doing!"

"It's a drill bit. Just an ordinary drill bit that I'm going to entertain you with. Our mutual Russian friends are quite skilled with them, you know; I do believe I'm going to have a limp for the rest of my life. But enough about me—it's your turn now."

"No, oh God, Stanley, don't! I'll do whatever you want, but don't torture me, please!"

Lagrange wept, the tears running down his face.

Stanley fixed the bit into place in the drill. As he set it up, he realized that he didn't want to torture Lagrange anymore, let alone kill him. He simply couldn't turn that drill on and make a hole in the knee of a living person. It wouldn't change a thing. It wouldn't bring Christine back. Or his old life. If he tortured and killed someone, he'd become just like Gagarin, a Russian maniac.

"Please don't torture me." Lagrange wept. "I've got lots of money here. You need money? Right? You can have it all. I have a safe, over there by that painting on the wall. There's a flash drive in there along with the cash. With it, you can access about $500 million in cryptocurrency. You want it? You can have it all. Take it! I don't mind."

Stanley set the drill aside.

"Fine, okay. Live if you must."

Lagrange sobbed even louder.

"Thank you!"

"Enough, enough, calm down."

"Thank you, McKnight, thank you!"

"Calm down. How do you open the safe?"

Lagrange was briefly silent.

"There's a sensor. My fingerprint opens it. You probably wanted to cut my fingers off, one by one. But I need them. I need them. Untie me and I'll open the safe."

Stanley sighed. He really couldn't do anything with Lagrange now. He didn't pity him. He despised and hated him, but torturing and killing a defenseless person went against his nature.

Stanley cut the tape binding Lagrange's wrists, then freed his legs. Lagrange got to his feet with a groan.

"Shit, I need a doctor," he said, limping and rubbing his wrists. He went over to the mirror, looking anxiously at the cut on his forehead.

"Where's the safe?"

"Safe?"

"Yes, the fucking safe with the 500 million in cryptocurrency. Give me the flash drive and I'm out of here. "

"It's over there," Lagrange said, waving toward a print of "The Yellow House" hanging on the wall.

Stanley walked over to the painting, examining it.

"Good quality...so open it."

Lagrange didn't answer, and Stanley was about to turn just as the other man's hands locked around his throat from behind.

"I'm not giving you anything!" Lagrange hissed. "Go fuck yourself. I earned that money. It's mine. Mine! And you're going to die. You'll die like your slut wife."

Stanley tried to break free, but it was too late. His throat was in a vice, and he was moments away from losing consciousness. He thrust his elbow backward and hit something soft; he repeated the blow, again and again, using his last bit reserves of strength. Lagrange shuddered and his grip loosened slightly. Using the momentum, Stanley drew in as much air as he could, then slammed his elbow back as hard as he could. He hit Lagrange in the solar plexus, and the other man flew back into the wall. Stanley turned, caught his breath for a moment, then rushed at Lagrange. But Pierre turned out to be a surprisingly skilled fighter, and was bigger and stronger than Stanley, despite the age difference. His blows rained down on Stanley's torso and head, but Stanley seemed to pay them no mind, focused on going for the throat. He managed to knock Lagrange down, but he was dragged down after him. Pierre got on top, pressing down on Stanley's rib cage. Lagrange got both hands around his opponent's throat and started to choke him.

Once again, Stanley was close to losing consciousness. As he grew weaker, his searching fingers found the drill on the floor. He slowly drew it closer until he got a better grip, then turned it on.

The drill bit entered Lagrange's right side, near the liver. Lagrange howled, and instantly let go, jumping up. Stanley jabbed again with the drill, but missed.

Lagrange stumbled backward, holding his side, and rushed toward the stairs.

Stanley rose slowly, breathing deeply, and followed the trail of blood on the floor. He took the knife with him.

Lagrange lay in a pool of blood on the second floor, six feet from the top of the stairs. With one hand, he pressed down on the wound in his stomach, from which blood spurted out, and with the other, he was holding the receiver of the stationary phone that had tumbled from its wall shelf.

Stanley stood over Lagrange and kicked the receiver to the side.

"Too late to call for help, old pal."

"I hate you," Lagrange rasped, blood trickling out of his mouth. "I hate you, you Russian bastard."

Stanley put his foot on Lagrange's throat.

"Au revoir, Lagrange. I'm afraid I'm going to have to cut your fingers off, after all."

Stanley shifted all of his weight onto his foot, and Lagrange's struggles soon ceased.

CHAPTER 52

I T WAS DRIZZLING AS THE plane touched down in New York, and the faint sounds of thunder were barely audible in the distance. Flights had been delayed due to the fog, and the flight from Havana landed hours later than scheduled, around seven AM.

Stanley opened his eyes when they came to a complete stop and the passengers were lining up to get off. His knee ached from sitting in the same position for so many hours, but he didn't rush to get up. He knew what was waiting for him out there; he just didn't know whether they would arrest him here on the plane or whether they'd let him get further into the airport first.

Stanley looked through the window. Airport employees in bright-yellow jumpsuits and fur-covered headphones slowly unloaded the luggage from the cargo hold; from this height, they looked like Lego figurines.

He closed his eyes. He imagined floating slowly along on his back. The water was almost completely calm, the waves of the turquoise Caribbean Sea slowly rocking him back and forth. The rays of the sun gently warmed Stanley's body, reaching through him to the sandy bottom below. He was floating next to a beautiful, deserted, sandy beach stretching out into the distance. Stanley wondered whether to keep floating, or whether it was time to swim back to shore, bury his arms and legs in the sand, and fall asleep.

"Stanley McKnight?"

Stanley jerked. He didn't want to open his eyes.

"I'm going to read you your rights," someone's grating voice said.

"Wake up, McKnight!"

Stanley slowly opened his eyes and looked up, squinting. A thin man of about fifty with nearly clear, fishy eyes stood over him. He was dressed in a black suit, and two more men in similar black suits stood behind him. The thin man stood with his hand at his hip, pushing his jacket back to show his badge and gun.

"Are you feeling all right?"

"I want to become a shell on the bottom of the ocean," whispered Stanley.

"Too late for that, buddy," said the man with a laugh. "I can't help you there."

"Then go ahead: read me my rights."

Through the fog he heard, "You have the right to remain silent." Stanley shut his eyes again, pulled by the intense desire to return to his daydream of the beach.

"Do you have any questions, McKnight?"

"No." Stanley shook his head.

They handcuffed him and led him off the plane. He limped more than usual from the sharp pain in his knee. On his way out, he caught the frightened expression of the stewardess he'd been flirting with. He winked at her, but she shrank back in fear, as if he were a serial killer. Stanley didn't care; he didn't care about anything at all.

Two hours later, the thin policeman and his partner put Stanley on a plane to Washington, DC. He left that airport in a police car, sirens on and lights flashing. Stanley hadn't been in Washington since he was a child. He noted their route before he dozed off, and thought they must be heading toward Langley.

"You look pretty good for a dead man, McKnight."

"But I feel like shit." Stanley sat on a metal chair that was screwed to the floor. Frank Dillon and Marco Monti sat across the table from him.

"We already said our goodbyes, you know. We thought the Russians must have buried our poor banker somewhere near Monaco."

"They tried, Frank. They tried. And thanks for the help there. I sure could count on you, you fuckers."

"We're not magicians."

"Oh, that I know."

"What did you do in Cuba?" asked Monti.

"I decided to take a little vacation after my old Russian client put a couple of neat little holes in my kneecaps."

"We didn't agree to that."

"Give it up, Monti. Where was I supposed to go? A Crimean health resort? They're all on your sanctions lists."

"You broke our agreement," said Marco. "All guarantees are now null and void."

"Go fuck yourself."

"And fuck you, McKnight! We'll see how fast you can limp away from all your new boyfriends in jail, pretty boy."

"I can't wait. Go ahead and send me there now," said Stanley, giving him the middle finger.

"You son of a bitch!" Marco jumped up.

"Take it easy, boys. Settle down," said Frank, raising his hands.

"You know where the most unpleasant people in the world live, Frank?" asked Stanley. "They live in Zurich and eat the worst food in the world. Have you heard of raclette? You think I came back here by accident? I'd rather go to prison here at home than be free in fucking Switzerland."

"You're a good patriot, Stanley," Frank said. "Now why don't you tell us everything. We'll help you."

"How?"

"By saving your ass."

"You already helped me once. People died."

"Stanley, please accept my sincere condolences. I am truly sorry about your wife. But we need to move forward. We have to nail those Russian bastards. Are you with us?"

Stanley remained silent, studying the large mirror on the wall. He wondered how many people were watching him behind it. Suddenly, he saw Gagarin's face before him, dotted with small drops of blood, the basement in Nice; then Shamil appeared, twisting the dial to send another electric shock.

"McKnight," Marco asked again quietly, "are you with us?"

Stanley shook himself.

"I'd like a drink," answered Stanley. "I had a bottle of Russian whiskey in my bag. And bring me some cigarettes. And ice, as much ice as you can."

"You're not at a goddamned night club in St. Tropez!" shouted Monti.

"If you didn't notice, the Russians did a number on my knees," Stanley said, putting his feet on the table. "Russian whiskey will help ease the pain. You want to talk—bring me whiskey."

"Okay, whatever. Monti, bring him what he asked for."

"Anything else, McKnight?"

"I want a guarantee. New appearance. New life."

"You'll have to remember a whole lot for that, Stanley."

"I know enough."

"It's not what you know—it's who you know."

Monti came back five minutes later with cigarettes, the potbellied bottle of Zvenigorod, and an ice bucket. Stanley poured himself a double, took a hefty gulp, and lit a cigarette.

"You drink like a fish," Monti said, shaking his head disapprovingly.

"Let me guess: you're all about the healthy lifestyle?"

"Uh-huh. I'm a vegan."

Stanley finished his drink and reached for the bottle to pour another.

"I can't stand people like you, Monti."

"Is that so!"

"You're a psychopath. Excuse my directness. Most psychos are obsessed with living a healthy lifestyle."

"He's a clever one, Frank. He knows it all."

"Oh, that's not my own interpretation. Psychologists have written about it. You're athletic, don't eat meat, are always choosing the healthiest food. This passion for healthy living comes from your constant fear of death. Something inside you, Monti, is whispering, 'Don't let me die, God. Monti hasn't lived yet.'"

"Have another drink, McKnight, and maybe you should start thinking about yourself."

Stanley paused to light a fresh cigarette, and asked, "Any news on Gagarin?"

"You haven't heard?"

"No," Stanley shrugged.

Frank exchanged a look with Monti, and the younger man dug through the papers in a red folder until he found the newspaper he was looking for. He tossed it on the table.

Stanley pulled it over and read the headline, "Tragedy on the French Riviera. Russian oligarch Viktor Gagarin drowns while diving from his yacht." Stanley checked the date; Gagarin had died about a month ago.

"Is this true? You believe this?" Stanley slapped his hand down on the paper. "That cocksucker probably staged his own death, changed his appearance, and is now hiding away somewhere. Singapore, maybe."

"Unlikely." Frank shook his head. "I think his own people killed him for the missing money. No plastic surgery could keep him hidden from the FSB. "

"And his wife? Mila?" asked Stanley.

"Killed herself. Couldn't stand the grief," laughed Monti. "The very same day. She hung herself with a shoelace in the bathroom at home."

"Well, well," Stanley sighed. "Money costs the most to women who marry for it."

"So, Stanley," said Frank, "we have a good offer for you."

"I'm all ears."

"You give us all the information you have. Tell us in detail what you saw and heard when you were hiding Russian money—their corrupt schemes, their front men, their offshore structures. The technical details aren't actually our main focus now, though. We managed to get enough of that through your flash drive. We need information of a more personal nature."

"Who's sleeping with who?"

"That too. What bad habits do they have? Political views? Do they believe in God and Judgment Day? Any compromising info that you know."

"Tempting. And then what? I'm found floating face down in the San Francisco Bay?"

"We'll guarantee your safety," said Frank. "No one will be able to touch you in the States. You'll spend one month working for us, and then...then we'll get you plastic surgery to change your appearance, and you'll live out the rest of your life in whatever section of this great country we choose for you."

"As far as the public knows, you'll disappear," added Monti. "You'll become just another banker who died."

"It sounds like a way out. What do I have to do?"

"Nothing much, really. You already know how to talk. You'll spend your days with our specialists, telling them everything you know. Then—freedom!"

"Well, not entirely," Monti clarified grimly. "You'll be under observation—for you own safety."

"Do I have a choice?" asked Stanley.

Frank shook his head.

"Okay, let's say I agree. Why not ask me to testify in court? Aren't you going to go after the Magnificent Five?"

Frank laughed.

"Where did you get the idea that we're trying to put anyone in trial or send them to prison, Stanley?"

Stanley ground out his cigarette.

"You're collecting compromising information, but you're not going after anyone?"

"No." Frank smiled.

"So what's the point of it all?" Stanley tapped his pointer finger on the rim of his empty glass.

Frank and Monti just went on smiling silently.

"Of course," said Stanley. "You don't want to put the dirty Russians in jail. You want to blackmail them. It's your best recruitment tool."

"He's quick," Monti said to Frank, pointing at Stanley. "A clever banker."

"You don't want to stop the Russian mafia. You want to manipulate them and get control over everything."

"Mafia? Bite your tongue, Stanley," said Frank. "'Mafia' is a chain of pizzerias in Brooklyn. What they've got in Russia and the former Soviet Union states is a system, a well-organized system of theft and money laundering, growing deep into the government like ivy on a tree."

"Is it really so bad?" asked Stanley.

"Do you know the size of the national welfare fund in Norway?" asked Frank.

"Over a trillion dollars, I read."

"Right. The national welfare fund in Russia is a tenth that size, and will soon run out. Now, do you know how much oil the two countries produce?"

"No."

"Russia produces six times more oil. How do you explain that?"

"Theft."

"Absolute and total theft."

"But isn't there theft in other countries? You're trying to say there's no corruption in Norway? No one in France steals anything? It's the same everywhere."

"True," said Frank. "It's like the old joke: 'Why did you arrest me? Everyone else is pissing in the pool too!' People are the same everywhere, but you Russians are the only ones doing it from high up."

"Very funny," Stanley said. "I still don't understand why you're focused specifically on Russia."

"Politics, Stan, politics," said Frank. "Carthage must be destroyed."

Stanley was quiet for a bit, flipping through the newspaper on the table. There was a photograph of a familiar Russian, a tall blond man, being led out of a police bus in handcuffs.

"I know him," Stanley said.

"That's the main opposition leader in Russia," Frank said in surprise. "How do you know him?"

"We were in a Moscow jail together. Not for long, though."

"He's a brave guy."

"Are you helping him?"

"No."

"Why not? You think he doesn't have any chance of winning?"

"Of course, he does," Frank said, raising his hands, palm up. "He's got a chance, as long as he doesn't get shot too soon."

"A cheerful forecast."

"Some more Russian whiskey, McKnight?"

The black Chevrolet Suburban was heading down a wet highway toward Georgetown Pike. The first snow had fallen, and turned immediately to slushy puddles. Stanley was feverish and had a cough. He'd also quit smoking five days ago, and he was wracked with desire for a cigarette. He looked out the passenger window at the bare trees outside, trying to take his mind off it by counting each tree they passed.

Frank Dillon was behind the wheel. He was in a good mood; McKnight had finished giving evidence, and all that remained was a couple plastic surgeries to change his appearance.

"Do you get depressed in the fall, Frank?" asked Stanley, suppressing a yawn.

"The only thing that depressed me is your sorrowful mug. Smile, my friend! You'll be a different person soon. You'll get a chance to start over. Have you picked out a new face?"

"I didn't know I had a say in it."

"Well, within reason. For example, do you want a bigger nose?"

"No."

"You could ask the surgeon to focus on your nose."

"I don't want a bigger nose, Frank."

"I just think it would suit you," said Frank, turning away from the road to give him a wink.

"No."

"I'm sure it wouldn't bother you."

"Fine, I'll leave it up to the surgeon. Happy?"

"Good."

"Let it be a surprise. I'll wake up from the anesthesia, walk over to the mirror, and ...surprise."

Stanley fell silent.

"Do you have any cigarettes?"

"Didn't you quit, Stan?"

"I did."

"So don't start again."

"I want to smoke one last cigarette. If I'm going to be gone soon, if they're making a new man out of me, I have to mark the occasion with a last drag."

"Look in the glove compartment."

Stanley dug around a bit until he found a soft pack of Camels, and lit one from the car's cigarette lighter.

"Nasty weather." Stanley exhaled with pleasure.

"Yes."

"Frank, you said you're going to pick where I'll be placed?"

"That's right."

"Could you put me in California?"

Frank laughed.

"I'll see what I can do, McKnight."

"Thanks."

"And I might be able to get you a job. At a bank."

"A bank?" Stanley took one last deep drag and tossed the cigarette out the window. "Fuck banks."

ABOUT THE AUTHOR

Before writing his first novel, Matthew A. Carter worked in the private banking industry in Switzerland and the UK. He also spent seven years in Russia as an investment banker and is fluent in Russian. He was born and grew up in San Francisco and studied economics at University of Southern California. He now lives in Zurich.

Made in the USA
Middletown, DE
08 August 2019